RAVEN

D0551882

RAVEN

by

Michael Murray

ibooks
DISTRIBUTED BY PUBLISHERS GROUP WEST

An Original Publication of ibooks, inc.

Copyright © 2004 Michael Harreschou

An ibooks, inc. Book

Distributed By Publishers Group West
1700 Fourth Street, Berkeley, CA 94710
www.pgw.com

ibooks, inc.
24 West 25th Street
New York, NY 10010

ISBN: 1-59687-167-9

10 9 8 7 6 5 4 3 2

Printed in the U.S.A.

<u>RANKS</u>

The following is a list of German military ranks and their Allied equivalents. Also included in the list are various terms used preceding and during the Nazi years.

SS	US Army
Reichsfuhrer-SS	General of the Army
SS-Oberstgruppenfuhrer	Lieutenant General
SS-Obergruppenfuhrer	General
SS-Gruppenfuhrer	Major-General
SS-Oberfuhrer	General
SS-Standartenfuhrer	Colonel
SS-Obersturmbannfuhrer	Lieutenant-Colonel
SS-Sturmbannfuhrer	Major
SS-Hauptsturmfuhrer	Captain
SS-Obersturmfuhrer	1st Lieutenant
SS-Untersturmfuhrer	2nd Lieutenant
SS-Sturmscharfuhrer	Sergeant-Major
SS-Hauptscharfuhrer	Master Sergeant
SS-Oberscharfuhrer	Technical Sergeant
SS-Scharfuhrer	Sergeant
SS-Rottenfuhrer	Corporal
SS-Sturmann	Corporal
SS-Oberschutze	Private

<u>Luftwaffe</u>	<u>U.S. Air Force</u>
Reichsmarshall	No equivalent rank
Generalfeldmarshall	General (5 star)
Generaloberst	General (4 star)
General der Flieger	Lieutenant General
Generalleutnant	Major General (2 stars)
Generalmajor	Brigadier General (1 star)
Oberst	Colonel
Oberstleutnant	Lieutenant Colonel

Major	Major
Hauptmann	Captain
Oberleutnant	1st Lieutenant
Leutnant	2nd Lieutenant

Warrant Officers

Stabsfeldwebel	Flight Officer
Oberfaehnrich	Sr. Off. Candidate

NON-COMMISSIONED OFFICERS.

Oberfeldwebel	Master Sergeant
Feldwebel	Technical Sergeant
Unterfeldwebel	Sergeant
Unteroffizier	Corporal

NON-COMM

Hauptgefreiter	N/A
Obergefreiter	N/A
Gefreiter	Private First Class
Flieger	Private

Lieutenant Colonels were often, in fact usually, addressed simply as "Colonel" to save time. This was true in both armies and air forces.

Waffen-SS officers and men could be referred to, and often were, in their army equivalent rank. A Waffen-SS Sturmbannfuhrer could therefore be properly addressed as Major.

The Waffen-SS were simply the armed SS. Waffen-SS were fully equipped with the latest infantry and assault weapons and were extremely well trained fighting units. While the Waffen-SS were sometimes tarred by the same brush as their more bestial brethren, and to be sure there were Waffen-SS divisions that were ruthless in the extreme, others were guilty of nothing more serious than fighting courageously a war that they could not win.

The Gestapo (*Geheime Staatspolizei*) or German Secret Police, was a Nazi invention of 1933 originally under the command of Reichsmarshall Hermann Goering, later headed by the infamous Heinrich Himmler. In the typical labyrinth of totalitarian governmental bureaucracy of Nazi Germany, the Gestapo and the SS were entwined with various departments that included internal espionage as well as intelligence and counter-intelligence. This is distinct from the Abwehr which was Military Intelligence headed by Admiral Wilhelm Canaris. (Canaris, it should be said, was vehemently anti-Nazi and anti-Hitler.)

Panzer. The German word for armor, but was incorporated into the reference for tank by the Allies. It was also used in the larger context of certain armed vehicles that supported panzer-led divisions or groups (*gruppen*).

Panzer Grenadiers. Infantry troops that were assigned to and fought with panzer divisions.

Abteilung. This could mean detachment, department or battalion, but the majority of the term referred to battalion-sized units.

Wehrmacht. Often confused as the German army. The Wehrmacht actually referred to Germany's military apparatus and all of its support units, Luftwaffe, Kriegsmarine, etc. Specific reference to the army was Heer.

FOREWORD

Historians chronicling the incredible ascendancy of Germany's Third Reich have paused in their retrospection to collectively shake their heads at the personality of its dominant leader, Adolf Hitler. Many of them would agree that had Adolf Hitler been a secret spy for British MI6 during World War II, he could not possibly have been more effective for the Allied cause.

From early recorded times there have been magnetic human beings who have risen from the masses to become important leaders of their tribes, regions, or nations. The means of their rule and the extension of their legacies have been achieved by their successes at force of arms. The Caesars, the Alexanders, the Charlemagnes, the Napoleons of the world, while having their detractors, all had certain shared personality traits that were vital to their grip on power. They were dedicated, focused, obsessive people.

Above all else, they possessed an intelligence that was unique to them. Because of this they believed that they knew, better than those they ruled, what was required to lift their peoples from the commonplace to an exalted plateau in the history of world domination. Certainly Adolf Hitler knew this. His aims for the German people were specific and they were well articulated. He was absolutely confident, unshaken in his beliefs, that whatever methods he chose to force the rest of the world to heel would be validated by the court of future public opinion. There is nothing on Earth that equals success and Hitler was, unarguably, a success at what he started out to accomplish.

Until a certain day.

Then everything changed.

But first, a brief review. Adolf Hitler, born in Austria, transplanted to Germany, a decorated war hero, received the Iron Cross Second Class for valor in December of 1914, and the Iron Cross First Class in August 1918, an unusually distinctive award for an enlisted man. He spent post-war months in 1918 recovering from wounds he received at the front. Extremely disenchanted with the terms of the Versaill Treaty, he railed in public at his own weak government for accepti those dictates. He took to the soap box and beer halls to vent his not only against the ineffective Weimar Republic, but at the nations against whom Germany fought, France, England and America, and the sinister forces that financed those nations: the Jews.

Hitler was not only an anti-Semite but an anti-everything; Asian, Negro, Armenian, Indian, to name only a few, who were not descendant from his mythical Aryan caste. But it was not enough to simply hate other peoples. Many persons shared Hitler's pathological dislikes in human beings. It was Hitler's ability to focus this hatred into a directed energy that carried with it a kind of social fission process where one German citizen shared his or her fervor of loathing with two more people who, in turn, passed theirs to four more.

Hatred and intolerance was no longer sublimated, was no longer an embarrassment, but was now a matter of pride and public policy. Hitler had created a source target at which the arrows of torment could be pointed to relieve the German people of not only their pain but their wounded egos.

To accomplish his goals he took a small political party, National-sozialistische Deutsche Arbeiterpartei, that was rudderless and weak, and injected it with the full force of his ambition to control the entire government, and single handedly built it into a dominant machine. That he could accomplish such a feat in a single lifetime would have been a crowning achievement for most dedicated men, but Adolf Hitler started his dark work beginning in 1920 and had himself installed as Chancellor of Germany just thirteen years later.

Hitler knew how to appeal to all levels of society, from the simple *volk* (people) to the industrial elite of the nation. That is not to say that all Germans approved of the hoarse, chest-beating Austrian, but Hitler was not out to achieve love: he wanted power. And he got it. They supported him financially while he positioned himself and his Nazi party for eventual succession to the reigns and trappings of federal authority.

Once he had accomplished this by becoming chancellor of Germany on January 30, 1933 cleverly having yet made no move that would derail his future plans articulated in his rambling book *Mein Kampf,* Hitler consolidated his power by polling 44percent of the votes in the March 5, 1933 election and, only days later, passed an "enabling" bill giving Hitler dictatorial powers over almost every facet of German civil and military life.

In 1934 Germany began a strong economic recovery. Hitler repudiated the Treaty of Versailles, thus lifting an enormous, stultifying, burden of national debt from the backs of the German people. Repatriations, payable to France and to England, no longer drained from the national treasury. No wonder the citizens of his nation, except for the Jews and other dismissable minorities, thought he was heaven's answer to their prayers.

In 1935 Hitler announced the introduction of military conscription. In the same year, at the Stresa Conference, he forced Britain to agree that Germany had the right to rearm.

Then, in 1936, delivering a diplomatic master stroke, Hitler used the excuse of a pact between France and the Soviet Union to remilitarize the Rhineland, a decision he made in opposition to conventional political wisdom.

Hardly pausing in his shotless take-over, he established the Rome-Berlin axis and shortly thereafter the Anti-Comintern Pact with Japan.

In 1938 Hitler forced the Austrian chancellor, Kurt von Schuschnigg, at Berchtesgaden, to sign an agreement that gave Austrian Nazis a free hand in that country. And later, when Schuschnigg attempted to repudiate the agreement, Hitler sent troops into Austria and occupied it proclaiming his move an *Anschluss* (union).

The world watched, slack jawed, while in 1939 Hitler sent his armies, unopposed, into the Sudentenland of Czechoslovakia, to "free" the ethnic Sudenten Germans.

Then in August, Hitler, needing to protect himself from fighting a two-front war that he knew was coming because he planned to start it, ordered his foreign minister, Joachim von Ribbentrop, to sign a treaty with the Soviet Union. It became known to the world as the Russo-German Nonaggression Pact, a base contract of protected aggression that Soviet Premier Joseph Stalin was only too happy to support.

With the Soviet Union in his pocket, Hitler attacked Poland, bringing that nation's armies to its knees in less than thirty days. In spring 1940 the German army conquered Norway and Denmark.

While the crumbs of victory were still falling from his voracious mouth, Hitler launched his military forces at France in May 1940, attacking through the Low Countries of the Netherlands and Belgium in a blitzkrieg of panzer choreography that remains to this day the classic blueprint of how future tank warfare would be waged.

Skirting the vaunted Maginot line, Hitler defeated France with insulting ease. It is a little known fact that it was Hitler who urged General Erich von Manstein to use his panzer divisions with foot soldiers assigned to each tank, to seek an unorthodox alternative to slugging it out with French forces in the Ardennes as was done in the previous war. On June 14th, 1940, the German Wehrmacht goose-stepped its way into Paris. Eight days later the Franco-German armistice was signed at Rethondes, near the town of Compiègne, the site of German humiliation twenty-two years before.

While Britain managed to rescue its expeditionary force (BEF) that had been pushed into the sea at Dunkirk, it had very little left of a land army to withstand the expected invasion by Germany's three hundred fifty seasoned Wehrmacht and newly forming Waffen SS divisions. While the British navy was clearly the numerical superior of Grand Admiral Raeder's navy, there was agreement among military minds that the British navy could not by itself repulse a determined German landing on its shores.

Not a single person in the world at the time called Hitler stupid. Monstrous, perhaps, egotistical to be sure, the two driving personality traits ascribed to Napoleon. But nobody for a moment believed that Adolf Hitler was anything but calculating and that his shrewd judgement proved to be absolutely rational.

The dictator of Europe now stood astride the Continent with France at his feet, Britain in death throes and reduced to begging America to enter the war, and the only potential military threat, Russia, meekly gnawing on the carcass of Eastern Poland and the Baltic states, Latvia, Estonia and Lithuania, thrown to her like bones to a starving dog.

With Germany's troops assembling along the English Channel in Calais, its Luftwaffe locked in combat with the gallant but reeling Royal Air Force, itself grievously damaged from relentless pounding of its airfields, it seemed only a matter of days, if not hours, before Hitler delivered his death blow upon the British.

Then, the impossible happened.

And the impossible is what this story is about.

BOOK I

From the Foreign & Commonwealth Office News
SPECIAL OPERATIONS EXECUTIVE (SOE): RELEASE OF
RECORDS.

The final set of Special Operations Executive (SOE) records, covering wartime operations in Western Europe, will be released at the Public Record Office at Kew on 23 July 1998. Foreign Secretary Robin Cook, said: 'The exploits of the brave men and women who served in SOE are well-known. These newly-released records provide a real-life history of the SOE, showing once again, how much we and Europe owe to them. We continue to be committed to greater transparency. This is the largest release of SOE records to date, and significant time and effort have been devoted to reviewing the 1,013 files involved.

CHAPTER

1

Two years ago I had finished a rather laborious study for a client of the H.P. Carlisle Foundation. I was looking forward to returning to the west coast and my golfing buddies for much needed outdoor recreation. I was only a contributor to a larger research project for which the foundation was a sub-contractor. The thrust of our work, while the nuts and bolts of it are classified, was an assessment of where the National Security Agency (NSA) stands in its capabilities of intercepting and analyzing electronic signal traffic. It is an overstatement to say that the NSA can no longer analyze a big city newspaper, as encryption expert Whitfield Diffie of Sun Microsystems once said, but it is fair to say that the NSA can only get to a small fraction of its intercepted data because of the unanticipated spread of new cryptology invented by the likes of George I. Davida from the University of Wisconsin, Martin E. Hellman of Stanford, and Philip R. Zimmermann from Boulder, Colorado. The NSA is becoming increasingly helpless in reading the newer stuff. It is like a farmer who hoards his bumper crop of potatoes in the basement which becomes rotten before he gets around to eating it all.

I am not a cryptographer. It was a challenge for me to remember my air force serial number back before Social Security numbers were used in the military. I try to remind myself that Einstein was not very good at math. In my former life with the military I was what the Intelligence community refers to as a tendency analyst. I looked at the data that had been collected either by human agents (Humint) or by satellite or land-line interception (Elint), then I tried to imagine what effects that data revealed about human behavior. If the data revealed that a certain third-world dictator had recently spent one-third of his country's gross national product on armaments and military training facilities, my job was to estimate his intentions. There is a lot of inductive reasoning in my sort of work which, I must tell you, made me a bit edgy. And here I am, still playing with the same dodgy guessing game.

I should make a caveat here. There were two other tendency people at Carlisle, Fred Burckhardt and Nina Parkinson, both of whom were probably better at what we do than I, but I've hung around the building longer than they so I hovered above them on the organizational chart, avoiding hard jobs by virtue of seniority. But when the request came down from Room D 400 or simply "the room," as we referred to it, to examine certain documents at MI-6 in London, neither my friend Burckhardt nor the lovely, fun-loving Nina Parkinson could remove themselves from their urgent work. Burckhardt made no effort to keep the laughter out of his voice as he congratulated me on nailing down a November assignment in sunny London.

Veda Lilliskov Lund, the Foundation's travel coordinator, provided me with a packet containing travel authorization, a letter of credit good at any bank in the world, a hotel reservation number, and tickets on British Airways from Dulles International to Heathrow.

Hardly pausing at the reception desk to show my tickets, I tried not to trot to the bar at the British Airway's travel lounge where I ordered a gin martini on the rocks. I'm one of those people who fear flying and I never let a chance to go by to innoculate myself when faced with leaving the ground. Acrophobia. Having said that, I will also tell you that I flew fighter aircraft during a five year tour in the U.S. Air Force, fifteen months of that time in combat over the skies of Vietnam. The reader might be surprised at the number of active pilots who cower when faced with the prospect of climbing a ladder to replace a burned out flood-light on their garage roof.

Once aloft over the Atlantic, I continued with the project of self-medication with another martini. As we cruised through the heavens faster than sound, I reflected on the nature of my contact at Vauxhall Cross, Jean Scheerer. I had known Scheerer casually over the past ten years that I had been with the foundation, bumping into him at the one of the many cocktail parties that inevitably preceded information swapping conferences. Scheerer was too young to have served in WWII, as was I, but he distinguished himself in the Cold War as a field man for MI-6. He was fluent in German, passable with Russian and French. Scheerer was tall, very good natured, and he had the delightful quality of never taking himself too seriously, contrary to the type of personality that attracts most spies to the business.

He was retired now and I was surprised that he could be dragged away from the shores of southern Spain where he spent most of the year to join me in vetting old MI6 files. The purpose of our meeting, according to Bradley Wallis, was to reconcile certain still-secret American OSS records with those of Britain's SOE, Special Operations Executive, most of which the Brits had recently agreed to make public. There was a number of activities and documentation that both the U.S. and U.K. were reluctant to reveal to the world, and I was named to serve on a joint review committee whose business it was to raise thumbs up or down on publication.

I checked into the Brown's Hotel on Albermarie Street in Mayfair, conscious of the chill in London's late night air. The differential from Washington at the time was only ten degrees but there was something about London weather that went right to the bone, at least to my bones, and my vicuna coat was still buttoned to the top as I entered my rooms and thanked the bellman. We, of the H.P. Carlisle Foundation, did not tip for services until departure where a pre-arranged amount was added to our bill.

Before I could mix myself a whiskey from the bar and settle in with my feet to the fire, the red message light was winking at me from the telephone. I pushed the proper buttons to receive my call-back numbers. There were two from the Foundation and one, as expected, from Jean Scheerer.

"I'm out of town for a few days," Scheerer's recorded voice came to me. "Sorry I couldn't be there to welcome you. There is a lady at 64 Vauxhall Cross by the name of Debra Mears who is expecting you. I hope to be back in town before you finish. My best to Linda, when you talk to her."

Thoughtful of him to remember Linda. They had met just once, as I recalled, and then only briefly. Not to mention the fact that Linda and I weren't married and still are not.

After a surprisingly good night's sleep I ate a typical American breakfast of bacon and scrambled eggs and reveled in strong French coffee. I drank three cups. Thus wired, I taxied to Vauxhall Cross, residence for MI6 on the South Bank of the Thames.

Ms. Mears was indeed waiting for me. She arrived at the visitor's check-in desk with a special pass already made out in my name, complete with a photograph laminated under the plastic cover. It must have been wired to her from the Foundation. Ms. Mears, "Call me Debbie, or Deb, as you like," was tall, blond hair, tending to over-weight and was probably older than her youthful appearance. While I took her age to be mid-to late-thirties, I subsequently learned that she had two grown sons, both in the military, one of whom matriculated at Eton.

Debbie, as I now chose to call her, led me to a basement room that was windowless, cheerless and would have been dusty had it not been for an air filtering system that processed all of the stuff people at MI6 took into their lungs. The door to room SB-301 was accessed by a combination lock that resembled a medium security safe. The door was set in concrete walls that were part of extensive British Intelligence archives, a good deal of which was created in this building and some brought from Whitehall well after WWII ended. Debbie worked the lock for me and, after opening the door, bade me enter but did not supply me with the combination.

"SOE material is here," Debbie said, waving her arms in a circular motion to include steel shelving containing cardboard boxes. "I think we have most of it but then one never knows when one deals with secret organizations, right? In any case I think we have all of what you need for your inquiries."

Strange that she should think so if neither she nor I would know if any of those materials were missing or not.

"But if you need anything, ring me up on the phone, right over there. My extension number is posted, ah, next to it. I'm only at the end of the hall. I make tea in my office, as well. Now, then," Debbie crooked her finger and I followed.

Within room SB-301were several smaller rooms, examination

rooms, they were referred to, and Debbie ushered me into one of them. "The drill," she said, "is to select documents you wish to examine and bring them into one of these." She went on to explain that the rooms were secure and that no one could look over one's shoulder. There was a single table, about thirty-six by seventy inches covered in ersatz oak-vinyl, and two chairs. Both of the chairs had arm rests but each had minimum padding on the seat and back, as if to discourage deep-digging into the nation's secrets.

"This," she said, handing me a plastic card with a magnetic strip, "will let you into the outer room. You can lock the door here, if you like, from inside. You may not leave documents on this table while you are not in the examining room." Debbie smiled at my arched eyebrow. "Yes, I know there is no way to enforce it but that's the rule. Do what you like. Well, that's it, then, isn't it? Remember to call if you need me. When you get hungry the food isn't bad here in the building. I can show you the cafeteria if you like."

I thanked Debbie and made a mental note to take her up on her offer for lunch.

"Oh, almost forgot." Debbie handed me a sealed envelope. It had been taped closed with a tamper-revealing flap. "These are the documents we're interested in."

As she closed the door of Room SB-301 I opened the sealed envelope and scanned the five page list. Each page contained approximately twenty-four references to SOE formation, operations, personnel, including cover names, as well as real names of the field agents to whom those cover names applied during a war that had been finished for more than fifty-five years.

It wasn't difficult to find the expanded files that documented those operations in the main room, and I found that I could carry two or three at a time to the examining room. My best plan, it seemed to me, was to begin alphabetically starting with the "A"s. I opened up my lap-top computer to makes notes, I plugged it into an electric wall outlet, then set about looking at what the SOE had done long ago.

The first operation I examined was Agrippa, and a field agent who had been dropped into Belgium from a Lancaster at night on the fifth of March 1944. He was a wireless operator sent as a replacement for still another three-man espionage team previously assigned to operate in Brussels. Unbeknownst to the SOE, and certainly not by "Brooch," the agent's field name, the Germans had already captured his team and had "turned" one of them. Brooch was followed by the Gestapo from the moment he attempted to make his first contact with "Jeanine," a member of the original team. The Gestapo hoped Brooch would lead them to still other members of cells yet to be discovered. But Brooch could only wait in his rented room for a call that never came. He was arrested forty-eight hours after his arrival in Belgium and his radio, buried near his parachute, was retrieved.

The story of Brooch was not unique to the annals of WWII field operations that took place in Western Europe. The Nazis had done an outstanding job of capturing large numbers of agents dropped into The Netherlands and Belgium after being sold out by a traitor in late 1942. The Brooch documentation continued for some sixty pages including equipment inventories, training regime, radio and language school, background investigation results, even post-war communique's regarding Brooch and other agents connected to him who were executed by occupation forces of the Third Reich.

Valerie Graimont was yet another agent slated for work in Brussels but lost in Holland when she was dropped there by mistake. She had been trained as an expert reception committee worker and saboteur. Out of a reception committee of twelve, not counting Valerie and her three man team, only one survived.

Holland was indeed a vast quicksand of unfortunate intelligence agents, one Edward Vanden Eykel served as an example. He was dropped twelve kilometers outside of Amsterdam, this city chosen by his controllers because it was a transportation center with rails and roads pointing all over Europe. It was Vanden Eykel's assignment to make his way to Lille, France, where he was to liaise with a German national sympathetic to the Allied cause. He was captured within minutes of touching Dutch soil and taken off to Gestapo headquarters where he was tortured. The report was truncated however, and Vanden Eykel's fate was not revealed in the folder. Further, the pagination on the dossier indicated that only four of twenty-seven pages were in the file. I wondered briefly whether the fact that pages had been removed was sinister, but reflecting that the mission had been undertaken in February of 1942, I could assume the missing pages were a product of careless bookkeeping or perhaps an air raid.

By mid-afternoon I had worked my way through more than forty clandestine operations to Blundell, Violet, an attractive agent, had worked in the Spezia region of Italy, her mission placing her with Piacenza partisans. Her mission was successful, I was pleased to read, and her reports tendered by Captain T.D. Gregg were interesting to browse. However, it had been a long day and there were few accounts that leaped off the page. I could find nothing that I thought should remain classified after this long period of time and I so indicated in my written recommendations.

By six P.M. I was closing the files on Operation Cawdor, field name Roland, in Belgium who, with "Necklace," had operated a courier service back to London, when I realized that I was famished. I dialed Debbie's extension and she picked up almost immediately.

"Mears," she said.

"I'm hungry," I said into the phone. "I don't suppose they're still serving lunch in the cafeteria?"

"No, but we have twenty-four hour food available. You'll just love the menu."

I assumed Debbie was being facetious about the food served at the MI6 mess but in fact I thought the offering was better than average for a swing shift. The buffet included two kinds of fish, plaice, a kind of flounder, and smoked kipper. I opted for Irish potato pancakes, grilled oysters wrapped in bacon and a tossed salad. Against my better judgement I ordered a liter of red wine, assured by Debbie that it was an above average table wine. It turned out that it was far less than average, but it was better than, say, "Night Train" which I once bought in a California drug store.

I almost embarrassed myself wolfing down my meal before Debbie had hardly swallowed her first bite, but after ordering a second basket of garlic bread and washing it down with yet another glass of wine, I felt physically and mentally on top of my game, as the British say, and Debbie was cheerful.

"How long have you known Jean?" she asked.

"Scheerer? About ten years or so. Why?" She had used his first name, telling me that she had not simply run across the man's name in a file.

"I just wondered why he roped you into this god-awful job," she said.

"As a matter of fact, he didn't. I work for the HP Carlisle Foundation. We do contract work from time to time for the..."

I stopped talking because Debbie was quietly shaking.

"What are you laughing at?" I said.

"I'm sorry. I wasn't really laughing. Was I? I don't think I'm speaking out of turn when I say that you wouldn't have come within a hundred kilometers of this project if Jean Scheerer hadn't asked for you specifically." Her Meryl Streep smile remained as she slowly lifted her wine glass to her lips.

"Hmm. You must know something, no, you must know a lot, that I don't know. In the first place I thought Jean had retired two or three years ago and, secondly, the job isn't very, well, sensitive. I mean, there isn't a war going on, I don't think one will start in the very near future, and the one I'm supposed to be interested in has been over for more than half a century. Right?" I said.

"Oh, yes. Right. Indeed."

"What the hell. He'll be back in a day or two so we'll find out for sure." I pushed the last piece of garlic bread into my mouth, totally aware that I had not left it for my host/guest, but thinking that if I could control the garlic bread I was in charge of the conversation. Three glasses of wine will do that to you. "In any case, he didn't have to do this, whatever this declassification program is all about, if he didn't want to."

"That's where you're wrong, August. I'm sorry, do you mind first names?"

"Of course not. Excuse me," I said, floating a hand through the air.

"I rather think you're his last hope. I mean, he has incredible pressures, and none of them are, well, to be taken lightly," Debbie said, finishing the last of her red wine sans garlic bread.

But she had certainly got my attention. "Really?" I said, leaning over the table as I lowered my voice. "What kind of pressures?"

"He'll tell you when he gets here," she said, the Streep smile turned wistful.

I found myself nodding off at my table by nine-thirty that night, a combination of wine with dinner and the difference in time zones on both sides of the Atlantic. By then I had worked through to *Backgammon*, an operation that sent an espionage team into Holland in late 1944 but which found its way into the Ruhr valley in Germany in order to carry out sabotage. The wireless operator was a talented Pole by the name of Katowski who played the piano at concert level and whose touch on a wireless key was distinctive in its perfection. Robin Katowski did not survive the war, a fact that made me personally sad as I read of his heroism in the hands of his Nazi interrogators. I scribbled my recommendation that the Backgammon file should be released, then I cleaned off my desk.

It was almost midnight when I arrived back at my room in the Brown Hotel, again by taxi. I washed my hands and face before going straight to bed and did not bother to listen to waiting telephone messages since, I reasoned, there wasn't much I could do with them until morning, anyway.

The next day I awoke and rose before dawn, reasonably refreshed, and ordered breakfast from room service. I showered quickly, then listened to my telephone messages from the day before. There was one from Linda, nothing urgent, she said, one from Danny Ryan in Mt. Juliet, Ireland, suggesting that we play golf that week, but nothing from the Foundation, a mild surprise. There were two from my colleagues with whom I worked on the NSA report and I typed replies to both and sent them by e-mail. Minimizing telephone time was almost a passion of mine.

I enjoyed every bite of breakfast, my favorite meal of the day, and started on my last cup of coffee before dialing Lynda's number in California. She answered on the second ring and, after an exchange of confirmations of mutual love, she read to me several pieces of mail that had been piling up in my almost two month absence. They included a request that I speak at the Renaissance Society, a New England historical institution who were not exceptionally well funded so that accepting their invitation to speak meant doing it pro bono. There was also a note from my literary agent of twelve years who, while referring in a vague way to the confused exigencies of the hardcover book market, would have to drop me from his active-writer roll. I didn't like the sound of that. It was as though I was some kind of failure in my business. Still, Len Gross did not know that my primary income was a product of my research work for the Foundation and he often urged me to "sit down, by god, and just write."

I almost worked through the lunch hour again but was saved from doing so by a call from Debbie. "It's Friday," she said. "Do you eat on Friday?"

"Naturally. Why would I not eat on Friday?" I said.

"I don't know. You Americans drink so much I thought you might just start drinking early and skip the food. Anyway," she said, "it's time to do one or the other."

I think I like this woman. "I'll be with you in fifty-four seconds," I said.

I ordered Scottish hen and leek soup and a large salad with bleu cheese dressing. The dressing turned out to be milky and bland, not enough garlic, and Debbie told me to always order the mustard dressing. She had shepherd's pie, explaining to me that she was once in love with a shepherd. I skipped wine, Debbie had two glasses of red.

"How are you coming?" she asked.

"Have you seen the list I'm working on?" I said.

"No, but I've probably seen a few thousand just like them," she said, glancing into the bottom of her glass with one eye closed, as though she had dropped something into the bottom.

"Then why didn't you do the job I'm doing?" I said.

"Not enough rank."

"No? Well, what rank do you think I have in the scheme of things?" I said.

"It takes a Minister's appointment to write off these security documents, that or represent a signatory to the National Secrets Act, like H. P. Carlisle Foundation. You see, Jean has already signed off on your list for the U.K. and you're doing the same for the United States," she said. Debbie poured the remaining drops from our table decanter into her own glass.

"What if Jean and I don't agree on what should be declassified?" I asked.

"Then it goes back to the Defense Ministry for further review. But the ruling will follow the negative input," Debbie said.

"Always?"

"Always. No one wants to be accused of jeopardizing national security, now do they? Better to err on the side of silence. That's what we do, you see."

"God. These things are more than fifty years old. Tell you what,

Debbie, why don't you just give me Jean's list and I'll write mine to agree with his," I said, only half in jest.

"He said you would say that," Debbie said.

"He did, huh?"

"Yes. Of course, you could throw caution to the wind, take me dining and dancing and try to make me give up the list in a moment of romantic weakness," Debbie arched an eyebrow.

"Then would you let me see his list?"

"No, but we would have had a wonderful weekend together," she said.

We did not have a wonderful weekend together. I worked past midnight that Friday night and got through the S's. By late in the evening I had hit a stride, a kind of zone, and my reading speed was in high gear. I was looking for names of people who's relatives might have been embarrassed by their husband, father, uncle, whatever, who might have been considered traitors or collaborators by a citizenry who was unfamiliar with the extreme measures of torture used by the Nazis throughout Europe. My concern was not only for British or American volunteers but for persons of all nations, not excluding Germany itself, or any of the Eastern bloc countries who were sympathetic or actively participating on the side of their German conquerors.

Names of people were not the only considerations I was bound to make about declassification. Some current organizations were outgrowths of WWII activities, the OSS becoming the CIA was one, and there were cases where moles might have been planted back in the forties that were still in place today, or whose contacts in other countries were active. There were special markings attached to the files for these cases, beige note papers with interrupted lines bordering the page, that warned me to pay special attention when reading and cross-referencing. I found myself simply marking the file "*Not recommended for publication.*" Debbie was right. I, like the rest of the bureaucrats, chose to err on the side of discretion.

It was one of these beige colored files code named RAVEN that caused me to pause. I scribbled the usual not recommended note on the transit slip and tossed it onto the top of the pile when, for whatever reason, I re-read the last paragraph of the cover sheet. It said "*TOP SECRET - EYES ONLY: Robinette.* I knew who Robinette was. The code word had come up during the NSA evaluation. For reasons that were never stated, all communications regarding SIS man Edward Boxshall, was sealed. Boxshall was a powerful influence in British Secret Intelligence Service, before it became known as MI6 at the outbreak of war in 1939. Boxshall was the Babe Ruth of big-league spies and he was a key figure in determining who would eventually form the nucleus of SOE. I re-read the Raven file.

The account was unusually short. It referred to a commando raid undertaken in August of 1940. It was a small but well mounted airborne operation that took place in the south of Germany, about fifteen kilometers north of Moosberg. The report indicated that it was the British 3rd Para-Commando that made a night jump into a wooded area between Munich and Regensburg. Thirty-six commandos made the raid and listed one "technical expert" as part of the raiding party. The apparent target was listed as a train track, presumably the one that passed through Moosberg. The commandos were "engaged," according to the report, and there was one survivor from the action.

One man out of thirty-six. Or thirty-seven, if one counted the technical expert. Street was stunned. God, it was a slaughter. And over what? A railroad track deep in Germany itself? The RAF had hardly begun bombing Berlin, never mind a raid as deep into Germany as Munich. I knew that British bombers had range enough to fly a mission of that length and return, but the risk of being shot down over heavily defended Germany on such a long mission would have been incredibly risky. And where were the names of the personnel who took part in the raid?

I had several immediate reactions to the report. In the first place information needed to make a determination was paltry. In fact it seemed suppressed. Then I felt the emotion of anger at the waste of so many gallant fighting men thrown against a railroad target. What in the hell could have been so important that the delay of a train - and that is all one could expect of wrecking track since it is so easily repaired - could be worth the sacrifice of an elite commando unit and a very brave aircrew? It certainly wasn't an atomic bomb. That would come more than four years later.

I picked up the telephone and dialed Debbie's extension. As usual, she answered at once. "August Street, Debbie," I said.

"Oh, I was expecting dead end but I guess August will do," she said.

"I've heard all of those jokes, thank you. I want you to tell me something," I said in what I thought was a no-nonsense tone.

"Of course. And I apologize for the stupid joke. It just leaped out of my mouth before I could retrieve it. I am in your debt," she said.

"Good. I want you to tell me how Jean Scheerer signed off on Operation Raven, 1940," I said.

"I can't tell you that. It's against the rules," she said.

"I don't care if it's against the rules. I want to know. It's important," I said.

"I could lose my job," Debbie said.

For a long moment I was silent. I felt foolish asking her to break a rule over a telephone. Then she said, "I'll be right down to explain to you why I can't give you that information."

"All right," I said, still mildly irate.

She arrived from her office in less than a minute. As she walked through the door of SB-301 she closed it behind her. Before I could say hello she said "Scheerer recommended against release."

"I thought so," I said, my frustration rising once again. "So no matter what I do the file stays sealed. Right?"

"I think that's about the all of it, yes," Debbie said, a twinge of a smile at the corner of her mouth.

"Well, hell," was all I could muster. I was far enough along on the project so that if I worked through the weekend I could be back in California by Monday playing golf at the club. "Can we get him on the phone?"

"I doubt it."

"Doubt it or know for sure?" I said.

"For sure. He can't be reached for any reason," she said, still standing though there was a chair near her.

"For how long? As long as I'm here in London? Until I finish this little exercise?" I wanted to know.

Debbie nodded. "As long as we're guessing, I think your guess is very good."

I considered for a long moment, watching Debbie's eyes. She let me look but not read. I briefly thought that she would make a hell of a field agent, then realized that she probably had been.

"Thanks, Deb," I said as she left the room.

I did not change my recommendation for release of the Raven file and went on to others. As I pored through the next stack I found the going more difficult. I began to distrust the contents of the reports, looking for double entendre or veiled meanings where, almost certainly, none existed. And I never got Raven out of my mind. Finally, exasperated, I pushed the stacks aside and retrieved Raven. I read it once again then I activated my modem and typed an access number that put me into Whitehall archives. There were two more passwords to insert before I gained the TO&E's of all British units active from 1939 through 1940. Several were classified Secret, but that level of classification was hardly what it seemed today. I was interested in commando units. From 1941 through 1945 there were several dozen, but in 1939 there were only five. Several more were being trained and assembled.

I used *search* to look up the Third Para-commando but I got the message *Access Denied*. I started to dial Debbie's number again but thought better of it. Instead I used the telephone to dial the H.P. Carlisle Foundation in Virginia and asked to be put through to Wes Claridge. I couldn't remember his extension number. Wes was somewhere in the building, I was told, but not at his desk. I said that he should call me back immediately, and said that it was an emergency. I left my extension number at the basement of MI6. I didn't care if my phone calls were being monitored or not.

Within a short period of time Wes returned my call. "I was eating a cheeseburger," he said.

"I know you wouldn't stop eating a hamburger for just anyone," I said. "I need the help of the best computer hacker in the world."

"You got him. Who's our victim?"

I explained that I needed to get into a certain data base and either remove a file or be told who gave the order to deny access.

"Hardly a challenge to my talents," Wes said. "I've got a slick idea for diverting money from the St. Louis General Dynamics overseas wire transfers into a Swiss account without them knowing it for five months. All you have to do is set up the account for us. I figure we could each take down fifteen million."

"Guys with a lousy eighty-five mile per hour fastball make that much money," I said. "I'm in a hurry, Wes."

"Okay. Wait a sec."

"Call me back," I said.

"Just hang on," he said.

I hung on. I could hear the unmistakable sounds of a long series of touch-tone sounds, rings, clicks, then modem sounds, and more clicks.

"Are you at your computer?" Wes asked me.

"Yeah," I said, turning toward the screen of my lap-top which was still where I had left it when access had been denied. The prohibiting message was no long there. In its place were several paragraphs of military exposition followed by two rows of names, ranks and military specialty codes. Atop the page read **THIRD- PARA REGIMENT COMMANDO** and the date of February 22, 1940.

"Got it?" Wes asked.

"Sure do, pard. Thanks very much," I said.

"Just get the Swiss account opened and I'll show you what hacking is all about."

I quickly scanned the names of the regiment, containing about four hundred in all. I saw no name that meant anything to me so I took my time reading the top of the TO&E which explained, in military shorthand, that after Operation Raven was launched, the remaining personnel in Third-Para Regiment were reassigned to new commando units currently training in the U. K.

Personnel chosen for Raven were underlined. With the exception of an inventory of arms, signed off by one Lieutenant Roe, there was nothing further.

The task that confronted me next I thought was going to be easy. I needed to find, and interview, the survivor of Raven. There was only one: Private Thomas Ross MacQueen, age nineteen. His home of record was Narberth, a small town west of Swansea near St. George's Channel. I called local telephone information for Narberth and asked for a listing by that name. There were two MacQueens but no Thomas. Or Ross. I thanked the operator and dialed the first MacQueen. A young man answered. I gave him my name and told him that I was with the H.P. Carlisle Foundation and that I had a small amount of money, some three hundred pounds, to pay to a Thomas R. MacQueen who would be about eighty years old. Was he, I asked, related to such a person or did he know him?

Was it a prize? Like an answer to a question on the radio? the young man wanted to know.

No. It was not. Do you know?

No, sorry to say, it wasn't him.

A woman's voice answered the next MacQueen call. She sounded firm in voice, I judged her to be in her mid-thirties to late 40's. She said that her name was Kathleen. I did not feel the need to use my cash give-away ruse, so I merely told Kathleen MacQueen that I was trying to locate a Thomas R. MacQueen. Kathleen informed me, without asking why I was looking for him, that her husband's name was Arthur.

"He would be an older man. Thomas MacQueen would be almost eighty years old," I said. "I don't suppose that could be a father, or even a grandfather. Or uncle."

"Well, if it is, it isn't one that I know. Nor Arthur, I'm sure," she said.

"Is your husband home now?" I realized after I got the words out of my mouth that I must have sounded impertinent.

"He's home," Kathleen said, her voice clearly not taking offense, "but he's asleep. He's had a long day. If you care to give me your number I'd be happy to have him call you in the morning. His day off, you know."

"Thank you. I'm staying at the Brown Hotel, in London." I gave her the number including the room extension so that Arthur could ring directly through.

"And what time would be most convenient, Mr. Street?" Kathleen asked.

"I'm an early riser," I lied, thinking back thirty or so years when that might have been the truth. "Tell Arthur that he can call at any time when he wakes in the morning. I'll be up and about."

Kathleen MacQueen assured me that he would call, and probably early.

I suddenly felt exhausted and realized that I had called the Mac-Queens at a late hour, especially this time of year when people tend to retire a bit earlier than in the summer months. I put away my unexamined ops files and stowed my laptop in its carrying case. I made sure the door to SB-301 was securely locked behind me then walked down the hallway toward the elevator banks. En route I tried

Debbie's door but found it locked. I knocked and waited a moment or two, but when there was no answer I continued to the elevator and into the lobby of 64 Vauxhall. Having forgotten to call a taxi from my cubbyhole in the basement, I used a public telephone near the security desk. Assured by the dispatcher that a cab would be there within the next ten minutes, I walked outside to await my transportation in fresh air.

As I leaned against a wall near the circular drive in front of the building, I buttoned the topmost loop of my coat, feeling that the motion was a futile one, that I was dealing with London chill that had no respect for the best of thermal clothing, even my top coat. Yet the night-time cold hardly distracted me from questions that had been swirling around inside my head about Raven.

CHAPTER

2

A near 100percent casualty rate for a mission to blow up railroad track simply defied my understanding of warfare at any level. Using highly trained, elite troops to undertake what seemed like a suicidal assault was even more mystifying to me. And then there were attempts to cover it all up. Otherwise, why did I have to hack my way into something as straightforward as an organization table for the regiment?

I neglected to take a shower before falling into bed and to sleep. For that reason my sleep was uncomfortable. I awoke several times wishing that I had at least pulled on my favorite flannel top before crashing, yet felt too tired to go to the trouble of getting up to locate the damn thing.

I still jumped when the telephone went off near my ear at a perfectly civilized hour, nearly seven thirty in the morning. It was Arthur MacQueen calling. I pulled myself into a sitting position to speak to him. I found that I sound like a drowning man when speaking over a telephone while prone, and I had the hope that Mr. MacQueen would not realize he had caught me still slumbering while the sun had long been up.

"Kathleen's told me that you're looking for a Thomas MacQueen," Arthur said. "Near eighty, you say?"

"Yes," I said, licking my lips and blinking my contact lenses back into action. "He was nineteen years old in 1940. An army veteran, in fact."

There was a soft chuckle from the other end of the line. "Afraid I'm a bit younger. Forty-seven. You didn't say why you was after him."

"Ah, well, it's a silly thing, really. We're trying to contact some of the old British commandos for a kind of reunion. Thomas was one of the fellows at the top of our list," I said.

There was a slight hesitation from Arthur at the other end. Was he waiting for me to add more?

"Sorry, mate. I love parties and we'd love to come to yours, Kathleen and me. We just had her twentieth school clam-ketch. Hell of a time, we had."

"So you don't know a Thomas MacQueen. Not a relative? He comes from Narberth," I said.

"Does he, now? We've been here, how long, now? Near fifteen years. Seems like I might have heard of a Thomas, given the last name we share."

"Yes, I suppose so. Thank you for calling me back, Mr. MacQueen," I said and hung up.

A hot shower did little to clear up the niggling that had crawled onto the back of my neck and would not go away. I ordered breakfast from room service, grateful once again that my expense allowance covered such things while traveling for the Foundation, and tried to become interested in the London Times newspaper. I found that while I was reading the words, none of them were registering inside my head. I had hardly put away one egg and a piece of toast when it occurred to me that I had to travel to Narberth myself. There were other steps available to me, even on a Saturday, that I might have taken to locate the man. An Internet telephone directory for the entire British isles, for example, or contacts with army veteran's groups. Even police or Scotland Yard could have helped. But for some reason that I could not explain I knew that I would have to see Narberth with my own eyes because according to his service records that was where Thomas R. MacQueen called home in 1939.

I called the concierge and asked that a rental car be made available. I said that I would appreciate whatever road maps the rental company could provide that could direct me to Narberth be included. The distance to Swansea, the concierge guessed at my urging, was approximately two hundred eighty kilometers from London and that Narberth was probably another fifty from there. It sounded like an easy four-hour drive but I took along a change of clothing, a casual outdoor jacket and, of course, my laptop.

The drive from London to Narberth was almost directly west on A-40. The sky was entirely overcast and it rained almost non-stop causing me to travel at a slower speed than usual and with lights on. My drive took me over the Cambrian Mountains which I thought was exceptional scenery, though hardly the kind of mountains that we have in our American West. I stopped once at a roadside restaurant in Pembrokeshire to eat a sandwich and drink a cup of coffee, arriving in Narberth after dark. I considered checking into a hotel straight away but, not wanting to lose any more time than was necessary, I decided to call Arthur MacQueen before anything else. As events unfolded, I was glad that I did. I used a public telephone and had a pen and notepad ready, hoping to invite myself to their residence. Mrs. MacQueen answered the telephone.

"Mrs. MacQueen," I said, "This is August Street calling you back. I'm very sorry to bother you again but I happen to be in Narberth, still looking for Thomas R. MacQueen. I wonder if I might stop by for just a question or two."

"Ah. Please hold on, Mr. Street," she said.

As I waited, the receiver pressed tightly to my ear, I could hear Mrs. MacQueen's voice and, less distinctly, Arthur MacQueen's responses. She seemed to be saying words to the effect that I-told-you-so. From Arthur a long silence, mumbles, then came his voice on the telephone.

"Arthur MacQueen here," he said.

"I'm really very sorry to bother you, Mr. MacQueen, but I'm still looking for Thomas. I was wondering if..."

"He doesn't live in Narberth," Arthur said, cutting in.

I felt a surge of excitement at his certain declaration. "I see. Where else then?" I asked, almost holding my breath.

There was a distinct hesitation on the other of the line and when Arthur spoke again it was with a kind of resignation.

"Saundersfoot," he said.

"Ah," I said, as though that explained everything and as though I knew where Saundersfoot was, which I didn't.

As if reading my mind, Arthur MacQueen said "Saundersfoot is a ways down the road. You take four-seven-eight south. Watch the signs and you can't miss the place."

"And how will I find him there?" I asked.

"The Wise Pelican. That's the name of the pub he owns. Mr. Street...."

"Yes?"

"I'm not sure what you intend for Thomas. He's my uncle. I don't think you mean him any harm or I wouldn't have told you where to find him. He's, he's had a hard life," Arthur MacQueen said, somewhat searching for just the right words.

"Thank you for your confidence, Mr. MacQueen. You're right, I certainly wouldn't say or do anything that would injure your uncle. I think he is a great hero," I said.

There was an almost audible sound of relief from the other end of the line. "All right, then. Goodby," he said.

The drive to Saundersfoot was, indeed, an easy one, and after only one wrong turn at the intersections of A477 and A478, I arrived in the coastal town just after eleven o'clock. I found a hotel by following the ratings of my Tourist Board guide which listed the Cliff House on Wogan Terrace as a three star guest house. I asked for and received a room overlooking the ocean, or the bay. The hotel's bar being closed for the night, a non-weekend, I had a drink of Scotch from a bottle that I carried with me as I surveyed the marina below and to my right. The boats in the moorage could hardly be seen through the drizzling rain but as I sipped my drink I felt reasonably good about my chances of finding Thomas R. MacQueen. I took a shower, read a few pages of a novel, then dropped off to sleep.

The next morning I slept in. It was almost ten when I rose, washed my face and shaved. I walked down stairs to the hotel's dining room. I was shown to a table near a large window with a pleasant view of the bay and the headlands on either side. I ordered coffee, stipulating that it be Italian, French, or any other very black roast, scrambled eggs and a croissant. I perused the local newspaper while waiting for my breakfast to arrive, then, because it was handy, found a telephone book in the small library connected to the dining room. I looked in the directory for a listing of MacQueen but found nothing. I did find, however, The Wise Pelican. After eating I dialed the number for the Pelican and asked the lady who answered the telephone how to find the place. I did not ask for Thomas MacQueen.

Returning to my room I turned on my lap top that contained a portable modem and checked my e-mail. There was a three day accumulation to wade through and I found that I could delete a good bit of it without responding. I spent the next hour and one-half answering those that were imperative, and felt a sense of relief when the last one was flashed off.

In going through my past week's notes one more time and reviewing the Raven operation in particular, it struck me again that the British government was attempting to cover up the fact that they had squandered the lives of their brave young soldiers. It also occurred to me that the cover-up was being advanced by Jean Scheerer. It was possible that if the entire affair became known, even at this late date, there would almost certainly be an investigation and that investigation could reach very high, indeed. Thus, in a state of some agitation, I walked under skies, now clearing, along quaint streets and businesses that had been carefully maintained with tourism in mind. There were plenty of eateries, specialty shops of all kinds including souvenir sellers.

I found The Wise Pelican two blocks back from the beach with a small alley in the rear that also serviced a bicycle shop and a takeaway sandwich business. The Pelican was well lit with the shades drawn back on large windows. There was a semi-circular bar on the far side of the room as one entered the premises, with tables and chairs filling the rest of the floor space except for a place where darts were played. The odor of deep-fry oil struck me immediately as the door closed behind me, and my mouth watering for the fish and chips it created. In addition to the odor of hot oil and fish, cigarette and pipe smoke hung in the air and stuck to the walls.

One man behind the bar served customers seated in front of him while he also made drinks for a waitress who distributed food and drinks to patrons at tables. The bartender was slender, well under six feet, wore his black hair slicked down and locked in place with shiny stuff. He was perhaps forty years old.

I found an empty table with a view of the entire room. A young waitress who appeared to have eaten too many of the establishment's fried foods took my order for the house specialty plus a pint of stout. I had never developed much of a liking for that British brew but I continued to order it when I visited the U.K. hoping that my taste would someday develop. The practical side was that there was never a chance of drinking too much while on the job, like today. I sipped the stuff as I leaned back in my chair to survey the room.

There were three or four tables occupied by people who appeared to be business types on their lunch hour. All had food in front of them. There were a pair of couples that were relaxed at their respective tables, drinking and picking at chips. At the bar were three patrons who appeared to be "regulars" whiling away the day, drinking their stout while gazing into the large mirror behind the bar. A newly arriving fourth customer was a portly, middle-aged woman carrying a woven straw shopping bag. She plopped herself onto a bar stool and greeted everyone around her, including the bartender, as old friends.

My gaze eventually fell upon an elderly man with full, grizzled hair, face clean-shaven, elongated square chin, sitting alone at a corner table, ignoring or indifferent to the sounds or presence of others in the room. The man was reading a book that he had propped upon an ashtray. At his elbow was a pint of ale that he infrequently lifted to his mouth although the same waitress who took my order made certain that the man's glass was kept continually filled. If the man noticed me looking in his direction there was no outward sign. He simply continued to read, his eyes seldom looking up from his book material.

I turned away from the man for a moment while my fish and chips order was placed before me and when I looked back at the table the man had shifted position somewhat. Then I noticed something strange. The man's left hand was a claw, the fingers curled and twisted tightly into the palm, the middle finger also curled but looped above the others giving an eerie image of a raptor's tool.

I judged the man's height to be over six feet. His well-worn jacket was herringbone, under which was a blue collar working man's shirt. His trousers were straw colored corduroy. He might have been quite handsome as a younger man. There was something else about him that for a very long moment I couldn't quite place, then it occurred to me that there was something wrong with one of his legs. The right foot turned toward the left, in a position that one could only call uncomfortable. Before I had finished my fish and stout I was all but certain that I had found my man. Leaving more than enough money on my table to cover my bill, I rose from the chair and crossed the room to his table. I stood motionless near him until he looked up from his reading.

I said, "Mr. MacQueen?"

The eyes that looked up from under heavy eyebrows now turned grey were intelligent and non-wavering. "Who are you?" he said.

"My name is August Street. I've come across your name while doing some historical research and wondered if..."

"For the army," he said in the same tone that he might address a draft-dodger.

"Well, not exactly," I said, instantly feeling that I was starting off my association with this good man with a half-lie. The sides of his mouth turned down slightly as I corrected my equivocation. "I'm an employee of the H. P. Carlisle Foundation. It is true that we do research from time to time for the government."

"Whose?"

"Whose? Ah, generally the United States government but there are occasions when the interests of the Unites States and the United Kingdom are the same. Then it's possible that the Foundation might do work for both." I must have sounded like an idiot, in fact I know that I did, just trying to be careful not to mislead Thomas MacQueen. I regarded him as a singular man who could live within himself and shut out others easily. Men of commando background are selected for, among other things, the ability to work entirely independent of outside support. To have survived what he must have gone through would have tested that part of his psyche to the maximum.

MacQueen turned away from me, without asking me to sit, and looked again at his book. "I'm not interested in either one of them governments," he said in dismissing me.

Without being asked, I pulled out a chair and sat facing him across the table. "Mr. MacQueen," I said, "I'm not any kind of representative of either government. I'm an historian, and right now I don't feel like a very good one. I have questions to ask you but I promise you that I will not write about your answers without your agreement."

MacQueen snorted as he raised his pint of dark beer to his mouth and drank deeply. He handled the suds like a man who drank with regularity but I saw no signs of dissipation about him. His waist was reasonably narrow and one could see the muscles were still hard around his neck and shoulders. My eyes moved again at his deformed left hand. The sleeves of his shirt and coat covered most of the forearm but the deep and terrible scars that had caused the limb to shrivel were clear. If his eyes had followed mine, he made no acknowledgment.

"Ahhh, ye don't even know what questions to ask. Go away, now," he said.

"I know that you were a part of Operation Raven," I said. He raised his eyes at this. "And I know that you were the only survivor."

"You're fifty years too late, Mr. August Street. I had something to say back then, but not now. No, thank you," he said, and turned back to his reading as though I was not there.

"Mr. MacQueen," I began, but he cut me off cold with a cocked eye that held me fast like an insect stuck through with a pin.

"Ye heard now, didn't ye?"

I had no choice but to withdraw.

I returned to my room at the Cliff House to think. Turning on my computer, I punched up my modem and checked my e-mail. I read through the stuff with little enthusiasm for its contents. There was one from Linda. She had tried to reach me in London to no avail. She wanted me to call. Because her message did not seem urgent and I was in no mood to chit-chat, I simply made a mental note to call her later.

I spent the day doing miscellaneous work through the computer but none of it was important and my mind wasn't really into the tasks. I put through a call to MI6 and asked for Debbie's extension. She did not answer but I was automatically routed to her voice mail. My message to her was that I needed to speak with Jean Scheerer and that I simply did not believe he was entirely out of reach. If he didn't carry a cell phone, I said, he must at least check messages on an answering machine every day. After hanging up I was painfully aware that I had long refused to carry a cell phone, regarding it as a tether around my neck. Scheerer and I most likely shared the same aversion.

I was determined not to leave Saundersfoot without learning what

MacQueen knew that I did not. As I strolled through the streets of the town, not fully appreciating the delightful scenery and seashore ambience that I might have enjoyed were I not preoccupied, I ran through a series of scenarios designed to pry open the man's mouth, if not his heart. I thought, for example, that I could have gotten authorization under the Official Secrets Act to force MacQueen to speak to me. But I didn't have the stomach for an approach of that kind nor did I think that MacQueen was the type of man who would collapse if threatened.

I returned to The Wise Pelican that evening. I occupied the same table I had earlier and ordered a lager beer, being in no mood for more stout. The smell of the deep fryer reminded me that I had not eaten since breakfast and I ordered fish and chips, calories be damned. MacQueen was not on the premises though I ate and drank slowly hoping that he might show up. I sipped at a second pint but when I had finished MacQueen had not appeared and I returned to the hotel.

After staying as long as possible under an extra-hot shower, my favorite method of relaxation, I lay on top of the coverlet reading a book I had found in the hotel's small library. It was Barbara Tuchman's superbly written *The Guns of August* which I had read before but still enjoyed.

The next morning I awoke still inventing and discarding ideas that might make the irascible MacQueen talk to me. More than once it occurred to me to offer the man some kind of remuneration for his story. It would not have been the first time that I had drawn a sum from the Foundation's discretionary fund to defray the expense for obtaining information otherwise impossible to get. We are, after all, living in the age of information and a good deal of it that we need had a cost attached to it somewhere along the line. By the end of an impatiently spent morning again walking through the town, I was among the first lunch diners in The Wise Pelican.

Recognizing me from my previous excursions there, my waitress seemed almost happy to see me. I appreciated her good cheer and we talked briefly about the weather, overcast but "stimulating" she said, because it was "brooding." I wondered if she wasn't interested in drama but decided not to ask. She said her name was Lydia. I asked Lydia about Mr. MacQueen.

"Oh, he'll be in, all right. He owns the place. Counts the money twice a day, that one."

She did not ask why I was interested in MacQueen and I did not pursue the subject. But I had hardly got beyond the first article in the London *Times* when the object of my interest walked in the door. I was sure that he saw me immediately but he made no outward sign of it. There were still fewer than five or six customers in the place and, after acknowledging the bartender and Lydia, he walked the length of the room to the rear. I could see that he had a pronounced limp as moved among the tables and chairs.

He sat at his usual table and, without asking, Lydia brought him a mug of tea and what looked to be a scone. I returned to reading my newspaper without attempting to catch his eye. After several minutes I had the feeling that he was watching me instead of the other way around. I resisted the temptation to look up for myself, instead burying myself in the editorial pages.

After what must have been half an hour, I closed my paper and casually looked in his direction. MacQueen was now regarding me quite openly.

I returned his gaze and for the most part of a minute we simply stared at each other. By this time I had jettisoned my idea of buying his story, not for any ethical considerations, but because I intuitively knew that such an offer would be ignored by MacQueen and perhaps even offend him. Eventually I turned my attention pointedly to another section of the *Times* and, trying to appear composed, began reading the sports section. While I follow sports in the U.S. I hadn't any idea of what English cricket or rugby was all about so that a large part of the articles made no sense to me at all. Still, I read each word as though I was a fan.

"So you won't go away," MacQueen said, standing at my table.

"No, I don't think I can," I said, quite honestly.

He continued to look down at me with something of a quizzical expression. Then he took a deep breath and slowly lowered himself to a chair opposite me. "Why is it," he said, "that I get the feeling yer trouble?"

I shrugged. "I certainly mean you no trouble, Mr. MacQueen. I'm only a reporter of facts." I was not comfortable with the impression that I must have been giving MacQueen so I tried to be reassuring.

"I should also tell you that I can keep a confidence. If you answer my questions and you want your responses to be kept confidential, I'll respect your decision absolutely."

His large head turned away as he looked out of the window that gave the best view of the marina and the Atlantic Ocean beyond. For several minutes he sat that way and I feared that I had said the wrong things or somehow failed to convince him of my representations of confidentiality. When he moved his attention away from the window it was to signal Lydia with a nod of his head for more tea. She brought a freshly filled mug and a second scone. While she was there she removed my basket of chips and, per my request, left to get me a cup of black coffee.

"What do you know about Raven?" MacQueen asked me.

"Very little. Only that the operation took place in July of 1940, and that it was launched by the Third Para Commando. There were thirty-six commandos and only one survivor. You. At least that's what the report said."

"What report?" MacQueen wanted to know.

I explained to him my assignment in London, that I was reviewing wartime documents that had specific names of places and people who were involved with espionage or commando activities. "There seems to be no reason for not releasing it all now, sixty years later."

I waited for a reaction from MacQueen but there was none. "In the case of Raven, on the other hand," I said, "there is more that is missing than what's there."

"That's because they want it that way, mate," MacQueen said with certainty.

"Why? What difference could it make now?"

"Because there's no statute of limitations on murder, that's why," the ex-commando said.

"Murder?" I said. "You mean war? Are you talking about the men who were behind the war? Churchill, Hitler, Stalin? Those people?"

"Exactly right on. *Those* bloody bastards," he said. MacQueen straightened his leg which caused him enough discomfort to make him wince. I suspicioned that it gave him far more pain than he allowed to show on his face.

"I think I could agree with you there," I said, settling back in my chair. We had found a common ground and I was beginning to feel the slightest bit of confidence that MacQueen could eventually fill in the Raven blanks. I would find out later that what I needed to know was far more than MacQueen would or could tell me. "If you don't mind, Mr. MacQueen, I'd like to sample a bit of your famous single malt whiskey. I would be honored if you'd allow me to treat us both." I made no apology for the early hour.

"Thanking you for your generous offer, Mr. Street, but you're in my place and while you sit at my table your money won't buy a drop. Lydie," he said, motioning to Lydia. When she arrived at our table he said "Fetch the Macallan Twenty-five from the basement. Mr. Street, here, intends to make a detailed report back to the United States of America about our whiskey. We'd best keep him on course."

As MacQueen and I resumed our conversation I saw that the bartender had gone to the far end of the bar and lifted a trap door. As his shoulders then his head disappeared down under, I could only assume that he had accessed the basement.

I was hard pressed to hold in check my curiosity about MacQueen's arm and leg but I refrained from asking so that I might have the aid of the magical malt that was even now being poured into our tumblers. The bottle, I noticed, was of clear glass and the fluid inside bright amber. It was less than half full and covered in heavy dust that the bartender was apparently not called upon to remove. I gathered that the Macallan was twenty-five years old when it was finally bottled but I had a hunch that another twenty-five might have passed from the time it was opened in this place of business. There was no ice offered, of course, nor water to dilute the stuff. After tipping the bottle for each of us Lydia stepped back but did not withdraw from our table, staying to watch with interest at least our first taste.

I raised my glass to MacQueen and said, "To your continued good health."

He nodded solemnly. "And to yours," he said as we tipped up our glasses.

The taste of that drink might have been the most flavorful one of my life or I might have simply thought so at the time. I've had good Scotch in my time just as I've had my share of sex. It has been said that all sex is good with some only better than others. I recall thinking at that time that Macallan had made himself a mighty sexy scotch.

"Thank you, Mr. MacQueen. That's a whiskey drink I'll remember until the old folk's illness takes away my brain."

MacQueen put his head back and laughed. For the first time I saw his teeth. They were remarkably white and seemed to light up his entire face, even though one of them had been broken off at an angle. MacQueen had not, for whatever lack of caring, had it capped.

"We're all here for a short while, aren't we?" he said. "First we're babes and our mothers suckle us and our fathers tend that we get enough food and mind his manners, not ours. Then we're off on our own for a while, at least we think we're on our own, then our brains begin leakin' out and we have to wear diapers again. Meantime, we got to get our livin' done, don't we?"

"I suspect you've done more living than most, Mr. MacQueen," I said.

"Tisn't true," he said, his head lowering a bit, but a whiff of his smile still remaining on his thin, bluing lips. "And you might call me Tom, since you won't go away."

"You'd flatter me if you called me August," I said, and meant it.

MacQueen poured us each another drink. This time I sipped mine and he did the same, the delicious bite tracing its trickle to the bottom of the gut sent back rewards to the tongue in both taste and touch.

"All right, then, what do you want to know?" he said.

I felt myself shrug. Everything. I wanted to know it all but hardly knew where to start. "Well," I heard myself say, "what kind of mission was it? I mean, the report said that you were to take out a railroad track. Surely there was more to it than that."

"Oh, yes, to be sure. Much more than that. We was to kill Adie, that's what it was about," MacQueen said, then sipped his scotch.

"Adie. Do you mean Adolf?" I said, certain that MacQueen would correct my erroneous conclusion.

But he nodded his head. "I do, indeed. Nobody less than the Austrian house painter, we were after. Schicklgruber his ownself. Strange, you know, me usin' his name like that. Schicklgruber. It was his real name, you know, but we had all kinds of names for him and we looked at all sorts of scrawlings of the man. Part of the dehumanizing process, we know now."

I agreed but said nothing, waiting for MacQueen to continue.

"What he was was a smart bastard. Very, very smart. And the ones he pulled in around him was smart, too, don't think they wasn't. They knew what they wanted and they got it. Oh, they was evil, all right. Damned sure about that, with no mistake, but when it comes to takin' over worlds, ol' Adie was as good as you'd care to come up out of the bag with."

MacQueen turned his head once more to glance out of the window, as though he suddenly had remembered an appointment that had to be kept. But he turned back to the table and reached for his drink, hesitated, then put the tumbler to his lips and drank.

"It was a rush, rush job. Hell, I was just a lad, eighteen, when I'd joined the army in 1938, and fourteen months later I was fresh out of commando training in the north of Scotland when they formed us up an asked who'd volunteer for a dangerous mission. Well, you've been in the military, right, August?"

I nodded that I had but did not feel the need to tell MacQueen that I was an air force type. I had never missed so much as a meal in the military and that included getting shot down over Duc Phu and being choppered back to my squadron the same afternoon. So I said nothing.

"It's either a joke or the best advice ever given when they say 'never volunteer for anything.' Comes to cleaning up the messhalls it makes sense, no denying that, but you tell a nineteen-year-old kid that you've got a dangerous deed to be done you'll have to beat the kid and all his friends back with a stick cause they're all wanting to go! No, there was no shortage of volunteers for that dirty piece of business they sent us on. Sent us on to die, no mistake."

My curiosity forced me to speak. "You say that as though they expected no survivors."

His response was a grimace. "Yes, well, that's a little further down the line, isn't it?"

Strange answer. In any case, why, I asked myself, *haven't I heard about an attempt on Hitler's life before? There were several, I know, but not by an organized Allied military raiding party.*

"Yes," I said, "of course. Please go on."

"Like I say, it was a rush. We had only three days to get ready, no training special to the landing zone. There'd be a train coming from Munich, Hitler's train, with him on board. Nothing fancy about what was to be done; we'd wait for the train, blow the tracks, and kill his bodyguards. And then Adolf. Just like that," MacQueen said. It was breath- taking in its simplicity.

"A very long shot. I suppose you knew that, of course," I said.

"The whole thing was a long shot, wasn't it? The war, I mean. There were all kinds of units wiped out before it was over. But we were the best, and we knew that, for sure. We'd take a damn lot of killin' we boys would. We had fine training, good tactics, the best weapons made, at the time. And we were a tough lot. No, we weren't afraid of any man or group of men, damn sure not the Fritzes."

"So how did it go, then?" I said, painfully aware that Hitler survived to the end of the war and that none of MacQueen's comrades did.

MacQueen shrugged. "Good as them things can go, I s'pose you'd say. We packed into a Stirling. They'd took off the guns an' such to save weight for a long trip. We went up with a bomber stream that night so's we'd appear like all the other ships, and we could slip right through keepin' out of searchlights by going a bit around the targets, you see..."

"Thirty-six. Plus the Stirling crew," I said.

"Aye, and the tech," MacQueen said.

"What tech?" I wanted to know.

MacQueen shrugged again. "Radio bloke, I guess he was. While we was knocking off the bodyguards and Adolf, the tech had something to do in the communications car."

"What?" I said.

"Don't know. Wasn't all that important, though, was it?"

I supposed that it wasn't. "What kind of range did the Stirling have?"

"I'm no expert of planes, but to Munich from Chelmsford was nine hundred kilometers. I've checked it since. The Stirling could do us that far and home, no question about that."

"So, when did you take off?" I asked, beginning to make shorthand notes on a paper place-mat upon which was a cartoon drawing of a pelican wearing a professor's gown and spectacles.

"Tuesday, August third, nineteen hundred and forty," MacQueen said.

Funny. There was no *action date* on the report at MI6. "Time?" I asked.

"Twenty-one thirty hours, or thereabouts. It was about as early as we could go and still have cover of night over the channel. We was probably about eleven thousand feet, cause we could breathe all right," he said. "But the tech. They had an oxygen bottle for that chap, just in case."

"Hm. You climbed out over the channel with other bombers in the stream. Now, what was the plan once you got to Munich?" I asked.

"North of Munich," MacQueen corrected. "There's the main line that goes to Regensburg from there. Nearest town, a village, really, was Pilz. Maybe fifteen kilometers from where we planned the bang-up. Moonless night and we had to find a meadow there, about three kilometers from the track itself. Plan was us paras would jump, lay over the day. Then the next night do the tracks and kill the bodyguard, and of course ol' Adie, and whilst we was doing that the Stirling would come back and pick us up."

God, he made it sound so simple. It was anything but, I thought. "How about German garrisons? Any nearby?"

"Well, we didn't know that, did we? I mean, intelligence that deep into Germany was hard to come by on short notice," MacQueen shook his head in memory. "Wasn't in the cards. We'd just have to lay it on and see how we come out."

I could feel the effects of the Macallan Scotch in my belly but I did not want more lest my awareness of MacQueen's words become dulled. But MacQueen poured himself another and, without asking, poured me one as well. I thanked him but took the smallest sip possible from the glass. MacQueen took a large one from his.

"The jump went all right, considering, though we lost one man but not much trouble with the tech. I doubt he'd jumped before. Two men were assigned to him, kind of to look out for him."

"Do you recall their names?" I asked.

"Acting Sergeant Collin Ferrel, Marion Clark, and Dickie Grafton. They was corporals," MacQueen said with no hesitation. "And fine men they was."

"You have a good memory, Thomas," I said, using his given name for the first time.

MacQueen slowly turned his head toward me, fixing his eyes upon me like a pair of gaffs piercing a fish's gill. "Not likely I'll ever forget, August."

"Even when the brain leaks?" I said, hoping to avert a storm with humor.

There was no acknowledging smile but he nodded his head in agreement. "Not even then. So they threw him out, the tech man. Down through the hole and his static line pulled open his chute. The rest of us dropped right on top of him, the plane circling."

"I don't suppose you remember the names of the flying crew?" I said.

MacQueen shook his head. "They wasn't any of us. Tell you, though, that navigator would make any father's son proud. Imagine tryin' to find a field of grass on a black night in a country you'd only seen on a map."

"So you found the drop zone?" I urged.

"Close enough. We had to walk a bit, but it was one hell of a job, considering no moon and no thanks to the fighter types. They was looking for us over Mannheim and then again near Stuttgart. We thought we'd bought it when night fighters was about but there was clouds, too, and that's where we lost em. Then, not long later, we went out. How often did something like that happen in one of these lash-ups?"

"Luck," I heard myself say.

"Yep, that it was. And that wasn't all the good luck we had. From the DZ to the main track me and Bobby Shaw found easy roads. Stumbled on it in the dark. A hikin' trail, it was. So we covered the way through woodlands and a valley on a' easy pace, the last kilometer uphill, but we wasn't even breathing hard when we got to the track. We was behind schedule so we put eight men out on the track while the sappers wired the trestle."

"A bridge?"

"Aye. A short one and not very high. It only spanned a small stream, but it would help us to turn cars over so that's where we put the charges," MacQueen said.

"The rest of us dug in among behind the tree line. We had to lay up in the day because the train was due at night, about fifteen hours."

"The Stirling?" I wondered aloud about the waiting bomber.

MacQueen snorted. "That I don't know. All I know is that it was there, waitin', at near midnight the next night when we got back. Course, anything could have gone wrong. The train might have been late. Or early! Yes, hell, we could'a missed her. Gone before us and there we'd be, strung out like laundry flappin' in the damn German wind."

"And was it? Late, I mean?" I asked.

MacQueen's lips pursed, then curled in a grimace until his mouth resembled an angry animal. "No, dear god, it was not."

MacQueen was silent for long moments, lost in a time and place known only to him and no other man alive. I refrained from speaking, waiting patiently for him to go on, if that was his wish. His eyes began to move ever so slightly, side to side, as if he were getting images into proper order, then he again began to speak.

"There was two trains. One that went ahead of Hitler's train a couple kilometers, maybe. We almost blew the tracks too soon, but Major Plith knew the difference at the last minute. So we let it go by. Then came the one we was waiting for. Nine cars in all, counting the locomotive. It was a big one, brand new Diesel, swastikas painted in red, white and black on the sides. It was pullin' two cars full of SS troops. Some was sitting on top, more down inside. They had a pair of machine guns mounted up there, MG-42s. Then there was the com car..."

"The communications car. How did you know which it was?" I asked.

"Aerials. No mistaken that one."

"Yes, of course."

"Then a kitchen car, then a dining room car. The sixth car was for staff officers. Beds and so forth. Then a map car, they called it..."

"Hitler's conference room on wheels?" I asked, actually knowing the answer.

"Righto. Then came Hitler's car himself. Gold swastikas on that one. Whole car polished and well-lit. Behind that was another car of SS troops. His personal bodyguard, you know."

I did indeed know. The palace guard. The hand-picked, fanatic Nazis were the creme de la creme of Germanic manhood, chosen for their fighting abilities and for their unquestioned devotion to their Führer. They were well-armed and very well trained.

"How many of them and how many of you?" I asked.

"It was almost two to one, they had us. No way to tell for sure. If we didn't have surprise, well...."

MacQueen tasted his Scotch again, sipping this time.

"It was a set-to, I'll tell you that. Bloody awful. When the tracks blew we was on em fast, tossing grenades into the two SS cars, and then using our Thompson guns. If I told you we didn't die easy, they didn't, either. We fired at near point-blank, barrels on our guns, on both sides, heatin' up, shoving magazine after magazine into em as fast as they emptied. One of them Krauts took half a mag from me and damned if he didn't come right at me, teeth bared, a hole in his damn chest as big as my fist. I clugged him in the head with the butt of my gun before the bastard fell. On and on we went, fighting first with guns, then we was down to knives. We carried them trench-stickers with the knuckle guards. I seen some of my boys clubbin' the SS with nothin' but their gun stocks, like a axe, we was so close to one another we could smell each other's breath."

MacQueen stopped talking and his eyes drifted again to look outside of the window, at a placid sea mottled with shadows of clouds gently moving shards of light across its grey waters. As I watched him in profile I believed I could see the boyish face that so many years ago had been horrified by free flowing blood.

"What about Hitler? Did you get near him?" I asked.

"Hell, I thought we killed him," MacQueen said, simply. "We all had assignments, you know. Mine was the last car, one of the SS guard cars. Me and my chaps 'd killed all we could find. Three of our paras went for Hitler's car with us comin' behind. We wasn't sure which one but it might have been the number eight car. I don't remember which it turned out."

"Do you recall the names?" I asked, almost holding my breath. "The men assigned to kill Hitler?"

"Marion Clark. He and me was close," he said. "And Dickie Grafton, he was another who went for Adie."

"And why did you think you killed him? Hitler." I said.

"Because Marion told me so. He and his mates blew open the car doors and went inside, firin' as they went. There was two officers with Hitler, Marion said, and he gunned em. Then he turned on Hitler and took a bullet of his own."

"Hitler?" I asked.

"No, Marion. Damned if Schicklgruber didn't shoot Marion with a pistol. The man was no coward, I'll give him that. Then Marion and his lads caught Adie with their Thompsons and that was the end of him. Damned if I know how the man pulled through," MacQueen said, his head shaking from side to side.

"They only thought they killed him. Obviously they just wounded him," I said.

"Well, I expect your right. I mean, the man survived, didn't he? Tough old cob, Adie must have been. Still, they said they shot up his face and set fire to him and his car with thermite."

"Marion said that?"

"He did."

Incredible. "Shot him in the face? Why?"

MacQueen shrugged. "Orders, I suppose."

"Did you believe him?"

"Marion? Of course I believed him, man! Damn, d' you think we'd come that far and risk that much just to let the target go? Why would he say it if it weren't so?" MacQueen laughed sardonically at the thought.

Indeed, I thought.

"And what happened to the tech?" I asked.

"Never saw him again. Him an' his two bodyguards went for the com car. Last I saw of em," MacQueen said.

MacQueen tossed off the last of his Scotch and began humming. His voice was a pleasant baritone and, without a thought, he began to sing, in a soft voice, a song the words of which were German. I leaned forward to hear them but could not make them out.

"You have a nice sound," I said, watching him carefully.

He stopped singing and regarded me fully. "What?" he said.

"I said, you have a good voice. What was that song you were singing?" I asked.

"It was *Der Panzerlied*," he said.

"And why do you sing that?" I asked.

"Because..." his lips remained partially open, then he closed them again with effort. "Because cannibals eats their killed enemies to destroy their spirits from ever coming back. So we sang the Fritz's songs. Killed em an' sang their songs for the same reason," MacQueen said. "Anyway, we made our way back to the Stirling, those who wasn't dead. That's all."

That wasn't all, of course. "How many? Who made it back to the plane, I mean?"

"Five. We lost thirty-one," MacQueen said.

My god. But," I began, confused. "You are listed as the only survivor. The other four?"

"We was shot down comin' home. Over Ameins, France," MacQueen said, his jaw set, teeth bared again in anguish.

"Flak? Or German fighters?" I asked.

MacQueen began to laugh, but there was no humor in his laughter. I reached for the bottle of Scotch, meaning to refill his glass, and mine. But he put his hand over it, pulling it away.

"You'd think as much, wouldn't you? That we'd almost made it home but then got ourselves caught by the Jerries."

"You mean to say it was something else? Engine trouble? What?"

"Oh, fighters shot us down, all right." MacQueen simply looked at me in a strange way, his head cocked, as though he were waiting for me to say something. So I did.

"One oh nines?" I asked.

"Beaufighters," he said.

I was stunned. I thought I hadn't heard right. "Beaufighters. Bristol Beaufighters? Is that what you said?"

"I did," he said, a warped smile tugging on his mouth.

"Jesus. What a ghastly mistake," I said, aware how inadequate my words must have sounded.

MacQueen chuckled. "Wasn't it, though? Yes, I thought that for a long time. A very long time. But consider this; our course was set for Eindhoven, the shortest route home. But the navigator heard our code sign over the wireless. Raven, you know. He gave the message to our pilot. We were diverted to Ameins."

"Why?" I asked.

MacQueen shrugged. "Our instructions, once we'd made contact with Bomber Command, was to fly a heading of three hundred five degrees for two minutes, three hundred forty degrees for two minutes, then back on three-five, then a vector to Ameins, so's they could verify our position on radar."

"That seems strange. There was a concentration of several Luftwaffe fighter squadrons at Ameins," I said, as much to myself as to Mac-Queen.

"Correct, but they wasn't up that night. Only two Beaufighters. The ones what got us."

"Beaufighters?" I said, incredulously. "Surely you mean..."

"I said they was Beaufighters. Wasn't just me. We all knew what they was."

Slowly, the horrific realization of what MacQueen was trying to tell me got through my hazy brain. "They shot you down? You mean, your own people shot you down? I can't believe it," I said, almost gasping aloud.

"We bailed out, thems that survived the fight, then we were captured and took to the Gestapo headquarters in Ameins. The Jerries meant to kill us all, I escaped," MacQueen said, then held up his gnarled and shrunken left arm. He did not need to pull up the sleeve for me to see that it was horribly mutilated.

"Alsatians. One of the damned animals from hell clamped on to me as I was goin' over the wall and he wouldn't let go. He shredded the skin down to the bone and then some and just hung there while I beat him on the head with a rock. Aye, and not a little rock, either. Even after the animal was dead I had to pull his jaws apart. Well, I was in France and I got to a farm, more dead than alive. Crawled into a haystack covered with tarp to keep it dry. Let me tell you something, Mr. August Street, there ain't no man that can't be made to cry. I prided myself on takin' as much pain as I thought the body could stand, but that night I cried my child's eyes out, my arm hurtin' as it did. I still dream about it, you know. Not the dog. The pain. I didn't care a whit if I died."

"But you lived," I said, softly.

"Yes. I was found the next day by the family, Paul d'Rouné. They hid me under a pile of potatoes in their cellar. The Germans searched for days. Those good people would have been shot if they'd caught me there but...Michele, Paul and Marie dRouné's daughter is my wife."

"Really!" I said, truly surprised and pleasantly so. "Then you went back after the war?"

MacQueen gave me one of his level eye contacts and shook his head from side to side. "I did not. I never tried to get back to England after the raid. I stayed until long after the war was over. In nineteen forty-seven I came back, wanting to testify against war criminals. Not Germans. Ours. But that never happened, as you know. I told my story to superiors, that we'd been.... Ah," MacQueen said at the futile memory. He turned away again and looked out of the window.

"That's it," he said. "That's all of it."

"It can't be all. Were you decorated? Your unit; did they receive a citation?"

"I said that was the all of it, man! Are you deaf? Do you not understand the English language?"

We sat in common silence for many minutes. I think we were both searching for words, at least I was, but none came. Finally I said "Tom, for whatever it's worth, I'm very grateful to you for...for everything."

I rose from the table and put my hand gently on his still strong shoulder, his right one, and squeezed. As I was about to let go he reached up and put his fingers around my wrist, and returned my pressure. In a sidelong glance I thought I could see tears in his eyes.

I left The Wise Pelican and returned to my hotel. In the next few hours I transcribed to my computer the notes I had made in my head of MacQueen's story. I re-read the list of thirty-six commandos and one tech.

I was exhausted when I had finished late that night and went directly to bed. It was near eleven o'clock the next morning when I arose and stepped into a steaming shower, scrubbing myself as much to start circulation to my brain as to remove sweat and dust, I stayed for a long while under the hot stream to rinse.

Just as I was turning off the water I remembered something that I had seen on the Three Para Commando special combat roster. I was still shivering with nothing but a damp towel wrapped around me when I raised the top of my portable and turned on the computer. I called up the names of the Three Commando paras and, there it was. One of the names had a very small asterisk beside it. The list contained thirty-seven entries. I had transcribed the list myself and I knew for sure that the asterisk did not refer to a footnote. It had simply been put there to denote that the man was somehow different from the other thirty six. I wondered if it was as simple as that, that the tech, A. Smythes, was indicated on the list with an asterisk.

Quickly I called the number of The Wise Pelican and asked the bartender for Thomas MacQueen. I was told that he was not in yet but that he likely would arrive within the hour. I asked the bartender for Tom's home telephone number but he refused to give it out. I told him that it was an emergency. After a lengthy pause the man gave up the number. My finger was shaking slightly as I punched the keys on my telephone.

MacQueen answered. "Tom," I said, "I'm very sorry to bother you at home, but I have something to ask you that is extremely important. Do you mind?"

He said to ask it. I slowly read off the names on the list but omitted one. "Do you know the men?" I said.

"Of course. My mates, Three Commando," he said.

"All of them. You're absolutely sure?" I said.

"Of course I'm sure. What're you about?" he wanted to know.

"How about this name: A. Smythes? That's spelled with an s on the end. Does that ring a bell?" I asked.

"Nope," MacQueen said.

"I don't know what the A initial stands for. Arnold, Arthur, Aaron, maybe. Does that make a difference?" I asked.

"Not a whit. There wasn't no Smythes," MacQueen said with certainty.

My spirits soared. "Smythes could not have been a commando? No mistake about it?"

"Look here, August. We trained together for ten months. Ate together, fought together, slept together, and for all I know we might o' buggered each other. One thing we knew were our mates and Smythes, whoever that might be, wasn't one of us."

Before August Street could hang up the phone he was stopped by MacQueen's voice. "Hitler's special train had a name. Want to know what it was? *Amerika*."

N ot here."
  "Damn. The man is absolutely elusive."
  "Yes, I'll just bet you've been calling all over the world trying to track him down."
  "Where do you think he is?"
  "I know where he is. He's in Saundersfoot,"
  "By way of Narberth, I suppose."
  "Yes. Well, he was yesterday."
  "Not today, I'll wager. If I know my man he was up early this morning, hard to the road."
  "Are you going to stop him?"
  The telephone line became a hushed silence for a moment.
  "I think not. Not now, anyway."
  "What shall I tell him if he calls? And he surely will."
  "Nothing."

A. Smythes. The "tech." The name might have been false, of course, but so far all of the others connected with Raven were correct. As I sat behind the wheel of my rental car en route back to London to write a summary to my declassification actions, I mulled over all of the things that MacQueen had told me at his public house. British fighters shooting down a British bomber? Purposely. I didn't believe it. I thought MacQueen was mistaken about this. The mission itself; kill Hitler? A very good idea by any point of view. Worth the risk of 37 men and an aircrew? Of course.

A very sad end, to be sure, but if they had pulled it off. *Ah, well.* I thought again about what MacQueen's friend, Marion Clark. They *had* succeeded, he said. They had killed Hitler. They had even shot him in the face and burned the body. A thermite bomb, he had said. Strange, that MacQueen could remember such detail about a killing that apparently did not take place. That bothered me.

After two hours on the road I stopped for coffee and a bite to eat. I found a London newspaper rack and tried to read it inside the restaurant but I found nothing in the newsprint that could tear my thoughts away from the Raven raid. I tried to imagine why the radio tech was along. It wasn't just for a ride. The man had been literally thrown from the Stirling. And with a bodyguard! Odd that on such a highly prioritized mission, the assassination of the leader of Nazi Germany, a mere radio engineer would rate so much valuable packaging.

I drank three cups of coffee despite the fact that the English still make the stuff as an after-thought. It was much too weak for me, but at least it was stronger than tea. I picked at a chef's salad before giving up and hitting the road again. Back on the highway, cruising as before, I tried to imagine what there was about the radio on Hitler's train that rated an engineer going along. A new invention? Like radar? Possibly, but there was no radar on Hitler's train. Back in those days a radar took a very large array of antennae, much larger than could be put on a train in 1940.

I knew next to nothing about radio, or radar, but by the time I had reached the outskirts of London, late at night, I no longer believed that Smythes was an electronics maven. He must have been something else.

Back in my room at Brown's Hotel in Mayfair I ordered a sandwich and pot of coffee from room service, then settled down to spend the day on the telephone. I began my search for A. Smythes by calling British veteran's associations, including all of the commando associations I could locate, and there were many. There were some Arthur Smythe's, without the s, and Arnold, Archer, and Armond listed on their registries but follow-up calls to every name beginning with A-r-g became a dead-end. And then there was the period following Arch on the Raven raid roster. Was that meant to be an abbreviation for a whole name? I thought almost certainly it was.

By ten o'clock that night I had nothing to show for my efforts but two sore ears from pressing a telephone against them, yet I had worked my way through the Imperial War Museum Locating Service, Royal British Legion, and the British War Veteran's Association. I quit dialing long enough to take an elevator down to the hotel bar where I drank two Irish whiskies. Upon returning to the room I found that I lacked the endurance to dial again so I showered and went to bed.

The next morning I ate a light breakfast and began the process all over again. That day was spent much like the one before with Smythes, Smythe, and Smiths singing around inside my head. Not all of the archive rolls had been computerized so much of the process became tedious. I had to prevail upon the hotel's management to put an extra telephone line into my instrument so that I could accept call-backs while I was dialing out. All of the associations and quasi-official offices were closed by 6:00 P.M. and, like the day before, I directed all of my calls to following up to private residences on leads that ranged from tepid to hot. None of them lead me to the A. Smythes I wanted to find.

At least, not so far as I could tell. And that was the worst part: I had a growing suspicion that became a certainty that my A. Smythes had somehow slipped through my fingers. My eyes were fatigued and my ears now ached when I quit late on Thursday evening. Since London was eight hours ahead of California time I could have called Lynda but the idea of yet another phone call, probably a long one, appalled me. Still, she was the woman I loved so I dialed all of the required numbers. Her telephone rang three times before her answering machine turned itself on. It was with mixed feelings that I left her a message that said the important things that I thought she needed to hear, but with no description of what I had been about that past week, and this time with no estimate for the date I would return to the U.S.

I was up the next morning feeling surprisingly better than I deserved after a very late dinner of ale, roast lamb, and potatoes. It tasted so good that I overate, then suffered from indigestion for hours that night before dropping off to sleep. I gathered up my myriad notes that took most of four steno pads, plus those made in my computer, and took a taxi to Whitehall to the Ministry of Defence building. I knew that Defence Ministry, at least the part I was interested in, was still located in the Old Admiralty building, a pile of stone and masonry that dated back to the eighteenth century.

Using my MI6 identification and pass, plus my H.P. Carlisle Foundation credentials, I was able to convince Dr. Geoffry Whalen, OBE, that my need to access Whitehall archives was part of my research for the joint National Secrets Act declassification project. That was true, of course, but the quest to learn the secrets of Operation Raven went far beyond my required duties within the project. It had become a personal quest for the total story. Following a map provided me by one of Whalen's assistants, I found myself located in still another basement level room, a room within rooms, to be accurate, where I could spread out on a large table with a plug for my computer adapter.

While the indices in the ministry files were at least as complete as that of MI6, they were far from universally computerized. So I spent the next three days with my eyes glued to micro-film viewing machines. At the end of that time I would have gladly paid for auto-scanners for the MOD out of my own pocket.

Psychologists say that there is only one thing that causes anger: Frustration. When I arrived back at the hotel on Saturday afternoon, literally locked out of my dreadful little rooms at Whitehall, I was angry enough to throw my wet umbrella across the room, leaving a mark on the wall, and kicking an afternoon newspaper from my doorway into the fireplace beyond. The Cyclopsian red eye of the telephone message service was stabbing me in my sore eyes, demanding that I pick it up. I was resentful, my throat dry as a bone, and in need of something, I cared not what, to go right. I snatched the phone from its cradle and sat down, seething, to make notes of all of the people and their numbers whom I had no intention of calling back. Fuck 'em.

The second one was from Debbie. "Hi, there, you handsome horse, you. I had to work this morning and I feel like I should have a treat this afternoon when I leave the office. If you don't want to buy me a drink I'll have to go down to the navy docks and try my luck on the first ship that ties up. It's almost twelve. Oh, by the way, this is Debbie."

I dialed Debbie's number at MI6. It rang five times and, because it was almost two o'clock, I started to hang up when the telephone came alive on the sixth ring. "Mears," she said.

"Street," I countered.

"Avenue," she said.

"Highway," I said.

"Circle," she offered.

"Way."

"Road."

"Freeway," I said, running out of thoroughfares.

"Is that a dirty suggestion? Is that what you colonials think you can do with us poor English girls? Have a free way? Do you think you can buy us a number of exotic drinks at a fashionable eating establishment, then spend lots of money on a lavish meal, pouring champagne continuously down our parched throats before taking advantage of our weakened state to put aside our clothes that we take off? Is that what you filthy curs expect?" Debbie said.

"Not all of those thoughts had crossed my mind, but some of them did. Let's eat, first," I said, more interested in her scenario that I was willing to admit.

I arrived by taxi at Vauxhall thirty minutes later to find Debbie waiting patiently for my arrival. She spotted me almost before the cab had braked to a halt on the circular entrance in front of the main building, and walked quickly toward the car. I was glad that I didn't have to step into the rain myself as I held the door for her to enter.

"Nice to see you," I said, more formally than I intended.

"I'm sure it is," she said, and threw her head back in laughter. Debbie was a woman totally certain of her female charms and equally aware of man's fundamental weakness. At my suggestion, she gave the driver directions for a restaurant called the Great Nepalese on Eversholt Street. "You'll love the food. It will taste much better tonight than it did when you cooked it yourself on the ice ledges of Mount Everest," she said with a perfectly straight face.

"But I never..."

"Are you going to tell me that I'm out with a man who never climbed Mount Everest? Please don't say that."

For the first time in days I relaxed, enjoying the sound of another voice. I felt better immediately and if I had been angry an hour ago, it seemed like a time in another life. On the way to the restaurant I told Debbie what I had been doing for the past week, though for some reason that even I didn't understand, I omitted telling her Thomas MacQueen's name. I did reveal to her in broad strokes of my fruitless endeavor to locate an A. Smythes, a member of a British commando special mission team.

At our dinner table I acquiesced to Debbie's offer to order the wine since her French was not only better than mine but her knowledge of the estates was far more refined. The bottle was a Bordeaux, excellent tasting to my palate as it must have been to hers because we finished that and ordered another before we were done with our masco bara, an hors' de oeuvre made of black lentil that tasted superb. We worked our way stolidly through a second bottle while our waiter brought bhutuwa chicken and mamoco, a kind of steamed dumpling.

We ate like trenchermen. I was more than a little impressed with the way Debbie could put away both food and wine while maintaining a figure that could only be described as delicious. I was aware, if she was not, that we were the object of many diner's interest.

She shook her head as she considered my monumental dilemma of finding the proverbial needle. "Can't be done, you know," she said. "They're all bloody gone."

"Who?" I said.

"The SOE. I mean, good heavens, that lot was what...in their late 30's to fifties when they put it all together? And it's been almost sixty years! Don't you see? Hell, if any of them were alive they'd be too old to talk." Debbie attempted a laugh but the wine had reduced her energy to a smile.

"Yes, but this Smythes guy..." I began.

"He's dead, too," she said, looking undecided at her sherbet dessert.

"How do you know?" I asked.

"Well, isn't he?" she said, sobering. "I hate sherbet."

It seemed to me that she had slipped for a moment and wanted to change the subject.

"You said that he was dead. Smythes. You said it like you knew."

"I should think he was. How the hell do I know? Let's see, Smythes -" she said, retrieving a small book from her purse and theatrically thumbing through the pages. "Smythes.... No, not here in my address book. But it's still possible that we have dated and that he is dead. I've had lots of those kinds of evenings. Excluding this one, of course."

I accepted Debbie's compliment but I was not about to dismiss the matter. "Then you know which Smythes I'm looking for."

"I certainly do not. Smythes? With an 's'?" she blinked her eyes, comically.

"Jean found him, didn't he?" I said. It was beginning to make sense to me, now.

I believed absolutely that Debbie lied to me. I also believed with equal conviction that Jean Scheerer knew something that I did not, else why would he avoid me? And, I was certain, that was just what Scheerer was doing. I therefore felt justified in taking the position that if Scheerer would not tell me what I wanted to know, I would extract it from him by any means in my power. Electronic search came to mind. Certainly better than driving bamboo slivers under his finger nails even if it didn't have the same emotional impact.

I was careful not to add any more alcohol to the wine I consumed at dinner so that by the time I returned to my hotel room at 0100, I was not seriously impaired. It was, however, too late to contact Wes Claridge at the HP Carlisle Foundation in Virginia and I did not know his home telephone number. I could have got it from the duty officer at the Foundation but decided, despite my zeal fueled by paranoia, to wait until the next morning to call.

My inner alarm jabbed me awake before 0700 at which time I called room service for coffee. It was still too early on the U.S. East Coast to call, so I ate my light breakfast, read the *Times*, ran through my ubiquitous e-mail, and then called up my electronic notes regarding Raven. I didn't like the idea of stealing from a colleague but the more

I thought about Scheerer dodging about Europe and avoiding my calls, the guilt didn't last long.

I tried my first call to the Foundation at noon London time, but Westbrook had not yet arrived. I was automatically routed to his answering machine but I hung up rather than leave a message. I tried again an hour later, 0900 his time, and by then the byte-meister was in.

"Did you know," he asked me after I told him who was calling, "that I was the University of Chicago's leading ground-gainer when I was there?"

"I didn't know they have a football team," I said.

"They don't now, but they did then," he said.

Why was I surprised? After all, Westbrook was a big man, over six feet and weighed well over two hundred pounds, some of it admittedly was excess, but I could imagine him with a flat gut. His face was slightly pockmarked, not severe enough to disfigure him but just the right amount to make him look rugged. And interesting. He had never married. Was he gay?

"Well, I'm impressed," I said, meaning it. "How well did you do? Your team, that is."

"We were zero and seven," Wes said.

"Not exactly a coach's dream," I said.

"Yeah, but then the University of Chicago didn't give out football scholarships, either," Westbrook said, proudly.

"Did you have any pro offers?"

"Yeah. From the Dolphins. Not an offer, exactly, but they said I had the same shoe size as Larry Csonka and said that their trainer wanted to meet me. I never tried out," he said.

"Their loss was our gain," I said, anxious to get on with my plea for help but concerned that I did not cut short the only man I knew who could make it happen.

Westbrook apparently felt my detachment from his football career. "So, what can I do for you, pal? Have you wised up to the possibilities of having our very own Swiss account?" he asked.

"It's looking better all the time," I said.

"Ah! I knew we'd make a team. You'll be the front man who looks like a typical corporate American shark and I'll be the inside man whom nobody suspects," Westbrook said.

"You talk like we're going to be caught."

"No. We're not. Not going to be caught. Don't think that way," Westbrook said. I could hear him slurp his morning coffee.

"I need your unique talents again, Wes," I said.

"Get in line. I'm still cleaning up some of the mess you left on your NSA report. It's a fucking oily, rag, pal."

"Wes, I really need help. I wouldn't ask you if there was..."

"MI6 again?" Westbrook interrupted.

"Yes," I said, feeling foolish. "Wes, I think I'm on to something very unusual. I don't want to go through the chairs for this one because I think they'd shoot me down."

"One of the Limey's locked you out?" he asked.

Something in Westbrook's tone of voice gave me an insight. "Actually, I need to steal something out of the bastard's secret files. He's pretty confident I can't get near him. He's one of the Brits' biggest spies."

"I love it," he said. "Who's the guy?"

"His name is Jean Scheerer. MI6. The information I want pertains to a 1940 SOE commando operation code named Raven. The key name I'm looking for is Smythes. I don't have a complete first name, just an initial, A.," I said to Westbrook.

"Do you care whether he knows we've hacked him?" Westbrook wanted to know.

"I'd rather he not know, but either way, I have to find the connection," I said.

"Well, that means I'll have to tip-toe around in there. Might take a little time. Better find something to do, today. Go to a movie or something. Are you at your hotel?"

I said that I was and gave him the number again, even though he said he still had it. After I hung up the telephone I considered doing just what Wes suggested, going to a movie. Or anyplace. I thought about calling Debbie to see if she wanted to kick around the city with me but I rejected that idea as quickly as I thought of it.

There was a well-stuffed chair in my suite that I had not yet used except to drop articles of clothing onto as I entered the room. Taking the television remote control with me I sat in the chair to begin surfing the BBC channels. I clicked my way onto an all news channel and slid back, deeper into the comfort of the chair. I wished that I had made myself a Scotch and water but felt entirely too relaxed to get back up and fix it. During a commercial message I closed my eyes, allowing my mind to drift back to my office at the Foundation, then to my residence in California, trying to remember my projected schedule for the next month. I was still thinking about a vacation that Lynda and I had for years talked about taking. It was a simple one, just driving up Highway One to San Francisco, hanging out with Laird and Judy Durham, eating good food in the city and drinking lots of Irish coffees.

It was dark inside the room when the ringing phone jarred me awake. I snatched the instrument from its cradle and my voice croaked. "Hello?"

"This is Westbrook. Can you talk?"

"Yeah. I guess I dropped off for a while. What's up?" I asked.

"I went above and beyond the call for this one, big boy. I want a bonus."

"Like what?" I asked.

"Why don't you introduce me to Lynda? You're gone all the time, anyway. She can't spend her whole life waiting for you to show up," Westbrook said.

His remark, meant to be humorous, struck a chord nonetheless. I had been avoiding the issue of my prolonged absences from her when my work for the foundation required me to be on the East Coast far too often. I determined to do something about it when I returned from this trip. "I'll ask her if she wants to meet you. If she does, I won't stand in the way of you two. Now, tell me what you have."

"The 'A' in Smythes stands for Archie. And you couldn't find Smythes because he wasn't military," Westbrook said.

"What was he?" I said, my pulse quickening.

"Civilian," Westbrook said.

"Yes, but what kind? I mean, what did he do? I figure he might have been an electrical engineer, some kind of specialist. The commandos referred to him as a tech," I said.

"Well, he might have been. Scheerer's files don't say. They pretty much match what you got in your computer on this declassification business, except for Smythes, of course."

"So? What did it say about him?" I urged.

"There was a copy of his birth certificate showing his date of birth as February 2, 1890, and the last place of residence as of August 1, 1940."

"Where was that?" I pressed Westbrook.

"In London. 12-C, Hammil Lane, near the Putney Bridge," Westbrook said as I scribbled down his words.

"How about family? A wife? Children?" I asked.

"One each. Wife's name Laverne, a daughter by the name of Rose, date of birth 16 August 1932," Westbrook said.

"You didn't give me the wife's DOB," I said.

"There is none."

"How about relatives?"

"None listed."

"Anything else?" I wanted to know.

"Well, there's a notation here. It says 'Hawkins, P-22, Burton Heath.'"

"An address, I suppose. Any indication of whose it might be?" I asked.

"Nope. That's all. And I mean that's everything I could find in any kind of combination with the word Raven. Hope it helps," Westbrook said.

"Maybe it will. Send me what you just said by e-mail, Wes. And thanks," I said.

I was under no illusion that 12-C Hammil Lane would have remained in a 1940 time capsule as I drove my rental car along Felsham Road and under the Putney Bridge. The entire area, once a prime target of Luftwaffe bombs during the Blitz of 1940 had, in the intervening sixty years, been entirely rebuilt and preserved as the worth of all London property rose to be among the world's most valuable. Riverfront locations, especially, were highly sought by developers in competition with historical preservation organizations who, often working in opposition, created a highly desirable city.

But in the years before World War II, the area was a slum.

The docks along the Thames served to support the vital lifeline of shipping that brought not only food and clothing to the UK but also the means of defending itself against the threat of invasion from Europe. If the British lost their ability to send ships to sea and safely retrieve them in large numbers, the future of England as a nation was in peril. So the waterfront was hit hard and all of the human beings that lived in that proximity were affected. Blocks upon blocks of houses were blown apart or burned. Casualties were high and it was almost impossible to find a man, woman, or child who did not have a neighbor or relative who was not among either the bombed-out or wounded or both.

As I drove along the miles of streets in Putney I thought about what it must have been like to spend nights in an air-raid shelter and days cleaning rubble from the streets. And if you were a child if would have been even worse. Consulting a current street map, I found Hammil Lane. Instead of the old "two up, two down" dwellings of prewar London, the short street seemed to be an almost continuous condominium, containing a five acre recreation park as well as smart shops and eateries that served that now upscale part of London that might well had been a camp site of Roman soldiers two thousand years past. It was not only clear that Archie Smythes was no longer a resident but that neither was there a 12-C.

I took the Chelmsford train from Victoria Station, judging that Burton Heath was near enough to that city to use local transportation to Hawkins, P-22, whatever that was. I had always enjoyed riding trains, probably because in the United States a train ride was a rarity and therefore a treat. Local milk-runs were not always convenient in the U.S., but Europe and Britain knew how to intelligently operate railroad systems so that it was hard for an American to have a bad experience. As I watched the scenery dashing by my first-class window the topography becoming not only rural but distinctly farm friendly as we traveled east by northeast. Industrial manufacturing entities became increasingly rare, bedroom communities gave way to genuine villages that contained shops, farms and scattered housing. Everything was green and it seemed to me that were I a cow this is where I'd want to graze.

I spent a good deal of my life torn between wanting to read a book and the pressing financial need to write one, but I had bought a current issue of the *New Yorker* magazine at Victoria Station. I opened the pages as the train pulled out of Brentwood, more than half way to my destination. After leafing through its pages, taking in the cartoons, I returned to the first page and, skipping through "About Town,"

I read through to the back cover. Chelmsford was only ten minutes down the track by the time I had finished and I had not heard an announcement for Burton Heath. After arriving at Chelmsford station on a nippy early evening, a baggage handler was kind enough to advise me about where to find bus service to Burton Heath. I changed my mind about the bus, however, at the sight of a taxi waiting for a fare into town. A cab offered the advantage of a car with a driver who knew the area sans maps, and who might even have an insight about deciphering Hawkins P-22.

As it turned out, the problem of finding P-22 was more challenging in London than it was in the rural community of Burton Heath. P-22 in notation stood for the postal route number twenty-two that served the Hawkins family on that route. Twenty-two was either the mailbox or a utility pole, the twenty-second along that route. I was greatly relived to have chosen the taxi.

The house was set back off a two-lane road several hundred feet. There was no gate to the swept-gravel entrance but a stone wall about three feet high started at each corner of the house and, at about two hundred feet on either side, gave way to split rail fencing. There was a barn in the rear, an equipment shed, and a pen on the opposite side of the property that we would have called a corral in the western part of the U.S. The house itself was two stories, the lower half constructed of local stone, the upper half was plaster, with three gables framing double-lancet windows. In all the property was well kept despite its age that might have reached back to the turn of the last century.

I asked my driver to wait in the driveway while I knocked upon the heavy wooden front door. I waited an appreciable amount of time and was about to knock again when the door opened. Before me stood a tall, slender woman whom I judged to be in her mid-to-late sixties. Her hair was perfectly gray, tied closely back into a bun. She was not wearing glasses and her eyes were dark brown but very bright in the way that they seemed to see everything before them at a glance. She held her narrow shoulders back and her chin high, as though she had been taught to be proud at some time in her early life. The woman said nothing but waited for me to speak.

"Excuse me for interrupting your day, but I'm looking for a certain party that might have lived near here almost sixty years ago. I don't imagine that you would know of a family, or part of a family, by the name of Smythes?" I asked, suddenly aware of what an incredible leap of faith I must have made from a scrap of information fixed on a partial operational report in London.

The woman stared at me, unblinking, one hand on the front door, the other resting easily on a denim-clad hip. She had dressed for work, judging by her chambray shirt and sturdy shoes. The lids of her eyes fell almost closed before opening again, the corners of her mouth twitching upwards as though she was hearing a familiar joke repeated yet again.

"And you are...?" she asked.

"My name is August Street. I am...doing work on a historical report for a London archive," I said, not lying but not wholly truthful, either. I wanted to avoid invoking government interest, sometimes a sore point for a large part of the population of independent people.

"My name is Rose Marie Hawkins," she said. "Before I married Roger Hawkins my name was Smythes. Would you like to come in?"

Struck almost speechless by the simplicity of facing a woman in real life that I was frankly skeptical even existed, I was at a total loss as to what to do next. Rose Hawkins saved me from embarrassment by suggesting that I might release my cab driver in the interest of saving money. Buses traveled the main road every ninety minutes until eleven P.M.., she said. Retrieving my lap-top computer and giving the driver a generous tip, I let him return to town but not before taking the trouble of writing down the telephone number of the cab company in the event that my stay with Rose Hawkins kept me beyond the hour of eleven.

The interior of the Hawkins home was a very pleasing, eclectic blend of time and choice in decor and furnishings. Its central aim, well achieved, I thought, seemed to be comfort over uniformity. The front door opened directly into the main living area, with hardwood floors covered with rugs of good quality. Immediately to the left in the living room was a small piano that appeared to me to be quite old but, like the rest of the house, well maintained. Without hearing it played I would have bet that it was in good tune. Behind the piano, in a nook at the far wall, were book shelves that began at waist level and ended at about the eight foot mark, accessible by a heavy wooden step stool. The book shelves were set into a wall of the house that gave way to a large picture window made of steel sash frame and which looked out onto the farm buildings I had seen from the front. The bucolic view included gently rolling hills and fenced pastures containing grazing cows. I thought I could see goats in an enclosed pen beyond the barn. I never understood why people raised goats for any reason other than pets. I knew my notion was parochial and ill-informed, so I made a mental note to ask Rose Hawkins about the subject at a later time.

"This used to be a much smaller bay window," Rose said, assuming that I was inspecting the west wall. "Roger ripped it out and replaced it with this," she said, raising her hand in a sweeping motion. "Then we found that we had to reinforce the next floor and, oh, what a task."

I could see that the second floor was buttressed with two six-by-six posts directly in front of the window on the outside. They obstructed the view in only a minor way and might even have added to the appeal of the building overall.

"Roger?" I asked.

"My husband. Roger passed away in 1984," she said without any dramatic overtone.

"Roger Hawkins?" I said.

"Yes. He was an only son but he had a sister, Helen. Would you like tea? I was just about to put it on," she said.

I thanked her and said that I would. She invited me to sit with a movement of her hand, then left the room for what I assumed would be the kitchen. The chair I chose was mohair wingback. Facing each other with an inlaid plain colored glass table between them were two sofas containing plump pillows. There was another table in the room, a game table, upon which was a half-completed jig-saw puzzle. On the walls were a good number of small, framed prints. I left my chair to look at them more closely. They were exquisite drawings and etchings of ancient Rome, some black and white, others in mauve, soft greens and delicate golds.

"They came from a 19th century set of books about the history of Rome," Rose said as she entered the room pushing a rattan teacart. It had a removable tray on the top, wooden spoked wheels on the front and small casters on the back legs. She smiled as she placed the cart conveniently near me. "I love this old thing. I think it's funky," she said.

"It sure is," I said approvingly. It was British-India, circa 1860, or a very good replica, a joy to behold. "Do you live alone, Mrs. Hawkins?" I asked, accepting the delicate China cup and saucer she offered.

"No," she smiled. "I'm sixty-eight years old and I have never lived alone. It isn't like that in the States, is it? You're an American, aren't you? Call me Rose, please," she added.

"Yes, I'm from California. I work mostly in Virginia but I think I'm going to try to stay home more when I get back from this trip," I said. "Are you remarried, then?"

"No. My mother - mother-in-law, that is - lives with me. She is ninety-one and would have trouble caring for herself. We're..." Rose searched for a word "...lucky to have each other. She's napping right now but she can be obstreperous at times when she is awake."

I have never been much of a tea drinker but the cup I tasted then was better than any I could remember. I said as much to Rose. She smiled her appreciation of my compliment and remained silent as she sipped from her equally delicate cup. The quiet between us seemed strange insofar as I, a perfect stranger, invaded her home without notice and without offering a good reason for staying for tea. As I cleared my throat in preparation to speak, I saw again the calm light of her eyes set off by the ever-so-slight upturns at the corners of her mouth, as though she knew what I was about to say.

"Mrs. Hawkins," I began, then quickly corrected myself. "Ah, Rose, would you mind terribly if I asked you questions about you and your family? You see, I don't have all of the..."

"Certainly not," she said, interrupting. "Ask me anything you'd like." She settled back in her own well-stuffed chair and regarded me quite frankly.

"Good. Well, if I'm not mistaken, you're from London, originally," I began.

"Yes. Putney," Rose said as my pulse quickened. "We lived on Hammil Lane. A pretty name for a dreadful place. It was a slum, you know."

Rose arched an eyebrow in question. I nodded my head but before I could speak she went on. "I left there when I was eight years old. It was during the Blitz and many of us children were sent to the countryside to avoid the bombs."

Of course I was quite familiar with the plight of England's children, driven from their homes by the Luftwaffe. Blankets of German bombers would fly up the Thames, using the great river as an easy navigation guide. It was easy to find the dock areas that they were looking for that way. Infant children, up to ages fifteen, along with expectant mothers and elderly people, patients and the blind who qualified for government assistance were relocated out of the combat zone. Almost a quarter-million children were evacuated from London as well as others in target areas such as Manchester, Sheffield, and Newcastle. Evacuees, in total, numbered into the millions and were scattered throughout the rural parts of the British Isles.

"I was sent here," Rose was saying. "To the Hawkins' farm," she smiled wistfully. "Many of the children weren't welcome, you know. I used to have nightmares about that, wondering if I was one of them."

"I don't think I understand," I said.

"Many of us came from the slums. We were dirty, often dressed in rags and we had lice and mites in our hair and all sorts of skin diseases. I can't forget that I arrived here without underpants. Imagine hordes of rag-tag children invading the countryside."

"Well, it was an extraordinary time. I'm sure people understood." I had not thought of the famous exodus in negative terms. I had always assumed that the warm-natured English populace held open their arms to the children willingly.

"We had no bath in our place in Putney, let alone a bathroom. It was a shared bathhouse that we'd use and we queued up for it. A once a week affair. Did you know that?" Rose Hawkins asked.

I shook my head.

"The same with toilets, of course. None in our flat. We had to go out in the cold and dark to the back yard. People in the country, like the Hawkins, bathed several times a week. Some of us hated it at first but most came to enjoy the experience. And it was indoors! Toilet, bath. Everything. As the months went by I found myself praying that the war would last forever so that I could stay here," Rose said, her chin rising ever so slightly.

"Did they treat you well? The Hawkins?" I asked.

Rose smiled wanly. "Yes. Well, it was a farm, you know, and we all had to work. I think that I did more than my share and I think that Edith would have been content to have me do it all..."

"Edith?"

"Hawkins. My husband's mother," Rose said, jerking her thumb over her shoulder toward another part of the house.

"Ah. Well, it seems like you got your wish," I said, crossing my legs.

"Mr. Street..."

"August," I said, interrupting.

"You didn't come all this way to Burton Heath to talk about me," she said, her tight smile widening.

"In a way I did," I said, politely.

"Thank you, but you came to talk about my father, Archie. That's so, isn't it?"

"But you are more than a minor part of what I'm interested in knowing about Archie. I'd like to know something about your mother, too." When Rose did not immediately respond I said, "Having said that, your father was, wasn't he, attached to a commando group for a special mission early in World War II?" The words were hardly out of my mouth when it suddenly occurred to me that Rose Smythes Hawkins might very well know nothing about her father's activities, secret as they were. And it was unlikely that he survived the war. I prayed that I was wrong.

"Yes. At least that's what he said."

MacQueen was not the only man to survive the raid into Germany. Archie Smythes must have made it back as well and he told his daughter about it. I began to feel a sudden surge excitement. Leaning forward trying to frame my questions clearly, I said, "He told you that when he returned, did he?"

"Well, not until after the war. It was almost five years later, wasn't it?" Rose said.

"Right. Rose, what did your father do? As a civilian, I mean. Was he some kind of electronics wizard, a radio expert of some kind?" I asked.

Rose almost spilled her tea as she laughed aloud. More like a guffaw. "Archie? A wizard? I never heard of that unless he got some acting part that mum and I were never told about. My father was a voracious reader, but no, he could hardly change a tire on a car. Not that we had a car, mind you. We were far too poor to even think of that. But Archie was completely inept at everything. When the war broke out in 1939 everybody found immediate employment except Archie. Eventually he swept floors at the Rolls-Royce plant in Croydon."

I looked closely at Rose's profile as her head turned slightly away from me, her eyes drifting toward the large window nearby. "How did you get along with your father?" I asked.

"Archie?" she said, as though we were discussing a total stranger. "All right, I suppose, what I saw of him. I was only eight, you know, when I went away."

"Yes. I take it you weren't close, then?"

For very long moments I saw only the back of Rose's head as she remained fixed upon a distant object in the fields beyond. I kept silent, and when at last she turned toward me her eyes were filled with tears. Before I could produce my own clean handkerchief she had found one of her own and dabbed at her cheeks. "Damn," she said. "After all these years, here I am crying over that man. To think I hated him so."

The force of her words silenced the next question that had been forming on my lips, so I remained quiet, waiting for her to go on.

"We were so wretched. He nearly killed my mother. Not with an axe, of course, but from work. She took in laundry and, by god, even as a child hardly old enough to walk, I helped. My mother's hands were cracked open from a day in hot lye, wringing out sheets, scrubbing other people's clothing in a big iron tub -."

Rose's voice broke, but after a moment she went on. "She'd sob at night from the pain of her hands and in her back and most of all from the pain that told her that her lot in life was never going to get any better. And she must have cried for me, too, cause she loved me. We didn't often have bread but when we did there was nothing to put into it but lard. Did you ever eat a lard sandwich, Mr. Street? Well, you can't believe how good one could taste to a starving child."

"What was your father...?"

Rose's lips quivered as she wiped at her eyes again, but her voice gained in strength. "Archie? Archie was an actor. That's what he called himself, anyway. Nobody else did. Not his mates down at the pubs and not even those he traveled with. Actors. The real ones!"

"Then why did he pursue the business? Or the art, I guess one would call it," I said.

Rose raised her eyes skyward, turned the palms of her hands covering her face, her head shaking. "I'm sorry, Mr. Street. He said it was because it was in his blood. I've tried to understand that. I really have, but I cannot. When I said that he did not have the talent to change a tire or tighten a leaking faucet or glue soles on our broken shoes, he was just as inept as an actor. He wasn't a handsome man, you know. Romantic roles would never have been open to him. And he had a rasping voice. After the war, as a teenager, we would go to a public place together and people would turn their heads toward him when he spoke. At age thirteen I was mortified." Rose dropped her eyes to her lap. "I suppose that was terribly selfish of me. But that's the way young girls are at that age."

I shook my head in sympathy. "Amazing. I suppose it's like gambling or drugs or alcohol when you get hooked. Just can't give it up. Even a gambler sometimes wins, but apparently your father didn't, eh?"

"There was a time, several months, in fact, that my father was actually paid for acting. His jobs were usually helping out on stage with the props or the lights, never more than enough to pay for his own food while he was on the road with one troupe or another, but in 1938 he got a part playing Hitler in a comedy. He actually sent money home to us every week. I recall how my mother and I ate. We filled the cooler with food, canned stuffs that would keep because we knew the money would stop sooner or later, and probably sooner. Sure enough, in 1939 it did."

"The war started in 1939," I said.

"Yes. Adolf Hitler wasn't very funny, then," she said.

At Rose Hawkins's invitation I stayed for dinner that night. I offered to take her into town to the best dinner that we could find, even lightly assuring her that my expense account was unlimited for all practical purposes, but she politely declined. She would have to get someone to watch over Edith and in the end it was much simpler to fix a good meal at home. There was no shortage of choice beef on the farm, she said, and she suggested we have broiled steaks, broasted leaks, asparagus and sourdough bread. "That's a California meal, isn't it?"

I agreed that it was, lacking only artichoke. I felt frustrated that I had not the foresight to at least supply wine with our meal, but Rose even had that. "Roger loved wine. He bought or traded for cases of the stuff. It's still in the cellar. I don't have much occasion. I'll just fetch it," she said, starting to rise.

"Let me go."

"Oh, thank you. It might be a good idea to have someone who knows something about wine look it over. Roger was fussy about how he kept it. Said he didn't want to cook it. Not likely where, it sits," she said.

I had neither the expertise nor the patience to assay Rose Smythes Hawkins's wine cellar but I managed to set aside for disposal a few bottles of Beaujolais that were some twenty years past their maximum drinking age. I brought up two bottles of Bordeaux and two Burgundy. Rose was already putting food onto our plates when I finished cleaning thick dust from the bottles and opened a Cabernet. Rose unabashedly lit two candles on the table and we sat down to eat in her pleasant, spacious kitchen.

"Delicious," I said, tasting first the meat, then new potatoes cooked with rosemary, garlic and olive oil. "I don't know where the rumor ever got started that the British couldn't cook."

"Oh, we can cook, it just doesn't taste good to most people," Rose said, looking down modestly.

She picked at her food, pushing portions of it from one part of her plate to another, sipping her glass like a bird wetting her bill. Eventually she gave up altogether the pretense of hunger. We exchanged very little talk during the dinner yet the exceptionally good grape wiped away any atmosphere of strain between us, at least on my behalf.

"I didn't have time to make a desert," Rose began as I put down my knife and fork for the last time and drained my glass.

"No need at all," I said, and meant it.

"I have a Cognac," she said, starting to rise from her chair.

"Not for me, thank you, but have one yourself, please," I said. The thought of Cognac sounded delicious but I needed to stay reasonably sober if I was to hear this woman's story, or Archie's story. Leaving the unwashed dishes behind us we moved into the living room and took the chairs that we had occupied earlier.

"I have a tape recorder, Rose. Rather than take notes I wonder if you'd mind my turning it on while you talk about your father," I said.

"I suppose that's all right," she said, but her hand went involuntarily to her throat in a brief display of nervousness. She flashed a tortured smile and said "Really, I expect you'll shut it off before I go very far. It's...well, fantastic. And it's what Archie told me when he came home. I didn't believe a word of it then and I still don't."

"But you remember it?" I asked.

"Oh, yes. I couldn't forget it. Not ever," she said.

"All right," I said, placing the small micro-recorder on an end table near her. "It was after the war, you said. Was Archie in the army?"

Unexpectedly, Rose put her head back and laughed aloud. It seemed out of character for her, knowing her even for the short time that I had. "The army, yes, I suppose we could say that."

"Then go on, please."

I leaned back in my chair and concentrated on Rose's words.

"Well, it was just following Dunkirk. The miracle, it was called, when the British Expeditionary Forces were evacuated from France. Really, we expected the Germans to arrive on our beaches at any hour. Churchill called it Britain's darkest hour. I was too young to appreciate its full meaning, but even now looking back, I think he was most certainly correct."

BOOK II

CHAPTER
5

I t wasn't the kind of noise that Archie was used to. High speed drills boring through steel blocks, a hundred motors spinning, turning lathes, running gears, and shouts of men and women who were in a hurry. His ears were injured in 1910 when he was only fifteen years old. It didn't seem so at the time. He was polishing the brass rail of a steam locomotive at the Victoria roundhouse when the engineer, following his own peculiar sense of humor, pulled the lanyard on the steam whistle and a very high decibel shriek filled the air only inches from young Archie's head. The tiny stereo cilia hair cells inside the ear were smashed flat and, while Archie eventually lost the ringing inside his ears, his hearing deteriorated rapidly with age. Because of his inability to dampen and separate noises, he frequently had headaches during his graveyard shifts.

Streaks of blue-orange August dawn was just framing England's skies when Archie punched out his time card and began shuffling along with other workers the half mile to the train stop for a twenty-three mile trip home. There was doubtless places to work closer to Putney but his lack of skills made job shopping a complicated undertaking so he put off the problem yet again this week. He would do it next week.

As he stood, holding a strap in a carriage car, he could look out of the windows facing north and see the smoke of fires raging from last night's raids on the dockland areas of Woolwhich and Silverton. The German bomber stream, now operating out of bases in France, used the Thames estuary as a navigation fix for their turn up the river that took them into the heart of the city. Archie did not deceive himself that he was a man of courage, and when the bombs began to fall back in May, first striking RAF air fields then later London, he was afraid. He, along with neighbors and strangers he met in the subway tubes, thought that it was the end. He thought England would fall and that he would have fallen long before, blown into pieces by the Luftwaffe. But as the days went by, the earth jumping underfoot, walls of houses crashing behind and beside him, he gradually lost the feeling of imminent death. He found himself looking forward to the following day.

Yet it was a relief to know that Rose was safe in a distant town, away from the bombs and, worse yet, away from the pervasive threat of invasion, the danger of which everyone was aware but seldom spoke about aloud. Burton Heath was the place stamped on Rose's processing papers given them by the Air Raid Patrol (ARP) at the Interior Ministry.

Rose seemed to have adjusted well to the sudden uproot. Unlike the other children on the packed train leaving Victoria Station for the northeast, she was not in tears. Nor was she smiling, to be sure, but she marched off quite bravely with her tiny package of clothing wrapped in plain butcher's paper and tied with a string while her mother wept openly. Archie had been on hand for that family epiphany unlike most other occasions, like Rose's brush with death from mastoid infection, and Laverne's pneumonia. He had only once before seen Laverne cry. He should not have been surprised, though, close as the two of them were. But Laverne quickly recovered knowing that her child was safe in the country while the damn Huns dropped bombs on those who stayed.

Archie tried to put himself inside of Laverne's heart and mind now that he was spending so many days at home. If she was happier now it was difficult to tell. There had never been closeness between them following the death of their first born to consumption before the little tyke was three. It was the place that killed him, Laverne said. Archie did not respond. She may have been right. By that time she was

MICHAEL MURRAY

pregnant with their second, Rose, and Archie had been laid off of yet another job. Laverne had been taking in washing and ironing that paid enough pennies to buy bread and to feed coins into the electric meter for lights.

Archie did not know what Laverne thought about him, about life or about almost anything that mattered. She was a woman who kept her thoughts to herself, her thin lips pulled resiliently across her teeth, eyes down. But he wanted to reach for the brass ring. He longed to be a movie star or a stage idol. Fame and money would be his if only the right role was up for grabs while he was there to snatch it. And that was the secret. Oh, yes, hard work was a requirement, for sure, but it always came down to being in the right place at the right time, and that meant being on the boards, or near them, when that right part came along.

He was like a gambler afflicted with the need to bet on the long shot, or on the turn of a single card. He knew that the odds were long and getting longer but he also knew that others won. Somebody had to win, why not him?

The soot in east London was always thick and very black. The smell of rank oil, rotting fish and vegetables, hot pavements and tar and a sense of surging pressure, the heavy used-up air was life in the city. Fires caused by the bombing maintained an acrid smell in the air while neighboring houses turned to rubble at night smoldered throughout the day. Then at night the bombers would come again, light new fires to be fought by auxiliary firemen. Archie had heard on the news that the night before London had been attacked by 348 German bombers and over 600 escorting fighters, on a single wave. More came later that night, dropping their bombs into the blaze below them. Worst hit was East Ham, Whitechapel, Southwark and the Thameside area of central London.

By the time he had arrived home a few minutes after 8:00 A.M., Laverne had already left for her job at the shipyards at Hoxton. She had responded to newspaper ads for riveters needed for government work, no experience necessary. Out of the house like a shot she went, and now Archie only saw her on Sundays and for a few minutes in the evenings before she went to bed and he went to work. Strange, he thought, here she was doing man's work building ships and she

70

seemed damned near happy about it. Not that washing clothes would make a woman laugh, but he thought Laverne had actually gained weight while she built steel bulkheads for the Navy. Yes, and with two regular sets of wages there was plenty of food on the table, that is comparing plenty against what they used to have.

Archie fixed himself a sandwich made out of that new American meat they called Spam. Tasted good enough for him and when it was fried, which is how they cooked it on weekend mornings, it was downright good. Still, he barely finished the last bite before the need for sleep overtook him. He fell onto his bed without bothering to wash the factory dirt from his body. He'd do it later.

Deep asleep, Archie snored through the crump of anti-aircraft guns, civil-defense sirens, and the screaming engines of fighter aircraft as RAF Spitfires and Hurricanes dueled with Luftwaffe ME-109s and FW-190s over the blue skies of England. He therefore scarcely heard the sound of knocking on the front door of their flat at mid-day. It was the third series of rapping along with the sound of a man's voice saying "Hello, anybody in there?" that finally caused his eyes to open. After more than a month on the job Archie had still not coaxed his mind into changing its circadian rhythm to work with his body, and his every instinct was to allow his eyelids to slam shut again.

But rise he did and it was only as he grasped the doorknob in his hand that he realized he was still in his skivvies, stained undershirt and with streaks of dirt still on his face. "Who is it?" he called through the thin wooden door.

"My name is Wiles, Mr. Smythes. Do you suppose I might come in and have a word?" a muffled voice came from the other side.

Wiles? Archie mulled the name through his sleepy skull but could not recall a debt collector or landlord by that name. Besides, he thought they were paid up on the rent as of four days ago. "Well, I'm not dressed," he said.

"I would be pleased to wait, Mr. Smythes," the distinctly cultured voice said.

It was likely not a salesman judging from the sound of a gentleman's speech, Archie thought.

"Just a minute, then." Archie looked about their single room for something to put around him. He found his well-used satin robe that he had picked up when backstage at the Sanderson Theater in Glasgow. It had in fact been tossed into a trash can in one of the dressing rooms but Archie never cared about that. He tied the waist sash into a formless knot and pulled open the door.

The man who stood before him was taller than Archie, and lighter and slimmer in the hips. A rather dull, blond hair was revealed when the man removed his bowler hat, and his navy blue serge suit was tailored. His nose was patrician, somewhat pointed and of generous length. His cheekbones were cut high but he looked masculine enough.

He offered his hand. "Edward Wiles," he said, smiling broadly behind perfectly formed, white teeth. Archie took Wiles's hand.

"I'm sorry to barge in on you at this hour, I know you work late at night. I'm on a rather pressing errand, you see."

Archie could not imagine what was pressing about the visit. What was pressing was his sudden need to pee. "Excuse me," he said, not sure that he shouldn't first ask permission. He waved his hand toward the only comfortable chair in the room, then left the flat through the rear door that led to the community toilet. The end of summer weather was a blessing as it was at the same time a curse. Archie was not chilled to the bones dashing along the pathway to the loo, but once there the stench of the toilet and attack of defiant flies was equally uncomfortable.

Upon his return Archie felt a pang of disappointment that Edward Wiles was still sitting in the chair, waiting patiently. He considered offering his visitor tea but was not sure where Laverne kept it if they even had any on hand. Archie turned around a wooden straight-back chair to face Mr. Wiles and sat, waiting.

"I saw you in a play last year, Mr. Smythes," Wiles said.

"Really?" Archie said, his surprise quite evident on his face. His was the face of a very plain man, one that looked packed together by a clay modeler who hadn't quite finished the job. His eyes, however, gave him whatever presence he was able to project in a room. They were dark and sometimes interesting, or so he had been told.

"It was called *Life Everafter*. In Bristol," Wiles said.

Archie tried to hide his disappointment. He had twice played the role of Adolf Hitler in comedy farces, and *Life Everafter* closed after one week. It was a bitter pill for Archie. He was surprised that Wiles had seen it at all, even more surprised that he remembered Archie's part and he said as much to Wiles.

"You're much too modest, old chap," Wiles said, his boyish smile once again spreading across his face. "I saw you in *My Brothers*, as well," Wiles said.

Another comedy, another Hitler role, though this play fared a bit better than *Life Everafter*. "Yes, well, I look like Hitler, once I get into costume," Archie said, his eyes lowering to his hands that he opened and closed.

"By Jove, man, there you go again! It's incredible. How do you do that so effortlessly?" Wiles said, greatly amused.

"Do what?"

"Your hands. Those are his mannerisms," Wiles enthused.

"Whose? Hitler's? I don't know why. Nervous habit, I suppose," Archie said, putting his hands into the pockets of his satin robe. "It closed last October, you know," he said.

"The play? Oh, yes, yes. I know it did. On the twenty-first, I believe," Wiles said, shaking his head in sympathy.

"Hitler wasn't funny anymore," Archie explained. "Of course, it might have folded anyway."

"I'm not so sure about that. Personally, I thought it was very good. And I thought you were crackerjack," Wiles said, his praise quite genuine, Archie thought.

"Is that so? Thank you. That's very kind. I, uh, didn't have a very successful..."

"And the German. Do you speak the language?" Wiles asked.

"Yes. As a matter of fact when I started school I spoke very little English. My mother was German, you see, and we spoke it at home. During *Everafter* I memorized the lines that were written in the play easily. And I had seen the man in newsreels. It was very easy for me to do. I was not a...a great actor."

"You're far too modest, Mr. Smythes." Wiles said, obviously impressed.

"Then *My Brothers* was a bigger part, and I wanted to be very good. I thought the play would run for a while so I studied German. Got pretty good at it, I suppose," Archie said, suddenly gripped by melancholy and wishing he were back in bed.

Sensing the actor's discomfort, Wiles leaned forward in his chair as though preparing to leave. Instead he fixed Archie in a steady gaze, humor no longer dancing at the corners of his eyes. "Mr. Smythes, do you suppose that you could do a performance for two of my colleagues tonight?"

"Begging your pardon? What performance would that be?" Archie said, dumbfounded.

"Your Hitler scenes. One or two should do it. We'd pay you, of course. Would ten pounds be sufficient? On second thought, let's make it twenty," Wiles said.

Twenty pounds! Good heavens, that was more than he would have made if he were on the road with the show for six months! Was this fellow serious? "Well, I haven't done the part for some time..."

"A year," Wiles suggested.

Archie swallowed, concerned that his lack of currency might cause the man to change his mind. "But of course I can do it," he said.

"Jolly good," Wiles said, rising to his feet. He retrieved a flat leather wallet from his breast pocket and withdrew a twenty pound note.

Archie started to put the palm of his hand toward Wiles but the gesture lacked determination. "No need for an advance..."

"Nonsense. I prefer to have the debt paid and off my mind. Please, you would do me a great service by accepting it now," Wiles said.

"Well, then, in that case," Archie said, almost snatching the bill from the gentleman's hand, "I will gladly help you out. And which theater will be used for the audition?" Archie naturally assumed that the other two men were play producers, possibly even motion picture executives looking for talent for a new show. A kind of cold fear crept into his gut at the possibility that these men might have seen him in some of his other tiny parts in which, as he had been reminded, he was perfectly awful.

"A special screening room. I'll jot down the address." Wiles used a fountain pen to write on the back of a small business card. Archie did not so much as glance at the card as Wiles moved gracefully toward the door.

"Eight o'clock, shall we say?" Wiles said. "Will that give you enough time?"

"Yes, damn right it will, Mr. Wiles," Archie said, his confidence buoyed by the feel of the twenty quid note in the pocket of his robe. He offered his hand first this time, and Wiles shook it before leaving.

By 6:00 P.M. Archie was preparing to leave the flat. He was finishing coloring his brown, graying hair to an almost black color, the more to resemble the dictator he would soon imitate. There was barely enough dye left from his long unused bag of stage make-up and he reminded himself that he would have to get more at the chemist's this weekend.

The rattle of the front door as it opened caused him to look up from his mirror over the sink. Laverne entered, a new metal lunch pail with her name scratched into its lid, strung over her shoulder with a loop of electrical wire. Her hair was contained within a bandana tied in a knot above her forehead, a gross work shirt worn under men's small size overalls that she had shortened in the legs. Archie thought Laverne epitomized the British female war worker appearing on propaganda posters liberally distributed about the UK. She had put on weight in recent weeks, it seemed to Archie, and looked the better for it though he would never have described his wife as an attractive woman. Still, with late afternoon sun framing her distorted body lines, Archie felt something compelling, even romantic, about his feeling toward her. She was, after all, a warrior united with many others in a common cause fighting for freedom and it gave her an indefinable stature.

"Hello, Laverne," he said.

"Ev'ning, Archie. Going out?" she asked, noticing that he was wearing his good trousers and newly repaired black shoes.

"Yes, I..." Archie hesitated to refer to his looming audition as a potential acting job. He could not bear to see the profound disappointment in her face were she to learn that he might be prepared to leave steady employment. Though he only earned £3 6d per week as a factory trainee, it was a fortune compared with his sporadic earnings in show business. "I have an interview for an office position," he lied, the twenty quid suddenly burning a hole in his pocket. How would he account for an advance on a white collar job?

"What kind of position?" Laverne asked, setting down her lunch pail and dropping a lump of coal into the firebox.

"It's, well, a kind of supply clerk sort of thing," he said, as he shrugged into a sweater that he would wear despite the warmth of the afternoon. His only coat was covered with dirt from the Croydon plant and its many round trips on tubes and buses.

"Hm. Then I wish you good luck," Laverne said, sighing deeply, fatigue now pulling down on her shoulders and head, and her rather long neck drooping forward. She sat heavily on the bed and began to remove her heavy work shoes.

With his back turned to Laverne, Archie removed the twenty quid note from his pocket and surreptitiously placed it under a heavy salt shaker. By the time he returned from his audition he would have concocted a convincing story about where it came from and, hopefully, that there would be more.

He was glad that he left Putney a full two hours before his scheduled appointment in Belgravia. Everything in the city was running slow and for twenty minutes busses and trains stopped during an air-raid alert. He used the trip to work on his long neglected lines. Having no script to refer to, he recalled them from memory. It was difficult at first for him to bring them up in any kind of flowing order, and for a time he fought back panic, often described as stage fright. But the more he concentrated on remembering the easier it got until, when the last stop had been reached, he was optimistic that he could acquit himself well enough. Clutching his small satchel containing his change of clothing, Archie stepped off the car at the South Kensington station in time to catch the bus for Belgravia, then on to Semley Place.

Referring to the house number on the card given him by Edward Miles, Archie arrived at an imposing townhouse, whitewashed and its grounds well maintained. Despite sandbags piled several feet high entirely around its walls and tape criss-crossing its windows to protect against bomb blast, it was a magnificent residence, far better than any he had been in. He felt an intimidating tingle in his stomach and he was gripped with an almost overwhelming urge to turn and run. So this was how the angels of the theater lived. While he yearned for success and the money that would flow from it, he never aspired to the kind of wealth it must take to own a home as fine as this one.

He used the large brass knocker, the head of a lion, to rap two times on the door. He was prepared to wait a considerable period of time for what he imagined would be a long trek within the house for someone to go from back to front. But the door opened wide after only a few moments. Behind it was a rather short man in a gray pin-striped suit that fitted him snugly, especially at the shoulders and chest. He had heavy brows and large ears with extended lobes, and with eyes set close together that were wintry blue and unsmiling.

"My name is Smythes," Archie said with more confidence than he felt.

"Come in, please," the man said and stepped back without offering his hand or providing his own name. "Mr. Wiles is in the study. This way."

Archie followed the man inside, passing two closed doors before coming to a third dark-stained oak door that had a large, gleaming brass knob on the outside. On the same wall, to the left of the door, was an oil portrait of a man in the naval uniform of an admiral, circa 1700 Archie guessed. Glancing nervously at pictures on the hallway wall behind him he saw that a common theme was military, depicting square-rigged men-o-war under full sail, some in battle, others at anchor, all British.

His escort opened the door, stuck his head inside, then turned back toward Archie. "All right, sir," he said, then closed the door behind Archie as he stepped through the threshold.

Inside the room appeared to be a library slightly modified to contain a small dais along with tall book shelves and comfortable furniture. Above the dais were rolls of what Archie believed were either screens or perhaps maps. There was a large window in the room but it was covered with heavy black or navy blue curtains. There were two men in the room in addition to Edward Wiles. It was Wiles who came toward him, hand extended.

"Ah, Archie, there you are. How good of you to come. Did you bring your costume?" he asked, omitting introductions of the other two men.

Archie lifted his satchel. "Yes. It's a bit wrinkled, of course. Long time since I've used it," he said, apologetically.

"No need to fret over what can't be helped. I say, why don't you just pop into that room there," Wiles said, nodding toward a second door, "and change. Let us know when you're ready."

The room in which Archie found himself was little more than a storage space containing miscellaneous office supplies such as paper, an easel, a ditto machine and the like. Connected to this room was a half-bath, elegant, Archie thought, by any standards. The water basin had tap handles that were as well polished as the shining door knobs he had seen since entering the building.

He opened his satchel and emptied it of his Hitler uniform, less boots and hat. There simply wasn't room for boots within the bag and, in any case, Hitler's usual uniform dress was oxford shoes, dark trousers with a split red stripe down the legs. It was these he pulled up around his waist, finding them just a bit large, the result of the workaday life he'd been leading since the outbreak of hostilities. The olive shirt he donned was short sleeved, made that way so that his Hitlerian jacket would fit more easily, its black and red swastika permanently attached to the left sleeve. As he fumbled to tie the black necktie into a proper knot, Archie was pleased to find that a small tie-tack, a miniature swastika, was still in the coat pocket. Aside from the fact that his clothing was rumpled, he thought he looked well enough dressed for any Nazi function.

Dipping once again into his satchel he withdrew the Führer's mustache and, using more pressure than when the gum was fresh, got it to stick to his upper lip. Finally, wishing that he had the German leader's hat, Archie pulled at his hair with his fingers until it fell across his forehead. His own hair was doubtless longer than Hitler kept his, but of course when the play opened, if indeed it did, he would be suitably barbered for the occasion.

Standing before a mirror attached to the back side of the bathroom door, Archie inspected himself. He was still critical of the wrinkled condition of the uniform but knew from experience that after he got into his performance that small distraction would disappear. He threw himself several salutes, the bent arm, palm outward that Hitler tossed about so casually in the newsreels, and the more formal stiff armed, fully extended Nazi party greeting with which the world had become so familiar. He even clenched his fist several times and brought it across his chest in the dramatic fashion as he had seen Hitler touch himself when he wanted the world to know that his words were heartfelt.

Satisfied, Archie opened the door but hesitated, waiting for Edward Wiles to somehow announce him to the audience. Sensing this to be the case, Wiles crossed the room. "Good heavens, Archie, if I didn't know better I would have thought it was the archfiend himself," he said, taking Archie by the elbow and leading him across the floor to the small stage under the map rollers. The lights in the room had been dimmed so that the audience, composed of Wiles and the two men Archie had seen when he first entered, were cast in deep shadow.

Three overhead lights serving to illuminate the stage area, were turned on making it almost impossible for Archie to discern faces in the room. It was a condition with which Archie was fully familiar and that distracted not at all from his work at hand.

He cleared his throat and spoke to his audience. "Bear in mind, gentlemen, that I haven't had a proper rehearsal and...and that it has been more than a year since the play was done...." His voice trailed off into a silence that was in itself intimidating, almost hostile. Maybe the producers had changed their minds about having him audition. Perhaps plans to produce the play itself had been changed and that he no longer figured into their scheme.

"Well," he began, "the scene is Adolf Hitler giving his reasons to his inner circle about why he wants the Jews out of Germany. But they are finding that the country does not run so well without the Jews. There are responses that I should be getting from other actors on stage and..."

Archie broke off, listening to talking coming from one of the audience. Then he heard Wiles's voice from the back of the room. "Make it a monologue, Archie," he said.

"It wouldn't make much sense that way, but I..."

"In German," Wiles said, interrupting.

Archie hesitated. He had not worked on his lines in German. It was enough of a struggle to recall them in English. He closed his eyes.

"Go ahead, my Führer," Wiles said in German, *"I am sure you will do very well."*

Archie nodded, blinked, then plunged ahead in German. *"I want the hook-nose people, the Jews, out of Germany forever. It is national survival. The Jews have been eating us alive, we Germans!"* he said, allowing his voice to rise. *"Wait. Leave a few. We need them to run the city. Ja, and we must have their art as well. Leave that."*

Archie had hooked his thumb into a side pocket of his coat jacket, and begun to pace the length of the dais. His free hand clenched and unclenched as his voice rose to dominate his imaginary staff officers.

"And where is the idiot Goering? Ah, you, German, there you are. I want you to stop eating so much schnitzel. Eat fettucini. Il Duce says that noodles are good for you. That is my order, Herman!"

Archie paused for audience reaction. When there was none, he then reminded himself that there likely would be none. As he continued to pace, gesticulating with his hands and upraised chin, he was not conscious that the character of the Führer had returned, and his delivery became effortless. Responses from other actors were not coming, of course, but he found that he could improvise the character into a monologue. He began to think that the scene, perhaps the entire play, should be rewritten as a one man show. Even though Hitler was no longer a laughing matter there might be....

"I beg your pardon?" he said, suddenly aware that Wiles was speaking to him from the back of the room.

"I said thank you very much. I think we have the insights that we need," Wiles said, moving into the lighted area of the room.

"Yes, well, I have some thoughts about how we could..."

"Would you mind waiting in the other room while we chat for a bit? We shouldn't be long, Archie," Wiles said.

Archie nodded and stepped to the door of his "dressing room." Once inside the storage area he regarded his appearance yet again. Peering carefully into the mirror, this he time attempted to be quite critical of the visage before him. He leaned closer to the glass, looking deeply into his dark eyes. He did not see the rage that he knew the real Führer had in his, but the rest of him was very, very close to Adolf. He pulled back from the mirror, inspected his profile as best he could see it, then shook his head. He knew that to fool an audience it only took confidence, not perfection of similarity. It was mannerisms more than physical attributes that created a character. People gained and lost weight, they went through life suffering cuts, scrapes, breaks, all sorts of things that changed their physical appearance, but personal habits were forever.

Archie sat heavily onto a straight back chair and considered the leader of the German nation. He was not ashamed to admit that at one time he was a strong supporter of Hitler's. Well, he admired him. Many English people did. He got things done when others had failed. He replaced bureaucracies in Germany that were holding back his people. The Versailles treaty *was* unfair to the German volk and everyone who was not a hypocrite would admit it. The Great War was as much the fault of others as Germany's. Oh, that wasn't to excuse them, not at all, but there was enough blame to go around, make no mistake. And when this fellow Adolf had nerve enough to speak out, they tried to silence him.

But he crossed the line with the Jews. And with others. And making war on Poland was wrong, too. Very wrong. Archie could feel his heart begin to pump as he thought about the Wehrmacht massed across the channel from Dover, just waiting to pounce. Schicklgruber and his pals were welcome to try, of course, but they'd bloody well die before they even got to the beaches. Hadn't they heard of His Majesty's Navy? The Home Fleet was the mightiest in the world and even a school boy knows that to land troops one must have ships to get them ashore!

Archie found a water glass and filled it. He drank it down and filled it again and began to sip. He closed his eyes, leaned back in the chair and realized that his body had been tense for over an hour and was now in the process of relaxing. He began to feel pleasantly warm as his hands, then his arms, went limp.

When he opened his eyes again his head was resting uncomfortably on his chest. He had no watch but even without consulting a clock he had the feeling that the hour was late, at least late enough so that using the best public transportation route to Croydon would bring him to the engine factory late for his shift. His foreman was the nastiest sort of monster, probably chosen for the job because of his traits of being a bastard. Archie rose to his feet and, as he placed his hand on the door knob, felt it open.

"Archie," Wiles said, as though surprised that the actor was still there. "Terribly sorry for keeping you waiting, old chap. We were discussing matters that were very important, I assure you. Come in, please," Wiles said, taking Archie collegially by the upper arm.

"Let me introduce you to my colleagues," Wiles smoothly went on. "MacLean Elliot," he said, presenting Archie to a man probably in his early sixties.

MacLean Elliot had brown hair which was rapidly turning grey, a square jaw, prominent cheekbones and deep, very light blue eyes. He carried himself with square shoulders, square chin held high, and was average height if not a bit under. He focused a frankly appraising gaze as he continued to measure Archie even as he did when Archie was performing. He merely grunted at the introduction and did not offer his hand.

"Sir William Schuyler," Wiles said, introducing the fourth man in the room. Schuyler, a very tall, slender man, untangled his knobby knees and feet and, rising from his sitting position, towered over the others. He extended his hand and Archie took it, almost wincing with pain from the strength of the old man's grip. Schuyler had an angular face that supported a large nose and only wisps of hair around the ears of an otherwise bald head. Schuyler, too, continued to observe Archie from head to toe as a commander might do when inspecting a significant military weapon.

"Well, now," Schuyler said, raising himself to his toes, then rocking back to his heels, hands clasped behind the back. "I don't see anything in your background that impresses me at all. Eh? Not at all, Mr. Smythes."

Archie was struck dumb not only because of Schuyler's directness but because of the huge, disturbing grin that spread across his face along with the insult.

"Well, I, uh," Archie spluttered, unsure of how the gangly, obviously important man, meant his comment. Was he talking about Archie's career in the theater? His military record? His entire life? "I suppose you might be right about that...."

"This man has insulted you, my Führer," Wiles whispered into Archie's ear in German.

For the flash of an instant Archie turned toward Wiles, confused, but then clenched his fist and raised it just above belt level. Redness showed in his fingers, as the fist moved up and down like a piston, *The Führer's* rage rising as though moving to the beat to an imaginary drummer. His eyes narrowed and his lips turned into a sneer. *"What? Idiot! You dare to question me, Adolf Hitler, the greatest military mind of this age? Of any age?"* Archie allowed his voice to raise to a shriek, spittle beginning to show at the corners of his mouth.

Schuyler staggered back at the force of Archie's blast as the Führer continued his tirade in German. *"I will have no officer on my staff, who questions my decisions. Do you hear? Take this imbecile from my sight immediately and find something for him to do away from Germany!"*

"Jawohl, mein Führer," Wiles said, playing his part.

Archie had thrown all of his indignation, pure spleen, into the character's outburst aimed at a subordinate. His face was flushed and his breathing had quickened. He turned away from the trio and paced the room while, apparently subconsciously, holding his left arm with his right hand across his chest.

Wiles watched in fascination. He lit a cigarette, inhaled, then blew the smoke out of his lungs.

"Put that filthy thingout!" Archie snapped in German.

"Excuse me one moment, Herr...Archie," Wiles said, winking at the actor. He turned back to his colleagues who spoke softly among their gathered heads before turning in unison back toward Archie. MacLean Elliot and Schuyler returned to their comfortable chairs, and listened, while Wiles continued to stand as he addressed Archie. "Look here, old man, what we're about to ask of you is very secret. What we discuss in this room must stay here. Do you understand?" Wiles began.

"You're not producers, are you?" Archie asked, taking a deep breath, knowing the answer before asking.

"No, we are not," Wiles said.

"Not in the film business? The theater?" he said, his heart beginning to sink.

"No, nothing like that," Wiles shook his head.

"Then there is no job," Archie said, defeated now.

Wiles's smile only flashed at the irony before his face sobered again. "Well, in the strictest sense of the word, there is a job. A very important one. Would you like to hear what it is?"

"Yes, of course," Archie said.

"You might want to sit down," Wiles said, indicating toward a leather covered chair.

"No, I think I'd rather stand," Archie said.

"As you wish. Now, Archie, a final warning. Any indication that you have breathed a word of what we about to tell you to anyone in the world, that includes your wife, your daughter, even anyone you should meet tonight, tomorrow or forever, will be grounds for the swiftest and harshest punishment possible. Do you understand in full what I mean?" Wiles said.

Archie experienced a certain fluid sensation in his knees, and for a moment his hearing dulled as blood rushed to his brain. Rather than utter a word, he merely nodded his head.

"Following what I am about to tell you, even if you do not accept our offer, you shall not be allowed to return to your home for a minimum of a fortnight. There is state secrecy involved and we cannot afford to let you roam about. Are we clear about that?"

Archie nodded his understanding.

"And I should add that if you accept the offer we are about to extend, you will be watched, twenty-four hours a day, every day, by a member or members of His Majesty's government." Wiles paused for a moment before continuing on. "I, and Mssrs. Elliot and Schuyler, are members of SOE. SOE stands for Special Operations Executive. It is our business to organize special warfare operations in enemy held territory. We," Wiles motioned his hands to indicate his two associates, "concern ourselves with clandestine operations in Europe. Do you understand so far?"

Archie nodded solemnly. "I think I do."

"Good. I can tell you that we here in the British Isles are, at this moment of time, in an extremely dangerous position. Our army has just been evacuated from Dunkirk and is in no condition to fight. The RAF is fully engaged against a numerically dominant Luftwaffe, both in bomber and fighter aircraft. Our navy is superior to the Nazis' but if Hitler is determined to invade the islands our fleet will not be able to stop him. We would be able to hurt him, to be sure, but his invasion would succeed. Do you still follow?"

Archie swallowed, and nodded once again.

"We know that Hitler's plans for the invasion of England is code named Sealion," Wiles paused for absolute clarity, then repeated the word. "Sealion. We don't know the exact date that he plans to execute his plan but he is massing the necessary armies across the channel even as we speak and his forces are building by the day."

Wiles regarded Archie at length, as though he was having second thoughts about continuing his revelations to an actor. "We have plans to kill Hitler," he said, simply. "In four days time he will make an address to a cadre of German officers that have been chosen to form two new Waffen SS divisions. This will take place in Munich. Himmler and other staff officers will be with him when he returns to Berlin by train. The Führer train is heavily guarded and travels with an escort train. No easy target. We might destroy the train with a squadron of Mosquito bombers but there is no guarantee we would get Hitler. No, instead we shall parachute in a special commando group to stop the train by first blowing up the tracks, then killing the SS guards assigned to it. Certain of those men will be specifically assigned to kill Hitler. Still with me, Archie?"

"I think so," he said, clearing his parched throat.

"Would you like a glass of water?" Wiles said.

"Yes, please," Archie responded, accepting water poured for him by Wiles. The actor glanced at Elliot and Schuyler who continued to hold him in unblinking stares.

"You see, we think it might be the case that Germany would be so traumatized by the loss of their leader that they might sue for peace. Or at least cancel his plans for invading England. That was our hope, but it was only a hope. Then you came to mind, old chap. We thought that if, out of the smoke and carnage of a train wreck, Adolf Hitler could emerge long enough to send a single radio message to OKW, Oberkommando der Wehrmacht, in Berlin, the exercise could be an assured success. Can you guess what that message would be, Archie?" Wiles asked, softly.

Archie, transfixed, shook his head.

"Stand down from Operation Sealion," Wiles said. "That's all. 'Stand down from Operation Sealion.' Hitler's last order before disappearing."

"Yes, but, I don't understand. I thought I did but if he is dead..." Archie halted, confused.

"In reality he will be dead, of course," Wiles said. "The commandos who kill Adolf will make sure of that but you, dressed in the appropriate uniform, will take his place. Appearing to be Hitler, you will have survived the attack long enough to make your way to the communications car and send your historic message. It will be witnessed by the communications officer and radio signalmen inside that car. After the message is safely sent, you will return to England with the retreating commandos aboard a Stirling bomber whence you came."

Wiles paused again, clearly this time to gauge Archie's reaction to a rather straightforward plan.

"And...you suggest that I should go with the commandos? That I should send the message?" Archie said, incredulous.

"Exactly. Of course it will be dangerous. I won't lie to you, it's a long shot. But I can tell you that the plan and you shall receive the full support of your country. And, should you succeed, it would be no exaggeration to say that you shall have the everlasting gratitude of your King and of the entire English speaking world. Well? What do you say?"

Archie sat down. "How long do I have to think about it?"

"Let's give it ten minutes, old man. We have a great deal to do, you see. You shall have to leave immediately for a commando training base at once. The Third Parachute Commando is in the final stages of preparing for the mission even as we speak, with or without you. We are moving rapidly in reaction to intelligence as it is acquired on the Continent. So, Archie, what's it to be?"

A single line? he thought. To change the course of history by delivering only a few words of dialogue? Was this not a role that any actor would die to play? He would be, without doubt, regarded as the key figure in affecting England's most significant military victory in history. He would be the rival of Nelson at Trafalgar. Still, Archie could hardly believe the words that came out of his mouth. "I'm an Englishman. Of course I'll do it."

Archie immediately felt sick to his stomach.

emergencies, they often heard, a catchphrase for everything needed and unavailable, wanted and denied, could hardly justify cutting off the village from the rest of the world.

While only a few miles away parachutists drifted down from the sky, and the oft heard carrump, carrump of explosives shook the earth, the town leaders demanded the commanding officer fully explain his latest outrage directed against Scottish civilians and tell them when the train would run again. Their demands fell upon deaf ears. Military secret, was all they received for their exercise.

Major Cedric Plith of the Third Para Commandoes knew, of course, exactly when the train would be allowed to resume its schedule through Galene. That would be August third, two days hence, the day he and his unit of volunteers would leave on their top-secret mission into the heart of danger. It would be a security blunder to advertise their departure date by naming the date when train service would be restored. It was impossible now simply because his commando sappers had blown the bloody tracks upon which it ran. Blown it, mind you, not once but three times, following three night time drops by his paras from a specially modified Stirling bomber.

As Major Plith, a young man to have achieved that much rank, escaped still another congregation of town's people through the rear door of his headquarters building, he stepped aboard a lorry that was headed the five kilometers to the track site. Major Plith was a natural worrier and he worried about the great number of items that could befoul his mission. It could be called off as quickly as it was ordered on. The communications gear aboard the Stirling had been acting up and, at his order, had been completely replaced with the newest equipment available. And new equipment, by definition, worried Major Plith. Navigation was a horror that was never far from his mind, even in his dreams. To find their DZ under the best of meteorological conditions seemed impossible for him to fathom, but adding to that fact that they would be deep into enemy territory without electronic aid was frightening. The aircrew assigned to this mission was the best that Special Ops could produce, and that was saying a great deal. They were the best of the best.

It was his attention to small details, a heart that refused to recognize fear when others were paralyzed by it, and a willingness to make vital decisions quickly, had catapulted Plith from the lower officer grades over his superiors to command a new kind of military warfare group. He had led his men back from the fighting in France and the beaches of Dunkirk to this place in Scotland where he and his men had been chosen to execute a mission which, if successful, could immeasurably shorten the war. Only Major Plith and four other men in the world knew its true objective and he would take his hand-picked group of soldiers into the jaws of danger without telling them, until it was over, what they were being asked to accomplish. Those who would die would never know, and those who lived would be owed a debt of large proportion by their nation. Plith never doubted that such a day in history would arrive.

"Sir!" shouted Sergeant Ferrel, snapping a salute to Plith as the lanky commander approached. Plith returned the sergeant's perfect military salute with a touch of his swagger stick to the brim of his garrison hat as he looked around at the work being done. Numbers One and Two squads were removing twisted railroad track and hammering down new lengths of the iron rail over a freshly filled hole made hours before by the new plastic explosive. Plith knew that his commandos were doing work normally accomplished by engineers but he wanted his men to be totally familiar with the thing they were assigned to destroy, and that included making it whole again so that they could once again destroy it. If they knew how it went together, they would know what it took to rip it apart.

"Where is he?" Major Plith said.

"He's over there, sir," Sergeant Ferrel said, falling into step with his commander as the two of them walked in the direction indicated. "He's been watching us all along, keen on the job, I'll say that. As long as he don't have to move, that is," Ferrel said with little attempt to hide his derision.

Major Plith could make out the form of the middle aged man sitting, as comfortably as possible, on the ground with his back propped against a rock wall. The man, dressed in a new, rather sloppy fitting army uniform, wore no rank nor unit badge. His rather shapeless body was in sharp contrast with those of the hard troops around him, a man clearly out of place.

"Have you talked with him?" Plith asked.

"Very little, sir. Routine, that's all," the sergeant responded.

"Good. That goes for the others as well."

"They've got their orders, Major," Sergeant Ferrel said, letting the major know that he knew how to carry out his duties. "Ah, Major Plith, sir," Ferrel began.

"Yes?"

"I have a question, if you don't mind me askin'" Ferrel said.

"I dare say you would. What is it, Sergeant?" Plith said.

"Well, sir, the man, Archie Smythes, is going with us on the bang-up, but he says he's never jumped before. No training whatever, he says. I'd say the blighter's scared and I believe I would be, too."

"Yes, well, we have no time to train him, do we?" Plith said.

"I suppose we don't, sir, but..."

"And even if we did, we'd risk injuring the man, so we might as well train him by jumping for real. See the logic, Sergeant?" Plith explained.

"Righto, Major, sir. Still, he thinks the Stirling is going to land and he's going to step out after," the sergeant said, eyebrows raised as he anticipated his commander's next response.

"I'm sure. Instead we'll simply throw him out."

"Like a sack of potatoes?" Sergeant Ferrel said, smiling at the very thought.

"Exactly like a sack of potatoes. If he jumps on queue, fine, but if not, he goes anyway. Who have you assigned to him?"

"Corporals Marion Clark and Dickie Grafton," Sergeant Ferrel said.

"Yes. Good men," Plith agreed.

"They're all good, sir, and I believe I could have picked any of them," Ferrel said, not hiding his pride.

"No question about it, Sergeant. Now, then, one more order that will no doubt strike you as a bit odd. Call Clark and Grafton over here and I'll tell them as well," Plith said.

"Yes, sir," Ferrel said, and double timed the short distance to the track where thirty men worked at replacing the iron rail line that they had destroyed only hours before.

Plith looked on as Ferrel spoke briefly with two of the commandos, then returned with them in company. The men stood at attention in front of Plith.

"Stand easy," he said.

Ferrel, Clark and Grafton stood as ordered, hands behind their backs, Thompson submachine guns slung casually over their shoulders, awaiting their commander's direction.

"You and your men know that you are going to fight a very determined enemy in Germany. An SS detachment guarding a train. What you don't know is who is on the train or why it is to be destroyed. Well, the time has come to reveal the purpose of our mission. Our target on that special train is none other than Germany's leader, Adolf Hitler."

Plith paused to note reactions from his NCOs. There was very little change of expressions on their faces, the result, Plith believed, of previous speculation.

"I suppose you might have guessed it would be something like that, given the size of the escort detail assigned to the train, and now you know. We all have our assignments and yours will be to make sure that fellow over there," Plith nodded toward Archie Smythes, "gets to the communications car. Once inside the comm-car he will impersonate the voice of Hitler. You will wait nearby until he is finished. After he exits the car, he will return with you to the pick-up aircraft. Do you understand?"

"Yes, sir," Corporal Clark said. "We're to see Archie there isn't bothered til he's done his business."

"That's correct, Corporal," Plith said. "Second squad attacks the Führer's car, Ferrel..."

"Right, sir," Ferrel interjected.

"I want Archie to enter the car with you. Got that? Right on your heels," Plith said. "When you have made sure Adolf is dead, off you go to the communications car."

"Yes, sir," the men chorused.

"Very well. Carry on with your duties while I talk with Archie," Plith said.

"Sir," Corporal Clark said, causing Major Plith to pause.

"Yes?"

"Archie don't seem all that, well, military. He don't salute right. I haven't seen the bloke march yet and I'm not sure the man can tell which end of a gun the bullet comes outa. So what is he, sir?"

"What he is is nobody's business, Corporal. He is not a soldier, I can tell you that much," Plith said.

"Ah, well, that's fine, sir. Just fine," Corporal Clark said, obviously relieved. "I'd hate to think we'd trained the likes o' him and come up with..."

"A bloke like him," Sergeant Ferrel readily agreed.

"The man is a civilian, in fact. He is a volunteer. And a very brave one, at that," Plith said, his voice at a slight edge.

The three commandos exchange quick glances. A civilian. Damn, that's a fine one.

"Right, then, we'll go over this again later. Carry on," Plith said as the three enlisted men stepped back and saluted.

Plith strode to the rock wall only a few hundred feet away. Archie's eyes were closed against the late afternoon sun, his knees drawn up to his chest, head resting lightly back upon Highland stone. A shadow cast across his face caused him to blink and to see the unmistakable, slender form of young Major Plith. He attempted to struggle to his feet but was pushed gently back by a firm hand on his shoulder.

"As you were, Archie. I'll just have a sit next to you," Major Plith said, squatting at Archie's side. "Sorry that we haven't had a chance to get to know each other but two days..." the major shrugged.

"Yes, two days," Archie seemed to want to say more but he choked slightly and remained silent.

"You haven't spoken to the men? About your mission, I mean?"

"No, of course not. I really wouldn't know what to say. I can hardly believe it, myself," Archie said. The actor bit his lip, feeling the growth of his newly developed mustache. It seemed strange to live with it day and night, not just while playing a role. It was grey, matching his hair, and it made him wonder if Hitler did not tint his hair and mustache. He shook his head before speaking again. "There isn't a chance they'll scratch the operation, is there? I mean, has anyone changed their mind?"

"No."

"Ah. Good."

Major Plith knew that Archie meant exactly the opposite of good. The actor was a frightened man. My god, who wouldn't be? He's not a soldier, he probably does not know how to shoot a gun, let alone hit anything with it. He's middle-aged, not able to leap over obstacles, swim rivers or fight a man with a knife. Were the situations reversed Plith wasn't sure that he wouldn't run, screaming, as far away from the nightmare into which the poor man had got himself. Not knowing a proper way to commiserate with his charge, however, Major Plith could only offer advice even he did not believe.

"We're keeping our fingers crossed that our target's schedule holds firm. If it does, we'll give old Adie the shock of his misspent life, won't we? You'll be in the company of the world's best, Archie, and it's our job to see that you get there to do your job and to get back safe and sound. We're dedicated to that."

Archie attempted to smile but one side of his mouth failed him and his lips sagged. "I know that, Major."

"Fine, then," Plith said, awkwardly. Major Plith wanted to know many things about Archie Smythes but was professionally reluctant to ask. Who he really was, where he came from, who his people were, was of no consequence to the success of the mission. "You've had no contact with people on the outside? Family, that is?"

Archie shook his head, his eyes dropping to his folded hands in his lap.

"I don't want to repeat the obvious, Archie, but you are forbidden to do so now. No calls, no letters, nothing to go outside this camp."

Archie nodded.

"Point of fact, you are not to discuss your mission with the other commandos with the exception of three, Sergeant Ferrel and Corporals Clark and Grafton. Is that understood?" Plith said, almost gently.

Archie assented again with his head.

"I have just briefed those men on our real target. When we are airborne I shall instruct the rest of the commando that we're after Hitler, though I would wager that those chaps have already figured it out. Now, then, I'm charged with explaining to you certain survivors benefits, national insurance, for instance."

Major Plith stopped when Archie slowly raised his hand. Shaking his head he said "Please. I don't think I could...that is, I don't want to hear it, sir." Archie struggled to find his voice. "My wife and...my daughter...."

Major Plith touched the civilian on the arm and squeezed, reassuringly. "Well, enough said that everything will be taken of in the off chance that we don't make it back. Standard stuff, and all that."

"God," Archie exhaled, "I saw myself as a hero. What was wrong with me to believe that? I'm not a hero, I'm a coward. I'm so frightened I can't keep food down and that which I manage to swallow comes quickly out, one end or the other."

Major Plith noticed that Archie was now trembling.

"I only hope I don't soil my trousers when we land," Archie continued. "Wouldn't that be the bloody end? Adolf Hitler shits his pants?"

Despite himself Major Plith smiled. Archie's eyes caught his and they grinned together. Then they began to laugh. Whether it was the unexpected release of tension each man was feeling or the pure comic element of a Chaplinesque vision of Adolf in stained dress uniform, neither knew or cared. By the time they had stopped their convulsed laughter they felt better.

"Well, old boy," Plith said collegially, "in a few days, when we've arrived home again, we'll drink to your very excellent joke." Major Plith rose, patted Archie again and, more sober, walked away.

For Archie, the wave of good cheer lasted less than a minute before the cold clouds of despair crept back into his guts.

On the afternoon of Wednesday, August 31, 1940, the Raven detachment of Third Para Commando was flown south to a secret staging area near Ramsgate. Ramsgate was primarily an RAF fighter support area but Special Air Mission (SAM) often served the needs of SOE when deep-penetration aircraft were required. SOE would later use the aerodrome at Suffolks for SOE Special Duty Flights and would eventually become permanently situated at Harrington RAF base.

The Raven commando remained on the field from 1303 hours when it arrived and 2300 hours. At that time it was scheduled to take off and fly among Bomber Command aircraft headed for targets over French channel ports.

Hot food was driven out to the Stirling bomber assigned to Third Para as it sat parked on the tarmac being refueled and last minute pre-flighting was accomplished by its aircrew. The thirty-seven man Raven detachment, including Archie Smythes, would have been far happier to stretch their legs while still on friendly soil, but were at the same time aware of the need for secrecy to provide them with the maximum chance of getting to their target and getting back safely.

The pathfinder aircraft of Bomber Command had departed an hour earlier when the big Stirling bomber, engines revving to a full 2600 rpm, received the green flare from the tower and Pilot Officer Ronald Kershwim released the brakes on his mighty machine to begin its ground roll. While the Stirling carried a maximum fuel load in its tanks, it was not weighted down with guns, ammunition, or bombs, and the big aircraft lifted off the runway with more than one thousand feet to spare. Kershwim turned to a heading of 185 to pick up the bomber stream that would hit targets in and around Rouen, France. The meteorological briefing forecast broken clouds at six thousand feet over the primary target area with scattered clouds at thirteen thousand. The flight plan called for a turn over Rouen onto a course of 79, ESE, which would take the Stirling over the heart of Germany leaving Stuttgart on their port wing, to a location approximately twenty-one statute miles past Augsburg.

The Stirling was still climbing through five thousand feet, turbo chargers full open, when Major Plith stood up from his bucket seat and placed himself in the middle of his men.

"Right, gather round now, fellows," he said, his voice straining to be heard over the roar of the pounding Rolls-Royce engines. His commandos, not yet harnessed into the parachutes but still strapped into ammunition, food and weapons carrying harnesses, pulled themselves into the tightest possible circle around their commander. Major Plith was authorized to reveal as much or as little about the true nature of their mission into Germany as he saw fit. Under the circumstances, Plith saw no reason to withhold anything from his men.

"You all know the mechanics of what we're about on this raid," he began. "We've blown enough track and attacked enough trains to give ourselves all the edge we need to pull this off successfully. We'll kill the SS on board that train to a man. I repeat, leave no one alive. With one exception. Sergeant Ferrel," Major Plith snapped, "who is that one exception?"

"The communications officer, sir. And if not him, the ranking man in charge of the comm-car," Ferrel responded without hesitation.

"Correct," Plith said. "Corporal Clark, what happens after Archie Smythes sends his message?"

"We kill the Huns commo boys and hot-foot it back to the rendez-vous point," Clark said.

"Right," Plith nodded. "Corporal Grafton..."

"Sir?" Grafton said at once.

"Have you the stomach for it, lad? To kill unarmed men?" Plith asked.

"Yes, sir. I see the why of it, Major, sir. You needn't worry about me."

"Good man. That goes for the rest of you. If one man falls, the next man has got to take his place. When we leave the fight behind us, there can't be a soul to tell any tale." Plith took the time to look each man in the eye and to hold that connection until he was certain of what he saw inside the man. "Now, then, in case none of you has divined who our target must be, I shall unburden you of wrong notions. We shall attack and kill no less a person than Adolf Hitler."

Plith waited for a reaction from his men. He was not disappointed. Most had indeed guessed but now that the fact was confirmed, every man nudged the man next to him, quickly shaking hands, punching shoulders, and otherwise showing their strong approval that such a prestigious target was to be the prize for their dangerous mission.

Plith continued. "Squad One will have to reinforce Ferrel, Clark, and Grafton when they hit the Führer car. Who are they to be, Corporal Lund?"

"Privates MacQueen and Shaw, sir," Corporal Douglas Lund, a sandy haired Highlander said without hesitation.

Plith smiled. "Got your Scots on the job, eh, Corporal?"

"That's it, Major, sir. When the stakes are high we clansmen are the answer," Lund responded without the slightest bit of doubt in his voice.

"Very well. That's it, then. A final word, don't bother Archie, back there. He's got a lot to think about and the less he knows about our end of the business, the better off we all are. Now get some rest. Two hours to DZ."

Maximum operational speed for the Stirling was 280 mph but realistic cruise was 235. While computing altitude and outside temperature the navigator could discern the pressure altitude and once he knew that he could compute true airspeed, or speed over the ground, and make corrections for the effects of wind. The Stirling was ploughing through bumpy skies with a thirty knot headwind that would put them over the target forty minutes later than scheduled. Such a deviation from ideal conditions had been taken into account when planning the mission, but the navigator was not pleased that meteorological conditions were other than predicted. What else could go wrong?

The flak over Rouen was as heavy as the Stirling crew had experienced in France. They knew that when it let up they would be hunted by Luftwaffe night fighters. They had no guns for defense but relied upon remaining inconspicuous among the hundreds of other aircraft in the bomber stream passing over the German occupied city.

At 2415 hours Flying Officer Kershwim eased in left rudder and rolled coordinated aileron to bring the nose of his Stirling around to a course of 79, the fires at the outskirts of Rouen's industrialized area, still burning, now fading in the distance behind them. The air was still turbulent at eleven thousand feet and Kershwim sent word back to the commandos that he was climbing to thirteen thousand. He was determined to find smoother air and also to find cloud cover created by the unstable summer weather mass. Thirteen thousand was about the maximum safe altitude before crew and passengers would have to use supplemental oxygen. Kershwim put himself on oxygen as a safety precaution and ordered his navigator to do so, as well. The pilot was relieved that the unseasonable cold at this altitude was sufficient to allow him to keep his engine cowlings closed during the climb without overheating.

Archie was keeping to himself, as ordered, in the rear of the aircraft. He was soon joined by Sergeant Ferrel and corporals Clark and Grafton who, from now on, would not leave his side until they returned to England. Clark noticed that Archie had a very large, oversized jump suit covering his uniform and that a special canvas kit was fastened securely to his waist. He wore his parachute, attached before he boarded the aircraft, even while the other commandos left theirs off, albeit within easy reach, until farther into the mission. Archie was reading a sheaf of papers and while Sergeant Ferrel was curious about its content, straining to see print in the dark was too much for him.

Sergeant Ferrel might have been surprised that Archie was reading a classified report excerpted from an MI6 commissioned study done on Germany's leader, Adolf Hitler. An ad hoc staff of psychologists at Oxford had assembled a several hundred page document that aimed at assessing the Führer's complete psychological history including, in the thirty page section now being studied by Archie, his personality traits. The Führer, according to the study, was absolutely confident that he and his decisions are correct. He once said in a speech describing his own conduct: "I follow my course with the precision and security of a sleepwalker," and to President Schuschnigg during the Berchtesgaden interviews: "Do you realize that you are in the presence of the greatest German of all time?" It was, Archie thought, an incredible self-appraisal. He wondered if any other leader in world history had such fantastic notions about himself.

He read on through the report, partly to distract himself from the fear that he felt for his own fate that lay just hours away. He regarded himself as the world's greatest military mind, the greatest of all architects, and an outstanding judge in legal matters. He was, in short, a genius in the broadest sense of the word. He was infallible and invincible. It was false, despite belief to the contrary, the report said, that Hitler was in touch with astrologers who advised him. Nothing was more foreign to his personality than to seek help from outside sources of this type. An informant from the Dutch Legation affirms this when he says, "Not only has the Führer never had his horoscope cast, but he is in principle against horoscopes because he feels he might be unconsciously influenced by them." Before the war Hitler forbade the practice of fortune-telling and star-reading in Germany.

Although Hitler had done considerable reading in a variety of fields of study, the report went on, he did not in any way attribute his infallibility or omniscience to any intellectual endeavor on his part. On the contrary, he frowned upon such sources when it came to guiding the destiny of nations. His opinion of the intellect was quite low. For example, he said "Of secondary importance is the training of mental abilities. Over-educated people, stuffed with knowledge and intellect, but bare of any sound instincts.... These impudent rascals, the intellectuals, who always know everything better than anybody else.... The intellect has grown autocratic and has become a disease of life."

Archie was pleasantly surprised to find that he could read with reasonable ease parts of the report that were quoted in German. He was not fluent, to be sure, but he felt a certain comfort with the language. He read that although Hitler was brought up a Catholic and received Communion, during the war he severed his connection with the Church directly afterwards. This kind of Christ he considered soft and weak and unsuitable as a German Messiah. He, the true deliverer of Germany's future, must be hard and brutal if he is to save the people and their destiny. Hitler had been known to acknowledge the salute, "Heil Hitler, our Savior," with a slight bow and acceptance. Archie wondered what it felt like to be Christ. *Bloody hell*, he thought, he would never know that emotion no matter how he "did" Hitler.

The turbulence had eased considerably as the Stirling bored through the night heading east. There was no light shining outside or inside the bomber save the faintest glow of a quarter moon that lit the plexiglass openings in the ship's hull where guns once were mounted. Because they had put a skin darkening agent onto their faces and hands, Archie could not make out the features of the commandos who, he felt, would often look in his direction. They knew he was not a soldier. For egotistical reasons he wished that he was. But he frankly lacked their courage, their strength, and their mental toughness. While he felt inadequate to them, he also felt comfort in being in their midst, among the strongest of the strong.

Major Plith looked at his hack watch for the tenth time in as many minutes, noting that the Stirling was now almost three hours into the mission. They should have arrived at the DZ fifteen minutes ago. Plith unfastened his bucket-seat belt and started to move forward toward the navigator's compartment when the Stirling suddenly lurched hard right, throwing Plith across the aircraft into the arms of men from number one squad. "Gotcha, there, sir," he heard from behind him as several strong hands steadied him. As he attempted to rise to his feet the Stirling banked sharply in the opposite direction, across the belly of the aircraft throwing Plith against the bulkhead whence he started. Reaching for a steadying handhold, Plith felt a sharp pain in his right wrist, jamming it against a fuselage reinforcement. He immediately knew that he had badly sprained it or even broken bones, but he also knew that he would not allow the discomfort from the injury to effect the mission in any way.

After pulling himself into his bucket seat, he remained attached to it until the Stirling stabilized. Looking down, Plith could see blinding fingers of brilliance stabbing upward into the clouds, arc lights sweeping the skies for the intruder airplane the Stirling, which had failed to send the Luftwaffe fighter command's recognition signal of the day. The fascinating lights of death from below blinked off, came alive, them fluttered away again as the Stirling roared deeper into heavy cloud. Turbulence returned with a vengeance, tossing the big ship about in the skies like a cork on stormy seas, it's joints and braces groaning with stress that tested the craft's construction strength. Then, as quickly as it had come, the thrashing was gone and the Stirling continued to drone through the enemy blackness. Plith once again moved from his seat and this time made it to the pilot's place of business. He spoke to Flying Officer Kershwim, a grizzled veteran whose age Plith guessed at about twenty-three, who was smiling as he felt Plith's presence.

"Bit bumpy for you, Major?"

"Just a bit."

"We had some company back there. A pair of Jerry night fighters stooging about. Gave the Fritzies the slip, though. Your boys all right?" the jaunty RAF pilot asked.

"Yes, they've been through worse. Tell me, how close are we to the DZ? My watch tells me we're overdue," Plith said, purposely making his demeanor equally nonchalant as the pilot's.

"Well, we've had head winds and deviations to deal with but Rusty, there," the pilot jerked his head toward the navigator's table, "will find it. He's getting a star fix right now. We're probably twenty out, now. I'll start a descent at this time."

Plith understood that they were about twenty kilometers from the DZ, though in what direction he did not know and, frankly, did not care.

"Very well, we'll be ready. See you tomorrow, same time," Plith said, and tapped Kershwim on the shoulder as he turned, his head stooped, to make his way back to the belly of the airplane and his men. He intended to give a thumb up sign to the navigator but that crewman's head was bent over his chart table with a small light illuminating his very demanding work. The commando could see a sextant lying nearby and decided to let the airman get on with his task without Plith's interruption.

At the far end of the aircraft Archie could feel tension mounting inside his guts, the violent turbulence of the airplane terrifying him. He felt increasingly nauseous and he knew that the cause was not motion sickness but cowardice. He began to feel the affects of creeping hysteria, a desperate need to escape with no place to hide. He began to quickly run scenarios through his mind that he might spring on Major Plith, that he was sick from a mysterious ailment, or that he had injured himself, or that he really could not speak German as he had promised his SOE handlers. He abandoned the last grasping notion as quickly as it arose simply because they, the SOE men, had heard him repeat the needed dialogue a number of times. They had rehearsed him.

"Right, lads," the major shouted above the roar of the bomber's engines, "check your chutes, no loose straps, now...We're ten to the DZ. Look at the man in front of you." As Plith spoke to his men he continued to make his way down the aircraft's belly toward Archie.

"Are you ready there, Sergeant Ferrel?" he said, a slight nod in the direction of Archie whose head was down, his eyes fixed woodenly on the deck of the plane.

"Ready, sir!" Sergeant Ferrel snapped back.

Major Plith turned his eyes toward corporals Clark and Grafton.

"Ready, Major, sir!" they said, almost in unison. Their instructions were clear: Archie would go out the bomb bay in the bottom of the plane at the jump signal, and he would go quickly, on cue.

Nor did Archie suffer under any illusion that the commandos would wait while he jumped of his own accord. It did not take a scholar to realize that the corporals behind him had orders to make him disappear out the belly of the aircraft should he hesitate at the opening. Well, maybe that would be the easiest, after all. If it was out of his hands then it was one less thing to be feared, his final failure of courage.

He had opened his makeup kit and liberally covered his head with the special hair dye provided him for the purpose of the mission. He made sure his mustache was covered with the liquid before removing the latex gloves and dropping them into the kit he would leave behind in the aircraft. From the corners of his eyes he could feel the stare of Ferrel, Clark and Grafton as they peered at him through the darkness of the bomber. He stifled a smile and instead glared back at them with all of the emotional energy he could muster, wondering if his own eyes held any of the magnetism of the Führer's. Their faces reflected back astonishment at the intensity in his eyes despite their earlier briefing from Major Plith that Archie knew his role well.

The commandos had checked and rechecked each other for equipment security when the bomber's crew chief moved into the belly of the aircraft with them. He knelt, unfastened the reinforced wooden hatch to let in a blast of cold, high-speed air. The man held up four fingers to Major Plith who nodded his understanding that they were four minutes to the DZ. The crew chief then pointed toward a pair of lights, one red, one green, mounted on a bulkhead near the flight deck. Major Plith again nodded his concurrence. The night now glowed red. When it changed to green, the commandos would jump.

"Smartly now, lads, jump positions!" Plith shouted, the noise of flight even louder with the opening of the jump hatch.

The commandos crowded close together, two lines of men leading to the hatch, last among them Archie with Ferrel directly in front and his two bodyguards touching him from the rear. There was no backing out now.

The commandos now heard the change of the great aircraft's propeller pitch as it slowed for the drop. They could feel a gentle buffet from the wings as flaps were extended to 20 percent, the nose raised slightly and a turn to the left begun by the pilot. Plith, unaware that he was holding his breath during these maneuvers, never took his eyes from the jump signal light. When it turned green he immediately dropped through the bay, followed rapidly by the two sticks of soldiers who had executed a similar drill countless times from towers, balloons, and airplanes. Archie, shoved stumbling along toward the abyss, strangely felt his fear leave him and replaced with the incredible combination of sensation and wonder. He was unaware that his feet were moving until the hole appeared under them. There was no need for Corporal Clark to push him, but he felt a hand on the top of his head which, he realized, helped guide him through the hole rather than "ring the bell" by hitting his head on the edge. In a single rush of cold air slapping him solidly against his neck, Archie was unaware that his static line had done its work until his chute opened above his head, his legs around his crotch pulled hard for a moment. Then there was no wind, no sensation of falling, only a relieved, even giddy feeling of swinging in the sky, much more pleasant than the summertime rides at Brighton.

Archie look about him and saw, reassuringly, his companions in what seemed almost like a gay adventure drifting down below puffs of white silk blossoming like cotton balls in the sky. He looked down but could not make out the ground. He had no idea how high they

He had, of course, failed to assume anything like the correct landing position he had been shown repeatedly in static drills of dropping off the back of a moving lorry or from an eight foot loading dock at the army camp. His left ankle cried out in the greatest pain but there were enough bruises on his upper body to cause one huge surge of pain in his brain. He was still lying flat on his back when he felt strong hands on his body, snatching at his release plate, then pulling him upward onto his feet.

"Come, there, Archie. Up you go, that's the fellow," a voice said into his ear, he recognized as belonging to Corporal Grafton. Grafton pulled Archie with one hand toward a nearby stand of forest while still carrying his own parachute, his submachine gun still strapped firmly across his chest. Corporal Clark, quickly gathering Archie's chute as well as his own, fell into quick-step behind.

Archie hobbled on his twisted ankle as best he could, and while the injury was painful it was not entirely debilitating. He thought the trauma would ease soon if he could just get his weight off the foot. He found himself leaning upon Grafton's strong shoulder, feeling just a bit guilty for adding to the commando's already heavy burden. They were well inside the tree line when Grafton halted, joining several other commandos responding to hand signals and quick flashes of red recognition torches carried by each man.

The entire detachment, it appeared to Archie, had gathered within a ten minute period of time, some men arriving at a fast trot having run all of the way across a drop area of more than a square mile. Others, like Archie, favored injured legs or held damaged arms near their bodies. There were plenty of bruises and cuts to go around, some quite severe. Archie heard that one man had been killed in the jump and that Plith immediately ordered the body buried and the grave obscured.

Plith, like the others, had removed his padded hat and buried it, along with his parachute, in a shallow hole dug among the trees in the forest. The commandos now wore knit stocking caps without insignia. Their submachine guns were now in hand and each man carried a rucksack containing rations, small amounts of first-aid material, a great deal of ammunition and explosives to blow railroad track. Key men carried communication gear, a main radio for contacting the airplane, Archie believed, and smaller radios for communication among the detachment. Every man carried a knife at his belt or strapped to a leg. The knife was large, it seemed to Archie, and combined steel knuckles at the haft for what was clearly for close-in fighting. The thought made him shudder in spite of his resolve to remain calm and collected. Already the extreme thrill of having survived, even enjoying, a parachute jump executed during war time was so fleeting he could hardly recall the sensations, and they were only minutes ago.

While outposts watched for intruders, Major Plith referred to a map spread on the ground before him. Sergeant Ferrel held a shrouded electric torch over the map and studied it with great interest.

"We're five kilometers from where we should be, as I see it. Here," he said, placing an index finger on the map. "There should be a power line there and there isn't one. Also a water tower over there," Plith said, pointing in a northerly direction. "Also not there. On the way down I saw a lake, so I know where we are. Here," he said, once again pointing with his finger on the map. "Do you agree, Ferrel?"

"I do, sir. We can pick up the track moving west," the sergeant said.

"Yes, but I don't want to get near that track yet. We'll move south first, about three kilometers to avoid the village. Pilz. Then we'll turn west by the river, marker twelve on your maps. We have to be here," Plith said, his finger moving to yet another forest location, "at C10:H2 well before dawn. We'll have to move along quickly. I want to be dug in and covered up before daylight. Questions?"

Plith looked up to ensure his non-commissioned officers were making appropriate marks on their maps. If he were wounded, killed or captured, the mission would then fall to the next man in line, Sergeant Ferrel, and if he were incapacitated it would befall the next in rank, and the next.

"Right, then, MacQueen and Shaw at the points. Quiet is the word, laddies. Use the knife where possible. All right, then..."

"Major Plith," Archie heard himself say, surprised at the sound of his own voice which seemed to be without quaver, almost sure of himself.

"Yes?"

"I'd like to remove this jump suit," Archie said, referring to the rather heavy, one-piece suit that covered almost his entire body. The night was still warm and he was sweltering with still another complete set of clothing underneath. He doubted that he could walk far without fainting.

Plith pursed his lips while considering for a moment. Then, with a twitch at the corners of his mouth, he said "Certainly, Archie. Let's bury the bloody thing right here."

As Archie peeled his way out of the bulky covering, he noted with amusement the faces of the commandos who had only known Archie as a reclusive "tech." Though his German uniform had been carefully altered before leaving England to appear to have been through a train wreck and a fire fight, there was no mistaking the beige uniform jacket and brazen black on white on red swastika on its left sleeve, the black uniform trousers with the wide red stripes. It was not the uniform of a German officer but, unmistakably, that of Adolf Hitler. There was an audible gasp as Archie stepped out of the jump suit and dropped it into a freshly dug hole in the soft earth among the tall trees.

"Ready, Major," Archie announced.

"So you are, Arch - er, Mein Führer. With your permission, we'll be off. Keep three meters and keep silent," the major reminded the men as he gave the signal to move out.

Following at forty meters from his point men, Plith's two squads of commandos followed, with every second man looking ahead and to his left while the man in front and the man behind looked ahead and to the right. Two trailing commandos had the job of walking forward while looking sharply with eyes behind their heads.

They moved through the dark of night over paths that had been worn by animals as well as humans, along the bank of a small river marked *Zcess* on their maps. The going was easier than he expected along a three kilometer stretch that lay east of Pilz. At the outskirts of the village, marked by a small but sturdy wooden bridge painted white, the commando file turned southeast, leaving the village on their right flank. Archie was suddenly pulled to the ground by the strong hand of Corporal Clark as the rest of the file, responding to a hand signal from the point men to Major Plith and then to the file, were down on their bellies, weapons poised to defend against an unknown threat.

Then they heard it again. It had moved. Still again the metallic sound clearly reached all ears of the prone British soldiers who held their positions until the word was passed down the line. A cow bell.

"Cor," the man behind Clark whispered, "I could ha' told 'em that. I milked the bastards long enough!"

The file was quickly on its feet again and began making a strong pace, now facilitated by traveling an unpaved but semi-hard surfaced farm road. As they were moving along a valley the road took an abrupt right turn toward the west, the direction of the village. Plith sent hand signals to the point men, MacQueen and Shaw, who led the way by abandoning the road and moved toward a range of hills that were twelve hundred feet in elevation according to the commando's field maps. Their planned route would not take them over the hills but about three hundred feet above the valley floor over a distance of two kilometers, leaving scattered farms on their right, to the north, and the railroad dead ahead, less than six hundred meters from their place of concealment in the woods.

The way out, theoretically, would be closer and simpler than the way they came in. They would meet the aircraft shortly after the shoot-out at a valley hardly fifteen hundred meters to the south, near the track.

They accomplished the march without incident, arriving in the wooded area at 0144 hours. Major Plith huddled briefly with his outposts, then placed lookouts at strategic points of their perimeters, while sappers, already practiced, moved out toward the small railroad trestle where they would place their charges. The rest of the Raven commando began digging holes and preparing camouflage inside the forest line in which they would spend the following day and part of the night waiting for the arrival of the Führer's train.

Archie was exempt from the work of digging and concealment. Not that he wanted special treatment, but he was not qualified to do either with expertise and, as well, he was considered too valuable to risk an injury or even, and it had to be taken into account, a heart attack. He had never been given a physical by the military such was the secrecy connected to the entire mission.

It was near 0400 hours when the sappers had returned from placing charges on the bridge, the shallow holes and vegetation had been covered, that everyone was well hidden inside. A distant light winked on inside a farm house and barn as its occupants prepared to meet the coming dawn. The nearest house, Archie guessed, was about eight hundred meters, a distance far enough from his location so that the possibility of an errant traveler discovering their hiding place was unlikely. That was what he kept telling himself until it became a prayer. Archie's hole was near Plith's. As tired as he was, as needy he was of sleep, his eyes would not stay closed as he willed them. Giving up, he whispered to the commando's leader.

"Are you awake, sir?"

"Yes. What is it, Archie?" Plith answered.

"Well, I was thinking about the SS. I know who they are, of course, but, well.... " Archie's voice trailed off.

"You mean can we beat them?" the major asked.

"Something like that, I suppose." Archie immediately disliked himself for casting doubt where it did not deserve to be and, by this time, much too late to do anything about.

Major Plith wanted to smile at Archie's fears. "Nasty bunch," he said, then lapsed back into silence. The source of his mirth was ironic: he was suffering from fear as well. There could be no illusion that the fighting would not be very bloody. Hitler's praetorian guard, the Schutzstaffel division, Leibstandarte SS Adolf Hitler, as it was formally known, was formed seven years earlier, in 1933, from young, fanatic

Nazi men. Commanded by Josef "Sepp" Dietrich, a former butcher, they were hand-picked for their blind allegiance to their Führer and their complete willingness to employ any form of violence to carry out his will. Their training was second to none in the world and the Leibstandarte division was the fiercest and best armed of all the Waffen-SS. Major Plith was told by a French infantry officer who did battle with a panzer Waffen-SS grenadier division, that they were fighters tougher than any of their counterparts in the regular Wehrmacht, with more esprit de corp, and that they had no heart. He hoped that he would never see them again in his life.

Major Plith shuddered at the thought of meeting these Nazi soldiers who were totally without fear on the field of battle if he did not have an edge. Well, we would see how well the bastards could do battle climbing out of a bloody train wreck, he thought.

"Beg pardon, Major Plith, is anything wrong?" Archie wanted to know.

"Nothing, Archie. Try to get some rest, now."

With the sun fully up in the region, the chill had gone and the weather was still warm. The commandos moved no more than was necessary, eschewing the risk of making any sound at all. Outposts were rotated every two hours and, while the men needed rest, few slept and those who could manage sleep did it with one eye open.

The commandos watched below them where the train tracks climbed a long upgrade until it reached the level track into the valley some two kilometers south, then began a 7percent downgrade. By the time the Führer train reached the trestle and its explosive charges, its speed would have reached something like one hundred kph. Major Plith had posted two men to the south who, upon spotting the target train, would confirm that it was the correct train by blinking an electric torch. The Raven commando would have at least four minutes to take their ambush positions. It was far more than enough time.

During the long day the commando detachment made careful records of each train that went through the valley. All traffic was under military control and priority, of course, but civilians could be seen sharing cars with soldiers, as well as trains dedicated to entire Wehrmacht units. There was one exceptionally long train of flat cars shipping battle tanks. They appeared to be the light Kps, loaded two to a flatcar, and Major Plith believed it was the entire 2nd Panzer

Division on the move. He would have given much to send radio messages to Military Intelligence but complete radio silence was vital.

The Third Para Commando's position was northeast of Landshut, about twenty kilometers from Straubing. The railroad lines out of Munich passed through Moosburg toward the Danube River in the east, or directly north to Regensburg and eventually Nuremberg. The Führer train would use the Straubing track, or so it was hoped. Major Plith was quite aware that military intelligence was always chancy at best and that sources deep inside Germany more often than not were no better than second or even third hand. As Major Plith watched still another troop train moving north, this time most of a division, he sent his prayers not to a divine being in Heaven but to SOE in London.

It was 1820 hours when Major Plith felt a tap on his shoulder. He had drifted off to sleep but awoke to Sergeant Ferrel's hand.

Ferrel, on his belly, silently pointed down the mountainside at the trestle. Plith put binoculars to his eyes and surveyed the track. At first he saw nothing out of the ordinary. Then he saw a movement. It appeared to be a man, but a closer inspection revealed that it was a boy, a teen, but not yet old enough to be serving in Hitler's army. Plith could make out that the boy had found the explosives strapped to the bridge. It was not just Sergeant Ferrel who was watching for a command from the para officer, but most of the other ranks as well. As Plith kept his glasses trained on the trestle, the boy left the site and began walking away, to the south, in the direction of the farm house where, presumably, he would report what he saw.

Plith turned toward MacQueen, the most distant outpost and closest to the boy's position, and gave a hand signal. Private MacQueen, anticipating the command, dropped his gear in place and, carrying nothing but his combat knife, leaped out of his hole and began racing for the boy.

MacQueen was fast as he ran flat-out, but the boy either heard or sensed the British commando's presence. He glanced over his shoulder and, seeing MacQueen advancing, immediately broke into a run. MacQueen had an angle on the boy but the German youth was also fleet of foot. It became obvious that it was a race the boy would not win, but the danger was in letting him get close enough to the house to set off an alarm.

Plith and his commandos watched as a group, desperately interested in their man catching the youth before it was too late. They clenched fists, silently mouthed encouragement for MacQueen who, if he lost the pursuit, their very lives would pay the wager.

Charging hard through wild grass that had grown waist high during the summer months, MacQueen changed directions several times as the boy twisted and turned, sometimes dodging behind a tree or bush, only to emerge again on the other side in a dead run.

Just when it seemed that the youth was going to achieve his goal, MacQueen caught up with him less than three hundred meters from the farm house.

As the Third Para Commando watched through squinted eyes, MacQueen tackled the boy, one hand going to his mouth to silence a scream, the other hand drawing the razor sharp combat knife along the throat. Through his binoculars, even from his distant point on the side of the mountain, Plith could see the wound open in the boy's neck, and the blood gush to the ground.

Plith continued to watch as MacQueen released his prey and, taking the time to cover the body with branches of vegetation then, staying low so as not to be seen from the farm, began moving back to the concealed location whence he came.

Third Para commando released a collectively held breath at the nearness of their own imminent discovery by the enemy. But Plith, as he sank back into his hole in the ground, shuddered at the ghoulishness of war that children were sacrificed so callously. He pitied MacQueen whom he knew to be a good man, scarcely older than the lad he had just killed. He would no doubt carry the emotional scar with him for life.

Without being ordered, MacQueen retraced the boy's steps to the mined trestle and, while Major Plith watched through his glasses, inspected the explosives connections. After several minutes MacQueen made his way back to his post and signaled to the main force that all was well. Plith checked his watch. Forty-two minutes until the Hitler train was due to arrive. Again the vagaries of Hitler's proposed schedule assaulted Plith's brain. The train might have passed through the valley the day before the commandos arrived. Or Hitler might have flown back to Berlin, leaving others to ride his train. Or he may have postponed his trip. Or changed destinations. Anything was possible.

Forty minutes came and went. At 2100 hours darkness was nearly complete and there was no moon to light their way. Wanting to maximize their advantage of surprise, Major Plith moved his men from their positions on the side of the mountain to an area much closer to the railroad tracks. They had hardly settled into the new positions when lights, seemingly from lanterns, appeared from the direction of the farm house. Turning his glasses in that direction, Plith counted three such illuminations, moving about the fields as though people were looking for something. Or someone. It was about time. Way past time, Plith thought, that a search party went looking for a young boy who did not return home. Plith hoped that because of the darkness of the night and the fact that the dead body was partially concealed, it would not be discovered until morning. If that was the case the commandos would be safely back in England. If they were not killed on the field of battle. And even if there was no battle, the Stirling would wait only until 0300 hours then, if they were not there, would fly back to England without them.

At 2156 a fast train crested the hill and, passing through the valley, roared over the trestle and out of sight. It was neither the SS security train nor Adolf Hitler's personal train. Thirty meters from Plith Sergeant Ferrel spoke in a near whisper to Corporals Grafton and Clark.

"Remember, if I don't get to the radio operator..."

"Yes, Sergeant," Clark said, interrupting. "I'll shoot him."

"Or Grafton gets him," Ferrel said, nodding his head. "It's got to be quick," he added.

They had planned the execution of the radio operator countless times. It was imperative that no signals leave the Führer's train until Archie was ready to send his directive to Berlin. They were, of course, counting on the personnel inside the communications car being dazed from the derailment. They could not allow a message to be sent to the security train that would precede Hitler's following train. If that message were to be sent, the commandos would be doomed.

The odds of the commandos wiping out the Waffen SS aboard a wrecked Führer train was better than even. But if the First SS detachment of security troops became alerted at the outset of the action, they would immediately return. The numbers against the commandos would then be overwhelming.

At 0015 there was still no train.

The men's muscles were cramped from twenty-five hours of no activity, their every move needing to be silent and close to the ground. The strain on their nerves was intense as each sound of an airplane, the rattle of a train, the lowing of a cow, plunged adrenaline coursing through the systems of the commandos. They ached for action, for the release of tension that had been steadily building since they stepped on board the first transport aircraft in Scotland nearly two days before.

At 0222 Plith was contemplating the bitter options before him. He could not allow his men to remain in their positions for another hour. As it was, they would barely make the rendezvous with the Stirling if they picked up now and double-timed all the way over the hill to the designated field LZ, never mind fighting a battle before leaving. Cursing at nothing and everything, Plith was about to send out his order to withdraw when a surge of excitement went down the ranks of the Third Para. Plith quickly looked at Sergeant Ferrel who now lay with his head on the track, listening.

Plith, crouching, moved to the track where he, too, placed an ear onto the rail. It was unmistakable. A train was coming. The commando officer moved away from the track to gain perspective and, looking south, he could hear before he saw a train clearing the rise of the mountain and beginning its downward entry into the valley. As the minutes passed the commandos could see a large locomotive come into view. The modern, fast, diesel driven locomotive was pulling only three cars. The first and third cars were nothing more or less than gun platforms for quad-mounted MG-34 machine guns.

Every commando was very familiar with the killing power of the MG34, a 7.92mm gun with a 900 pm rate of fire that could be used in either anti-aircraft or infantry roles. But they had never seen the guns mounted in quads or, for that matter, even in pairs. Configured in this array the firepower directed at ground troops challenged the imagination of the commandos. Each modified flatcar, fortified with hardened steel shields in front of each set of guns, supported two sets of weapons or a total of eight guns that could be brought to bear on a target.

The second car was a specially constructed armored troop transport with gun ports on each side. On the top of the car were shielded firing positions that troops from within could quickly occupy, able to defend against either a ground or air attack. Plith and others had estimated that the personnel car accommodated fifty troops and their weapons. As familiar as they were with this efficient war-making machine, the British soldiers swallowed with great relief when the Waffen-SS train passed their position and faded into the darkness beyond.

Major Plith and his men tensed now, knowing that the Führer train would be close behind. An icy calm seemed to settle over the men. There were small, nervous movements of hands touching cocking bolts, going to boot knives, magazine pouches or a grenade hanging by its handle on a strap. But these were nothing more than absent-minded tics, the actual checking of weapons and equipment done with care a hundred times before.

Plith watched Sergeant Ferrel who, with his ear once again to the track, slowly raised his hand, held it aloft for a long moment, then snapped it down. Ferrel, Plith, and the others close to the track, now moved away from the area which, in scant minutes, would be the site of a train wreck.

Archie could feel his hands shaking. It was worse than stage fright, a malady that had taken over his senses only once in his life, then never again. But the remembrance of those awful moments leading up to his first real performance was living hell. He could laugh about it now when, in retrospect, nothing more was at stake than his pride, a puffed ego. Now it was his very life. The shaking did not stop as the train approached. In fact it became worse. He was not a religious man but prayed that some miracle would occur to make it all go away, to allow him to regain control over the involuntary spasms that seemed to progressively affect his whole body.

Virtually hypnotized by the events that were unfolding before his eyes, Archie watched the sappers as two of the men took prone positions at the of electrical leads that ran out from the explosives under the train trestle. It was not left to a single electric generator to detonate the explosives, but the explosives experts employed two sets of leads, independent of each other, originated under the track and snaked half buried in the grass to generator boxes two hundred meters from the track.

Archie could see the sappers calmly attaching their live leads to terminals atop the generators, then he saw each man draw the plunger out of its resting position. Major Plith was lying next to the sappers. They would blow the track at his command even though they knew exactly when that command should be given, having rehearsed the action countless times. As the train approached Major Plith placed a whistle between his lips. No commando would move until the whistle had blown. Plith wanted an absolutely coordinated attack and if there were any last moment changes required when the train derailed, he wanted all of his men in place.

The entire Third Para Commando could see the Führer train as it began picking up speed on the downhill valley run. It was a large locomotive that stood twenty feet high and housed two diesel engines that generated eight hundred ship horsepower each. The entire loco-motive was painted a metallic black, shining like a Teutonic knight's ghostly armor, and on each side were large emblems of Nazi power, black Swastikas against a field of white and red. As the giant machine continued to accelerate along the valley Major Plith could feel the ground under him tremble, the sound of its sixteen wheels screaming against hardened steel tracks, the explosive noise coming through exhaust portals on its huge, deafening, diesels.

Major Plith could clearly see the other cars behind the engine and oil car. Counting the engine and oil car as a single unit, the second car was the galley. Car number three, a custom manufactured car with fire-ports on each side, contained Waffen-SS troops. Car number four was easily identified as the communications center with several antennae protruding through its roof. Cars five, six and seven were believed to be Hitler's personal bedroom and salon, the map room, and his staff accommodations. These three cars were to be attacked with equal ferocity and thoroughness since it was not possible to be one hundred percent sure in which coach the Führer would be found. Car number eight was identical with number three, an SS fighting machine.

Major Plith's plan, the one the commandos had practiced relentlessly until they executed to his satisfaction, called for fourteen commandos to await in ambush positions at either end of the train so that their dispositions would put them nearest the SS cars. However, with one man killed on the jump, thirteen men would attack car number three, the first SS car, with fourteen men attacking car number eight, the last car on the train and the second SS car. That would leave two commandos assaulting the communications car, two men hitting the staff car, and two the Hitler car, number six in the train. That left the map car, number five in the train, unassigned; but it was anticipated that the map car would not be in use at this time of the evening. And even if it were, commandos could finish it up after hitting the com car and Hitler's private car.

Suddenly, before Archie's eyes, the trestle disappeared in a thunderous roar. Wooden components of the bridge simply evaporated in the air while pieces of steel track and reinforcing straps were blown into pieces, thrown upward into the sky. Archie followed them as best he could until they reached their apogee, then slowly began to rain down. Just in time he remembered his careful briefing which included keeping his head down until the explosion was well settled.

Archie was unaware of the sound that had preceded the detonation, but within a few heart beats the speeding train reached the spot where the trestle had been. There was no time for the engineer to apply brakes, to blow a horn, or to issue any kind of warning. It simply pitched forward into the stream bed below, while the trailing oil car telescoped into the engine, immediately killing the three man crew.

The galley car jack-knifed into the air and rolled down the elevated rail bed onto its side. Car number three, with its SS troops inside, careened completely off the tracks and, like the galley car, fell nine feet and rolled onto its side at the bottom of the shallow creek bed. Like an accordion squeezed by giant hands, the other cars of the trains crashed into the one in front, then skewed off the rails and, with the exception of cars number five and seven, rolled onto their sides.

The shriek of steel against steel, roaring aftershocks of the explosion from the massive collision assailed Archie's hearing system, sending concussive waves through his skull. His nearly overwhelming urge was to leap to his feet and run, but in the next moment he dug his fingernails into the soft earth and willed himself to disappear into it.

Then, after what seemed an incredibly long period of utter silence save the occasional snap of stressed metal, ruptured air hoses or groaning remnants of timber, Archie heard a high pitched whistle, loud, shrill and sustained. He opened his eyes that had been tightly shut, in time to see the men of the Third Para Commando rushing toward their assigned targets. He became aware of strong hands under each arm, pulling him to his feet.

"Up you go, Archie. That's the man. Stay on our arses, now."

Corporals Clark and Grafton were propelling him forward, and while his instincts were urging him back, his heart was compelling his feet to move. He knew his role and he found that he was anxious to play it. He could hear the sounds of automatic gunfire and felt the concussions of grenades going off all round him. Detonations erupted from explosive charges, he assumed they were hand grenades or satchel charges of some kind, tossed into the windows and doors of the cars containing German troops. The distinctive roil of Thompson submachine guns were comforting to Archie's alert ears and for a time, as he moved forward, he thought all would be well, easier than he once feared.

But then came responding fire of Nazi automatic gun fire, clearly nothing like anything that the British commando employed, and Archie was aware of the damage that real bullets were doing. He could hear the grunts of men being struck, seeing them fall, some to remain motionless on the ground, blood pulsing from their wounds, others getting up onto their feet to continue their charge despite wounds. As Archie was guided toward the rear of the train near the connection of the communications car and Hitler's personal coach.

Releasing Archie's arms to leave their own hands free, the commando corporals kicked open the door of the communications car and dove inside. Archie could see flashes of gunfire and heard the reports of the submachine guns that he knew were British. But before he could follow Grafton and Clark inside, he was arrested by a sight that he caught first in the corner of his eye. He saw a commando fire his submachine gun point blank into the body of a black-clad Waffen-SS man and, literally cut in two from the blast, the fanatic Nazi managed to plunge a knife into the side of the commando. The commando staggered, reached the hilt of the German knife and pulled it out of his rib cage, then, as he attempted to extricate himself from the death grip of the Nazi, stuck the same knife through the SS man's neck. Taking a deep breath, the commando threw himself back inside the ruptured door of the overturned car, followed closely by three more commandos. There came a cacophony of gunfire, poured out of metal barrels like a hundred firecrackers exploding simultaneously.

"Archie! Damn your eyes, get in here!"

It was the sound of Clark's commanding voice. His head snapping back toward his assigned station, Archie entered the communications car. Inside were three dead men and a wounded commando. Archie saw with alarm that the wounded man was Corporal Grafton. Even with blood streaming from his mid-section through holes in his battle dress and fingers clutching his guts, Grafton motioned toward a terrified German soldier standing in the middle of the smoke-filled car with his hands held high over his head.

"Do not move or you will die," Grafton said to Archie. "Tell the bastard that in German."

Archie understood exactly what the commando needed to convey to the frightened soldier and, as he turned toward the enemy, the young man, a bloody gash oozing blood over one eye and onto his cheek and neck, his uniform singed and torn by the impact of the train, managed to click his heels and pull himself to attention.

"*Soldier,*" Archie began.

"*Jawohl, mein Führer,*" the soldier said through pained lips.

Archie and Grafton exchanged puzzled looks, but it was Corporal Clark that was quickest in understanding the event.

"He thinks you're Adie," he said to Archie.

It seemed so obvious after the commando said it. Archie turned back to the quivering soldier.

"*I have an urgent communication. Contact OKW. Immediately!*" Archie ordered.

For a long moment the radio technician stood frozen by indecision, the apparition of Adolf Hitler, the nation's leader, giving an order in the company of two English fighting men. Was it possible or was he hallucinating?

"*At once!*" Archie barked in German, allowing his voice to rise in crescendo. The force of his tone bolted the soldier into action. Without questioning the order, the German radio man moved to a large short-wave radio and took a seat before it. "*OKW,*" he mumbled nervously to himself as he began to rapidly turn pages of his worn code book.

"*I want a voice line,*" Archie said, his voice deep, husky, singular to the delivery of the German leader.

"*Ja, mein....*" the young German throat constricting, collapsing under the awesome presence of Germany's modern Messiah. He had only seen Hitler on those rare occasions when he was boarding or debarking the train. He had never spoken directly with the great man.

When the wireless operator had secured an open line on a radio telephone for his Führer, he stepped back and stood at attention.

The sound of gunfire from other cars, diminished substantially from the moment of the initial attack, punctuated the atmosphere inside the communications car as Archie perched himself upon a seat in front of the console.

Reacting to a scratchy distant voice in Berlin, Archie pressed the transmit button and spoke into the mouthpiece. *"This is Adolf Hitler speaking. Do you recognize my voice?"*

"Jawohl, mein Führer," the voice said.

"Who is this speaking?" Archie said.

"I am Colonel Rudolph Eck, sir, duty officer, Oberkommando das Wehrmacht," the voice unequivocally said.

"Very well," Archie rasped. *"I have been attacked. British raiders have destroyed my train but my Leibstandarte SS has prevailed. Do you understand?"*

"Attacked!? Sir, I shall..." Eck began.

"Silence!" Archie shouted into the radio, keying the duty officer off the air, then listening for his response to Archie's order.

"Yes, sir. Of course," the colonel said, his words clipped.

"I now have the situation in hand. More important, I have an order for General Keitel. Keitel is to affect an immediate stand-down from Operation Sealion. Did you hear me quite clearly, Colonel?" Archie said into the microphone. He was surprised, even at himself, how steady his voice sounded.

"Yes, sir. General Keitel is to cancel Operation Sealion," Colonel Eck repeated.

"He will notify Manstein and General Rundstet. My order is to be carried out immediately and unconditionally. I will return to Berlin very soon. That is all."

"Jawohl, mein Führer," Colonel Eck responded before Archie clicked off the radio-telephone for the last time. Corporal Clark put the transmitter out of business permanently with a burst from his submachine gun.

"Let's get the bloody hell out of this place," he said. "Archie, give us a hand here with Richard."

Corporal Grafton was weak from loss of blood, his body sagging up against the bulkhead of the car.

"You go first," Archie said in perfectly clear English to Corporal Clark. "I'll bring him."

"No, you first," Corporal Clark said, pushing Archie, who now supported the wounded Corporal Grafton, out the door. Archie had hardly stepped out of the communications car when he heard a burst of automatic gunfire behind him. He knew the German radio operator was dead.

Major Plith and Sergeant Ferrel hit the number seven car containing either Adolf Hitler or his staff while a fierce battle from within the last car, the Waffen-SS and the commandos, continued to rage. The window in the door of the seventh car had been shattered as a result of the wreck itself, as most of the windows had been, and Plith and Ferrel each tossed a grenade into the car before kicking it open wide and stepping inside. The resulting explosion left the men inside the car either dead or dazed and the commandos quickly finished off those still alive with point-blank submachine gun fire. Within the car were customized sleeping compartments, private ones for the highest ranking officers and doubled beds for officers of field grade and below. While the two British commandos worked their way through the car, shooting off locks and kicking open doors that were not locked, they gunned down their targets with unerring lethality, the result of assiduous practice and well developed technique. There was some return fire but it was attempted with pistols and usually from a dazed defender.

One pistol shot, however, delivered by a German colonel, caught Sergeant Ferrel on the hip and completely severed a web belt supporting a satchel which, a short time before, had contained a dozen hand grenades. Ferrel was amazingly unhurt by the parabellum round. The colonel, whom Plith recognized from photographs as Kurt Offenrude, died quite bravely.

Plith's rapid mental recapitulation listed among those killed in the staff car a colonel-general, whom he did not recognize but who was expected to be on board according to the intelligence report, three full colonels, including Offenrude, and two aides de camp, one a Gestapo major, none of whom Plith was familiar. Plith was disappointed that their luck did not put him into Hitler's coach, but it was impossible to tell which was which until the action began. Still, he and Ferrel finished their job in scant minutes and, hardly pausing for breath, leaped beyond the map car and went for the number five coach. That, by order of elimination, had to be Hitler's.

Firing had stopped inside the railroad car, the once lush interior now a shambles of fractured and burnt materials, windows exploded out, a disintegrated sleeping chamber with nothing but charred stuffings of the bedding remaining. Bodies littered the floor. All were dead of multiple gunshot wounds or concussion, made evident by rivulets of blood running from noses, ears and mouths. Uniform trousers were often dark with blood around the anus caused by the blast of grenades or concussive explosives. Blood spatters smeared the paneled walls as well as soaked into wool carpet floor coverings.

One figure was caught while responding to the call of nature at the time of his death, gunned down wearing nothing more than dress tunic with trousers down around black boots. Two Waffen-SS troops lay lifeless a few feet inside one of the passageways into the Führer car. They were fully dressed, wearing the black helmet with distinctive SS runes on a field of white.

They had not died easily. Plith saw at a glance that the two personal guards of Adolf Hitler were well over six feet in height, broad in the shoulders. Over their black uniforms were battle harnesses that contained several pouches that held magazines for their automatic weapons, the MP38, often incorrectly referred to as Schmeissers but was in fact designed by Vollmer. Major Plith was not surprised to see that the 9mm submachine guns utilized by Hitler's personal SS were customized with a folding stock for close-in work and probably employed hand-crafted magazines that would have been virtually jam proof.

The SS men had dozens of holes in their bodies and heads, testimony to the firepower it took to bring down the Nazi gunmen.

And at a cost. Three dead British commandos, one lying prostrate over a dead Waffen-SS man, and one commando seriously wounded, all of whom had slugged it out toe to toe with the SS troops, lay within feet of the open door.

Plith and Ferrel heard two pistol shots which they recognized as not a British weapon, coming from the remaining compartment of the car, followed by two extended bursts of submachine gun fire, clearly the reports of the Thompson weapon carried by the commandos.

Guns raised, ready to fire, Plith and Ferrel charged into the compartment. It was charred and splintered like all the rest of those on the train, but this one was different. This was the dictator's personal study and Hitler lay on the floor of the car, fully dressed save his black boots, field green uniform tunic secured by only a single button in the wrong buttonhole. It was as though the German leader had been interrupted during a time of repose and had hastily risen to greet visitors. Plith could see that his upper body had been turned into a red mass from close range firing of the .45 cal Thompson. Hitler's lifeless body lay on its back, and near his outstretched arm was a 9mm Walther PPK, the favorite sidearm of the officer corps.

There was a second man in the confined space: Corporal Marion Clark.

"The bastard shot me," Clark said as he managed only with difficulty to eject a spent magazine from his submachine gun. Major Plith could see blood oozing from Clark's rib cage. Clark's knees sagged for a moment as the commando officer rushed to the corporal's side.

Plith could see that the wound was bad but perhaps not fatal if he could stem the bleeding until the aircraft arrived.

"Take it easy, Corporal," Plith said, gently lowering the commando to the floor of the car and groped in his own kit for a battlefield pressure dressing. "Ferrel," Plith said to his sergeant.

"Sir?"

"Finish the job," the major said, jerking his head toward the body of Germany's late leader. Plith unfastened his own grenade bag and tossed it toward the sergeant.

Every man in the raiding part knew the assignment of all the others. There was no hesitation as Ferrel opened the major's bag and withdrew two explosive devices, both thermal. The first would burn the body to which it was attached, the second would explode one minute later with enough power to leave literally no trace of the charred remains. The plan was to leave no piece of Hitler's mortal remains so that confusion would be maximized and Archie's message accepted at face value.

Archie arrived on the scene while Ferrel was putting the finishing touches to the body and connecting the fuse system. The sight of

Adolf Hitler caused Archie to halt in his tracks. In a single glance at the fallen dictator, however macabre, Archie felt a connection, strong and emotional, the likes of which he had never felt before. If pressed at the moment to have described it, he might not have got the words out in any form of sense, but there was no question in the soul of his being that he had met the dictator in a crossroads of karma, his and the Führer's. Unaware that the sounds of battle around him had ceased and that the quiet of the night was interrupted only by crackling fires set off by burning fuel and incendiary devices used in combat, Archie knelt unhesitatingly by the body of Hitler.

The once demonic eyes of Adolf Hitler were looking fixed sightlessly back into Archie's. But the actor was not repelled, not fearful in any way. Instead, he leaned closer, looked deeper, wanting to remember every cell of the man's face, the strong chin, the ears that had listened to the screaming devotion of a million German citizens held in his hypnotic embrace. It was like looking into a mirror.

And Archie wanted to know how it was possible.

The British actor, without a conscious effort, took up the Walther automatic pistol from the floor, its grip and slide still wet with Hitler's blood, and held it in his own hands. For a very long moment he sat in awe.

"All right," came Plith's commanding voice, "everybody out. We're torching the place."

Plith was helping Sergeant Ferrel with Corporal Clark, weak with loss of blood but still able to help his own cause.

"Hear me, Archie? Time to go. Get out of there," Plith ordered, his voice escalating with authority.

Reluctantly, Archie followed the commando out of the Führer's coach and into the night air filled with the acrid smell of cordite, away from the burning train.

Plith blew his whistle once more. There was no response. Despite the shrill signal to reform, there was no answer from a living commando. After waiting several moments, surveying the scene from one hundred meters and seeing nothing, Plith heard a faint voice. Racing to the site of the third car, the last SS car, Plith located the source of the sound. It was Private Thomas R. MacQueen, a hole in his leg and a wound that seemed to be a knife slash in his gut.

"How bad is it, man?" Plith asked the wounded man as he quickly placed a tourniquet above the commando's bleeding leg.

"'Tis neither deep as a well nor wide as a church door, but twill do,'" the grinning soldier quoted Shakespeare. "You help me out of here, Major, and damned if I won't set you for a pint when we get back."

"That's a wager I'll not let you off from, boyo," Plith said, laughing at the Scotsman's cheek. Plith helped MacQueen to his feet and the commando, using his Thompson as a crutch, limped along until he joined the others.

"Right," Major Plith said to his men, looking closely at his watch, "we've got forty minutes to reach the rendezvous with the Stirling. If we don't run into trouble, we'll make it."

"We will make it, Major," Sergeant Ferrel said as he began to look for other members of the elite commando team as they climbed out of the wreckage of the train, forming up in front of Ferrel. Plith counted only seven men, not including Archie, and three of his remaining fighters were wounded, corporals Grafton and Clark, and Private MacQueen. The shock of such great loss was momentarily staggering and Plith fought off a wave of grief for the brave young men who had died. He shook his head to clear his thoughts. He would have to act decisively if any of the others were to be saved. "Let's be off, then. Check your gear. Archie, move along, man," Major Plith said, urging the actor into step with the commandoes.

In thirty minutes of quick-march Plith had led his reduced command three kilometers from the ambush site to a meadow where the Stirling bomber would pick them up. Corporal Clark could not walk but was carried, more dead than alive, by others who rotated the burden. Dawn was breaking behind broken skies in the east as Plith and Sergeant Ferrel hurried to set out marking flares so the Stirling crew could land.

They were still in the process of completing this task when Plith heard the low whistle from MacQueen who had remained on the nearby hill as lookout. Plith could easily read MacQueen's hand signals: enemy approaching. Plith turned to Sergeant Ferrel but the sergeant had as well read MacQueen's signal and was already running toward their defensive position on the knoll. Above them, the faint drone of a multi-engine aircraft could be heard as its crew searched for its rendezvous point.

Falling onto his stomach atop the knoll Major Plith looked toward the road that led from Pilz. Plith did not need binoculars to see German trucks carrying troops in at least two-company strength, along with what appeared to be an automatic weapons platoon. His heart sank. An effective defense was out of the question. If he hesitated for too long the Germans would trap the Stirling and its crew on the ground. He made an instant decision.

"Sergeant, we just ran out of time," he said. "You and MacQueen douse the flares. No point in throwing away a perfectly good air machine."

The flares could be easily extinguished by mashing their burning ends into the ground. Without them the aircraft would assume that the worst and would return to England without touching down.

It was quite clear to Archie what was happening. They would die here. Even he, an untrained civilian, could see the inevitable. Strangely, he felt no fear. In the place of fear there was something else. For a moment he groped about in the recesses of his mind to find the proper name for what it was that he now felt. Satisfaction? Yes, certainly. He had been, if only for a few moments, on a world stage. He had delivered his lines in his role of the most important leader on Earth. And he was obeyed. After years of indifference to his acting by yawning audiences, skeptical producers and rude directors, whole nations now waited with bated breath for his next appearance. His next utterance.

There was something else, too. He was alive. His heart was pounding, adrenaline surging through his body, flowing hot to his brain. He felt, for the first time in his life, incredibly strong. He was capable of anything.

"Never mind that order, sergeant," Archie snapped at Sergeant Ferrel. The timber of the actor's voice froze the British commando in mid-stride. Archie's tone had been clear, authoritative, as though he had been giving orders all of his life. Archie stood to his feet, slapping dust from his disheveled uniform. He paused, looking down at the still prone Major Plith. "Stay under cover until you see the Germans turn away. Let the flares burn. The pick-up plane will need them."

Archie turned his back to Major Plith and his remaining com-

126

mandoes and began walking steadily down the hill directly toward the advancing German column.

"Archie!" Plith called out hoarsely. "Get back here! Do you hear, man? That's an order. Halt, damn your eyes, or I'll shoot!"

Major Plith raised his .48 caliber Wembley revolver and aimed it between Archie's shoulders. As his finger took up the slack in the trigger as he had been so carefully trained to do, Plith felt his hand begin to shake. He was aware that his men were watching him intently. They knew very well that their officer had been ordered to kill the actor rather than let him fall alive into enemy hands. They also knew that if Major Plith pulled the trigger the shot would instantly give their position away to the Germans. Plith might kill Archie but he would have killed them, as well.

Plith watched silently as Archie walked stolidly ahead, not giving so much as a glance over his shoulder on his way to meet the field-grey uniforms below.

Major Plith gently thumbed down the Wembley's hammer before holstering the gun. Using silent hand signals Plith directed what was left of his commandoes in a line of retreat toward the meadow. The sound of the Stirling was growing louder to their ears.

CHAPTER

9

A t the house in Belgravia, an armed dispatch rider arrived from the communications center at Whitehall on his first of a dozen deliveries for the day of August 4, 1940. It was 0427 hours when the courier, a sergeant in the Royal Marines, delivered a sealed envelope marked MOST URGENT - SEMLEY PLACE into the hands of MacLean Elliot. Elliot scribbled his name on a signals receipt pad proffered by the courier, dismissing the Marine with a brief nod of the head. The house was in the process of having its basement converted into its own communications center but, for the next week at least, they would have to rely upon Whitehall couriers. Elliot opened the envelope with eager anticipation even before he entered the map room where, only days before, Archie Smythes had given the audition of his life.

Elliot was in shirt sleeves, the unlit stub of cigar crunched between his tobacco stained teeth. He wore corduroy house slippers over one blue sock, the other black. His hair was tousled, the result of an abbreviated nap from which he awoke as the messenger arrived.

"Is that it?" Edward Wiles asked, emerging from a bathroom cleanly shaved. The lines under his eyes had deepened from lack of sleep in the past fortnight. And he had lost six pounds of weight from an already spare frame in favor of coffee and cigarettes over solid foods.

He wiped his face with a hand towel and moved nearer Elliot, bracing himself for the bad news he was certain had come.

"Yes," Elliot said, slowly lowering himself to a leather covered chair.

"Well?" Wiles urged.

"There must be a mistake," Elliot said, reading the shortly worded document yet again.

"Here," Wiles said, taking the signal from his colleague's fingers, "let me." His brows knit as he said "Raven accomplished. Archie stayed."

"What do you make of it?" Elliot said.

"Stayed," Wiles said, rolling the phrase around in his head. "Not killed. Not captured. Not wounded. Stayed."

"My god," Elliot said. "They got the blighter. What? He says, 'Raven accomplished.' There can't be any mistake there, can there? They killed Adolf."

"Yes," Wiles said, still staring at the paper in his hand. "So it would seem."

"Well, I daresay you don't sound as though you quite believe it, Edward," Elliot said.

"I believe it. That they attacked the train and killed Hitler? Of course I believe it. Why would I not? It's the rest of it I don't understand. Archie stayed. Would you know what Major Plith means by that?"

"Wounded, I should say. They probably couldn't get him out. We expected high casualties, it was likely not possible that all the wounded could be carried back to the DZ. Major Plith would have finished him off, poor chap. But that's war, eh?" Elliot pulled at a suspender strap that wanted to slip from his shoulder.

"Hm," Wiles said, managing to remain skeptical with only a grunt.

Sir William Schuyler arrived. Unlike his two senior SOE colleagues he could not sleep on sofas or in chairs. He had taken an apartment nearby for a period he thought would likely last the duration of the war, in which he could get proper rest and escape ringing telephones when they threatened to overwhelm his senses. Schuyler had hardly broken pace as he scooped up a cup of tea and garnered a scone. It was prepared in the kitchen and served round the clock in the house's dining room.

"The first signal has arrived, I take it," he said to neither colleague in particular.

"Yes," Elliot said, "how did you know?"

"Because you both look like you'd lost the rubber. Your man was no good, now, was he? Eh? I thought not. Any word on how close they came?" Schuyler, ever the pessimist, exuded what struck the others as near satisfaction at the confirmation of his direst predictions.

"As a matter of fact, Sir William, the raid seems to have succeeded," Wiles said, dropping the deciphered message into Schuyler's lap.

Schuyler read the note in a glance and, like his associates, immediately frowned. "What's this? What does it mean?"

"We were just discussing that. Any light you might shed would be more than a little appreciated," Wiles responded.

"By Jove, they seemed to have got the little corporal, what? Good for them. Any word from Plith on casualties? They must be back by now," Sir Schuyler said, his stork-like legs crossing as he sat in his favorite chair and pushing a nearby button to summon an aide.

"Sir?" a uniformed junior officer said upon entering the house's innermost sanctum.

"Has SDF operations reported the Raven flight in?" Elliot asked the lieutenant.

"Not yet, sir." The officer glanced at his wrist watch. It was just beginning to get light outside, a few minutes after 0500 hours. "We have no idea what time they would have left Germany and they would only break radio silence in an emergency, Colonel." The junior officer used MacLean Elliot's former service rank.

"Badger them, if need be. Use a land line to call our Ramsgate people. We want to know immediately anything they might have heard," Elliot said, waving away the junior officer.

"Well," Elliot said, consulting an ornate timepiece on a nearby table, "I suppose we had better inform the PM."

"Inform him about what?" Wiles said. "We don't have the whole picture yet, do we? I think we had better wait."

"We bloody well will," Schuyler said, brushing crumbs from his lapels. "He's so deeply into the romance of clandestine warfare that someone in this lash-up will have to stay sober enough to rein the man."

Wiles knew that there was a certain amount of truth in Schuyler's assessment of Mr. Churchill but he, Wiles, thought that Schuyler had it backward. It was the Prime Minister's very gallant and innovative vision of how the war should be fought that had made SOE possible on such short notice. And the PM had literally leaped out of his afternoon nap bed at the first suggestion that Hitler's train might be attacked by commandos. The very idea of killing the house painter on the fly set fire to the war leader's eyes, setting him to pace furiously, dressing robe billowing, behind his desk at Number Ten Downing. If SOE had done nothing further in the war than attack Hitler's personal train, even had the dictator escaped with his life, the SOE would have fulfilled its promise in his eyes. No, approaching Churchill with as much information that they now had on the strike would not daunt Edward Wiles.

"I suggest to you that waiting very much longer will not please the PM when you eventually see fit to give it to him. He is as anxious as we to know every event, every signal, as soon as it arrives. But of course, that's entirely your decision, Sir William." Wiles, by using Schuyler's peerage title, had placed all of the ensuing responsibility for communicating with Number Ten Downing on him, the senior member of SOE.

"Thank you for that keen political analysis, Edward. If you were on the other side I'm sure England's chances of winning this war would not be good. Still, I agree that we should wait a bit longer before making the trip," Schuyler said, meaning that electronic communications was out of the question. They would have to travel to Downing Street to deliver their assessment in person, whatever it turned out to be.

A steward knocked at the door, asking if any of the gentlemen cared to see a breakfast menu. Wiles and Elliot both wanted to eat but their stomachs rebelled at the notion. "Just coffee for me," Wiles said while reaching for the red telephone direct line telephone at his elbow, the one that would connect him with Whitehall signal center. Raven was not their only mission but its potential impact on the war, if their fragmented report was accurate, dwarfed all other missions. He asked one of the WAAF operators what signals, if any, had arrived for the Executive. She replied that another courier was en route to the house even as they spoke. He thanked the girl who sat at her radio for fourteen hours per day before hanging up the telephone.

Wiles shook his head at Elliot's questioning arched eyebrow, and awaited the arrival of Wiles' coffee and Elliot's tea. Schuyler opened a leather document case and, withdrawing from it a thick file, began studying the logistical requests for radios, weapons and additional personnel to support teams recently dropped into northern France.

Less than fifteen minutes passed which, to Wiles, seemed like hours, when the third dispatch of the still very new day arrived, this too marked MOST URGENT, SEMLEY PLACE. While any number of cover sheets arriving at Semley Place were thus marked, what was different from this signal was accompanied not only by its courier but by the WAAF radio operator who received the message.

She was young, Wiley could see, probably in her very early twenties. Her hair was a lusterless brown and she wore glasses that made her hazel eyes seem larger than they were. She might have had a shapely figure, but it was only speculation because her blue uniform of the Women's Auxiliary Air Force hung from her shoulders and hips in rather straight lines. Wiley, nevertheless, thought her attractive but reminded himself that everyone that age is appealing. Her name, he knew from talking with her countless times by telephone, was Kendel Grigg. He invited her to sit.

"Have you spoken to anyone else about this signal, Miss Grigg?" he asked. Radio operators at Whitehall were chosen by SOE were trained to identify the keystroke of team members who were dropped into enemy occupied territory. Their transmission idiosyncrasies were immediately identifiable by the operators in London so that if an impostor's hand were sending signals from Europe, it would be known. The SOE operators, therefore, were carefully chosen and jealously coveted for their expertise in reading between the lines of messages transmitted from Nazi occupied countries.

"No, sir," she said, perching on the edge of a sofa, calm, but very much aware that she was being scrutinized by important men in British Intelligence.

Elliot was conscious that his fingers were trembling as he opened the heavy enveloped sealed with equally heavy tape. He extracted the grainy message paper from the envelope and read it quickly twice. It was longer than the first Raven signal, but frustratingly lacking in the detailed information that Elliot and his coconspirators badly needed. He passed the message to Wiles who also read the material more than once, then passed it on to Schuyler.

Wiles turned to Kendel. "This came in the clear?" he said.

"Yes, sir. The aircraft was under attack, as you can tell. We assume that there was no time to code the message," the WAAF said, lifting her eyes to meet Wiles's.

"But they had one-time pads aboard," Wiles pressed.

"Indeed, sir, but they take time, too, don't they?"

Wiles glanced at Elliot who nodded his head. Even though the tear away pads, each page useless until matched at the receiver's end of the transmission, still had to be chosen letter by letter. It was not a slow system as encryption goes, but not fast, either, especially if one's airplane is on fire.

"'Five and crew going down,' the radio man said. What do you suppose that he meant? I mean, he didn't say bailing out," Wiles continued to address the WAAF.

"No. We assumed the pilot planned to crash land," Kendel said.

"You assume," Elliot said, stuffing his hands into his trouser pockets as he pursed his lips doubtfully.

"Yes, sir. I assumed," Kendel admitted but without including an apology.

"Of course you do," Wiles said in her defense. "That's why you are here. You know these men and their habits far more keenly than we." Wiles turned to Elliot. "They may not have had enough parachutes on the way home."

Elliot hunched his shoulders, pulling his head further down to examine his unpolished shoes in detail.

"How do we know that there were not, say, ten commandos, five of whom jumped and five stayed aboard the Stirling?" Sir William's scratchy voice interjected.

"That's possible, of course, sir, but I doubt the radio operator would have put it that way. I would think five commandos, plus the crew of the bomber," Kendel said without hesitation.

"Well, bloody hell, I can read that, can't I? Why didn't he say five commandos plus the crew? Five *what*? Monkeys? Pineapples?" Sir William rudely snapped.

Wiles was prepared to respond but Kendel was not intimidated by the intemperate old man.

"Since commandos were the only other personnel scheduled aboard the aircraft, both going and returning, sir, I assume that the radio operator was referring to commandos." Kendel clamped her lips together tightly.

"There you go again. Assuming. So you assume, eh? Well, there was a civilian along on the mission, now wasn't there? Eh? And what I want to know is..."

"I think you've told us everything you could, Miss Grigg," Wiles said, pointedly interrupting the senior SOE officer. Their radio operators were absolutely dependable security risks but there was still no point in revealing more of the Raven mission than was absolutely necessary, even to their own staff. Especially in the strange odyssey of Archie Smythes.

"Yes," Elliot quickly put in, "I agree. Don't you, Sir William?"

William Schuyler snorted his displeasure but asked nothing further of the harried WAAF.

"You may go back to your duties, Miss Grigg," Wiles said, then added: "I say, when was it last you slept?"

"I don't rightly recall, sir. But I am a bit tired," the young lady admitted.

"I'm sure of that. I want you to go directly to your barracks..."

"I live with my mother off station," she said to Wiles.

"Ah, yes. Well, then, go home and sleep until you are called. I'll notify your section chief."

For several minutes silence prevailed within the "game room" as the map room was often called by SOE insiders. Wiles poured cold coffee from a porcelain pot and, lifting it to his lips, quickly replaced the cup into the saucer. He did not want to interrupt the concentration in the room by ordering fresh. Instead he took a seat in a chair opposite the end of the leather covered couch.

Elliot crossed the room and, selecting a map from many contained in rollers suspended from the ceiling and pulled it down. It was a map of Germany. Donning reading glasses, Eliot examined it for the uncounted number of times since Operation Raven presented itself two weeks prior, this time leaning closely so that he could see the smaller towns and hamlets near the action area.

"Damn," he said in frustration. "Where do you suppose the man could have got?"

"Who? Archie? Where is not the issue, is it?" Sir William said, his mischievous smile baring crooked teeth. "We need to know if he is insane, eh? Well, don't we? And we need to know what the fool's intention is."

"I think you're correct, William. He'll be dead soon, in any case. We should be elated that the monster from Austria is gone from the face of the Earth. Blast it," Elliot said, then looked again at the time. "We simply have to inform the PM. Which of us shall go?"

"With all respect, MacLean, let's pause just for a moment more." Wiles stretched his legs and arms, holding his interlaced fingers high over his head as he rolled his eyes at the vaulted ceiling of the room.

"Pause for what?" Elliot said, turning toward his colleague. "We have all of the intelligence we are likely to get in the next several hours. And we can't put off informing Churchill that long about what we know."

"Yes, but he's going to ask us for our conclusions. Now, I don't know about you, but I haven't yet reached one. Further, I think we should project more than one ending scenario."

"For the outcome of the war? That isn't our domain, now is it?" Elliot pressed, turning once again toward the map of Germany.

"No, of course you are right. But to imagine that the German nation would suddenly throw up its collective hands and surrender because its Führer is dead, I suggest to you is dangerous wishing. There are any number of Nazis would could continue the conduct of the war quite ably, I should say," Wiles said, his eyes still focused on a place in the distance.

"Damned if that isn't so," Sir William snorted. "There is no telling what kind of damage we've done to the Huns but their ranks are still teeming with rabid dogs. And they'll fight. That's what they're bred to do."

While Wiles could not agree with Schuyler's metaphor, he appreciated its thrust. The ranks of Nazi Germany could easily produce strong military leadership, perhaps even stronger than Hitler's. The quality of the German general staff made Wiles shudder just to think of what might happen if the likes of Heinz Guderian, the genius of Germany's tank blitzkrieg, or von Bock, or General von Manstein were to be given free rein of Nazi military power. Surrender was not part of their vocabulary. No, they must use caution making assessments about the effect Hitler's death will make on Germany. Over-optimism would serve them ill.

Edward Wiles sketched his thoughts briefly for his two associates, then added "I don't think we're in any position to make accurate judgements about what all of this means. Frankly, I was so keen on getting on with the task of blowing up the arch fiend that I didn't think of step two."

"Good heavens, Edward, surely you're not suggesting that we acted rashly," Elliot said.

"Quite the contrary, I think we moved boldly and with a well conceived plan. We took advantage of a rare opportunity. I am only saying that we are at the place where we should ask ourselves, 'What now?'" "Hmm. Didn't we agree that it's a political question rather than a military one? I, for one, am for visiting Number Ten Downing. Sir William? Will you carry the message?" Elliot announced.

"Of course, dear boy. Wouldn't miss it for the world," Schuyler said, untangling his legs and rising from his perch.

"Well, and there you are! Come in, come in, gentlemen. Sit down," the Prime Minister said, sweeping an arm toward comfortable chairs. "Weldon, bring us some tea," he said to an aide. Then, to the SOE men, "Brandy's the ticket for us, eh? Right there, Elliot," he said, gesturing toward a bar which resembled, when closed, a small armoire. "One for me, as well."

Wiles shook his head at the silent inquiry by Elliot. It was far too early for him and, he knew by experience, that if Elliot put brandy in his own glass he would only wet his lips. Schuyler, on the other hand, was entirely intimidated by W.C. though he did his level best to appear perfectly at ease.

"Good morning, Prime Minister," Sir William said, somewhat unctuously. "Good of you to work us in to your busy schedule."

"Yes," Elliot said, bringing three snifters of the amber liquid to Churchill and Schuyler, while keeping one for himself, "very good indeed."

"Not drinking to your own success, Edward?" Churchill chided Wiles. The PM chuckled at Wiles's arched eyebrows at the suggestion that England's leader already knew the flavor of their intelligence report.

"Thank you, no, sir. I'm looking forward to the tea." As though on cue, a white jacketed mess steward arrived pushing a well polished mahogany tea service cart which, Wiles had been told on an earlier visit, the PM had acquired in South Africa while serving in a much earlier war. With a nod of thanks, Wiles silently accepted a filled cup and saucer from the steward.

"To good friends and last goodbys to our enemies," Churchill lifted the glass to his lips among murmurs of "hear, hear." In the process of his drink Churchill's silk robe slipped open at the waist exposing his bountiful girth and spindly legs dangling below baggy undershorts. The few hairs left upon his head were disarranged, though his visitors knew that he had not just arisen from bed. He padded on flapping slippers around his large desk and took the least comfortable chair among his guests to complete a circle of four.

"Now, then, let's hear it all," his lips almost smacking with delight.

The PM reminded Wiles of the American comedian W.C. Fields in so many ways that the SOE officer allowed himself half a smile. Churchill's sharp eyes, never missing a thing, caught the amusement in the younger man's demeanor but assumed they were sharing the SOE officer's enjoyment: the recent violent passing of Adolf Hitler.

"It would seem, Prime Minister," Schuyler, assuming his prerogative as the senior officer present, "that what we are about to tell you will not come as a complete surprise."

Churchill puffed mightily on his cigar but waved airily as though his knowledge was of no significance.

Schuyler struggled against the acidic taste in his mouth at the thought that Raven security had been so easily breached. He wanted to ask the PM the exact source of his information, but it was not his place to do so.

"The Raven mission went off as planned, Prime Minister..." Schuyler began.

"Killed the bastard, did they?" Churchill interrupted, grinning hugely.

"Yes. It was elements of the Third Para Commando, thirty-six men, including their officer, Major Plith. Gallant soldiers, all."

"Yes, yes. Go on."

"Well, to be quite candid, Prime Minister, we do not know all that we want, indeed, not all that we shall know, given time. We have received two signals from Raven. The first was from Major Plith while they were airborne. It was 'Raven accomplished, Archie stayed.' That was all. Then..."

"Stayed?" the Prime Minister leaned forward in his chair. "What do you mean by that?"

"Archie was the actor that we..." Schuyler began.

"Good God, William," Churchill shot back, omitting the SOE man's title, "you don't have to remind me who Archie is. We monitored his message to OKW, for heaven's sake. What do you mean, he stayed?"

Schuyler swallowed hard, mentally chiding himself for not realizing the obvious, that when Archie successfully transmitted his message from the Führer's communications car to Berlin as planned, Churchill would have been instantly notified.

"Unfortunately, that is all there was to the signal and we have not yet had time to receive independent reports."

"He may have been wounded and unable to return to the aircraft, Prime Minister," Elliot put in. "We're speculating, of course, but there are any number of possibilities why he could not have returned with the others."

Churchill was suddenly on his feet, pacing, head down, cigar smoke wafting in trail behind him. "But that was not to happen. Surely you recall we talked about such an eventuality. The game would be up if...if any part of the man were to be discovered. At this point it may well be that OKW is in the process of cancelling Sealion. Well? Think about what would happen if Archie the actor were to stumble out of the carnage of the train. Killing their leader and attempting to trick them might very well compel the swine to try crossing the channel at all costs. Damn, I wish I had turned you down when you threw in the bloody actor's role and simply killed the house painter!"

There was a lengthy silence in the PM's office while he puffed and paced and others sent their thoughts through cross country jumps.

"Is that all?" the PM snapped, frustrated.

"No. There is more," Schuyler pressed on with his report. "Approximately one hour and forty minutes later, a second signal arrived. I had the radio operator report to us in person. The second message was sent in the clear. It said, 'Five and crew going down.'"

"Crashing? No parachutes?" the Prime Minister asked.

"So it would seem. Our wireless operator thought the pilot was attempting a forced landing," Schuyler said.

"When can you obtain intelligence on that?" Churchill snapped, his glee over the death of the German dictator almost entirely vanished.

Schuyler turned to silently query his colleagues.

Wiles answered, directly to Sir William. "It depends upon where the machine went down, of course. We'll alert our teams along the course line the Stirling was to follow and have them investigate. We should have something within twenty-four hours, I should think."

"Make it sooner," Churchill gruffed.

"Of course we will, Prime Minister," Schuyler agreed arching a reproving eyebrow in Wiles' direction.

"Thank you, then" Churchill said, signaling the end of the interview. Schuyler turned to leave, as did Elliot, but Wiles remained where he stood.

"At the risk of pointing out the obvious, Prime Minister, what about Archie?" Wiles said.

Churchill turned toward Wiles. "What about him? His job was done, wasn't it? He must be dead by now."

"Possibly," Wiles said. "Even likely. But what if he isn't?" Wiles waited for a reply.

Schuyler provided it. "What are you suggesting, Edward? That he is not? My God, I should imagine his life expectancy could be calculated in minutes after the SS got their hands on him. Sorry to say, of course, but there it is. He should have gone out with the others."

"Assuming he was able," Elliot added.

Elliot's reminder was ignored as irrelevant.

"I invite you to imagine, Prime Minister," Wiles continued, "that Archie Smythes is not simply roaming about the forests of southern Germany, lost, with smoke and soot rising from his burnt Nazi uniform. I am suggesting that Archie might have decided to try it once more, and that is why he remained behind."

"His own choice?" Schuyler snorted. "Nonsense, Edward. We've taken all of the Prime Minister's time as it..."

"Suppose for a moment," Churchill interrupted, "that you are right. That Archie believed that he could continue his masquerade for one more act. If that were the case, I should not hesitate one moment to order his death to preserve the security of this otherwise incredibly successful undertaking."

Churchill underscored his conviction with a vigorous nod of his head. Schuyler and Elliot, grim faced, their muteness supporting the Prime Minister as they turned their eyes back toward Wiles. But Wiles, strangely, was smiling.

"Indeed, Prime Minister? And, sir, with respect, how would you go about that?," Wiles said.

As the British leader considered the question, he very slowly bent his knobby knees to sit in his chair behind his desk.

"Ironic, isn't it, sir?" Wiles went on, "We send commandos to assassinate Adolf Hitler, succeed beyond our wildest dreams, then end up having to do the whole thing over again just to kill an actor. Impossible, of course."

Schuyler placed his hand against the wall, as though to steady himself.

"Damn it, Edward," began Schuyler before clamping closed his mouth. He wanted to lay all the blame on the junior SOE executive but realized that he had nearly acted in bad form. It was the kind of admonition a senior would deliver to a junior in private. And deliver it he would.

Unlike the taciturn Schuyler, Churchill enjoyed an occasional use of theatrics to win his point. He allowed his eyes drooped a bit, his lips pressing tightly together, and he touched his temple with a fore-finger as he considered his options.

"And do you have a course of action in mind, Edward?" Churchill asked Wiles.

"I think I do, sir, though I would be the first to find it full of all sorts of flaws. It seems to me that if Archie were to have survived the action at the train, and if he were to have fooled the Germans long enough to give one more order, we should take advantage of that fact by calling the shot, if you'll accept a billiard metaphor," Wiles said.

"You mean tell him what order to give? From London?" Churchill said, his face beginning to brighten. It was the sort of joke that would appeal to him on a personal level. On the level of a war-maker, the idea had obvious attraction.

"Yes, sir, exactly," Wiles responded, calmly.

"Damn," Churchill said, placing his now cold cigar into his mouth. "I hope you won't disappoint me, Edward, by admitting that in the end you have no way of contacting Archie to let him in on our game." The PM phrased his statement in the form of a question.

"I think it is possible," Wiles said. "Ernst Dietrich was a medical doctor who matriculated at the Max Planck Institute in Berlin. He left Germany in 1916, the year his son, Stephen, was born. In the summer of 1936 Stephen was about to begin his last year at Yale University. It was the summer before, when he was touring Berlin, when we met. We shared the love of airplanes," Wiles said.

"Among other things," mumbled Elliot.

"Edward..." Schuyler began but was waved silent by Churchill.

"Where is Dietrich now?" the PM wanted to know.

"He is still in Germany, sir." Wiles said, a corner of his mouth turning up. "More specifically, he is a major in the Luftwaffe.

"Ah," Churchill said, leaning expansively back in his chair, obvi-ously in less discomfort than moments ago. "Dropping bombs on our airfields, I presume?"

"No, Prime Minister, Major Dietrich is a fighter pilot stationed in France. He is a highly respected squadron commander and seems destined for higher rank. He has been supplying us with intelligence for a full two years," Wiles answered.

"Blast it all," Elliot said, "a blind man can see where all of this is going. Prime Minister," he said, turning toward Churchill and delivering his words with force. "In all candor, I do not share Edward's apparently unshakable confidence in Stephen Dietrich. I believe he is a double agent. And even if I am wrong, the damage that he could do to cripple the war effort is enormous."

"What reason do you suspect his loyalty, Elliot?" Churchill asked.

"Dietrich is fully engaged in leading his Staffel on fighter sweeps over the Channel even as we speak. Our chaps in MI5 confirm that he has shot down four of our aircraft and probably more. Hardly the work of an agent loyal to the Crown!" Elliot pounded a fist into the palm of his hand.

"MacLean is correct, of course. But after all, Dietrich's military assignment is to fly German fighters. If the man is to be of any use to us at all he has to demonstrate proficiency in his work. I daresay that a certain amount of tragedy goes with his covert role of serving England. Rather than damn the man for doing a very nasty job, we should thank Providence that we have him where he is and when he is," Wiles said.

"But...." Elliot began, then was interrupted by the Prime Minister's raised hand.

"Gentlemen, we are but a few weeks from one of the greatest military defeats in the history of the Empire. When our forces swam from shore to waiting boats from the shores of Dunkirque they appeared more like drowning rats than fighting men. The equipment of an entire army was left behind to the pleasure of the victorious Hun. Even as we are gathered in this room, we are stringing barbed wire along the beaches. Old men and their dogs watch for landing craft from France while we scurry about trying to refit and rearm. Gentlemen, we could not repel a determined landing force at this time. The nightmare outcome of this war which we all fear could occur months, weeks, even days from now. We are, to coin a phrase, hardly in a position to shun a helping hand. We'll use this Dietrich chap. And we'll pray to God that the man is what we hope."

The room was silent for several moments. Then Churchill offered a smile to the SOE men. "Elliot, old boy, have a cigar," Churchill said. "Franklin went to the trouble of sending these by destroyer. Lend lease. I'll probably have to pay him for them later. Meantime, let's you and I enjoy them." The PM reached across his desk and raised the lid of his humidor.

With taste buds virtually leaking from the redolent bouquet, Elliot stepped forward and grasped one of the lovely Dunhills.

"Take several," Churchill said with a smile and conspiratorial wink.

Schuyler would later swear, in utter disgust, that MacLean Elliot had made an oinking sound as he rutted among the tubes of Caribbean tobacco.

"Dietrich...one of your secret weapons at SOE, eh?" the PM said. "I admire your ingenuity in recruiting the man. And protecting him. It only convinces me of the soundness of my judgment in giving you gentlemen the ball with which to run, if you'll allow me a rugby metaphor. But it is clear to me, as surely it must be to you, that if the beleaguered British people have a magic genie who will grant them one more wish, as their trusted leaders we should use every bit of our skills in making that wish become reality."

The prolonged stillness that followed was all of the assent Churchill needed from the SOE.

"But if Smythes is dead...." Schuyler began, his voice trailing off.

"Then we've lost nothing," Churchill said, "except an actor."

CHAPTER 11

Never, in the history of the tiny village of Gebirgs Sicht, had there been such a show of military might and fanfare as that which descended about the town in the past fifty-nine hours. Virtually the entire population of four hundred and ten stood outside their homes or businesses, while volks who had come in from their surrounding farms to gather in the streets, standing in awe of a Heers Kampfgruppe which had taken up tactical positions in a twenty-five kilometer perimeter around the entire village. With the four thousand man Kampfgruppe were their troop carrier vehicles, machine gun units armed with MG34's and infantry grenadiers.

Placed strategically among them was the 44th Panzerjager Battalion, as well as the 1st, 2nd and 3rd Regiments of the famous Gebirgsjager (Mountain) Division which had fought its way from the Polish campaign through France, glorifying itself in the Aisne crossing of the Mass, Aisne and Loire rivers. Their armored vehicles included the newest versions of Germany's battle tank.

The inner perimeter, surrounding the Hütte-Krankenhaus, Cottage Hospital in Gebirgs Sicht, consisted of I, II, III/ (Waffen)SS VT Standarte Das Führer and two of their SS Panzer regiments.

Overhead were several Fieseler Fi 156 reconnaissance aircraft executing concentric search patterns in a thirty kilometer radius of the village while elements of the Jagdgeschwader 4, flying Bf109's, operating out of Munich-Handorf, flew sorties at the farthest edges from the concentration of forces.

The British raiders for whom the Germans searched were, of course, long gone, the tire tracks of the Stirling found almost at once. It's final fate was reported within hours by Luftwaffe Nachtjagdgverbande (night fighters) after it had been shot down over occupied France.

The presence of so many fully manned and heavily armed military units was to protect the important patient inside the small Hospital of Mercy, as it was named. Small in size, hardly larger than the nearby Bruchlar Inn, the hospital was originally established to serve a bucolic agrarian population of nearby villages. Though few in number, its three man staff of doctors were young, professionally competent, drawn to the area by their enthusiasm for winter and healthy rural life style. Innsbruck and its irresistible winter sports was less than a two hour drive. Their medical equipment was more than adequate for the day and their surgical capabilities easily supported most of the cases required by the community and beyond. The Hospital of Mercy received a measure of federal financial support that paid for a full housekeeping staff, four nurses in training, five acute care emergency practitioners, augmented by volunteer nurses from a nearby nunnery, The Little Sisters.

Despite its well deserved reputation for competency, it was clearly not the equal to any of the great hospitals to be found in Berlin nor, even closer, Munich, where Adolf Hitler should have been rushed. Instead, upon his own firm orders given to the hospital administrator and relayed to anxiously awaiting staff and Nazi party hierarchy wringing their hands in the tiny lobby of the institution, Hitler would remain in his private room on the second floor until further notice.

What further notice? The question was asked of Doctor Fredrich Möeler, the only physician the Führer allowed to attend him.

"Until Herr Hitler says otherwise," the thirty-eight year old medical doctor responded, as he attempted to hide his inner pleasure at the frustration so obvious on the faces of many of the most important people in Germany.

And the extent of his injuries? Again, from bureaucrats and media from all over the world that jammed the small hamlet, the sober Möeler said that the Führer was in very good health, that his prognosis for a full recovery was excellent. However, the Führer had been subject to violent trauma, including nearby explosions and personal combat, that his condition called for continuing medical vigilance and evaluation. Concussion had occurred and until the Führer felt that he was recovered sufficiently, he would remain right where he was, room number five, Hospital of Mercy.

In response to questions pressed by personages awaiting the Führer's summons, Dr. Möeler described Herr Hitler's activities in his room.

"He rests, of course, at my urging. He speaks sparingly, that is he does not waste his resources by talking obsessively. He reads almost non-stop. We supply him with books from our small hospital library and I have found his appetite for literature of almost any kind quite stimulating. His strength seems to be returning before our very eyes. He often rises from bed to move around his room. The Führer, as you know, is a man of uncommon courage and uses no pain-killing drugs. I and my colleagues have discovered no broken bones. He has suffered concussion, not severe, and a badly twisted ankle, but there are no wounds that would keep him from discharging the duties of his office."

Archie wore bandages upon his head to cover a self-inflicted glancing blow to the head. It was part of his prop, a means by which he could drift into or out of awareness if and when the situation required. He hoped the highly visible bandages would act as a reminder that he had suffered a blow to the head and that whatever confusing behavior that he might exhibit could be explained by that trauma.

His contact with hospital staff had, at first, been daunting. He expected at any moment to be discovered for the impersonator that he was, that something in his speech would have given him away, or that his eyes would reflect the fear of a cornered animal. He strained to overhear the telephone call to police or army authorities that would denounce him not only as the impostor discovered but the murderer of the real leader of the German nation.

But no such call was made.

Nor did Archie perceive the hesitation of doubt or suspicion on the part of staff. On the contrary, he began to almost enjoy the deference he was shown, the way in which every hospital employee stood as far from him as possible when not directly engaged in a task of treatment, the dropping of eyes when his own were cast in their direction, the near genuflections that sprang spontaneously from nurses and nuns within his proximity.

His responses to questions from doctors, Does this hurt, sir? And here? Could you describe discomfort in your neck area, Herr Hitler? were as brief as possible, the sound of his voice seeming weak to him, but also understandably so. But as the hours progressed, he refused to take any medication that would induce drowsiness, his confidence gradually increased. His speech became less cryptic and he formed more complex sentences as he watched the faces of attending staff. When no suspicion appeared he ventured even more complete statements. He forced himself to make and sustain eye contact. He noted, with satisfaction, that others dropped theirs before him.

The books that he read were, at first, very simple ones. They were not for his entertainment but to give himself a crash refresher in German. There was one nurse, Hildegarde Bartholoma, who was particularly receptive to his light-hearted discussions of the material he had read. She would later enthrall other staff members telling in precise detail what the Führer had said to her about stories he had read. Hildegarde could not have been more surprised about the Leader's gentle nature, a side of him that the radio and newsreels had not revealed.

Archie, at his request, was also supplied with a copy of his own book, *Mein Kampf*, which he turned to scanning at all hours of the day or night. He explained to Hildegarde in a very fundamental way, what were his thoughts behind his writing that appeared on the page. But Archie was increasingly aware that the important officials waiting in halls and lobbies and grounds of the hospital were running out of patience. Joseph Goebbels was among the more strident of the congregation, all but threatening the medical staff of sabotaging the war effort by holding the Führer away from the throttles of communication so necessary to driving the engine of the German nation.

Hermann, Göring too, railed against the medical staff and guards who prevented Herr Hitler's closest friend from visiting at his bedside. Even when it was explained to the Field Marshal, that it was only the Führer's orders they were carrying out, the willful Luftwaffe commander insisted that he should be the exception.

More than once Sepp Dietrich, commanding general of the elite Leibstandarte-SS Adolf Hitler Division, had to personally intervene when an official of high government rank threatened an officer or hospital staff member for access to room number five. Ironic, such events, since Sepp Dietrich, a ruthless and physically action-oriented man, was anything but patient himself.

Goebbels, Dr. Möeler sensed, was much more than a simpering underling. He was dangerous to those who might attempt to reduce his influence with Hitler. If Möeler only realized that Goebbels was not in close favor of the Leader because of his frowned upon sexual relationship with a half Jewess actress, he might have been less concerned. But Möeler was careful to show not only deference to the Minister of Propaganda but to explain to him that he, Möeler, was acting upon the express will of the Führer.

Among the Party supplicants waiting for the merest lifting of the Führer's finger, was Rudolf Hess. Hess, Archie knew, was deputy party leader. He was the same man to whom Hitler dictated *Mein Kampf* in the days of his confinement in Landsberg Prison following the now famous 1923 Munich Beer Hall Putsch. Archie knew very little about Hess except that he, like virtually all others, viewed Hitler only from a respectful distance. Hitler had never in his life formed an intimate friendship with anyone and Archie counted upon this fact to keep others as far from him as possible.

It was as if Hitler had a large imaginary circle around his body into which no one dared enter except by permission, and Hitler never gave permission. So Hess, like the others, waited obsequiously for Hitler's summons.

As Archie nervously paced the room and, alternately, fell onto his bed, argued with himself for reasons to delay. He knew, sooner or later, that he would have to face someone who knew Hitler. Reasons were many, but to continue to delay was could be dangerous. As a matter of fact, he reasoned, the sooner he faced an important figure in the Nazi hierarchy the more effective his avenue of escape would be, i.e., to suddenly relapse into whatever real or imagined medical condition caused by the action at the train.

He hoped the lateness of the hour would help provide sympathetic light shadow for his appearance. Inhaling deeply, warding off a shudder that threatened to shake his body, Archie pushed a button to summon staff. Within moments a nurse answered his call. Her name was Geraldine, he remembered, and she seemed the least intimidated in his presence than any of the others. She was tall, and had a rather deep voice for her rather angular features.

"Herr Hess. Is he still waiting?" Archie said to the nurse.

"Yes, sir. In the entry."

"Ach. Good, old Rudolf," Archie said, wondering if the nurse would laugh at the absurdity of the statement. But Geraldine could not read his mind and she did not laugh. "Well, then, send him in."

Archie began to fight panic the moment nurse Geraldine exited the room to do his bidding. He had caught a glimpse of the black uniformed SS guards standing within the halls of the hospital as Geraldine passed through the open door. He could not run. There was no escape. Archie snapped on a dim lamp near his bed before crossing the room and turned off the wall switch that controlled the overhead lighting. The room was cast into a place of soft illumination and shadows. Yet Archie struggled to suppress the black fear that was welling up in his throat. He imagined that Hess would, at any moment, throw open the door, point a long finger directly at Archie and shout "Arrest that man! He is not the Führer, his name is Archie Smythes and he is English!"

Archie instinctively pulled his head into his neck to avoid the blows that would fall upon him. Rifle butts would smash into his ribs and jackboots would kick him into unconsciousness before they dragged him outside where he would be shot. Archie put his hand out to the nearby bed to steady himself before falling. He was thus touching the mattress of the bed when the door suddenly opened to reveal the unmistakable visage of a square jawed Rudolf Hess standing framed within. A large SS soldier waited patiently for the Party deputy to step fully inside the room. It was Archie who, it seemed, had to deal with the awkwardness of Hess's mesmerized gaze at the sight of the bandaged Adolf Hitler standing before him.

"Come, come," Archie said, hoping he sounded at once calm, in command of his faculties, but gruff, clearly impatient with events that had caused him to lay aside the affairs of state.

Hess's mouth twitched into a series of small smiles as he thrust his head down, bowing slightly but unmistakably at the waist. Archie found it strange that one man would so revere another man, especially one whom he has known for so long, that he would lower his head in abject submission.

"My Führer," Hess said, his eyes wide open with relief.

Archie did not offer his hand while Hess, anything but smooth and confident, actually checked a half step toward his leader then stepped back again to remain at a respectful distance. "It is good to see you looking so well. Battle reports have been difficult to verify and we feared for the worse. The swine who attacked you have been destroyed, of course."

"What's that?" Archie blurted.

"The filthy English air pirates, Führer. Their aircraft was shot down over France while the survivors attempted to steal their way home in the night."

"Good. Good," Archie said, momentarily sickened. "All dead then, eh, Hess?"

"Killed or captured. Ten bailed out and all rounded up by elements of the Wehrmacht near Ameins. They are all in the hands of the Gestapo as we speak. They will undergo exhaustive interrogation, then hanged, of course," Hess said, his eyes bright for the first time since he entered the room.

He wore clothing that did not fit him exactly right in spite of a tailor's best efforts. He had on a civilian suit, grey double breasted pin-stripe, of good quality wool, Archie thought, and a small Nazi party pin in the left lapel. A man Archie guessed was never at ease, the Nazi party deputy wore his hastily knotted tie lapped over his white shirt, giving the impression that Hitler's aide had been sleeping in his clothing. Probably true, Archie guessed. Hess's eyes were disconcerting to Archie. Unlike others whom Archie had met since posing as the dictator of Europe, Hess's gaze did not avert when Archie's eyes met his. Hess, indeed, stared, as though something magical was about to emanate from within Hitler's earthly body.

"Of course." Archie searched for a fitting comment but came up with only "Swine."

"The lowest kind," Hess eagerly agreed. Then, "You look quite robust, Führer. Considering the battle."

"Yes. Well, you know that I have an iron will, Rudolf."

"Yes, yes. No, ah, pain, then?"

Archie shook his head, not willing to agree that he was fully recovered. "The news of...of my near death must have frightened the German people," Archie ventured.

"No, Führer, not at all. That is, there has been no news released about the cowardly attack. Goebbels has seen to that."

"No news? Why not?"

"But why should there be? What do we gain by admitting that the British could fly so deeply into Germany? Our air defenses are quite secret."

"But the train...my train, was destroyed. SS men were killed," Archie said, caught off balance.

Hess was silent for a long moment as he considered the non-problem of controlling the news. "But, with respect, Führer, what do we gain by allowing the British to know how close they had come to killing you?"

"Has it occurred to you, Rudolf, that the British might already know that fact?" Archie allowed his voice to rise in volume and timber while responding to the absurdity of Hess' reasoning. He liked how he sounded. And how he felt.

"Yes, of course you are right. Er, shall I instruct the Minister of Propaganda to prepare a news release, then?" Hess asked.

"Ach, no. Not until I have thought about the form I want it to take. Now, on another subject, Hess...."

"Yes, sir?"

"I sent a message to OKW from the train. It regarded Operation Sealion. Was it received?" Archie said, his voice steady.

"I was not in contact with Headquarters, Führer, but if you gave the order, I am sure it was carried out." Hess' chin pulled back, the heels of his soft leather street shoes coming together as though to enunciate the certainty of Hitler's total authority.

"Well, I want confirmation, Hess. After all, I was fighting for my life at the time!" Archie reminded his servile associate.

Hess' eyes lit anew at the very thought of his leader's heroic actions. "If only the nation, the whole world, could have seen you, Führer, they would tremble to think of it. That Germany is led by a man of unconquerable will."

"They must know that by now, Hess."

"Yes, but..."

"I am going to sleep. Are there many outside waiting to see me?" Archie said.

"Many. Göring is quite insistent..."

"Yes, yes."

"And Reichsleiter Bormann," Hess added, as though biting into a lemon.

"What does he want?" Archie asked, unsure who Bormann was or, more precisely, what he did.

"He insists that you be moved to Obersalzburg, Führer. We have explained to him that your doctors have forbidden a move, but he does not want to listen. You know Martin," Hess tossed in.

"Yes, it sounds just like him," Archie cautiously agreed.

"I have tried to limit their number but it is difficult. Not much is generally known. If you could make an appearance, a brief one, it would be good, I think."

"No. No, I...I have other plans. You send out the word, Hess. Tell everyone that you have seen me. We have talked. I am conducting the war. In fact I am working on new orders for the entire war effort and they will hear them shortly. But we don't want to rush."

"Rush what, Führer?"

"Rush my recovery, Hess! That would be utterly idiotic! My health is what is important to Germany. It is vital." Archie felt a surge of confidence in his character. If Adolf Hitler was anything at all, he was totally selfish.

"Without question, Führer! I could not agree more. There is, possibly, an exception you should make."

"Yes?"

"Field Marshal Göring. He is highly agitated and says that he must see you at once, never mind, you will pardon me for saying, Führer..."

"Yes, yes, what did he say?"

"Never mind your condition. No matter what your wounds, is what he said," Hess concluded.

"Ah." Archie could well imagine why the overweight Luftwaffe commander was so disturbed. No doubt it was the conduct of the air war over England. It had to be won to invade Britain and if there was to be no invasion.... "Rudolf, speak to the Field Marshal personally. Tell him to...to carry on. I will meet with him in due course."

"Due course. I understand, Adolf," Hess said, in a rather touching attempt at personal affection.

"That is what I said. Due course. Go now, Rudolf. And thank you for coming," Archie said, turning his back on Hess.

Hess stepped smartly backward as he reached for the door. "I will remain nearby, Führer."

Archie lay on his back staring straight up at the ceiling, exulting, marveling that he was still alive. While there was no applause at the end of his very important scene with Hess, Archie knew that his performance was good. It was better than good, it was excellent! He began to feel almost giddy that his role was received by such an significant critic apparently without reservation. Archie's thoughts bolted to Göring. He most certainly knew why the corpulent field marshal wanted to see Hitler so urgently. It was about Sealion. And it was about the air war going on even now over the skies of England, preparatory to invasion.

Archie wracked his brain to recall how well Göring knew Hitler in relation to how well Hess had known the Führer. Was it just as well? Not quite as well? Or, horror of horrors, much better? Did Hitler and Göring share intimate information that the field marshal might expect to discuss? Almost certainly true, but how to circumvent such an event? Archie could feel sweat break out on the palms of his hands. He had to say something to Göring about the conduct of the air war. But what? He could not very well order all of the Luftwaffe down, could he? No, it would not only be the end of his charade but the order would probably be ignored, anyway.

And the other generals? What would he say to them?

I f Stephen Dietrich inherited anything of his parent's genes it was a willingness to work hard. He was an excellent student at university, his respected position on the dean's list a result of that inborn work ethic as well as a facility for remembering almost everything he read, including seemingly inconsequential details. He had only to peruse his text books once, at the beginning of each term, to be able to pass any test given in that discipline be it history, mathematics, literature, philosophy or languages. He was fluent in German and French before arriving in high school so that his studies in those arts were no challenge at all.

He was catholic in his interests and spent not an inconsiderable amount of time in high school shop, particularly mechanics where he and three other boys rebuilt a Gnome-Rône 14N, fourteen cylinder radial engine. Their shop teacher had no expertise with such a complex power system. He acted as an observer, rather than instructor, while the teenagers attacked the water-damaged engine, cleaned its parts, then reassembled the power plant. Dietrich himself built a test stand for the engine and when the boys lit it off it ran better than new.

The roar of that engine never quite subsided in Stephen Dietrich's ears, its throaty resonance reaching deep into his entire body's muscles and bones. Though his academics never suffered, Dietrich decided to forego the study of medicine, as his father had wished for him, and aimed for a career in aviation. During the 1930's, while the world drifted ever more deeply into economic depression and social unrest, building aircraft, the high performance kind, languished at the very end of national budget priorities. America was going nowhere fast in developing low wing, high-speed performers, while Italy and Germany seemed committed to the construction of dominating military designs. The summer before beginning his senior year at Yale, Dietrich used the excuse of the summer Olympics to underwrite a trip to Europe. He promised his father that he would broaden his intellectual horizons, but more important in Stephen's mind was to see the fastest, highest flying aircraft in the world.

Dietrich was certainly not blind to social events that were sweeping through Germany and other parts of the world. Benito Mussolini, Italy's Fascist dictator, was regarded as a political threat to Europe's democratic governments and it seemed clear that Germany, under the strong leadership of Chancellor Adolf Hitler, was developing national resolve to thrust itself into a position of prime power on the Continent. The times were exciting for a twenty year old college student and Stephen Dietrich wanted to see them first hand.

Dietrich had seldom thought much about antisemitism or, for that matter, racism in any form. Still, his attitude about the historical persecution of Jews was unsympathetic. If he were a Jew, he thought, he would accept abuse from no man. So why did they? But while his visceral connection to Jews was tenuous, he did not like the way they had been treated in Nazi Germany. Dietrich despised bullies. He did not like big ones, skinny ones or fat ones, smart ones or dumb ones. He simply could not allow himself to let powerful people step on weak ones. While Dietrich was well short of six feet in height, he was muscular, quick and coordinated. Most important, he was almost entirely without fear.

When Dietrich met Edward Wiles, an Englishman ten years his senior, the two men were staring into a cobalt blue sky watching an ME-108 do aerobatics in an air show at Tempelhof. The year was 1936, two days before Stephen's birthday.

"He won't finish," Dietrich said aloud but to no one in particular as the ME-108 began a loop.

"Yes, he will," came another voice near him. The voice responded in German but the language was acquired and the speaker's English accent was not disguised. "But at the top he'll split-S."

Dietrich turned to regard a slender man several inches taller than he, and Dietrich thought the man could afford regular treatment by a dentist, judging from bright, even teeth behind an easy smile. "The present regime doesn't like its pilots embarrassed," the Englishman said.

As it happened, they were both wrong. The pilot merely took a longer "down hill" run, a shallow dive, before bringing the nose up. With the extra speed built up, the ME-108 pulled neatly through the loop. Two years later, when the first iteration of the ME-109 appeared, it would have more than enough power in its Daimler-Benz twelve cylinder V block engine to complete that maneuver and many others with dazzling ease. But neither man could foretell the future.

"And what do the British have that is better?" Dietrich asked.

"Well, for one thing, we're not interested in building fighters," the man lied without blinking. "But Supermarine has a rather spiffy seaplane that just might win the Bendix races this year."

"Ah, yes," Dietrich said, "with the new Merlin engine. You have supercharged the machine. Tell me, how much altitude can it reach? Thirty thousand? Probably more, eh?" Dietrich could see a flash of something in the Englishman's eyes at the familiarity with which Dietrich referred to the newest model.

"Of course I don't know that. Should I take your word?" "Why not? We're your cousins," Dietrich said in perfect English, relishing Wiles's surprise as he abandoned German.

"You're American! Good grief, man, your German is perfect. At least I think it is. My name is Edward Wiles," the Englishman said, extending his hand.

"Stephen Dietrich. I was born in Germany but I grew up in America. You're British," the compact American grinned at his new acquaintance.

"Guilty. What brings you so far from home? Visiting relatives?" Wiles asked.

"On my mother's side. My aunt and uncle. Their name is Schrieber and they live in Koblenz. They have two daughters, Sheilah and Janette. I'm told they are skinny, homely, and too young yet to be interesting. I've been putting off seeing them until I've taken in all of the air shows I can find."

"And the Olympics?" the Britisher asked.

Dietrich shrugged. "Might be too late to get tickets. They must be half over by now. How about a beer?"

"My treat," Wiles said, as they moved toward a tent that sold refreshments of all kinds. "You must fly, then, Stephen?"

"Simple stuff. J-3's, a Ryan, Waco. You know. But I'm still a year from graduation so money and time are tight," Dietrich said.

"Two steins," Wiles said to the man pouring dark Bavarian beer behind a wood plank bar. "Do you mind?" the Englishman said of ordering for them both, extracting paper money from his wallet.

"Never complain when the other guy's buying. I think my mother told me that. How about a wurst? On me," Dietrich said, ordering the plump meat products as the beer was set before them.

"So," Dietrich said, "I'm sightseeing. What about you?"

"Vacation," Wiles said, the rest of his words drowned by the sound of yet another high performance engine. As though on cue, both men rushed to the door of the tent and looked up. What they saw was a pug-nosed, low wing aircraft mounting a radial power plant that lifted the plane effortlessly from its fifty foot altitude into a steep climb combined with an aileron roll.

The two men exchanged puzzled looks, watching as the aircraft disappeared into the distance.

"What the blazes was that?" Wiles asked, a wurst dripping in his hands.

"Search me, but that was a real piece of equipment." His head swivelled as he scanned the airfield for a similar shape, to no avail.

Passing overhead was a formation of six Ju-52 Junker tri-motor passenger airplanes which, even to the poorly informed observer, was but a thinly disguised bomber.

"Ever fly any of those?" Dietrich asked of Wiles.

"Only as a passenger. Lufthansa has a number of them on regular routes. They're noisy bastards, but they're very well built. Nothing to go wrong, you see," Wiles said.

"Do you fly for a living?" Dietrich wanted to know.

"Wanted to. I was in the RAF for five years before I pranged my kite," Wiles laughed ruefully. "I walked with a limp until about a year ago. Broke both legs below the knees."

"Really? How did you do that? Smash it up, I mean."

"I'm embarrassed to tell. Usually I have an exciting adventure story to get my sorry ego rescued, like testing a plane in a power dive or something, but the fact is that I attempted to take off without removing the tail chock."

"Jesus," Dietrich said, his eyes closing partially, as though he could see the whole thing unfolding, and as though but for the grace of God.... "And they mustered you out?"

"Yes. So now I look for places to sell Scottish wool," he shook his head at the irony. Wiles felt very much at ease with himself even though a good bit of what he had said was a lie.

But Dietrich didn't know that. He liked the Englishman at once.

Olympics fever had taken over Berlin if not all of Germany in 1936. Everywhere one looked swastikas festooned major streets, hanging from windows, light poles and rooftops to support the awarding of the Olympic games to the New Germany. It was proof that Deutschland had risen above all other cities and nations in this prestigious social fiat.

For the next three days the new friends frequented all of the night clubs and alkohol-stangens they could find in Berlin, with Wiles insisting upon picking up most of the checks over the increasingly pro-forma objections of his new American comrade. There were women everywhere they went, some of them attractive, but most of them drawn to the older, more cosmopolitan Wiles, leaving Dietrich to scramble for what was left. Some were too old, even for Wiles, many were too fat, or far too tall for Dietrich who, often as not, had trouble seeing over their shoulders while dancing.

Wiles did not dance, claiming that his air crash injuries kept him off his feet. That was not true. As a matter of fact Wiles had been professionally instructed in the art of dancing. His perfectly healthy legs could gracefully carry him across any ball room floor when the need arose.

Still, Dietrich was a gentleman to the core and, with Wiles, shared the keenest sense of humor. One needed a sense of humor in Germany of the 30s, they agreed. The night spots they frequented were increasingly patronized by military officers. The Treaty of Versailles,

MICHAEL MURRAY

denounced by Hitler in shrill tirades, had brought no negative sanctions against Germany and as the military machine increased in size and efficiency, unmistakable pride was plain on the faces of men and their women all over Germany.

In the early afternoon on the first day of September, still warm with a hint of continuing warm fall weather, Dietrich, waiting for Wiles to make his appearance, took a table at Das Wasserhahn (The Faucet), a bistro unremarkable from countless others among the streets surrounding the Kurfurstendamm, or Ku'damm as it was called by the city's cognicenti. Das Wasserhahn, however, seemed a bit livelier than most with current music played loudly from a machine behind the bar, and a noisy clientele for so early in the day. Dietrich had chosen a sidewalk table and ordered a glass of French wine from the waiter. He intended to give his body a day off from terrible abuse, promising his kidneys that they would have to process less than a pint of spirits, two glasses of wine or one quart of beer. Pleased in advance with his own discipline, he sipped an estate bottled Burgundy and nibbled his way through a small bowl of salted nuts.

Dietrich was aware that classes would start at Yale in less than two weeks. As it was, he would have to register by wire since registration was four days away and, clearly, he could not make it to Connecticut by then. There was a flying boat service from San Francisco to China that had been in operation almost a year, but it was Dietrich's belief that the first "Clipper," as Pan American called their seaplane, should have been scheduled between New York and Europe. That's where the future of international commerce lay. Meanwhile he would have to reschedule himself once again, cancelling his booking on the steamship *Hamburg*, which was sailing today from Bremerhaven without him, to another that would leave...when? In two days? Three?

He had ordered a second glass of wine when he heard his name called from a table across the wrought-iron fencing that surrounded the bistro's outside tables. Well, it wasn't his name, was it? It was more like...

"You. Yank. Yes, come, we'll buy you a beer!

He turned in his chair. There were two men in uniforms, seated at a table covered almost entirely with empty steins, plates containing congealed grease from now cold wurst, and red wine spilled atop its linen spread. The uniformed drinkers waved away an attempt by the

160

waiter to clear their mess, preferring, apparently, to wear the exhausted bottles and glasses as their badges of honor. After wagging at the waiter, they beckoned again to Dietrich.

"Come, we have questions about America," the taller of the two men said, a large smile fixed firmly on his, clean shaved, elongated face, eyes alit.

There being few people in the café who might have been Americans, Dietrich rose reluctantly to his feet and moved slowly toward their table.

"Here, sit. My name is Hartung," the tall, lean, blond offered, his hand outstretched. Dietrich took it and found that the man's fingers were long and his hand muscular. Dietrich could not help but notice that his uniform was field grey and that his black collar tabs were overlaid with silver jags in the form of SS, silver piping throughout the uniform. A "Schirmmutze" (peaked) hat hanging casually from a corner of Hartung's chair contained silver braid and a small skull in its center. A death's head. "My friends," he said, "call me Bunny."

Dietrich looked for a hidden joke, as though his leg was being pulled, but if it was so, it was in good fun. "Dietrich," he responded in German. "Stephen. And you don't look much like a bunny."

Eyes widened in the faces of Hartung and his friend.

"Guter Gott!" Hartung said, suddenly laughing, "we took you for American. But you are German!"

"No, you were right the first time. I'm American. Born here in this city. And you?" Dietrich nodded toward the second man. He was not as tall as Hartung but wider in the middle, a year or two older, and fuller in his florid face. Dietrich guessed that the man spent a good deal of his time with a bottle in his hand.

"Friedel. Frederich, lieutenant, Luftwaffe," he said, laughing at himself, Dietrich thought.

Friedel wore the cuff title of dark blue woolen material with *Geschwader Hindenburg* inscribed upon it in aluminum thread. The uniform itself was cut of fine blue cloth, a silver eagle worn over the right breast pocket, a swastika gripped by the bird's talons. His epaulets were gold and silver while lapel badges were gold. Over his left breast pocket was yet another bird of prey, gold, wreathed in intricately woven aluminum thread. Dietrich recognized it as the Bomber Gold Clasp. He would have cut a dashing figure, Dietrich thought, but there was no dash in Friedel. The collar of his dress white shirt was unbuttoned and his grey tunic was held around his expanding waist by a single button. He had been drinking heavily but, like Hartung, seemed light of heart, certainly not depressed.

"Jesus, man, we could sell your clothes to any Berliner on the street!" Friedel laughed at the thought. "Look at those pants. And shoes."

Dietrich was aware that he was wearing cream colored corduroy trousers, argyle socks and Scotch brogues. For the first time in several days he was not wearing his collar open but his gold and navy blue striped tie burned a hole in his blazer pocket.

"As a matter of fact," Dietrich said, calmly, "Berlin men walking around city streets look like they're on their way to work feeding animals in the zoo."

The uniformed men stared at Dietrich for a long moment, then burst into gales of uncontrolled laughter. "Waiter! Waiter, you son of a pig!" Friedel called loudly to a waiter at another table. "Drinks all around here. *Schnell.*"

The waiter's nose lifted slightly and the man sauntered to the table, languidly dumping an overflowing ash tray onto the ground, caring not at all that a good bit of the ash fell onto Friedel's uniform trousers.

"Speaking of pigs," the waiter said, dryly, "your Fraulein called. She can't meet you tonight because the fleet is in and she is working the starboard watch."

Dietrich, frozen in his chair, at his elbow heard suppressed air escaping. The source, he saw, was Bunny Hartung giggling, a kind of reverse snort, like a man with a sinus problem. Dietrich looked at Friedel's reaction to this gross insult.

With a face that did not flicker, Friedel said, "Then my credit is good. Maybe we'll switch to brandy. Make it the best you have, Pinky. Something better than you clean the toilet with."

"But we don't have anything better than we use on the toilet," Pinky said, equally straight faced.

"All right, if that is the best you have, you dick-licker, bring it out. We are getting dry," the bomber pilot said.

After the waiter had left Hartung said "Friedel and I used to work here. Behind the bar."

"Do you prefer the work you do now?" Dietrich said.

"Of course. We are building a new Germany. Then a new world. It is demanding business," Hartung said.

"He means that he has less time to pound his pud," Friedel said, making a masturbation gesture.

"Freddy," Hartung said as he crossed his highly polished boots and leaned back in his chair, "someday you will learn that pud pounding is one of the greatest sources of relaxation known to man. To say nothing of keen insights that often accompanies ejaculation."

"Well, I can't say the money is better." Friedel turned directly to Dietrich. "We got lots of tips working here, you know. And we fucked every girl who walked in," Friedel added, lighting another cigarette.

"You mean I did," Hartung said, nodding to Dietrich, "because I am handsome, as you can see."

"And suave," Dietrich added, beginning to enjoy the atmosphere.

"Yes. Very suave. Women would walk over Friedel's head to get to me. They would leave little holes in his face from their spike heels," Hartung said.

"You know, that happened once," Friedel said, leaning across the table toward Dietrich. "I had a little apartment on Lichtenstrasse near the university..."

"*I* had an apartment on Lichtenstrasse," Hartung corrected.

"The lease was in my name," Friedel said.

"It was in Ulrich's name." Hartung turned to Dietrich. "Ulrich Richman was a Jew. The Gestapo threw him out."

"But I fixed Ulrich up with my ex-wife," Friedel said. "It was actually a move up for him. Sheilah loves him."

Pinky returned with snifters of brandy. He placed the glasses in front of each man and kept one for himself.

"To new friends," Hartung said, raising his glass toward Dietrich.

"Have one for yourself," Friedel said testily to Pinky. "My treat."

"I have already done that, corporal, and one for later, too," Pinky responded before leaving the table.

Dietrich had noticed the left sleeve cuff title, embroidered in silver thread against black background read **Adolf Hitler**. He knew that the Schutzstaffel, or SS, was an elite group of young fighting men who were tall, physically fit, rejected for so much as a dental filling, and fanatically dedicated to their Führer, Adolf Hitler. It seemed to Dietrich, curious to separate fact from fiction, that Bunny Hartung might fit the first two criteria for service in the SS but there seemed to be nothing fanatic about the man, at least on the surface.

"I see Adolf Hitler's name on your sleeve," Dietrich ventured. "What does it mean, exactly?"

"It means that we need another drink, Pinky," interjected Friedel in a loud voice.

Lieutenant Hartung smiled, drunkenly, "I thought about sewing my own name there. I have a spare tunic for when I go on leave. It says 'Bunny Hartung Division.'"

"He works for a swine," Friedel said as Pinky arrived.

"More brandy, Pinky. And don't piss in my glass this time," Hartung said.

Dietrich quickly produced Deutschmarks. "Let me buy."

"You're our guest," protested Friedel, lacking conviction.

"Does that mean that I can't treat?" Dietrich demurred.

"Of course it does not," Hartung said. "The first thing we learn in officer's training school is to allow others to buy our drinks. I'm surprised that Freddy, here, could so easily forget his duty. And don't call my general a swine."

"What general do you mean?" Dietrich asked, interested.

"SS-GruppenFührer Wilhelm Beckman. Wilhelm Beckman is a swine, to be sure. Blood thirsty, petulant, money grubbing and follows his dick because it does all of his thinking for him. And those are his good qualities."

"Do you have to work for him?" Dietrich asked.

"No, but I am counting on the man..."

"Pig," corrected Friedel.

"...to keep me out of the fighting when the war comes," Hartung concluded.

"Bunny does not believe in fighting," Friedel winked at Dietrich.

Hartung nodded. "I have no natural enemies. Besides, I don't think I would be very good at it."

"But we Germans have natural enemies. You should know that, Bunny," Friedel admonished. "Do you have American cigarettes, my friend? No? Someday you will take up smoking, I promise."

"But Friedel, here," Hartung said, his eyes following two attractive girls on the sidewalk, "can drop bombs and has no idea where they land so war will be fine with him."

"Nonsense. I am a born killer. Blood letting is my life!"

"I should tell Ingrid you said that. Ingrid is his mother. I love her. She would weep to hear you speak that way. No wonder she tried to give you away at birth. You probably have the sign of the Anti-Christ on your body. You did not imagine that Friedel, here, could have a mother, eh? I have known him since he was five."

"No, that's not what I thought," Dietrich said, caught up entirely in the occasion. "I'm listening to you two talking about war. Is there going to be a war?"

"His boss owned all of the illegal gambling machines in Germany at one time. Beckman. The Weimar government sent him to jail so he joined the SS. You could enlist directly from your own cell, then," Friedel said, dryly, while reaching for one of the recently arrived brandy snifters.

"Freddy," Hartung said, lighting a cigarette, "someday you'll go too far and I won't be able to save your fat ass from a concentration camp."

"So, Stephen, do you have a sister who would like to get to know a humble but loveable bomber pilot?" Friedel asked.

"As a matter of fact, I do. She's only twelve years old but she's crazy for uniforms."

"What did you study at school?" Hartung asked. "Business? That's what Americans are best at, eh? You must be rich if you volunteer to pay for drinks."

"I attend college. Yale. And I'm not rich, but my father is comfortable, I suppose."

"And is he a businessman?"

"Doctor. He wants me to join him in practice some day, I think," Dietrich said.

"But?" Hartung said.

"What makes you think there is a 'but'?"

Hartung shrugged. "Am I wrong?"

"I suppose not. As a matter of fact, I'd like to be doing the same thing Freddy, here, is doing..."

"Getting drunk?"

"Let this incredibly intelligent man finish," Friedel said, pounding his fist loudly on the table, causing customers to look in their direction.

"Fly airplanes," Dietrich said. "Not bombers. Fighters."

"Isn't that wonderful?" Friedel said, careering his head first at Dietrich, then at Hartung. "I think we could find this fine fellow a little ME-108 to have some fun in, eh? We're always looking for new recruits."

"I doubt if Stephen would have much stomach for fighting the Frogs. Or the Brits. Especially the Brits, eh?" Hartung said, a small rivulet of brandy escaping his glass and falling to his lower chin.

"You haven't answered my question. Is there going to be a war?" Dietrich pressed.

For a long moment the two German officers looked with sudden interest in the bottom of their glasses.

"Yes," came a voice from behind them, "I am waiting breathlessly for that answer."

"Edward!" Dietrich said, jumping to his feet. "I want you to meet a couple of new friends of mine. Don't let the uniforms fool you, they're professional drunks."

"My kind of people," Wiles said as he found a chair and pulled it to the German's table.

"Bunny Hartung, Freddy Friedel, my friend Edward Wiles," Dietrich said as Wiles shook hands all around.

"English! Pinky, bring gin and bitters for our cousin! Where the hell is that wretch?" Hartung said.

"In point of fact I don't care much for it. Sorry to spoil a sound tradition. I'll have German beer, if you don't mind."

"Of course we do not mind," Friedel said. "Pinky!"

It was several moments before the diminutive waiter navigated his way through the tables to their side, but when he arrived he was carrying a shot glass of gin on a tray as well as what proved to be tonic water.

"My God, you are taking too long. This will never do. Put that on our bill, will you, Pinky?"

"I have already put in on the American's bill, just as you signaled to me," the waiter said to hoots of laughter.

"Lies. Lies," Friedel said, "don't listen to him."

"Another round for everyone. My treat," Wiles said, producing cash from his wallet and laying it on the waiter's tray. "This looks like a serious afternoon."

"Another enlightened foreigner. Where were you hiding when I was working the other side of the bar?" Hartung wanted to know.

"In any case, I'm here now, and I can't wait to hear about the war. When will it come? Try to be exact so that I can report back to my superiors."

"There will never be a war between the Third Reich and England. We are the same people. The Führer says so," Friedel said, slurring his words.

"Is that so?" Wiles asked.

"I think he did say that," Hartung agreed with his friend.

Hartung finished his brandy and waited for the next round of drinks. The Germans were clearly drunk and Dietrich was well on his way. Wiles poured tonic into his gin and proceeded to sip.

"Well, then, I am hugely relieved," Wiles said, taking another sip.

For a long moment Friedel regarded Wiles without smiling.

Then he said "It's a good thing the Führer said that, Englishman, or you would get your ass kicked. You know that, don't you? This isn't your good old days, my friend. Those days are over. Germany is strong again, and we are getting stronger each day."

Dietrich noticed Wiles's nostrils flare slightly but admired the man's continued composure. "Yes, I'm sure that's the case, Friedel, old boy. Always is with Germany, eh?"

"What do you mean?" the bomber pilot said, his lower lip drooping into a sneer. "You doubt my word? The Luftwaffe is second to no force on Earth. We don't need boats anymore, to get to you."

"Yes, Edward," Hartung said, leaning toward their most recent acquaintance, "you English will have to protect your sheep against our bomber pilots. The Luftwaffe falls in love easily and you wouldn't want your flocks to be defiled."

Hartung laughed until tears appeared in his eyes, as did Dietrich. Friedel did not immediately join in the fun, but continued to glare at the Englishman.

"Our sheep will survive," Wiles said, his wide grin a bit forced, Dietrich thought. "And so will we."

"Jesus, I hope I'm not going to spend my last night in Berlin fighting over British sheep...." Dietrich began.

"Last night? You mean you are returning to America so soon? I still have questions to ask. Do Jews own all of the buildings in New

MICHAEL MURRAY

York? Could I find work as an escort to a fat rich American woman? I must know these things so that I can make travel plans," Hartung said.

"How does your Führer get away with his treatment of Jews?" Dietrich said, the naivety of his question was framed by an open, inquisitive face. "Yesterday two of our athletes were prevented from running their one hundred meter relay because they are Jews."

"That's not so," Hartung shrugged.

"But it is so," Dietrich persisted. "It was in all of the newspapers."

"You mean the foreign newspapers," Hartung said.

"Well, yes. Marty Glickman and Sam Stoller trained for the event. They are our fastest sprinters," Dietrich said.

"So? Why did they not run, then? We had nothing to do with it. The Führer certainly did not."

"The papers said...." Dietrich began before being interrupted by the SS officer.

"Don't believe what the foreign press says about Germany. Especially what it says about Adolf Hitler. They spew out propaganda against the Leader. Pay it no mind."

"Propaganda? Why would they do that?" Dietrich wanted to know.

Hartung laughed aloud. "You are not very political, are you, Dietrich?"

"As a matter of fact, I'm not."

"Well, you should live in Europe. You would change. The world envies us. Adolf Hitler has reformed our currencies, revitalized industries, built autobahns...."

"And persecuted Jews," Dietrich insisted.

"Social progress. Jesus, look around you! Berlin is the capital of the world. Energetic! We have progressed. America and Britain are still starving their people. It is true, isn't it, that in America people stand in bread lines? Well, that was long ago for us. National jealousy, my friend," Hartung said.

"I must say, Bunny," Wiles said, "you don't sound much like the way I envisioned an SS officer."

"Trust your original instincts," Hartung said. "It is safer."

"I don't see what's frightening about them," Dietrich said, tiring of the subject.

"We Germans are frightened of nothing. They are sucking our life's blood," Friedel said.

"You mean your money?" Wiles asked.

"Yes. They own the banks. And mercantiles. You must know that, as an educated American," Hartung said, turning to Dietrich.

"That's bullshit," Dietrich snorted.

"It is? Then that settles it," Hartung said, breaking into laughter. He, too, was weary of discussing Jews.

"But even Jews have beautiful daughters," Friedel said, his head lolling, his eyes shifting into and out of focus. They came to rest on Wiles. "You."

"Edward," Wiles reminded the Luftwaffe pilot.

"I know that. Do you think I don't remember? You're not drinking."

"Sorry. I shouldn't want to dash the party, should I?"

"We have been here too long," Hartung said, standing unsteadily. "I know a bistro on Wollenstrasse where we can get the best blintz in the city. Come, we'll all go. I have credit there."

"I'm starving," Dietrich agreed, feeling the relief in his legs as he stretched upward from his chair.

"Very kind of you to include me, but as a matter of fact I'm meeting some friends in Bergstrasse. Can't do both, sorry to say. But you go ahead," Wiles said, gently pushing Dietrich's arm. "I'd ask you to go with me, Stephen, but it isn't my party. And you'll have more fun with Bunny and Freddy, anyway."

Dietrich's reaction was immediate. He knew very well that Wiles was not telling the truth. The two of them had planned to take in the Schinkel Museum and then a play. Dietrich, momentarily confused, walked the retreating Britisher to the sidewalk. They spoke in low tones.

"Edward, don't pay any attention to Friedel. He's just drunk," Dietrich said.

"They do have a nasty side, don't they? But this is as good a time as any to say goodbye, Stephen. I've enjoyed your company enormously." Wiles shook the younger man's hand.

"You're leaving Germany?"

"Yes. I've stayed too long. But you haven't been here long enough. I think you should stay right here. In Germany. You could become one of them."

"That's ridiculous. I'm an American. I can't...."

"You might be doing a much bigger thing for America than returning to college. Think very carefully about it. And if you ever need to contact me, place an advertisement of the personals in the *London Daily News*. Just say that you have a silk hat to sell at a bargain price. Can you remember that?"

"Of course, but really...."

"These highways they talked about. They may serve the people of Germany someday, and if that happens, fine. But what they are really being built to serve is Hitler's Wehrmacht. He'll be moving his panzers and convoys of infantry on these highways. Do you know where they lead? The borders. Arnhem, Dusseldorf, Köln, Wiesbaden in the west. Bremerhaven, Flensburg, Hamburg in the north to the port cities. So he can supply his naval units, his submarines."

"But how...."

"He's rearming, Stephen, and there can be only one result from a well armed nation in the hands of a tyrant. I'm sure you agree when you think about it."

"I don't see how that effects me."

"It will, someday soon. Those fellows like you, Stephen. So you start with an advantage."

Before Dietrich could respond Wiles had stepped into pedestrian traffic and was gone.

BOOK III

13

A rchie had ordered that Hess accompany him aboard his personal aircraft, a customized Ju-52 tri-motor. As the plane began letting down at Tempelhof his fighter escort of thirty ME-109s moved into concentric patterns above the field as the Führer's pilot lined up on the runway. There were three logical destinations that Archie could have chosen after leaving Gebirgs Sicht. One was directly to another hospital in a bigger city, such as Berlin. But Archie had dismissed the idea almost as it came to mind. He could not hide forever behind teams of medical experts. That would be dangerous.

He could have traveled to Hitler's residence, Obersalzburg, where he could have lain up for as long as he pleased. No one would criticize him for recuperating there, and he would be in control of the war from his bedroom. But there were risks as well. He would be in the proximity of servants, cooks, gardeners, perhaps even pets. Hitler had a dog, didn't he? Maybe not. But the very idea of an intimate location frightened him more than the thought of a more impersonal office in Berlin.

Surely the leader of Germany would have living space in the Reich Chancellery just has Roosevelt lived in the White House and Churchill occupied Number Ten Downing. Better to face the music there, if an orchestra of Jew haters and their fanatic followers were to provide the dirge. Hess was apparently fooled, and his presence at the side of the Führer would lend a certain unspoken provenance as Archie moved through Hitler's milieu.

"Rudolf," Archie had told Hess before enplaning, "I find at times I have memory lapses. Since the blow to my head. And the explosions. If I forget a name...."

"Of course, Führer," Hess responded at once.

"My head hurts and I do not want to talk to anyone. Do you understand?" Archie said.

"You may rely on me absolutely," Hess said, nodding his head to indicate his understanding and, implicit, the need for absolute confidentiality. It would not serve the Nazi cause if it became known, even among the inner circle, that the Führer suffered any mental impairment.

Skies were cloudy when the tri-motor taxied to a remote spot on the tarmac, and there began a light, late summer shower as Hitler's armored limousine raced from its waiting position to the side of the aircraft. Trailing cars of SS personnel took up discreet positions near the door of the Junkers where Hitler would deplane out of sight of the public.

Kempka, Hitler's personal chauffeur, opened the rear passenger door for his leader, stood unmoving as the Führer, dressed now in a fresh uniform, placed his feet carefully onto special steps that had been provided.

That his knees were near jelly in the way they shook, Archie knew would be ascribed to reasons other than the fear in his heart that clung to him like an arctic fog. Nor did he feel that he need smile to anyone, nor extend his hand in greeting, given his recent narrow escape with death and, as far as anyone could tell, his continued weakened condition. Archie looked only briefly into the face of his driver and, on impulse, winked at the man. The driver smiled slightly and, just as slightly, nodded curtly.

"Direct to the Reichschancellery, Erich," Hess said, not realizing that he had performed his first small rescue for Archie.

"Welcome home, sir," the man said.

"It's good to be back, Erich," Archie said, falling back into the soft velvet cushion of the Mercedes.

With small swastika pennants jutting from the fenders of the Führer's car, a heavy escort of black uniformed SS troops riding motorcycles front and rear, the now swollen entourage of vehicles quickly accelerated from the Tempelhof complex onto an improved highway, completely unknown to Archie, then north toward the center of the city. Archie had been to Berlin only once in his life, a brief two day visit picking up day money by helping a stage production company moving props and lighting equipment from Britain to the Continent. He had seen Berlin only through the windows of a briskly moving truck and he thought it ironic that he was now seeing it again through a briskly moving vehicle, with rain and fog obscuring his view.

Yet even through the impending darkness of an overcast day Archie could see that Berlin was blessed with many lakes, parks and rivers that seemed to magically appear everywhere he looked.

Even so, he looked anxiously for signs of recognizable landmarks, seeking the reassurance of the familiar. His motorcade passed over a canal which Archie incorrectly assumed was the River Spree that ran through the center of the city. He caught sight of a sign that said Potsdamer Platz as his limousine turned east.

Archie could not help but notice citizens stopping to gawk at what had to be the extraordinary sight of Adolf Hitler's personal car and large armed escort race at high speed through the streets of Germany's capitol. He felt a surge of excitement, a certain lift to his ego, as he returned the looks of admiring Germans watching their leader swept so smartly along, so close to them.

"The Honor Courtyard, Erich," Hess said to the driver.

Archie could see that they were now driving east on Voss Strasse, a huge building on his immediate left. While there were no signs identifying the edifice, Archie knew without being told that this was the Reichschancellery. The mass of sculpted grey concrete reached, Archie thought, between sixty and seventy feet high and ran the entire length of the street, well over one thousand feet. In the middle of the building stood black uniformed guards wearing the coal bucket helmets distinctive to Germany, in front of a very large entrance. High above the oversized doorway was a giant eagle gripping in its talons a swastika, official emblem of the Nazi party, now Germany's national symbol.

Slowing somewhat, Hitler's automobile retinue continued to the end of Voss Strasse then, turning left onto Wilhelmstrasse, turned sharply again into a courtyard at least two hundred feet long and half as much wide. Archie could see through the windscreen that he was at another entrance to the building, this one framed by four huge Doric columns, with two heroic statues of muscular nude men-gods, one clutching a flame, the other a sword, again with swastika affixed.

As Erich Kempka swung the car around, he had hardly braked to a halt when he was out of his seat and opening Archie's door. Wondering if his trembling limbs were visible to others, Archie prayed that he would not collapse, and that he would find the strength to walk forward. His prayer was soon answered as he managed to step from the limousine without tripping. He paused for a moment, trying not to gape, wide eyed, at the massively imposing building. Sensing without looking that Hess had arrived at his side, Archie stepped forward and ascended the steps of the Reichschancellery. Still another giant, stone carved bird of prey, framing the ubiquitous swastika, hovered above the tallest door Archie had ever seen in this in his life. This was the main entrance to the Chancellery. Two SS guards opened the double doors to admit the Führer and his Party Secretary, Hess.

Archie strained to appear not to gape at the walls and ceiling of the vestibule of light red walls and the darker red floor of Saalburg marble. As he entered the Mosaic Hall, more than one hundred fifty feet in length, Archie walked with measured steps, passing along Austrian marble under a ceiling of forty-five feet, gold eagle ornamental frames calling attention from a red background. Above Archie's head was an artificial skylight that shown indirect light to give a natural appearance, an effect that Archie attempted to see without raising his eyes like a member of a sightseeing tour.

From the Mosaic Hall Archie and Hess entered the center part of the building, the Marble Gallery, with high marble framed windows opening directly onto Voss Strasse. The huge, cavernous room, almost 500 feet long, was more than daunting to Archie, it was intimidating, just as the real Adolf Hitler intended it to be. The Führer had envisioned marching subjugated ambassadors and heads of states down the very steps Archie was taking, giving the impression that the Third Reich was dynamic, solid as its rock and marble, and lustrous in its future. Furniture of expensively upholstered chairs set upon opulent carpets with a table at their center were conveniently placed near every office door. Artwork abounded in the form of painted pictures, tapestries, candelabra attached to walls.

The Marble Gallery, a place designed for waiting was busy with government officials tending their business, passing from one office to another, papers and document cases in hand. Archie was acutely aware that he had instantly become the total focus of attention, with all eyes overtly or covertly studying him. Conversations suddenly became hushed. Archie's eyes shifted slightly to Hess's.

Anticipating Archie's unspoken thought, Hess said "The attack is still secret, Führer. No one knows..."

"Nonsense," Archie said, surprising himself with the forcefulness of his own impatience. He simply did not believe that such a secret could be kept even in the controlled environment of the Third Reich. Having said that, Archie was pleased that the event that put their leader in hospital had circulated, all the better to mask any eccentricities he might exhibit.

Archie had no idea where he was going. Would the real Hitler go to his quarters? If so, where were they? Instinctively, Archie paused in the center of the Marble Gallery, opposite the entry doors from Voss Street. He looked to his right at very tall, very ornate, double doors which had a golden eagle, wings extended, with the ubiquitous crooked cross of the Reich in its grip. Two SS guards stood at the door, eyes looking ahead, focused at a very distant place. It was clearly an important portal. But to where? Archie felt that he should enter and, if necessary, ad lib an excuse for going inside. He was, he reminded himself, lord of all he surveyed. Archie turned toward the doors and took only one, rather tentative step toward them when the SS men, anticipating his desire, pulled smartly at the gold plated handles and opened them. Archie stepped inside.

Without any question his instinct was the right one. It could have been nothing but what Archie had hoped it was, Adolf Hitler's office.

Immediately noticed, across the expansive room, were giant double doors, almost twenty feet high, that overlooked the Reichschancellery gardens. The room was, Archie guessed, nearly one hundred feet in length and about half that wide, with a very high ceiling consistent with the construction of virtually every part of the building. The ceiling, which Archie tried not to linger upon, nonetheless arrested his upward gaze with cassettes of palisander wood inlaid with other woods. There were cartouches above each door on the east end, the right side of the room which, Archie assumed, would likely lead to other offices. Secretaries, perhaps, and other staff. There was a fire-place, a long sofa, coffee table and overstuffed chairs at that end of the room. A fourth door, this one behind Hitler's desk, was almost certainly a private entrance for the Führer, and would lead to wherever his living accommodations were.

The entire room was covered with plush carpet and, at Archie's left, the west end, was a massive, hand-made desk, surrounded by three well padded chairs, one of which was a wingback. The room was breathtaking red, set off by the gold gild of the cartouches, wall lamps and the Nazi eagle and swastika above the entrance door. As Archie moved into the center of the room a heavy set man dressed in a blue serge suit appeared from nowhere and helped Archie out of his greatcoat and hat.

"Good afternoon, Führer," the man said.

"Yes, yes, good afternoon," Archie answered back in German.

"Something to eat or drink, sir?" the man said, obviously an aide of some sort, though his name and face meant nothing to Archie.

Archie considered for a moment. He knew that Hitler was a picky eater, a vegetarian, in fact. But what did he drink? No liquor, he was sure. But coffee? Tea?

"Tea," Archie said, turning toward his desk as though anxious to get to work, then he added. "And cookies."

The aide bowed, slightly, then turned toward Hess.

"Tea for me..."

"Don't let me keep you from your duties, Rudolph," Archie said, interrupting. He was afraid of being left alone to fend for himself but he was even more frightened of a prolonged conversation with his long time associate over tea and cookies.

"Ah, yes, of course, Führer. Thank you. If you need anything at all I will be..."

Sweeping into the room through a door as yet still open, a stout man with thinning hair, uniform tailored to fit perfectly and radiate each ribbon and insignia, came to a halt a respectful distance from Archie. Held under his left arm was a leather document folder, more than an inch thick. Clicking his heels with a penetrating snap, raised his arm in the full party salute.

"Heil Hitler," the man said, his lips set tightly upward as though his forced smile was mortised in place. "We are elated with your safe return, my Führer! Welcome."

"Yes," Archie said, returning the man's salute with only a half raised arm, bent at the elbow and extending to the shoulder. "Thank you. It is, ah...good to be back."

"I was just leaving, Bormann," Hess said to the new arrival. "The Führer still needs rest."

"Of course. I have been in constant communication with the Führer's doctors in Gebirgs Sicht. I am fully aware, but thank you for reminding, Herr Hess."

Archie detected a frostiness in Hess's voice, reflected in return by the man Hess called Bormann. Clearly these men did not like each other. At the risk of alienating Bormann, Archie approached Hess and extended his hand. Hess took it with what Archie thought might have been gratitude.

"Thank you, Rudolph," Archie said as Hess bowed at the waist before departing the office. The doors behind him were closed.

Archie, in his readings over the years of Hitler and his mannerisms, struggled to recall the figure of...Martin! Martin Bormann. Bormann's exact rank, or function within the Third Reich was not clear to him. The safe thing to do was to let Bormann execute his duties until he, Archie, could surmise what those duties were.

"I am about to have tea, Martin. You may join me," Archie said, turning his back on the Nazi party man.

"Thank you, Führer. I took the liberty of asking Otto to include another cup for me," Bormann said, following Archie toward his desk.

Archie sank into the large, padded chair behind the huge writing desk, devoid of all signs of clutter, including papers. Archie closed his eyes for a moment and tried to imagine pictures he had seen of Bormann, grasping at images that danced like a kaleidoscope inside his head. In his mind's eye he associated Martin Bormann with snow. Certainly not a holiday setting. Or was it?

"Führer," Bormann said, sensitive to Hitler's eyes drooping shut, "I will put aside all of the other business awaiting your decisions until you are improved, but there is a single item that I must be clear about...."

Bormann allowed his voice to trail off. Why? Was it a simple test? A trap of some kind? Archie was aware that Bormann had not reached such an intimate position so near Hitler without possessing the ability to intrigue.

But Archie was prepared. "My order regarding Operation Sealion," Archie said, with certainty.

"Yes, of course," Bormann said, his eyes diverting to a teak service cart covered with a stark white linen napkin. Otto quietly placed before the men French la Moge teacups before them and poured tea from a gleaming silver tea pot. Cookies were then placed near the Führer and his secretary. Neither Archie nor Bormann bothered to thank Otto as he placed the cookies and withdrew.

"Well? What about it, Bormann? I have reasons for my decision. You must know that," Archie said, examining a cookie.

"Yes, sir. No question, Führer. It is only that your determination has caused massive changes up and down the command structure at OKW. And other commands...."

"The Luftwaffe," Archie said, relishing the actual flavor of the tea as he lifted the cup to his lips.

As Bormann started to open the folder on his lap he stopped, his hand held motionless as he regarded Archie. His eyes narrowed as though to improve his vision.

"Your ring, Führer," he said.

"Yes?" Archie said.

"You are not wearing it," Bormann said, disbelief in his voice. The Führer's party ring was sacred and expected that he would wear it to the grave.

"Did you by any chance hear, Bormann, that my train was attacked by British commandos?" Archie said, bitingly.

"I have heard of nothing else since it happened, Führer," Bormann said, nudged off balance.

"I had taken it off to wash my hands when the British swine blew up the tracks. The ring was beside me when we went over," Archie said, his heart sinking. Then he added, "Have another made for me. And my reading glasses. They were lost, too." Archie was having difficulty reading without corrective lenses. He was far sighted and found himself holding books and now documents at arms length.

"Of course, Führer. Ah, but you must have another pair. Perhaps in your desk?" Bormann's eyebrows rose.

"Yes, they are somewhere, but I want my others replaced as well."

"Yes, sir," the Nazi said, then turned back to his sheaf of papers. "Reichsmarshall Göring telephones ten times a day. I am sure I don't have to tell you that he is difficult to contain. And I think in this case one can understand his need to communicate with you."

In an effort to gain vital seconds to think, Archie placed a second cookie into his mouth and took his time about washing it down with the tea.

"Tell Göring that I shall see him...I shall see him tomorrow at two o'clock. I intend to sleep in. And you may tell the others...."

"Keitel."

"Yes."

"Manstein."

"Yes, yes, Martin. You know who should be here. The fewest number, of course," Archie said, dismissively.

"I think we could keep the number to ten," Bormann said.

"Six. No more than six. And I want their files. I want to look over each man's dossier before the meeting. Including Göring's. See that I get them by eight o'clock tonight. I have something in mind for them all."

"Very well, Führer," Bormann said, making a note in his folder, just the hint of a smile tugging at the corners of his mouth. The inner elite of the Party held many of the old line Prussian generals, especially the ones with vons in front of their surnames, in contempt, and the thought of embarrassing them in any way was pure pleasure for Martin Bormann.

"And now, leave me, Martin. I intend to rest."

Without hesitation Bormann got to his feet, clicked the heels of his rich, hand sewn black leather boots. He lifted his hand, palm outward, in the abbreviated Nazi salute. Archie had turned away from the departing Bormann, pretending to close his eyes until the Nazi had gone.

The main door had hardly clicked closed when Archie was on his feet, nervously glancing through the drawers of Hitler's desk, not in the least knowing what he was looking for. He was like a school child who, left alone in a candy store, was unable to decide which flavor to try first. Then, in the middle drawer, were a pair of spectacles. He tried them on and, to his great relief, seemed to improve his vision. Seeing nothing else that leaped out at him, he turned to the door behind his desk. Pushing it carefully, he put his eye to the opening. Then considering how foolish it might look for Adolf Hitler to be peering sheepishly through his own office door, he swung it back until it was fully opened. Then he stepped through.

Inside the door was a narrow landing with hardened concrete walls on either side. Directly before him was a flight of steel stairs that led to a basement. He followed the stairs down, about fifteen feet in elevation, and was then faced with a concrete passageway that ran east and west. He took a few steps in the direction of west, then reconsidered, turned around, and began walking east. He passed through a doorway and was continuing ahead when two uniformed officers rounded a corner, talking as they walked. When they sighted the Führer they immediately halted, moved to a side of the passageway and snapped to attention. They did not salute nor did they utter a verbal greeting. However, feeling a compulsion to acknowledge their presence, Archie nodded his head and said, "Good day."

The officers each uttered a suitable short response and, after Archie had passed, continued quickly on their way, talking now in soft tones. As with most congested headquarters, the need to salute among all ranks, from the bottom up, was suspended for practical purposes. If saluting were required half of the working day would be taken up with the endless raising and lowering of hands.

Archie arrived at a second door, this one appearing to be blast resistant in its construction. The passageway continued straight ahead or branched left. He was at a loss as to which way to turn. He was about to continue straight ahead when he spotted yet another person approaching him, this time from the left, or northern, passageway. The figure was a woman, quite young, wearing a white dress and an apron. Like the two officers, the woman moved to the side of the passageway and waited for the Führer to pass.

But Archie paused near her. As he approached he could smell the redolence of kitchen food that clung to her clothing. He smiled.

"Young lady," he said, "what is your name?"

"It is Natalie, sir," the young woman said, visibly nervous. She seemed truly pleased at meeting Adolf Hitler and, Archie thought, why not?

"Natalie, I have become lightheaded. I would like you take my arm and walk me to my quarters. You see, I do not want to ask one of my aides. You understand?'

"Oh, yes, indeed. I would be honored," the girl said, accepting his proffered arm. As Archie felt the faintest pressure on his arm toward the northern passageway, he responded with his feet.

"You work in my kitchen, Natalie?" Archie asked, genially.

"No, my Führer, I am assigned to the chancellery kitchen. To your kitchen I have brought a special...." Natalie stopped mid sentence, then glanced guiltily up at Archie.

"A special what?" he asked, curious.

"Your favorite desert. Custard pudding with raisins." Natalie's smile turned at once to a frown, even a bit fearful. "I think it was to be a surprise."

"And did you make the desert?" Archie said, pleased.

"Yes. I hope you like it."

"I know I will like it," Archie lied. He hated raisins in anything but under the circumstances he would savor them. "And I will pretend to be surprised."

He had said exactly the right thing. Natalie glowed as they walked along the passageway and turned into another stairwell and descended to the third level. Foot traffic became more frequent here, though certainly not busy. Housekeeping personnel saw him but their contact with the Führer was not so unusual so that they went about their chores with nothing more than polite smiles while averting their eyes.

The walls of the bunker were made of reinforced concrete, well lit and decorated with pleasing works of art, many of which were seascapes and landscapes to give the psychological feeling of open space. After several steps following the last flight of stairs Natalie hesitated.

"I am not sure of your suite, Herr Hitler. Could you tell me, please?" she said.

Archie's heart fluttered in mid-beat, a sudden coldness in the pit of his stomach. He let his breath out slowly, gathering himself.

"I am feeling much better, now, Natalie. You run along. Thank you."

Natalie actually curtsied as Archie turned from her.

In fact, as he now considered his surroundings, there was, for all practical purposes, only one way to go, and that was through a doorway which was grander than the others and above which was a small cartouche of an eagle and the Nazi swastika above it. He opened the door. Before him was a wide hallway with four doors on the left, one on the right. As began to walk he passed by the first door and continued to the end of the hall. Opening the door in front of him he discovered yet another flight of stairs, these going up. He closed that door and looked to his left. After a moment's hesitation, he opened that door, the next to last. It was a spacious office, or meeting room. On the other side of the office a door was open and Archie could see that it was a bedroom. As he crossed the office, his boots silent as a thick carpet muffled his footfalls, a stout woman wearing a housekeeping dress was emerging from within. Putting her mouth to her lips to stifle a shriek, eyes wide open, she quickly regained her composure when she recognized the figure before her.

She curtsied. "Oh, sir, I am so sorry!"

"No need," Archie said, enormously relieved just as the housekeeper was, but for very different reasons. He offered the woman an avuncular smile of reassurance. "I intend to rest. Is my bed ready?"

"Yes, indeed, sir. I have just finished with today's dusting."

The cleaning woman stood aside as Archie stepped inside. She smiled nervously once more then, hurrying out, closed the door behind her.

His suite was Spartan compared with the opulence upstairs, but Archie supposed that the basement of the Reichschancellery was built like a secure vault or, because there was a war in progress, a bomb shelter. His sleeping quarters, less than half the size of either the living room or office, contained a few pieces of art work to satisfy even the most discerning sleeper, with a connected living room that was spacious with two large sofas, area carpets, and a number of comfortable chairs. A profile photograph of Eva Braun in a gold frame resided upon a table upon which also supported an antique vase full of fresh flowers.

There was, in addition to the large office, or work room through which Archie had entered, still another meeting room. It was smaller, but with a conference table in its center surrounding by leather covered chairs. He had no intention of sleeping, of course. He was far too tense, too fearful and, he had to admit, at a loss of what to do next in his role of Adolf Hitler.

He eased himself into a chair and put his head back as he tried to think. He felt like a prisoner. Strangely, he missed the comfort of Laverne. God knows they saw each other only occasionally over the years, and even then there was no particular warmth shared in their condition of none too genteel poverty. Still, he clung to the solace of what might have been.

Clearly, whatever urged him to stay behind as the commandos left Germany, was impulsive and not thought through. He had titular control of the German armed forces but did not have the vaguest notion of how to command those forces in a military conflict. He did not even know of what the forces were comprised. He knew that there were such things as army, navy and air forces. And tomorrow he would be faced by military experts of high rank, as well as members of the Nazi party apparatus. He had to tell them something! But what?

Archie once more felt icy fingers reaching into the bowels of his being as fear momentarily paralyzed him. He tried to close his eyes, desperate to relax so that his mind could function, but it was impossible. As he forced them shut, they would immediately come open, wide awake, leaving him with the corrosive fatigue of gnawing fear.

Was the real Adolf Hitler ever afraid? Why should he be? He was one of the most powerful men on the planet. He had armed guards, even whole armies, assigned to do nothing but keep him comfortable and alive. So why would he ever be afraid as Archie was now?

What Archie feared, of course, was innocent betrayal, a failure to recognize someone or some thing that the real Hitler should have known. But how to overcome such an obstacle?

Gradually, an image began taking shape. It had worked with Hess. And with Martin Bormann. He would know something about critical staff officers because Bormann would provide such documents before the meeting tomorrow. Why would not the same technique work on others near him?

He began to rummage through Hitler's desk. Almost immediately he found a list of numbers in a top drawer under to the telephone. There were several, as expected. Among them were Erich Kempka, his chauffeur, Julius Schaub, after which was the notation *helfer,* or aide. There was Bormann, of course. Under the listing for Reichschancellery Security included, as Commander RSD, Standartenführer Robert Hebert and below that was Obersturmbannführer Jon Vass, possibly Hebert's deputy. There were other names whom he did not recognize, but in front of the two colonels were the now familiar lightning runes of the SS.

Licking his dry lips, Archie picked up the telephone and dialed the extension number for Hebert. There was a click after the second ring and a voice at the other end of the line identified itself as Standartenführer Hebert. It was pronounced with a silent H and the e like an a, the way the French would say it.

"This is Adolf Hitler," Archie said, his voice full of the dictator's timbre, more from fear than anything else, but seemed to Archie to convey the real Hitler's sound. "Come to my quarters here, in the bunker. And come alone."

"Jawohl, sir. At once," the SS man snapped into the telephone.

Archie would later learn that SS-Standartenführer Hebert's quarters were within the Reichschancellery complex and that underground barracks for the elite SS guard were but a few dozen meters from there. It seemed to Archie that he had hardly unbuttoned his tunic and sat behind his desk when there was a single rap on the door.

"Come," he said.

A black uniformed SS officer stepped inside the door and closed it behind him. The SS man clicked his heels smartly together and stood at attention. "SS-Standartenführer Hebert, sir," he said, simply.

"Yes. Ah, sit down, Standartenführer," Archie said, waving a hand toward one of the chairs nearby.

The SS officer, Archie noted, was tall, at least two inches over six feet, and carried himself erect with shoulders back. He was in his early to mid-30's and appeared to be in excellent physical condition, a safe assumption regarding all members of the fanatic SS. Hebert had rather small eyes and a narrow face, his lips were thin and well compressed. He was, Archie thought, the perfect specimen upon which to hang a uniform.

"Now, then, Standartenführer, what is your duty assignment?" Archie said.

The SS officer was, if only for a moment, surprised. "Sir? It is to provide your protection. That includes my detachment, of course."

"That is correct. Exactly correct," Archie said, rising from his desk to begin to pacing the room.

"Listen carefully, Standartenführer," Archie began, using a low, conspiratorial tone of voice, "what I am about to tell you must remain an absolute secret, only to be discussed between you and me. It is never to be revealed to anyone. Never! Do you understand?"

"Yes, my Führer," the SS officer said, sitting even straighter in his chair, his black uniform with silver collar trim framing his intense face. In Archie's mind, Hebert was the very essence of the Teutonic soldier.

"Very well. Do you know what happened to me ten days ago in southern Germany?"

Without hesitation Hebert nodded his head. "Yes, sir. Your train was attacked by British commandos. I have been fully briefed, so far as we can reconstruct, sir." Standartenführer Hebert kept his responses brief, very much aware that it was Hitler's place to talk, and his to listen.

"God has spared my life, Hebert, so that Germany will be led by the only man in the world capable of uniting its people in common cause. It was a miracle that I was not murdered. A miracle."

"Yes, sir. We are all relieved to...."

"Germans would be dancing in the streets if they but only knew how close to death their Führer had come. No question."

Hebert remained silent as Archie completed a circuit of the room. Archie then leaned forward, looked directly into the Standartenführer's eyes.

"I was betrayed," Archie said, simply.

Hebert leaned forward in his chair, eyes narrowing. "Betrayed?"

"Yes, of course. At the highest level. I have suspected for some time that I have a traitor in my midst. How else do you think the British knew the precise movement of my train?" Archie said, completely ignorant of the answer to the question he posed. "I know nothing about him, only that he is very close to me. I will not divulge to you my source of this information, but I assure you, Standartenführer Hebert, that the spy is very real. It is possible that he is no one less than a British agent. Do you understand so far?"

Hebert was rigid with anticipation. "A British agent! In a German uniform?"

"Is it so hard to believe? There are many ways it might have been done. What I can tell you for certain is that it was this same traitor who planned to assassinate me. So, are you quite clear on that, Standartenführer?"

"Absolutely, my Führer. The swine will be caught, I promise you," Hebert said.

"I am relyingon you to do exactly that. But there is to be no alarm given. You and I will be vigilant and, in due course, we will know everything. Also, Hebert, it may be more than one person. The British are noted for their spy systems, are they not? And betrayal is like a virus, it can find a host then spread its infection to others. As a security man, Standartenführer, you know this to be true."

"Yes, of course, Führer. Er, if I may..."

"Of course. What is it, Hebert?"

"We in the SS have known for some time that certain members of the General Staff, and certain of their subordinates, have been critical of the Party from its very beginning...."

"Exactly!" Archie pounded his fist on his desk. "This is a time in the history of Germany where we must be strong. We must have wills of iron. Always vigilant. Now, Standartenführer, I will want you to carry out certain, shall we say, confidential tasks."

"You have only to order, sir," Hebert said, evenly.

"Good. The first thing I want are dossiers on all of those persons with which I come in daily contact. Every individual, no matter how trusted. If they are on my household staff, high party officials, even my personal valet, and I want each dossier with picture attached. Understand?"

"Perfectly."

"Do not initiate any investigations unless I say so. Just a brief description of the person and his or her assignment, and the picture," Archie said. He did not want to become overwhelmed reading long, unproductive documents. "A single page will suffice. And I want you to bring me a filing cabinet for this room. With a lock on it. These files are to be kept away from my secretaries."

"Yes, my Führer," the SS-Standartenführer responded.

"You may deliver the first documents tonight. Surely you must have a number of previous security investigations in your possession. Am I correct?"

"That is so, Führer. Our files are quite extensive," Hebert confirmed.

"Good. Put what you can into a case and bring it to me here. We will use the same document case to pass other papers as they come into your hands. And one other thing, Hebert," Archie said, his voice conveying a personal association. "I want Fraulein Braun kept away from me until I tell you otherwise. Where is she now?"

The SS Standartenführer's eyebrows arched slightly, but only slightly. "She is presently at Obersalzberg, sir. In her apartment, I believe."

"See that she stays there. I shall remain here for some time. That is all, Hebert," Archie said, nodding curtly.

The SS officer stood to his feet, clicked his heels smartly as he nodded his head and, despite the informality of his surroundings, gave the Nazi salute with arm fully extended. "Heil Hitler," he said.

Archie lifted his own arm, but only from the bent elbow position, palm upward.

Gruppencommodore Major Stephen Dietrich had led elements of Jagdgeschwader 3 on their third sweep of the day. JG3 had scored well against RAF fighters sent up to intercept Luftwaffe bombers hitting targets in the south of England. The wily British had the advantage of waiting until German bombers were well over the Channel before scrambling their Spitfires and Hurricanes, thus giving Dietrich and his fighter group precious little fuel with which to engage the enemy. It was Dietrich who devised a delayed rendezvous strategy where his staffelns could meet the bombers after delaying their own takeoffs from bases on the French coast. Using this technique, they increased their own time over targets by some ten to twelve minutes. In addition to being a highly respected and tenacious fighter pilot, Dietrich was also valued as an outstanding tactician of aerial combat.

His well known American heritage, far from causing suspicion, was celebrated across the Luftwaffe and he was proudly conferred the nickname of Yank among his German peers.

He had chased a lead Hurricane from its attack formation at 28,000 feet and began turning and rolling with it in frantic maneuvers that took both aircraft down to the deck. Dietrich had the slower, less agile

British fighter in his gun sights more than once but did not fire. He not only admired the skill of the RAF pilot but on this date in late August Dietrich had far more urgent business to attend to. It was late in the day and the last rays of the sun were settling over the coast of Britain when Dietrich allowed the Hurricane to slip away to the northeast and, presumably, the safety of his own field. Dietrich did not himself turn 180 in the direction of Bergues, France, where he was stationed, but dropped onto the deck and, a scarce ten feet from the top of the cold whitecaps, flew at full throttle on a predetermined course for England.

Within a few short minutes he gently pulled back on the stick of his ME-109 and, almost clipping leaves from trees as he flashed over British countryside, began to look for a secret airfield near Northiam. Dietrich peered hard through his clear plastic windscreen for the landing markers that he had to locate within a few minutes lest his fuel force him down onto a plowed field, wrecking his aircraft in the event. He pushed his flying goggles back onto his leather helmet and, circling low, at last located the critical landmark, a farm silo with three bands of white, vertically painted stripes on its north side. Not daring to break radio silence, Dietrich changed his propeller pitch and gunned the Messerschmitt's engine three times. As if by magic a large haystack became illuminated at its top and runway lights winked on and off at either end of an unimproved strip, then remained on. Dietrich lined up his fighter for a final approach knowing that the lights would be lit for less than a minute. His first attempt would have to be perfect.

He reduced engine power, then threw the switches that would lower his hydraulic landing gear and flaps. Immediately the high performance fighter began to sink. Dietrich calmly added more power as he simultaneously pulled back on the stick, raising the aircraft's nose and "hanging" it on its prop in the execution of a short field landing. As he flared the fighter he could almost at once feel its three wheels touch ground and he began gently braking the plane. After a short roll out, Dietrich kicked hard left rudder, spinning his machine around on the runway. He taxied to a covered location which supported camouflage netting, impossible to spot from the air.

He cut the fuel supply to the twelve cylinder Daimler-Benz engine and was climbing out of the cockpit before the propeller had stopped turning. He was quite aware, as he stepped onto the wing root, that his legs ached from cramps and his body was sore from the strain of pulling continuous Gs during a long day of combat flying. But he had much to accomplish before he could find his way back to the comfort of the officer's mess in Bergues. And a couple of smooth cognacs.

His feet had hardly touched British soil when a fuel bower pulled up next to his aircraft and two RAF mechanics opened the fuel caps of his machine.

"Not too much. I don't want to arrive back from a sortie with full tanks," he cautioned the refuellers.

"And how much, sir?" one of the ground men asked.

"About two hundred litres should do it," he said, removing his flying gloves.

"Have a cuppa."

Dietrich turned toward the voice of Edward Wiles, who stood holding a thermos bottle and a large mug in one hand. Wiles extended his free hand to Dietrich.

"Hello, my friend," he said.

Dietrich squeezed the man's hand with force. "I hope to hell this is important, Eddie," Dietrich said, mangling Wiles' given name, continuing a tease that was now four years old. "First things first. Have your men fire a few holes into my ship. Make damn sure they don't hit anything vital. Put a couple through the engine section but take the fasteners out, first, and open the cowl."

"Right. You can supervise the job," Wiles said. Wiles noted, with satisfaction, the growth of maturity in Stephen Dietrich the German commanding squadron leader from the callow college youth of only four years ago. The young Dietrich, awed and wonderfully stimulated by the huge wide world before him, was playfully indecisive, often uncaring of the planet on which he frolicked. Now, hard of eye, his deft intellect straddling the complex intelligence work of two warring nations, Wiles could only admire the American's ability to remain focused.

Dietrich still wore his Luftwaffe uniform, a blue one piece cotton flying suit lined with synthetic fur, black leather jacket with gold epaulets, an embossed metal eagle over the right zippered pocket, a wide leather belt around his waist that supported a holster for a 9mm pistol and a compass. In his hand Dietrich held an inflatable life vest that he had removed for comfort while on the ground. He could not help but wonder what must have been going on in the minds of the British ground personnel who were obliged to service a Nazi fighter aircraft and take orders from its pilot.

The ground crew were hand picked personnel, as were the entire complement of the two dozen men who operated the tiny, ultra secret airstrip for SOE. Their discretion could be absolutely counted on and their skill levels at the top of their fields. It took only a few minutes for the bullet holes to be fired at angles into the ME-109 to make it appear that a following aircraft had done the damage.

"You," Dietrich said to one of the mechanics, "cut this oil line. Then bind it up with tape. It needs to last for the flight back."

One more bullet was fired, this one cutting the chosen oil line. There were two ways Dietrich could return late to his Jagdgeschwader without arousing suspicion. One was by bailing out anywhere over France, allowing himself to be picked up by the occupying army. Or he could damage his airplane, then later claim that he had landed in a grass field, repaired the machine himself, then continued back to Bergues. There were risks in either case. Contrary to what some people might believe, bailing out of a fighter aircraft was inherently dangerous with a good chance of being killed or badly injured as part of the exercise. Dietrich had been forced to leave his plane when a Spitfire had shredded his vertical stabilizer and he had lost control over Calais. He had barely two thousand feet of altitude when he managed to free himself from his safety harness and drop out of the very tight cockpit. It was not an experience he cared to repeat again unless there was no other choice. So he would carry through with the more elaborate scheme of choice number two.

Dietrich turned back to Wiles. "I don't know that I can do this again."

"I can't express to you the gratitude of the Crown, Steven. The Prime Minister himself asked me to tell you that."

"Is that so? How is Winnie?" Dietrich said, drinking deeply of the tea which was only lukewarm. But it tasted wonderful.

"He is not sleeping well. Your bombers keep him awake."

"Ah, well, then, we'll just have to ask Göring to stop it all," Dietrich said, leaning tiredly against a fender of the fuel truck. "It must be a hell of a strain on him."

"As a matter of fact, it is," Wiles said.

"I'm sorry, Eddie. It is a crummy war. Sometimes..." Dietrich's voice trailed off.

"Sometimes what? Hard to remember which side you're on?" Wiles said.

Dietrich smiled. "I fly with men, not animals, Eddie. They are courageous. They're good fun to be around. They like girls, just like you and me. Well, maybe not like you. Anyway, it isn't pleasant to see them die."

"No, I'm sure you're right. I sit at a desk while you do the fighting and dying," Wiles said.

Dietrich knew that if Wiles could have it the other way around, he would leap at the chance.

"What happened with your people in Pilz? I went to a hell of a lot of trouble to get you that information," Dietrich said with a trace of disgust in his voice.

"It worked out very nicely, Steven. Better than we had hoped."

"It did, huh? Well, we flew air cover around some little town down there where Hitler was recovering. So you wrecked a train and killed some troops, but this war is still going on," Dietrich spat. His life was always at stake, not just flying fighter aircraft in battles over Britain's skies, but in gaining vital intelligence from under the noses of the Gestapo and paranoid Nazi party members and transmitting the stuff back to London. Having a hash made of his work was doubly disheartening.

"That's why you're here, Steven. He didn't recover."

I t took Dietrich most of an entire day to locate the whereabouts of Hauptman Frederich Friedel at his current station of Foucarmont, forty kilometers from the French coast. Like many forward bomber bases, Lufflotte II, KG 4 flew from grass runways. As Dietrich made his base leg turn onto final approach he knew that the Luftwaffe High Command assumed their Channel bases would become unnecessary by the time fall weather made unpaved fields unuseable. The battle for air supremacy would be all over by then with Germany the obvious winner. Reichsmarshall Göring had personally promised as much to the Führer.

After parking his Me-109 in the place directed by ground crews, Dietrich removed his parachute, as well as his helmet and life vest and dropped them onto the seat of the plane. He declined the offer of motorized transportation to flight operations in favor of walking the short distance from the maintenance area to administration. He asked one of the duty sergeants the whereabouts of Captain Frederich Friedel and was told that KG 4 was on operations but should return from their mission within fifty minutes. Dietrich knew that precise forecast meant that Friedel's He-111 would have exhausted its fuel supply by then. It would either be back on schedule or it would likely never return. Dietrich left word for Friedel that he would be at the officer's mess.

He had not seen his boisterous friend for six months, their duty assignments being the cause. So Dietrich was anxiously looking forward to the reunion, brief though it would have to be. He felt guilty that his real objective was to find and speak with Bunny Hartung as soon as possible, but the situation presented to him the night before was urgent in the extreme.

It was warmer inside the mess than outside and Dietrich, removing his leather flying jacket, was pleased with his decision not to wear a flying suit over his uniform for the short hop from Bergues. There had been no need to climb to altitude. There was less than a half-dozen officers eating or drinking in the mess, none of them giving Dietrich more than a cursory glance as he sat alone at a table. The place would fill up, he knew, when Friedel's unit returned from its mission. He recalled that he had missed lunch, his orderly allowing him to sleep late the first morning of his leave. He ordered a roast lamb sandwich and a cup of coffee. A slaw that came with it was surprisingly tasty. Dietrich was developing a taste for cabbage in its many forms uniquely prepared by German cooks.

He finished his third cup of coffee and was not looking forward to another, his mind reeling with possibilities presented by yesterday evening's extraordinary revelation by Edward Wiles. He tried to imagine what he might do if he were in the boots of this man, Archie, who now occupied the Reichschancellery and controlled the mightiest system of armed forces on the face of the Earth. Well, he wouldn't simply issue an order to stop the war, would he? Edward was quite right that it couldn't be done that way. Hitler, Archie, would have to nibble at the problem, at least in the beginning. He had already succeeded, according to Edward, in causing the German army to remain on this side of the Channel. Or so they thought. Dietrich, personally, was skeptical about the claim. His unit was still battling desperately for air superiority in the skies over England, an absolute must before an invasion could be mounted. So if Archie had succeeded as Wiles claimed, why was the air battle still raging? Wiles had said that Archie almost certainly did not know what to do.

The actor's real identity might well have been discovered by the time Dietrich was able to get to him, if indeed it was possible. Archie was not, after all, a military man, and had no idea how desperately the British military was being threatened by the continuous pounding of RAF air bases. And with the heavy losses being inflicted upon Fighter Command. Unsustainable, Wiles had said. Dietrich experienced a strange feeling of elation to hear the highly placed British master spy make such an admission. Dietrich's ostensible business as a Luftwaffe pilot was, after all, to shoot down British aircraft. And he was succeeding! But Dietrich was, on the other hand, in opposition to the continued success of the Third Reich, and his exhilaration was short lived.

He had no direct access to overall Luftwaffe losses other than his own unit. According to the Ministry of Propaganda German planes and aircrew lost in battle were very light, certainly far more favorable than that of their opponent, the RAF. Dr. Goebbels predicted a very short war, indeed, and from Dietrich's limited perspective the chief of the Nazi's information agencies might be correct. England was all alone, that was for sure, and Germany was more than a match for Britain's armed forces in almost every respect, save naval units.

Dietrich was gazing into the bottom of his empty coffee cup when Friedel lumbered through the door, his helmet, goggles and life vest still carried in one hand. He hung these impediments on a wall hook at the same moment he spotted Dietrich seated across the room.

"Good God!," he hollered for all to hear, "Look who is taking a day off from the French whorehouses."

Heads turned to see the object of Friedel's accusation as Dietrich got to his feet to put his arms around the larger pilot. Still in a bear hug, Friedel was not yet done baiting his friend.

"No! Please, no! He is a major, now. Every man in his squadron must have been shot down. We are losing the war," Friedel said, throwing his head back, leading gales of laughter at Dietrich's good natured expense.

"Guten tag, you drunk," he said.

"Sit down, Yank, and I'll buy you a man's drink. Vegan," he called to the locally born bartender, "two brandies here. You remember Pinky, Stephen? At Das Wasserhahn in Berlin? He is a corporal in the Wehrmacht and you will never guess what his job is, eh? He runs the officer's mess at Neubiberg."

"At last the army finds a fully qualified man for the job," Dietrich said. "I can't drink with you. I still have to fly."

Dietrich was struck by the dark circles under Friedel's blue eyes, the cheekbones made more prominent from loss of weight and, no doubt, sleep. Dietrich noticed Friedel's left hand, kept rather low and out of sight, had been burned and two fingers had become shriveled stubs, not yet fully healed. They must have caused him great pain.

Friedel followed Dietrich's gaze. "I never played with my weenie with that hand, anyway. So I am lucky. There must be a god. Prosit!" he said, raising his glass.

"I'm sorry about your hand, Frederich, but as long as you can wipe your ass you can still stuff your face with schnitzel. How have you been, otherwise?"

"How do you suppose a handsome Luftwaffe pilot can be? I am a part of the greatest force in the history of the world. We are just finishing off the pesky little Limeys and then soon I will be fucking their sisters right in Piccadilly. How could I not be wonderful?"

"I couldn't be happier for you, then," Dietrich said, watching while Friedel gulped down his brandy.

"Vegan, bring two more," Friedel said.

"No, really, I can't, Freddy." Dietrich demurred.

"Bring two anyway, Vegan, one for my other hand," Friedel laughed. Friedel appraised his American friend with studied interest. "By god, the war suits you, Stephen. You are not a little boy, anymore."

"I might have grown up even without the war," Dietrich said.

"You must be what, a gruppe leader?" the bomber pilot said. "Congratulations. You deserve it more than most. I'll never live to see it for myself'"

"Don't be silly. It will all be over, soon," Dietrich said, rhetorically.

"Yes? Then I am greatly relieved. The way we are losing men and machines I would have thought the factories could not keep up."

More than one head turned toward Friedel's voice. Friedel leaned forward toward Dietrich. "In three days this month we lost one hundred ten of our planes. Think of it, Stephen. Three days."

Dietrich knew exactly what Friedel was talking about. Those black days were only last week and the fighter command had lost thirty five. It was not reported to the public, of course, but the word among pilots and ground crew went around the squadrons like a gasoline fire.

"Still," Dietrich said, "the RAF is losing."

Friedel's voice dropped even lower, to a near whisper. "You don't believe that, Yank."

Dietrich shrugged. "We have more planes than they. You don't need a slide rule to figure it out."

But Friedel was right. Germany was losing its best pilots to the RAF Fighter Command because of stupid planning at the top. JG-52 had lost all three of its squadron commanders escorting the cumbersome Ju-87 dive bombers on raids over England, sacrificing the superior speed and altitude advantage of their Messerschmitts to stay with the dive bombers. They were easy pickings for the Brits who waited for them at 30,000 feet. Still, the British could not afford to trade aircraft with Germany because she would lose.

"Are you still flying the He-111?" Dietrich asked.

"Yes. A little too slow and too little bomb load to do much damage. We did a very nice job in Spain, you know," Friedel sighed. "Nobody shot back at us. But against fighters that are 150 kph faster.... " Friedel merely shook his head as he finished his third glass of brandy.

"You're after shipping?" Dietrich said, aware that Freddy had hunted British merchant shipping the last time they had met.

"Airfields. And shipping, too, but mostly airfields, for whatever good it does," Friedel scoffed. "They simply repair them again."

"So," Dietrich said, getting to the point of his visit, "I have a few days off. I wanted to find Bunny. Do you know where he is?"

"Of course. He is fucking his way through the entire city of Paris. Where do you suppose he would be? He has been here to see me twice, already."

"How is he?" Dietrich wanted to know.

"He is no longer an aide to that filthy wretch, Beckman. Did you know that he is now a hero of the Reich? Not Beckman, that asshole. Bunny. It's true! He commanded a Panzergruppe against a French strongpoint in the Ardennes and knocked it out from the rear. He wins an Iron Cross Third Class, the stupid fucker."

Dietrich could clearly see the pride in Friedel's eyes for his childhood friend. "And this was the man who joined the SS to stay out of the war," Dietrich said.

"And like you, he is promoted. He is now SS-SturmbannFührer Hartung."

"Well, then he will survive. There is nothing left to fight over. Hitler will be satisfied with what he already has. France is no small prize, you know," Dietrich said, believing that the two belligerents, Britain and Germany, would somehow come to terms.

"You think so, Yank? Good, then I will have a drink on it. Vegan! Bring me a bottle so you don't have to run your legs off."

It was quite dark when Dietrich left his Me-109 under the vigilant eyes of German sentries who guarded all of Le Bourget airport in Paris. He was able to arrange transportation from the motor pool that took him to the west bank. Knowing that he was not far from the street he needed to find, Dietrich dismissed the car and driver in favor of walking the old streets of the city. The city was in a stateof quasi-blackout in recognition that there was a war going on, but no bomb had been dropped on Paris from either of the warring parties, so there was enough illumination to make navigation easy.

Like any other tourist following a city street map, he craned his neck as he walked along the Quai De Celestins, taking in the facade of Notre Dame. Unable to spend the time to look inside, he turned left on Henri IV to Avenue Saint Antoine. Rather than taking a slightly longer way around the Place Des Vosges, Dietrich walked through the narrow Rue De Birague. The square of apartments by which he strode included one which was lived in by Victor Hugo, but Dietrich had no time to appreciate the historical significance of that fact. He emerged at the literal doorstep of the address Friedel had scribbled on the back of an envelope: Pavillon De La Reine, 28 Place des Vosges. De La Reine was a building six hundred years old, now a hotel, and now the residence of SS officers of the 1st SS-Panzer Division, Leib-standarte Adolf Hitler.

As he stood before the gates of the hotel on Rue Des Francs Bour-geois, he became aware of civilian pedestrians watching him. The Parisianers, when he looked their way, some who quickly averted their eyes but not before Dietrich recognized hatred in their glares. He tried to rationalize how he would feel if he were French and his country had been overrun by an invading army, especially a German one. Their enmity was not hard to understand.

He was saluted by the SS guard at the entrance to the hotel's courtyard. At the end of the stone walk the door to the lobby was opened for him by a white uniformed attendee whose sight was fixed on a place in space. Dietrich stopped briefly at the desk to enquire the room number for SS-Hauptsturmfuhrer Hartung. The clerk showed only the slightest hesitation before obliging Dietrich with the second floor number but also adding that the Hauptsturmfuhrer Führer was "entertaining" at the present time. Would the major like to be announced?

Please.

Sounds of loud music, male and female laughter reverberated throughout the hotel despite the thickness of the old stone walls. Hartung's room, as he opened the door, appeared to Dietrich to be incredibly small, and the lady of Bunny's choosing, although in bed, seemed to be practically in Dietrich's lap. Bunny did not want to release Dietrich from his clutch, insisting on tossing him to and fro until he let go the Luftwaffe pilot with a fling onto the bed.

"Meet Doniele," Bunny said, referring to the giggling French lady who, without a stitch of clothing that Dietrich could discern, occupied the middle of the bed.

"Well?" Doniele said to Dietrich in French. "Is that all that you are going to do, sit there and twist your fingers?"

Dietrich's French was awkward at best but there was no question that he was being invited into, rather than onto, the only bed in the room.

"You are too kind, miss, but my mother would not understand," he responded to gales of laughter from both Doniele and Bunny.

"God," Bunny said, reaching for a full bottle of wine, two others nearby quite empty. He poured two glasses to their brims. "How long has it been? Let's see, were we at peace or war? Friedel called to say you were on your way. Another girl is coming. What is her name, Doniele? No matter, Dietrich is a rich American. She will love him. We all love him. I got you a room in this hotel, Stephen. It was full, you know, but I had a full colonel kicked out on his ass. A quartermaster officer. He keeps the units supplied with rubbers here in Paris." Hartung paused long enough to swallow half the contents of his glass. "Drink, Stephen. I will order another bottle."

The wine was superb and Dietrich had no more flying to do that night. Dietrich broke off a piece of rye bread and dipped it into the red wine. Delicious, he thought. And it was just as well that Bunny was well into the grape.

"Do you and Friedel have the same mother? You're alcoholics. He probably takes his cognac on missions in his Heinkel," Dietrich said pretending disgust.

"Remember that we were drinking when we met in Berlin. It just tastes better, now. I think wars are good for liquors. It elevates even the worst to a much higher level. What a relief to discover French wine."

"Your glass is empty," Dietrich said. "Doniele, would you be wonderful and get us another bottle? No, make it two more bottles,"

"I can have it brought up," Hartung started to protest, then caught Dietrich's imploring eye. "But," he said, turning to the girl, "maybe it would be faster?"

Doniele pretended to pout, but her sense of humor remained high as she slipped into a dress and, without hose, high heeled shoes. Hartung admired her with lecherous eyes. He stepped to the door with her. "Take your time. This lion of the skies and I need to talk privately. I'll call you."

After the door to his room closed Hartung put his glass aside, not bothering to take the last swallow. "All right," he said, dropping onto the bed wearing only his shorts, stockings and a silk robe that was at least two sizes too small. His fine, blonde hair hung loosely over his ears, conflicting with the firmly enforced regulations of the Schutzstaffel. "What is it you have to say that you cannot say in front of my precious little French whore? Actually, she loves me. She says she will continue to work while I am off fighting the war. Now, is that love or is it not?"

"Bunny, I need a favor," Dietrich said.

"Name it, *mon ami.*"

"I need to meet Adolf Hitler," he said.

"Adolf Hitler?"

"Yes. The SS guards him. Everybody knows that. I hope that you can arrange it," Dietrich said.

"This is a joke, isn't it?" Hartung said but without laughing. "Ask me to do something else. As a matter of fact, I am willing to give up Doniele for as long as you are in Paris. Will that do?"

"I'm serious, Bunny. Can you do it?"

Hartung shook his head as though to clear it. If mere words could sober a soldier, invoking the Führer's name would accomplish the trick. It was true that the SS was a close fraternity and it was more than possible that Bunny might know someone assigned to the Reichschancellery. Or knew someone who knew someone.

"Stephen," Hartung said, "I am not willingly into your business. I like you. You're a little queer, and maybe that's why I like you. But you have to tell me some reason why I should even try. Do you understand? Consider how many people want the Führer's time. Heads of states. Gauleiters, generals. I need a very persuasive reason to even try. And I am sure I cannot do it even then."

Dietrich knew the question would be asked. The only answer he had, however, was itself an act of desperation. He wanted to open his mouth to say the words but he hesitated, knowing that the next step would place him in a position where there would be no retreat. He may very well be the instrument of his own death.

"So?" Hartung asked, not really eager to hear his friend's response.

"I know who supplied the British with the information about the Führer's train from Munich," Dietrich said, evenly.

For a long moment Hartung remained expressionless. He had known one of the officers aboard the train as well as one of the other ranks.

"Stephen, do you know what you are saying? Do you have any idea what could happen to you if you said this to anyone but me?" Hartung said, his voice lowering.

"Yes."

"What you are saying is true?"

"Yes. It is absolutely true. But I will inform no one but the Führer himself. That is my requirement for revealing the spy," Dietrich said, feeling his mouth go dry at the sound of his own voice.

"God damn it, Dietrich, you stupid son of a bitch!" Hartung said, his anger flashing as he got to his feet. "Think of where this puts me! I don't want to be involved but I am. Unlike you, I'm not crazy. I can't withhold information or blab it out loud just as I please. And neither can you, except you're too stupid to realize it."

"I'm sorry to involve you, Bunny. There isn't any other way. If there was, I would have done it. I promise you."

Hartung's anger passed as fast as it arrived. He put his arms around

Dietrich. "This is not America, my friend," he whispered into Dietrich's ear. "The closer you get to the power in Berlin, the less your life is worth. In trying to save Hitler's life, you might lose your own."

and recall even small items after reading material only once. He now knew, through the ever malevolent Martin Bormann, that General Blomberg's wife had once posed for pornographic pictures. While Archie might have enjoyed viewing them, he felt that the sexually puritanical Hitler would have violently disapproved. The malignant Bormann spoke forcefully against Blomberg's return to duty despite strong voices among the Army General Staff that he be brought back to prominence, his great talents of organization utilized.

He also knew that Göring, his political crony and now head of the Luftwaffe was greedy, venal and incompetent and that while he had persuaded the real Adolf Hitler that his air force could annihilate the British Expeditionary Force on the beaches of Dunkirk, he had failed. He cringed (according to Bormann's personal notation on the file) at any kind of reminder of that gross miscalculation. Now, with his promised destruction of the RAF, the field marshal's prestige was again in plain sight for all to judge.

Archie immediately recognized each officer from the photos that accompanied his file. Herman Göring, overweight, nervous, thin lips turned upward in a silly effort to seem pleased with himself despite his failures as a military leader; Alfred Jodl, Hitler's military gofer, slight of frame, ambitious but content to walk in the shadow of the great Führer; Chief of Staff Wilhelm Keitel, called the oiler, behind his back. He was a man who disliked friction, some would say confrontation, so that Hitler would never have to worry about arguing with Keitel; Gross Admiral Erich Raeder, old school, a man who believed in Hitler because Hitler believed in his navy and its vital component of the Third Reich; and Franz Halder, Chief of General staff, hair cut very short, intense, almost ritualistically correct, the master of self-discipline within a factory of Prussian approbates.

Martin Bormann had insinuated himself into the meeting of military men, taking a chair placed, by him, respectfully to the side and slightly distanced from the group of distinguished military officers.

Archie had rehearsed his lines, intending to keep this dramatic vignette as brief as possible. If he exhibited tremors, and he felt that he was, he would attempt to transform his visage of fear into an image of anger. He was, after all, a victim of Göring's military sloth and the army's inability to properly guarantee his safety, even deep in the heartland of Germany. He had a right to be in a rage, he reminded himself. Nor did he, as Supreme Commander of the Armed Forces, have to explain his motives to anyone, not even to the bemedaled assemblage in his office.

"Let me thank you all for your kind solicitations during my recent hospital stay. I can tell you that I am now quite recovered, except for occasional spells of dizziness and forgetfulness. But even these minor inconveniences are fading with each hour. In short, they have not yet made the British bullet to put through my heart!"

The High Command officers chucked fully, even softly applauded their leader's uncompromising spirit.

"Führer," Göring said, leaning forward in his overstuffed wingback chair almost, but not quite, coming to his feet for his soliloquy. "May I say that I speak to for the entire High Command when I say that it was Providence that spared you for your continued leadership for Germany's..."

"Yes, Herman," Archie interrupted, "I have already said that." Archie recalled a notation in Göring's file, possibly placed there by Bormann, that Göring had never had an original idea in his life. He carried within him unbridled ambition minus the ability to innovate.

"Of course, Führer," he said, rubbing his hands together in revolving motions. "I only meant that we want to welcome you back."

"Thank you," Archie said, his nerves beginning to cease their jangling as he watched Göring's eyes shifting about, as though to draw support from the others when, clearly, none was needed.

"May I speak forcefully, then? We received your signal concerning Directive Number 16," the Luftwaffe commander said. "You were fighting for your life. So we were told. And your communication, well, to call off the operation...we assume you meant until your return to Berlin."

"I am disappointed with our progress, that is why I am ordering a stand-down," Archie said.

"But why?" Göring persisted. "We are winning the air war above England. Our armies are ready to cross the Channel even as we speak. There is no question we could lay waste to the British army, what is left of it," he said, gaining confidence as he spoke. He rose from his chair and stepped to the huge garden window and looked contemplatively out.

"General von Halder?" Archie said, noticing that the Chief of Staff had leaned forward in his chair, wanting to speak.

"My Führer, within certain parameters, the Field Marshal is correct. The General Staff firmly believes that our opportunity for defeating the British army has never been better than at this moment. If the Luftwaffe can succeed..." He allowed his voice to make the proviso.

"We are only a few days from certain superiority in the air," Göring snapped, petulantly, still gazing through the thick glass of the window. "That is why we should continue our plans."

Generals Keitel and Jodl, nodding in agreement with their colleagues positions now that others had spoken, felt it was now safe to appear properly aggressive.

"That British weakness is clearly supported by every intelligence assessment at our disposal," Jodl said. Archie knew that Jodl often spoke his mind at strategy meetings, contrary to what others believed of him.

Without looking in Martin Bormann's direction Archie nevertheless knew that the Reich's Secretary had not taken his eyes from the Führer. Was he suspect? Had he somehow slipped out of Hitler's character as he was conducting a high level meeting, perhaps even a momentous one? In any case, Archie had a strategy that had arisen from the dossiers he had read from the night before.

"But there are other problems that have not been addressed. Is that not correct, admiral?" he said, turning to Raeder.

"Of course," Raeder said, sitting ramrod straight in his chair. "Our High Seas Fleet is not yet the numerical equal of the British navy. We would be able to support a limited beachhead, with every confidence of success, but landings on a wide front are, in my opinion, out of the question at this time."

"I disagree," General von Halder said sharply. "If Field Marshal Göring is correct then you shall have the Luftwaffe to handle the British surface fleet, *ja?* Isn't that what this is all about? If we have command of the air, it is not necessary that we control the ocean ship for ship." Halder looked around him for consensus.

Heads nodded. Even Raeder, lips pursed, did not object to the Chief of Staff's reasoning. Having made his point, he remained silent.

Archie's fists were doubled atop his desk. It was, he recalled, a gesture Adolf Hitler had often made when tensions were high, and certainly the room was charged at this moment.

"Well, when the Luftwaffe defeats the RAF we'll revisit Sealion," Archie said, rising to his feet. "Until then, I want no more execution of the Directive without my express approval."

As it seemed he was about to close the meeting, as indeed he was, Jodl spoke from his chair. "Führer, I assume it is still your orders to proceed with planning for operations Sunflower, Cyclamen, Felix and the other contingencies?"

Archie was vaguely aware that there had been invasion scenarios for Crete, the Balkans, moves in North Africa and elsewhere, but these references were impossibly complex for him. His grasp of Sealion, as far as it went, was tenuous but at least Admiral Raeder's position vis-a-vis those of the army generals was straightforward and easy to understand.

"Yes, of course. Now, if you will excuse me," he said, closing the meeting, "I have other work to do."

The officers stood quickly to their feet and filed their way toward the door. Archie could feel Field Marshal Göring's lingering eyes upon him but kept his own averted, looking down at his desk which, by now, had papers neatly stacked to one side.

Bormann, however, did not immediately leave the room with the others. "Führer, I have a great many calendar items that need your immediate attention. Can we meet later in the day, perhaps?"

"Not today, Martin. You have been doing good work, as usual. I am counting on you," Archie said, fearing the proximity of the highly perceptive man. Archie nodded his head toward the folder of papers Bormann clutched under his arm. "Leave those. I will look at them later. Martin, on your way out, I want you to send me a new secretary. Have her report to me at once."

"Yes, sir. Er, is there anything wrong with Gertrude Junge or the others in..."

"I have no complaints. I want a new face, that's all," Archie said, bruskly.

"Of course, Führer," Bormann said, his fingers tapping his leather file case, reluctantly allowing his control of the Reich's important paper to pass from his control. "One other thing," he added, his voice pitched low although the others had by now passed from the room.

"Reichsprotector Himmler is most anxious to see you. I have been told him that you are ah, recovering from your wounds, but he is most persistent."

"Good old Heinrich," Archie said, masking, he hoped, the dread in his voice. "Tell him that I'll see him soon." Archie reached for the gold plated door knob.

"Yes, but when?" Bormann gently continued.

"Soon." Archie said, turning away from the omnipresent man.

Among the documents left upon Archie's desk was an effusive communique from Il Duce who, still titillated by his own courage in declaring war on the Allies in June, urged a meeting soon, that they might discuss the pressing issues of expanded areas of influence. Il Duce was, of course, particularly interested in southern Europe and North Africa, despite his own military misadventures there. He hinted that he was quite ready to occupy Greece, lacking information of the Führer's intentions that might conflict, and was well passed the mere planning stages. Archie regarded the man as odious but, at least according to past correspondence between the two dictators, the real Adolf Hitler had held the Fascist leader in the highest regard. Archie, looked very closely at Hitler's hand written notations. He attempted to duplicate, as closely as possible, the letters as he jotted brief comments on the pile of papers before him. At a total loss as to what to respond to the Italian leader, he merely wrote "patience" in the margin of the man's communiqu and put the letter aside.

There were a dozen men to be awarded the Iron Cross for bravery three days hence, a ceremony over which he was expected to preside. One of the recipients was a Luftwaffe pilot in a bomb squadron. Also, in a separate ceremony, decorations for General Heinz Guderian, chief architect of the successful panzer Blitzkrieg through France, and a Knight's Cross for a brilliant young newly appointed general, a panzer division commander by the name of Erwin Rommel.

He was also scheduled to inspect new garrisons posted along the French coast near Calais, an important defensive area that would be vital in the unlikely event that the conflict would ever find its way to this side of the Channel.

There were a myriad of requests for public appearances; a speech at the WWI Deutschland Veteran's Association; the Gauleiters's national meeting in Stuttgart; a Hitler Youth parade down Unter den

Linden with one hundred divisions of young boys under age fifteen at which the Führer was expected to attend. Work on the teahouse atop the Berghof was long complete and there was increasing pressure from Bormann, whose idea it was to build the mountaintop retreat in Berchtesgaden, to acknowledge its architect, Philipp Holzmann and Professor R. Fick who drew the plans, as well as certain of the workers who had built the magnificent building 1800 meters high on the top of Kehlstein Mountain. While Archie was not comfortable at high elevations, he could appreciate the series of photographs that chronicled the construction project. He would simply have to make the time.

By far the most pressing business on his desk involved the war against Great Britain. There were detailed reports of U-boat activities against shipping of all descriptions, a great many of which seemed to Archie to occur off the east coast of America. Tonnage reports indicated a form of strangulation of supplies for Britain by U-boats choking off the western sea approaches. Archie was impressed because he could see that the U-boat fleet, under an admiral by the name of Karl Doenitz, was very active with as many as sixty-five boats on patrol at any one time. But what effect was it having on Britain's war effort? Was the loss of shipping critical? Or were the losses acceptable? Should he try to stop the activity by submarines? If so, by what logical justification?

Then there were the Luftwaffe reports about the campaign against the RAF. An almost endless stream of data describing sorties flown, types of aircraft delivering bomb loads, losses of all types inflicted upon the RAF and those suffered by the Luftwaffe was put before him. But what did it all mean? Was Germany winning or losing the war? Could factories maintain a flow of replacements in aircraft that went down on either side of the channel? He studied target damage assessments and scheduled mission plans, but they were only numbers. As in shipping, Archie had no basis on which to make his judgements of how the war was progressing and on who's terms. He began to feel a sense of futility, like a burglar who had managed to break into a business without detection only to find that he did not know what to steal.

At some time a woman appeared through the secretariat door. She was tall, blond, athletic in appearance, approximately in her mid 40s but who could have passed for much younger. "My name is Berta Holz, Herr Führer. Herr Bormann has directed me to report to you."

"Yes, er, sit down, please," Archie said, shifting awkwardly in his own chair behind his massive desk. "I should start by telling you that I have been recently in battle, of a kind...." he began, awkwardly. "You are nodding your head?"

"Oh, pardon me, sir, but most of us are aware." Berta said with confidence.

"I suppose that would follow. Well, then, I will tell you that I suffer from temporary forgetfulness. Bormann knows this, a few others do, and now you, as well. It is not a terrible thing but I don't wish my temporary condition to become common knowledge outside of this office. You understand."

"Yes. You can trust my discretion, sir," Berta said.

"Good. When I push this button, then," Archie said, nodding his head toward an array of signaling devices at his fingertips, each with a small printed identifier attached, "I want you to come into this office and assist me."

"I would be honored. Ah, is Frau Jung leaving her post, then?" Berta wanted to know.

Archie shook his head emphatically. "She is being assigned to a more important position. Please inform her of that when you leave. Tell her that her promotion is a result of her excellent work for me in the past." Archie made a mental note to find Frau Jung a suitable place of employment on the other side of Germany. Women who knew Adolf Hitler, like Eva Braun, worried him in a special way.

The next several days settled into an almost bearable period of responding to pressing needs of the various documents contained in Bormann's folders, with Berta shouldering the responsibility of carrying out the administration of both his annotated and oral directions.

Bormann popped into and out of Archie's office frequently and called several times from his office within the Chancellery, once to ask if Archie felt sufficiently recovered to resume his schedule of morning military briefings. He had left Berta with a list of officers that he, Bormann, thought the Führer would profit most by their attendance. Such a daily briefing schedule was vitally important, a fact recognized by even the military naive Archie Smythes, and he could not help but say that indeed the briefings should begin again. He did, however, feel a measure of confidence, having survived one such affair without discovery and apparently satisfying the omnipresent and paranoid Martin Bormann. He had, in addition, been giving long evening hours studying the files brought to him by SS Standartenführer Hebert in a series of discreet visits to his quarters. From the folders he could surmise that the security details at the Reichschancellery were many and complex, yet most of them came under the purview of the RSD or *Reichssicherheitsdienst*. The RSD, under the titular leadership of Adolf Hitler, was a part of the SS, the Leibstandarte Adolf Hitler Division. Ostensibly, the RSD reported to Chief of OKW, General Keitel, but in fact no such reporting ever took place except on organizational charts. Hebert had between 120 and 135 men on duty at the Chancellery at any one time, depending upon Hitler's schedule.

This did not include Hitler's on-road escort which were troops from SS-Leibstandarte AH who rode in armed personnel carriers in front and in the rear of Hitler's own armored limousines. Apart from the ride from Tempelhof to the Reichschancellery, Archie had not witnessed the elaborate protection designed to keep him safe.

Archie had read the dossier on SS-Sturmbannfuhrer Otto Günsche, and it said that his current assignment was the personal security of Adolf Hitler. Archie made a mental note to have Günsche reassigned elsewhere, just as a precaution. He also made a list, this time on paper, to have Otto Meyer, a valet, replaced immediately. Meyer had a minor blot on his record, public drunkenness, but Archie seized on it as an excuse to get rid of the man. Another valet, Wilhelm Schneider, had once been described as having a weakness for gambling. The entry in this dossier was notated neither by Martin Bormann nor Standartenführer Hebert, but to Archie it didn't matter. He would have the man transferred at once.

Still another dossier, this one on a man by the name of Heinz Linge, another SS man, had been recommended by Obersturmbannführer Jon Vass for valet duty which, Hebert pointed out in his memorandum to Archie, also included the physical ability to protect the Führer in a fight and, if need be, step in front of a bullet. Archie agreed to the proposed assignment: anyone, except those who were there before.

Archie perused the briefing schedule, noting that one agendum included a report to be delivered by Colonel von Eck to Hitler and his Army Chief of Staff, Franz Halder. It was the same Colonel von Eck who received Hitler's order from the train cancelling Directive #16. The Luftwaffe daily report would be given by Col. General Neumann. Also present would be Keitel and Jodl. Berta also noted that Reichsfuhrer Himmler be allowed to add his name to the list. Archie could not refuse.

In his office near the Reichschancellery only a few doors down from the Führer's, Party Secretary Rudolf Hess labored mightily on the myriad projects that the Nazi party was committed to. What was once largely a national organizational problem, Hess now had to think about on a global scale. In the last four days he had eaten lightly, left the office only for periods of vigorous exercise, and as briefly as possible whenever other duties required his personal attention. He was thankful that the tasks of administering security for Hitler was in the capable hands of Standartenführer Hebert and his deputy Obersturmbanführer Jon Vass, while he dedicated himself to the task of dealing with party functions at every level. Now there was the additional problem of addressing the Führer's fear, and a very real one, that there was a British agent placed in a high position within the Third Reich.

Hebert was quite right to take Hess into his confidence. Hess, too, had considered such a possibility.

But for different reasons.

Hess had requested not only copies of those files Hebert had been able to secure but had also managed to obtain documents from among the active data repositories of the Gestapo. It was they who specialized in the investigation of military officers. To obtain such jealously guarded records from competitive organizations is not always easy.

Ferreting out individuals who could betray the Fatherland and Adolf Hitler, literally one in the same, was hard work but one which was already producing a fruit that stimulated Hess's as well as the Standartenfurher's taste. He had fashioned a list of two dozen souls who had questionable political antecedents also the opportunities to have made contact with the British government. Hess was in the process of further refining the twenty-four names into an even smaller number preparatory to undertaking further, more incisive, investigations when his adjutant knocked on the door then, per officer protocol, entered the room.

"Yes, Meisner?" Hess said without looking up.

"Sir, Sturmbannfuhrer Otto Hockië is outside, sir. He requests that you see him."

"Sturmbannfuhrer Hockië? I don't know him. What does he want?" Hess said, slightly annoyed at the interruption.

"He is from Reichsmarshall Himmler's office, sir. Investigations, I believe. He would not say his business to me."

"Hmm. Well, if he sits in a chair at the Reichsmarshall's office I suppose he should get two minutes of my time. Tell him that, Meisner. Only two minutes. Then show him in."

Otto Hockië, contrary to current height requirements of Hitler's praetorian guard, was a short man, his hair worn in a brush cut and bore a livid scar on his left cheek. It flashed through Hess's naturally skeptical mind that Hockië might have administered the facial mark of courage himself. Hockië clicked his heels, thrusting his arm upward.

"Heil Hitler," he said.

"Heil Hitler," Hess returned as he remained seated. "Well?"

Hockië pointedly waited until Hebert's assistant had left the office and closed the door before speaking.

"You will excuse me, Herr Sturmbannfuhrer, if I urge you to be brief. I am doing important work for the Führer and time is of the essence," Hess said, officiously.

"I understand completely, sir. What I have to say will not take long. To be frank, I have no idea to make of it myself. I am the investigating officer in charge of determining the facts about the attempt on the Führer's life. My duties necessarily took me to Gebirgs Sicht, the hospital there. I looked at the site of the attack. I saw the bodies...."

"Yes, yes," Hess snapped, impatiently.

"...and I interviewed a good many people, even the farm family who's son was killed by the British soldiers...."

"They were not soldiers, Hockië, they were criminals," Hess corrected.

"Yes, of course. I interviewed one of the Heer survivors from the train," the Sturmbanfuhrer plodded on.

"There were no survivors," Hess said, but his attention was now focused on the SS officer before him.

"True in a technical sense. That is, every man on the train is now dead, but the radio operator did not die at once. While they worked on the young man in the same hospital in which the Führer was recovering, he lived for twenty-four hours. I was with him in the final hour of his life."

"And he could speak?"

Hockië nodded. "The operator had six machine-gun bullets in his chest and stomach. I told the doctors that they were not to attempt to save his life because it would mean sedation and he would have died, anyway. And no pain medication. I had him injected with stimulants so he could be fully awake as I questioned him."

"Very good, yes. So? What did he say?" Hess said, now sitting quite straight in his chair.

"He said that the Führer was with the British commandos."

"What else?" Hess wanted to know.

"That is all. He said that when the Führer entered the communications car he was with the British commandos," Hockië said, satisfied now that he had captured the Party Secretary's attention.

"There were no other words? How did he mean it? Did he say the commandos were holding the Führer in their grasp?"

"No, sir. He only said the words that I relate to you. He was quite delirious, in and out of consciousness," Hockië maintained.

"Yes? And what do you make of it, Sturmbanfuhrer?" Hess asked.

Hockië considered for a moment. "Naturally I have pondered the meaning of the soldier's words. I have tried to assume the man was totally coherent, and I have tried to connect such coherence with rational meaning. I have failed. Further, I have discussed the fact with my superiors, even with Oberstrgruppenfuhrer Heydrich, to no avail. Having said that, I believed it my duty to report the event to you."

Hess rose from his chair, began to pace his comfortable office. Then, clasping his hands behind his back, he said, "It means nothing. The words of a man in delirium, raving just as you or I might babble as we attempt to describe a fierce battle in which we had been fatally wounded," Hess shrugged his shoulders dismissively. For several long moments Hess dealt with the disquiet that had invaded his sanctum.

"And now, Sturmbanfuhrer, I shall allow you to return to your more important duties," Hess said, pulling his shoulders back into a more formal position.

Sturmbannfuhrer Hockië brought his heels together to produce the proper popping sound. "Heil Hitler," he said, giving the Nazi salute before spinning on his heels and letting himself out of the room.

Hess slowly returned to his chair and turned back toward his dossiers. But for a very long time he could only stare blankly at words that no longer registered in his brain. Unwanted cerebration, wild and dangerous, had destroyed his concentration.

CHAPTER
16

The occasion was a reception in the great hall of the Reichschan-cellery for the observance of the 1933 Enabling Act. Decreed by Hitler only seven years prior, the Nazi party became not only the official representative of the German people, but that was the only political party allowed in the nation. It was the epiphany of the Party from which all growth in modern Germany could be traced. The huge room, with its giant chandeliers suspended from the high ceiling, ornate tapestry gracing two walls, and hand-crafted furnishings made in Salzburg occupying the outer edges of a giant carpet, was now set with tables covered with linen cloths. Elegant foods of all description graced a service line which included sculpted ice as its centerpiece. Among the invited guests was the handsome young architect and builder of the New Reichschancellery, Albert Speer, lately officially named Reichsbuilder. Although totally obsequious to his patron, Hitler, Speer attracted admirers as he sipped champagne in one corner of the vast room.

Other dignitaries included Foreign Minister Joachim von Ribbentrop, a coarse, one-time wine salesman turned Anglophobe; Joseph Goebbels, Minister of Propaganda and his wife; Secretary of State Dr. Stuckart and his wife; Reich Ministry of Justice Freisler; Foreign Office Secretary Otto Luther and other party members that included Martin

Bormann, Herman Göring, and Heinrich Himmler. Archie had made his entrance as late as possible, putting it off partly out of fear and partly because he wanted a full room that would allow him to leave one group of people for another should they become uncomfortable to him.

He was tense as he moved among the guests of the Third Reich. He recognized most of those he would be expected to know by their photographs contained in the now massive number of dossiers supplied him by Standartenführer Hebert and Bormann, and acknowledged new faces as they were introduced. Uniforms were de rigueur and they began to blur as he greeted his guests, shaking hands, forcing a smile, then going to the next. He took no particular note of a young Luftwaffe major whose hand he shook but, as he turned away, thought he heard the word "Archie" called softly behind him.

It was such a shock to his system that, after an instant, he believed it was nothing more than his imagination. Even so, he did not turn to the source, if indeed there was a source, but continued to move about the room. He felt his body tremble again and wondered if his agitation was visible to others. He placed one hand over the other as he sat in a comfortable chair and nodded agreeably to a white coated waiter who, after a slight bow at the waist, asked the Führer if he would care for tea and lemon cake. He said that he would, grateful that there was a table nearby on which he would be able to set the cup without spilling its contents.

A knot of people coalesced about him, straining to remain at a respectful distance but, after all, meaning to make their Führer comfortable among their warm friendship. Joseph Goebbels was nearest and seemed quite pleasant. He was, it seemed to Archie, genuinely concerned about the Führer's physical comfort. It was perhaps, Archie thought, because of the Propaganda Minister's own discomfort of having to live with a club foot all of his life and suffering emotionally from his subsequent failure to do military duty in the last war. Archie knew Goebbels to be a man with an abiding interest in the theater, an activity Archie would have given much to discuss with him but feared he would somehow give himself away in the event. Still, Archie was paying attention to an idea that Goebbels had for a dramatic new film that would feature not actors but real fighting men, and to be done by the incredibly talented female director, Leni

Reifenstahl. Out of the corner of his eye Archie could see yet another uniform, also in dress white tunic like his own, but with the silver and gold wings of Luftwaffe. It was, yet again, the young pilot with whom he had shaken hands minutes ago and who had, Archie believed, almost stopped the very blood from flowing in his veins. He turned slowly toward the major and looked into his blue eyes and sandy colored hair. Smiling broadly, the major allowed himself to move closer to the Führer than perhaps protocol would permit but said in German, *"Having a good time, Archie?"*

Others standing back, including Goebbels, did not clearly hear the words of the decorated Luftwaffe officer, but Goebbels was near enough to pick up the word Archie. The Minister of Propaganda turned quizzically toward the pilot, regarded him appraisingly, then glanced at the Führer. Hitler seemed not in the least upset at whatever it was that the pilot had said so that Goebbels merely believed that he had heard incorrectly. Arch? What kind of arch? Still, not wishing to be rude, the Propaganda Minister returned the pilot's smile.

"I don't believe I have had the pleasure, Major...?" he said.

The major clicked his heels and, bowing slightly at the waist, said "Dietrich, Herr Minister. Stephen Dietrich. Forgive me, sir, but the fellows in my squadron made me promise to extend their deepest best wishes to our Führer. I hope I have not been impertinent."

Dietrich seemed to be a poster image of what the German fighter pilot should be. He wore the prestigious Iron Cross 1st Class at his throat, as well as the Silver Class Day Fighter awarded for 60 combat missions, and the German Cross in Gold placed upon his right breast. He might have been a few inches shorter than the ideal matinee idol but he had a fine physique, broad shoulders and just the hint of swagger that one would expect of a hunter of the skies. The Führer, too, seemed taken with the young fighter pilot, apparently not able to take his eyes from him. Goebbels felt compelled to remove the silence that ensued as well as sensing a unique moment of military opportunity.

"I see by your badge that you are in Fighter Command, Major," Goebbels said.

"Yes, sir. I have the honor to command 44th Squadron, Jagdeschwader3, Fightergruppen West."

"And you are stationed where?" Goebbels asked.

"Bergues, France, Herr Minister," Dietrich said, still holding an empty champagne glass in his hand.

"Fill the Major's glass," Goebbels said to a passing waiter. "What machine do you fly?" he said, turning back to Dietrich.

"The Me-109. We have just been upgraded with the E model. An excellent aircraft, we think."

"Tell me, Major Dietrich, what do you think of the British pilots?"

"They are flying Hurricanes and Spitfires, and the Spitfires are a very fast, very maneuverable aircraft. The Brits are well trained and they are courageous."

"Ah, chivalry. It is good to respect one's adversary," Goebbels observed, turning to Hitler for confirmation. The Führer seemed, strangely, to be following the conversation but contributing nothing. It was uncharacteristic for the German leader to remain totally withdrawn on the subject of war and warriors.

Goebbels continued. "So, when will you finish them off?"

"With respect, Herr Minister," Dietrich said and, turning toward Hitler, "my Führer, I am only able to shoot down the one who is unlucky enough to fly into my gun sights. It is for the generals to tell us when we will win."

"Thank you, Major," Goebbels said, dismissing Dietrich since he had taken up quite enough of the Führer's time.

Dietrich took one step back, clicked his heels as he nodded his head in a military bow, and turned to go.

"I would like to hear more about your airplane, Major," Archie said, at last rousing himself from some inner place and time.

Dietrich turned back.

"Have you seen the Mosaic Hall? They are made of Saalburg marble. Come," he said, rising from his chair.

The interior of the Reichschancellery was all but deserted save for the omnipresent SS guards stationed at key places within the grand walls.

"Did you see the sculptures representing the Army and the Party as you entered? You came through the Honor Courtyard, *ja*? They are among the most beautiful ever created in Germany," he said as they strolled along the block long hallways of the chancellery. "Ah, here we are. You see? The mosaics were designed by Professor Kaspar."

Archie was not yet sure with whom he was talking. The major might be more than a Luftwaffe pilot; he might also be assigned to the Gestapo. Or the dreaded SD. Or any of the myriad agencies of betrayal and death spawned and cultivated by totalitarian regimes.

"You said that you have a friend by the name of..." Archie looked over his shoulder once more, assuring himself that they could not be overheard.

"Archie," Major Dietrich supplied. "Actually, he's not a relative." Dietrich switched to English. "He is a British actor. And he is either quite brave or very foolish."

"Foolish," Archie said in English, "is charitable. I am a coward. My knees are weak even as we stand here speaking where we can't be heard. I often feel that I am about to cry and at this moment I wish to god I was sitting in The Lion's Den on Pinkney Street having a glass with my mates. Are you really a major in the Luftwaffe, or did you steal the uniform?"

Dietrich smiled, and when he spoke again he reverted to German. "I am what I told Minister Goebbels and I fly missions against the British. I'm sorry about that part of it but it is vital to my deep cover."

"You're British! Thank god! Can you get me out of here?"

"I'm not British, Archie. I'm American. But I work for the SOE in London. And I can't get you out of here," Dietrich said. There was a moment of sad silence as Archie knew at once Dietrich was lying and Dietrich knew that Archie knew better. "Not yet, anyway. I have directions for you that come from London. From time to time I will receive orders from there and I will pass them on to you. It will work the other way as well. I will get certain information from you and I will relay that information back to London."

Archie nodded balefully. He had expected something like this. Or death before the people at home could reach out to him.

"How?" he began. "I mean, what will be the mechanics? How will I contact you?"

"You will take an interest in me. You will enjoy hearing my tales of aerial combat and from time to time you will have your adjutant or secretary summon me from my unit to come to wherever you are for lunches or dinners or even weekends at Obersalzburg, for example. We will go for walks as a friendship develops. Whatever happens, make no notes. Trust nothing to paper or film. Spies and counterspies are everywhere," Dietrich warned.

"Why don't I just appoint you to my staff here at the Reichschan-cellery?" Archie asked.

"That is a possibility in the future, but for now I have to drop out of sight for hours at a time or even days at a time. If I were in Berlin, here in this building, it might be dangerous to arrange," the Luftwaffe pilot said.

"Yes, I see," Archie said, a feeling of disappointment pulsing through him.

"By the way, Archie, the Prime Minister conveys to you his personal congratulations. He sent word to have me to tell you that you have not only saved lives in this war but might have saved the British Empire itself."

Archie only nodded, at a loss as how to express his gratitude for Churchill's great compliment. In his uneven career as a professional actor, he had received very little praise.

"Now, Archie, listen carefully. You must order the Luftwaffe to change its primary target campaign," Dietrich said.

"What? I don't understand," Archie said.

"The bombers are hammering British airfields. The losses of planes and pilots is too great. If Germany keeps it up the RAF will not be able to sustain itself. Do you understand?" Dietrich said calmly but forcefully.

"I think so but how...?"

Archie and Dietrich became aware of a presence in the hallway. It was Martin Bormann.

"They are waiting for your speech, my Führer. When should I tell them you will be ready?" Bormann said, his eyes not missing Dietrich standing by Hitler's side.

"At once, Bormann," Archie said.

As Bormann withdrew Dietrich smiled. "If you don't mind, Führer, I'll skip the pep rally."

Pep rally? Archie thought on his way back to the Reception Hall. *What was a "pep rally"?*

Archie was about to make his way to the dais when he felt a light touch on his arm. It was Bormann.

"Führer," he whispered, eyes shifting among others in the huge room, then back to Archie, "the Luftwaffe officer you were with..."

"Major Dietrich," Archie said, impatiently.

"...is an American. I have a very large file on him," the Deputy Party Secretary said.

I t was 1:00 A.M. and since early afternoon Archie had been staring
blankly at Luftwaffe estimates of what they were facing on the
other side of the Channel. The RAF order of battle was, as far as
could be determined, approximately 600 front line fighter aircraft
existing on August 2nd when Field Marshal Göring issued the Eagle
Day directive to destroy Britain's air defense system. These very
excellent airplanes were dispersed among sixty airfields from 92
Squadron of Spitfires in the Pembry Sector to 54 Squadron in the
Catterick Sector with Tangmere and Duxford and many other sectors
thrown in. There were about fifty-nine squadrons, Luftwaffe Intelligence figured, among that many combat capable fields.

And this did not include bomber bases. However, RAF Bomber
Command provided little more than harassment to the German war
machine, most of their targets being French coastal cities with occasional raids on newly acquired Nazi ports in Denmark and Holland.
The battle of fighter aircraft in the skies above England as Germany
sent its bomber fleets aloft had been fierce from the outset, each side
realizing that the stakes were nothing less than total conquest of the
ground below.

For the fourth straight day after receiving London's orders through
Dietrich to shift Luftwaffe bomber strikes away from RAF airfields,

Archie had felt like a total failure. It was a familiar feeling. He had often played an understudy who, fully costumed, nevertheless waited in the wings for the real actors to find need of his questionable talents. Now he sat behind his massive desk in the Führer office looking at piles of strike photos, intelligence reports and battle estimates. It was hard for him to separate truth from distortion, the real from the wished for. But if he must give the order for the redirection of Luftwaffe he must have strong justifications or at least a one, singular, dramatic rationalization to offer his air marshals. While Archie could palpably feel the power of the absolute ruler that was Adolf Hitler, even Hitler had to make a certain amount of sense to his subordinates lest they work behind his back to undo him.

At 10:00 A.M. he would preside over a strategy meeting with Luftwaffe general staff. He considered rescheduling, putting off the meeting until he had not only worked up his nerve to issue what would surely be understood as a questionable strategic maneuver, but might even seem irresponsible. But in the end his belief that Britain desperately needed relief and its RAF was days, perhaps even hours, away from total collapse. No, he had to act now, even if he was inviting mutiny. He peered again at a damage assessment report, his eyes watering from the strain that comes from overuse, when he thought he heard a dull thump, then another, and still another.

His first thought, he later realized a silly one, was that it was terribly late for crews to be working on the Reichschancellery. For a few moments he even thought that exigencies of the war were strange indeed when a light began to blink on and off near the telephone near his Fuhrerbunker private telephone.

"Yes?" he said into the mouthpiece.

"Martin Bormann here, Führer. Did you feel it? The bombs! Berlin has been bombed!"

"Bombed? By the British?" he blurted, stupidly, he thought.

"Yes, of course it was the British. The swine. I am trying to get a damage report now. Nothing yet, of course. I don't even know how many aircraft were involved."

"Or," Archie said, becoming alert, the kriegmeister, "how many were shot down. Call me immediately when you know," he said and hung up.

Bombed. Well, I'll be boiled and plucked, Archie thought. *Good for*

*you, boys. We'll see how the damn Huns like the taste of their own
medicine.* He was almost sorry that the bloody things hadn't fallen
much closer so that he could get a better feel of them. He wondered
what the city looked like now. He had the urge to walk outside the
Chancellery for a look, but quickly overcame it. He wondered if air
raid sirens had sounded and searchlights lit the sky, like at home.
Silly. Of course there would have been. The moment had lifted him
because, he thought, it was almost like hearing from home, like getting
mail while serving overseas. He laughed at the thought. He was jerked
back to the problem at hand when his telephone rang again.

"Sir," a Reichschancellery operator said into his ear, "Reichsmarshall
Göring is on the line."

The last person Archie wanted to talk to was Göring. He had spent
the past many days avoiding the man and had not the faintest idea
what to say to him under these conditions. He needed time to think.

"Tell him I am asleep. No, wait. Have him call Bormann. I'll...I'll
see him tomorrow. In the morning," Archie said and hung up the
phone.

Exhausted, yet exhilarated, Archie fell into his bed and willed
himself to close his eyes and sleep. He found that he could do the
first but the latter did not come easily.

At Number Ten Downing Street Churchill was holding a meeting
of his own. Smoke spewed from his cigar like a screen laid from the
stacks of a destroyer at sea He had been engaged in painting an oil
scape of a Scottish Loch from memory and he clutched in his hand
a brush, waving it alternately at the painting and at the man who sat
across the small room from him.

"Damn it, man, this wasn't a bloody target to bomb, it wasn't a
machine works, a submarine pen! It was a political statement that
you made!"

"But, sir," retorted the object of the Prime Minister's wrath, Air
Marshal Edgar Ludlow-Hewitt, "I regard Berlin, as do my target
selection officers, as another city to be struck. I should not want my
crews to imagine that we're showing partiality to any..."

"Oh, dash it all, Edgar, that's nonsense you're saying and you know
it. 'Another city,' bugger all. You sent your entire command after
those monsters because you are frustrated. Now that's the truth of

it," Churchill said, plopping into his swivel chair then, immediately, popping right back out.

Ludlow-Hewitt's chin jutted, lifting the blossoming waddle clear of his blue RAF uniform shirt. "I won't say that I didn't damn well want to send a five hundred pounder right down Adi's bloody ventilator shaft."

"Damn good thing you didn't," Churchill said, peering into a seascape of the HMS *Hood*.

The Prime Minister's utterance sounded strange to the Chief of Bomber Command, even given the stress of war when men sometimes vocalize things that they do not mean.

"I beg your pardon?" Ludlow-Hewitt said.

"Nothing. Nothing at all. But look here, Edgar, I don't want any of these giant raids mounted, at least not against Berlin, unless you first trot the idea by me."

"I'm afraid I can't do that, Prime Minister," Ludlow-Hewitt said, not without, Churchill thought, a tinge of regret.

"Eh? What's that you say? Can't?" Churchill said, turning toward his senior airman.

"I suppose 'can't' isn't quite right. Will not, is better. It simply isn't possible to run an aerial war if I have to clear everything through your office. I mean, suppose you're off in Northumberland, talking to a labor meeting, or stamping around a town on the coast when I want my damn planes to fly. Nonsense," he said, reaching for his pipe-tobacco.

"Whiskey?" Churchill asked.

"A bit early. But it might settle my stomach," Ludlow-Hewitt said, accepting a drink from Churchill's very excellent bar.

"I hope I haven't contributed to an ulcer, old boy. Got one coming on?" Churchill asked. "Cheers," he said, tossing off his drink.

"I'm a stoic, Prime Minister. You have to be in my business, in case you haven't surmised as much. Wouldn't want your job, come to think about it."

Churchill fell again into his chair and, for a time, stayed put.

"What were your losses last night?"

"Heavy," the bomber commander said.

"Any reports on damage done to your target?" Churchill wanted to know.

Air Marshal Ludlow-Hewitt allowed his eyelids to close, the first time, he thought, in eighteen hours. When he opened them again the Prime Minister still waited for an answer.

"I did not send reconnaissance aircraft over for pictures," he admitted.

It was Churchill's turn to consider for a moment, his anger now replaced for admiration for RAF crews that fly off into the cold night, knowing that their chances were very good that they would not return, that if they were lucky they would suffer capture. That they would die was even more probable. And that they did it for some ill-defined, obscure effect that they may have on the war, never failed to fill him with a kind of choking awe. Of all of Britain's fighting arms, the Bomber Command suffered the most horrendous losses. And yet they never shirked their duty when called.

"I see. If it means anything to you, Edgar, I believe you were right. Whatever damage done to that huge city in a single raid will not be dramatic."

The Commander in Chief of the Bomber Command nodded his head. "It'll be a long war."

"Tell your boys that His Majesty's government is very proud of them. Will you do that for me?"

"Of course I will."

"And Edgar, no more Berlin raids without chatting with me first."

Waiting for him in his conference room were Chief of OKW Wilhelm Keitel, OKW Operations Officer General Alfred Jodl, Army C in C Field Marshal Walter Von Brauchitsch, Luftwaffe General Albert Kesselring and, of course, Field Marshal Hermann Göring, Luftwaffe. In addition each general officer had brought staff officers to do their secretarial chores, part of which was to bear witness to their own orders, given or received, for their own protection.

Cigarettes had been hastily extinguished before the Führer entered the room, but Archie could still smell the acrid remnants of polluted air and he marveled again at how many similarities he shared with the late, real, tyrant.

The group, surrounding the large conference table in the room adjoining his personal office, had been talking with some considerable animation, Archie thought, about the recent raid on the city by the RAF. He had indeed received a report about the raid. He had spoken directly with the Berlin Sector Commander, Luftwaffe Colonel Danz Unruh, before finally accepting one of Göring's frantic calls.

"Sit," Archie said as he entered and took his place at the center of the massive table. For a long moment, and for dramatic effect, Archie looked at each man around the table. By now he was intimately familiar with not only their war records as soldiers but their personal lives as well. In some cases he knew the names of their children and in all cases their wives. Family was still considered very important among the hierarchy of the German general staff. Without the proper pedigree one was not considered eligible for promotion if one married too far below one's social station and, while Hitler personally despised the aristocratic social stratums of Germany, he remained impressed with titles and nobility. He was unwilling to completely disregard the caste system that had developed over millennia and was not above using mistakes of the heart to get rid of high ranking officers who, for one reason or another, displeased him.

"This morning, in the darkness, the shining symbol of the Fatherland was bombed. I want to know why. I seem to remember a certain promise made to me and to the people of Germany." Archie was speaking, of course, of Göring's rash statement that no enemy bomb would fall on Berlin adding, in his bellicosity, that if one did "You can call me Meyer." Archie had no trouble hiding his secret feelings of delight by using an old actor's trick of transposition. Laughing can appear to be crying and visa versa. It was no challenge for Archie to shake with what appeared to be rage. "Well? How did the British gangsters penetrate our air defenses? How many of them did we shoot down?"

"My Führer," Göring said, his hands wringing just below the top of the conference table, "the raid was nothing more than a suicidal nuisance attempt to, ah, to make it seem like much more. The British sent a few bombers..."

"How few?" Archie thundered, totally enjoying the Luftwaffe commander's discomfort. "Be careful now, Herman. There were hundreds! The raid lasted over two hours! I could feel the bombs from my bunker. They woke me up!" he lied.

"It is true," Luftwaffe general Kesselring said, easily, calmly, from his position near his chief, "that several hundred RAF bombers penetrated our defense system. It was bound to happen. It is dangerously naive to believe that we could go through an entire war without receiving strikes on all of our cities, including Berlin."

In the face of such rationale Archie could feel his pretense ebb. He was very familiar with the record of this high ranking general who, truth be known, was the master tactician for the entire air fleet. He was fifty-five years of age, from Bavaria. He had masterminded the concept of close air support for ground forces during the Polish campaign, having himself been an artillery officer in World War I along with his army colleague, General von Bock.

Archie had read a summary of Kesselring's concept of first eliminating the enemy's potential to continue an air war, then using his own terrifying dive-bombers to support Panzer grenadiers action on the ground. Kesselring was a master organizer and a tactician of the first rank. Still, Archie's plan did not include agreeing with anything General Kesselring had to say.

"All very fine for you, Kesselring. You have an entire air force to protect you. And I have a bunker with concrete above my head. But what of the German people? Not so good for them, eh? I don't want excuses, Herman," Archie continued, turning back to Göring, "I want British blood to flow. Our fighter defenses should be so deadly, so efficient, that a British bomber crew will refuse to fly if it is ordered ever again to bomb Berlin!"

"Hell," the overweight field marshal said, but nevertheless diverting his eyes from Archie's. "Kesselring is quite correct. The British pilots are determined. They are well led and their machines...."

"Their aeroplanes are second rate," Archie said. "You told me that yourself. I have notes of that meeting!" Archie said, truthfully. Berta Holz had included it in a file brief she had prepared for him prior to the morning meeting.

"They are better now," Göring said, lamely, "and they sent over six hundred aeroplanes. Some are bound to get through. Even to drop their bombs, but we shot many down. Most, probably. I don't have all of the reports, yet. We are men of war, Führer, you and I. We know how these things go."

Archie had no idea how these things went, but would a super egotistical personality like Adolf Hitler let such trifles deter him? Archie thought not. Therefore he could not allow himself to become reasonable.

"I know no such thing. Tell me, Hermann, if it was you flying one of the British bombers...."

"Stirlings," Kesselring interjected, dryly. "A very good aircraft."

"Stirlings," Archie acquiesced, "would you be afraid to fly over Berlin?"

"I am afraid of nothing," Göring said, smiling, and waited for others around the table to agree with him. In point of fact, there was nothing cowardly about Hermann Göring, especially in the sky where, in the war just past, he had been the last commander of the Richthofen squadron.

"Then you have failed!" railed Archie. "Any airman asked to attack Berlin should be quaking in his flying boots!" Archie smashed his fist into the conference table. It was the first time he had demonstrated such rage, either acting or in real life. For a moment he worried that he might have overdone it but, in a quick assessment of the others in the room, he felt he had succeeded in setting them back in their chairs.

All except Kesselring.

Archie thought he detected in the general's visage just a ghost of a smile.

For several minutes the various generals around the table offered their less than passionate views on this milestone in the war. It was not, as far as he could discern, a matter of monumental importance to any of them, especially given the fact that they had all been bombed at one time or another in their careers and that the city of Berlin, with its four and one half million inhabitants, could easily survive terrorist attacks for the Duration and, indeed, should expect to. It was, to put it into perspective, a relatively small price to pay compared to that which front line troops had sacrificed in blood to historically change the entire geopolitical map of Europe.

Archie could feel the momentum shift away from him, if it had ever been on his side. Even Göring, slouching back in his wingback chair, talked about new features that were being installed on his Messerschmitt 110C models; e.g., advanced RDF navigation systems, an improved supercharger to reduce time to climb, as well as the latest iteration of the FW (Focke Wulf) 190D that could achieve 685 kpm at 10,000 meters. It was the air superiority fighter that the Luftwaffe had been waiting for. No enemy fighter, let alone bomber, was its equal. If Churchill dared mount another raid on Berlin, the crews would all find graveyards throughout Deutschland.

It sounded very strong. And convincing. But Archie noted that Kesselring's amused smile remained on his thin lips.

"They have not hurt us," Archie said, interrupting. All heads turned toward the Führer, "but we will hurt them. I want new targets for the Luftwaffe. I want London struck and struck again! I want their cities crushed. I want their schools and their hospitals leveled!" he allowed his voice to rise in pitch, and wondered if he had sounded evil enough invoking schools and hospitals to be destroyed. He did not think it was possible for target teams to single out schools in London or anywhere else. At least he hoped to God that it wasn't, but he believed he sounded sufficiently furious to get the point across. He thought about London, and he knew that his own daughter, Rose, was safely in the countryside, and that Laverne had complete access to bomb shelters constructed for defense workers. He knew that. But he knew others in London would die because of his directive. He shook his head, refusing to imagine the event.

"I'm afraid that isn't possible, Führer," Archie heard the voice above the others around the table who began talking all at once, none in favor of his order.

"What's that? Of course it can be done. Who said it could not?" Archie looked around the table. On Archie's part, it was theatrics. He knew who had spoken.

"If we divert from our plan to destroy the RAF we will not defeat the British," Kesselring said. "We have them now almost beaten. We are destroying their planes in the air and on the ground. They cannot possibly last another month. Two at the most."

Archie noticed that Göring's eyes were shifting between his top general and undisputed master tactician, and his Führer, the man who supplied the largesse for Göring to live his life of luxury and hedonist pleasures.

"We will defeat the British if we destroy that which they love most. London," Archie insisted. "The Crown exists for them there. When they see the walls of Westminster Abbey crash to the ground they will weep for relief. They will sue for peace. England is London. London is England. Also, General Kesselring, there are more than sufficient targets of military value to justify continuous raids on the city," Archie said, allowing his voice to ring the bell of finality.

"Allow me to point out, Führer," Kesselring said, leaning forward in his chair, the smile, if there ever was one, now gone, "that the British army is defeated. We should have finished it off on the beaches of Dunkirk but we did not. Its soldiers are now, like wet rats, drying out back in their homeland, perhaps having a pint while they rest. But they are in disarray. They are no longer a fighting army. All that protects them from literal annihilation is the RAF and the RAF, I suggest, will cease to exist in only a matter of weeks. Or even days. They will be defeated, but only if we execute our battle plan and our target register."

"As you have designed it," Archie said, surprising himself with his courage to speak forcefully to a master strategist.

"Yes, sir. As I and my staff have designed it. I am afraid there is no other way," Kesselring said.

"No other way? No other way, General Kesselring? The object of our commitment to the war is to win it. Is that not so?" Archie demanded, rhetorically. "And how do we win a war? I have demonstrated that quite convincingly in Czechoslovakia, in the Sudentland, in Poland. In France. I believe I know how to win a war. While the German General Staff twiddled its thumbs for four years in the last war, I set about winning this one in a matter of weeks! And I am telling you, General Kesselring, that to win a war you convince your enemy that it is he who cannot win it. And if he believes he cannot win the war, you have won." Archie said, leaning on the table with his fists clenched. He allowed his gaze to fall upon each senior officer present.

"We are going to bomb London. We are going to reduce the British city to rubble and we will convince Churchill and his sheep that they cannot win the war. Are we all quite clear? Eh? As of immediately, the Luftwaffe will stop the stalemate and start winning the conflict with that fat, cigar smoking bastard on Downing Street. That is my final decision in this matter."

With that Archie pushed back his chair and strode from the room while others in the room quickly came to their feet and waited until he had gone.

BOOK IV

CHAPTER

18

Archie had begun the day making two speeches, minor ones, the first to a breakfast assemblage of Gauleiters from the German protectorates of Bohemia and Moravia, the second in the afternoon to shipyard workers in Hamburg. The activities had no special significance to Archie but had been on Hitler's previous schedule as devised and maintained by Martin Bormann. He had not the faintest idea what the real Adolf Hitler had planned to tell the meeting of Gauleiters, except that it was intended to support activities proposed by SS-Obergruppenfuhrer Reinhard Heydrich, nor did he have any notion what activities Heydrich had proposed. Military, he supposed. In any case, Archie had no intention of asking. There was a limit to his crutch of temporary amnesia resulting from the assassination attempt. No, he would simply entertain the gauleiters through their coffee and pastries then leave for Tempelhof.

"In Germany," Archie said from the head of a table that had been set up in the Reichschancellery dining room, "the people, without doubt, decide their existence. They determine the principles of their government. In fact it has been possible in this country to incorporate many of the broad masses into the National Socialist party, that gigantic organization embracing millions and having millions of officials drawn from the people themselves. This principle is extended to the highest ranks. Like you, my comrades."

As Archie reached for a glass of water before him, he could easily see chests swell in the rapt group turned toward him, hardly a movement to create a distraction as the Führer continued is incredibly enlightening speech.

"For the first time in German history, we have a state which has absolutely abolished all social prejudices in regard to political appointments as well as in private life," Archie said, waiting for knowing smiles, sardonic nods, or possibly even laughter at his ironic words.

Nothing of the sort.

He continued, "I myself am the best proof of this. Just imagine, I am not even a lawyer, and yet I am your Führer!"

The applause was spontaneous, exuberant. Several of the gauleiters rose to their feet, eventually all of them were standing before reseating themselves.

"It is not only in ordinary life that we have succeeded in appointing the best among the people for every position. We have Reichsstatthalters who were formerly agricultural laborers or locksmiths. Yes, we have succeeded in breaking down prejudice in a place where it was most deep-seated, in the fighting forces. Thousands of officers are being promoted from the ranks today. We have done away with prejudice. We have generals who were ordinary soldiers and noncommissioned officers twenty-two and twenty-three years ago. In this instance, too, we have overcome all social obstacles. Who can tell, perhaps one day an actor may be your Führer!"

Appreciative laughter and bright, unblinking eyes lit up the loving faces of the Third Reich's guests.

Hauptman Pilot Frederich Friedel lumbered around his parked Dornier 217E, swathed in his bulky flying suit, the bottom of which was tucked into fur lined boots made by Germany's new ally, Czechoslovakia. He carried leather gloves, lined with rabbit fur, tucked into a wide leather waist belt. His zippered flight suit, worn over his regular uniform, was causing him to perspire in spite of the fact that the sun had set more than two hours ago. It was a balmy night, even for late September, and he was anxious to complete his preflight inspection of his new aircraft. Like most of the pilots and crew of Kampfgeschwader 1, he had survived too many missions to deceive himself that he would continually come back from them all. He believed, and history would prove him correct, that he would simply fly combat until he was captured or killed, that Herman Göring and Dr. Goebbels notwithstanding, the war would not be over very soon. The British fighters showed no signs of weakness in the ferocity of their attacks nor their number diminishing.

It was good, he thought, that the Luftwaffe had switched from day to night bombing. The air groups were suffering fewer aircraft and crews shot down, but the number was still far too great for what they bargained for at the outset of the war.

Friedel carefully ran his fingers over the control surfaces of the wing, checking rigging alignment, then pushed and pulled them to judge freedom of traverse. He glanced at the tires to make sure he would not be taking off on a flat, and he worked his way to the tail assembly, feeling and moving the horizontal stabilizers and vertical rudders.

"Ludi," he said to his bombardier and nose gunner, "look at the maintenance sheet. See if they replaced a brake cylinder." Dark blue brake fluid covered the tire of the port side main gear, but it could have happened during the cylinder change.

"No, sir," Ludi Schollz said, flipping through the squawk sheets. "Nothing here."

Friedel frowned. Aborting the mission was not much of an option. As long as the aircraft could fly, he would have to fly. Losing one's brakes on a landing rollout was an unwritten acceptable risk.

"Well, Freddy?" Ludi asked, squatting to look at the leaking cylinder. He knew that while the braking system should have been redlined there was no danger of losing all hydraulic pressure in the airplane's systems because of redundancy.

"Well, what?" Friedel snorted. "We fly. What the fuck do you think? And if we don't die we find the line chief when we get back and we kick his stupid ass!"

The others of his crew of four were already aboard, checking their weapons, loading ammunition belts into them and determining that their radio leads for intercom were working.

Once into the cockpit of his bomber Friedel set to work on his navigation checkpoints, committing his mission profile to memory; time to start engines, time to climb to 5,000 meters, at the very limit of the Dornier's maximum ceiling, and a run to target at 500 kph, much faster than his old Heinkel 111. He would use the Luftwaffe's nav/beams, radio frequency transmissions sent from points in Holland, Belgium, and France, to navigate toward London where he would find tonight's target in the Thames estuary. There was the Woolwich Arsenal, the Beckton gas works and a large number of docks as well as the West Ham power station. Friedel was fully aware that he and his comrades were placing a maximum number of aircraft into a concerted number of raids aimed at finally breaking the back of the British people and their overall ability to wage war. If London cracked, they will have won the entire war.

Friedel also knew that for one of his bombs from his paltry capacity of 2,000 kg to fall on a vital target, especially at night, would take the hand of Providence to accomplish. More likely he would kill a mother and her two children. Or that he would dig a huge hole in the middle of a British golf course. God, he was glad he would be unable to see it.

He made a spinning motion with his forefinger at the ground crew and, closing the fuel mixture lever and priming the starboard engine, cracked the throttle slightly, then pulled the starting lever. The fourteen cylinder radial BMW engine began turning slowly, then coughed, caught, and settled into a throaty rumble. With the starboard engine generating power for the electric starter on the port engine, Friedel began the start-up procedure and, after ten blades, the engine caught and growled itself into a confident, steady, roar. He checked the magnetos first on one engine, then the other, determining that both ignition systems were on line. He lubricated the pitch controls on each propeller, then brought each back to climb and taxi position.

"Pilot to crew," Friedel said as he pulled the control yoke into his lap and turned it right to left to test full traverse, "everybody on board? High turret," he intoned.

"Hans, Hauptman," the top gunner reported, then followed by the other three who acknowledged they were on board and prepared to fly.

"Good. No one stayed behind. You are all good little Germans. I am so proud. Before you know it we'll be back and I'll stand for the beer. All you can drink!"

He kicked off the brakes and called his taxi turns by radio to the rest of the ground traffic, working his way from the dispersal area to the active runway.

"Do you promise, sir?" Christian Weisel said from the waist gun. "I am thirsty right now."

"Of course, I promise. And I'm going to have them put saltpeter into your swill. I don't want you to get that little waitress in the NCO mess pregnant. For your own good. All right, radio quiet, now," Friedel said, pushing the throttles to the forward stops as the Do 217 began racing down the newly paved runway, picking up speed until it virtually groaned at its full bomb weight, yet lifted off the ground at 110 kph. It was not necessary for Friedel to do much. The engines were contra-rotating, negating the need to offset torque with the rudder pedals, and he had cranked in enough trim so that the nose of the machine pointed itself gracefully above the horizon and into the blackness of the night.

He put the Dornier into a 190 kph climb and began the ritual of instrument scan; checking all gauges with practiced eye, engine temperatures, tachometers, vacuum in inches of mercury, oil and fuel pressures, airspeed indicator, turn and bank coordinator to maintain the aircraft in level flight without ground reference. His heading was going to be 71 magnetic, a course that would take them over Boulogne, France, when the ship would have attained cruise altitude. This was important to Friedel because he wanted to pick up as much speed as possible in level flight before turning out over the Channel on a 110 heading. If he could coax the Dornier into its maximum designed altitude before the turn, he would be able to drop the nose and, using high power settings red-lining the engines, if necessary, pick up additional knots on the run through enemy fighter space.

His course, verified and updated by his navigator every few minutes during the flight, would take them well behind Margate, England, where there was a heavy concentration of Spitfire squadrons, and onto Sheerness where he would make another 20 left turn and run up the winding Thames River.

At night, without clouds, like this, the Thames reflected the moon and made the bomb run seem like a daylight training exercise in its simplicity. Friedel much preferred dark nights and clouds nearby in which to hide. In this so-called "bomber's moon" he would be at least as visible to the RAF fighters as his targets on the ground. He shuddered at the thought, then forced his attention onto other cockpit business.

Fifty-two minutes into the mission he was bearing down on the British coastline. He had not managed to attain the altitude he hoped for over the French coast and was indicating only 390 kph instead of the 515 maximum kph the machine was designed to fly. The specs on the airplane were, he knew, skewed in favor of the manufacturer when it was selling the plane to the Luftwaffe and not in favor of the crews that flew it into combat. Friedel therefore felt no obligation to execute the mission profile as the planners had drawn it up. Passing over the British coast at 4,200 meters, he lowered the nose slightly, rolled in corresponding trim, and leaned his engines to the max. Up ahead he could see shafts of searchlights on the ground stabbing through darkened skies like multiple fingers of a ghostly hand from the grave, reaching up for him and his crew. He knew they had been picked up on radar and could expect fighter interceptors any time. He could not guide on the searchlights even though they waited for him every time he flew a mission, because the Limeys moved the damn things at least every two days. If a lazy Luftwaffe pilot followed the lights in order to find his London target, he would likely drop his bombs into cow pastures outside the city.

"Night fighters!" came the shout over the intercom.

"Call it out, Hans," Friedel said, in a voice much calmer than he felt.

"My five o'clock, one thousand meters," the high gunner said as he fired his rear-facing gun for the first time.

Friedel waited. In his mind's eye he tried to imagine that he was the enemy pilot closing in on the Dornier. He would be gaining approximately 450 meters per minute on the bomber, coming from below and climbing, so Friedel counted to himself and when he got to ten he kicked a hard left rudder, rolled in all of the aileron he had, then pulled the yoke back into his lap. He held the four G turn for several seconds until, in his imagination, the Spitfire pilot had rolled his own aircraft into a tight turn, then Friedel shoved the yoke full forward, kicked opposite rudder, rolling the ailerons to the right. This time he did not pull the yoke back all the way into his lap but pushed the nose of the bomber down sharply. The maneuver allowed him to pick up precious airspeed while he dove for the protection of a clouds 200 meters down at his three o'clock.

Out of his peripheral vision he saw the night fighter's tracers gliding past his port wing root, a beautiful pattern of light flashing near him, trying gracefully to tear his aircraft apart, set it afire and kill him and his crew. Friedel thought he had made it into the cloud cover free and clear when he felt the dull thuds of machine gun rounds stitching his starboard wing and into the engine. It was the work of the first fighter's wing man, Friedel thought. For an instant he felt anger at Hans for not telling him there was not one but two fighters on his tail, but dismissed the notion at once realizing that even if he had known there was probably nothing he could have done differently to avoid the hits.

"Right engine on fire, boys," Friedel said to his crew. "Time to get out! Go, go," he urged even as he actuated the fire extinguishers placed inside the engine cowling. Even if they could have put the fire out it would not survive the return flight.

"Ludi, drop...."

But his bombardier had already toggled the bomb load and began his own climb out of his nose position toward the escape hatch he and Friedel would have to share to exit the burning plane. Friedel struggled mightily to hold up the port wing by standing on the left rudder and cranking in full aileron to compensate for the immense drag on the right side and increased torque from the starboard engine which was still producing power. It meant death for them all if the aircraft rolled while they were trying to get out. There was no way he could see behind and below him inside the airplane but he could now see Ludi, with smoke beginning to fill the cockpit, wrestle to twist open the escape hatch in the glassine nose. The navigator, delivering a desperate kick, popped out the hatch cover allowing high speed cold air to race through the aircraft.

Friedel saw Ludi dive head first through the small opening and, setting the controls on auto pilot, positioned himself to take the next leap. He let go the controls and moved to the hatch. The Dornier immediately began to roll inverted, and what was "down" one second before was now "up" for Friedel as he struggled with all of his strength against the forces of gravity. As the burning aircraft continued its irregular rotation through space, Friedel relaxed for one second as he waited for the ship to roll just a few more degrees, easing the G forces pulling him back inside.

He waited too long.

The wing, now completely engulfed in flame, exploded.

It was late on a February afternoon when, returning from Hamburg, Archie had a chance to examine the papers over which Bormann, for the past several days, had beamed his unqualified approval. Archie knew that the thick file folder that the Deputy Party Secretary kept nudging toward him had something to do with the after-action reports following the Polish campaign. They were disturbing and he put them away. Archie longed instead to read something other than accounts of Teutonic saber-slashing. While the war seemed to grind on with some sort of automata propelling it, Archie acted out his scenes with increasing confidence. He was, however, being pressured by social forces to make a trip to the Berghof in Obersalzberg, his "home" and the retreat of the topmost officials of the Third Reich.

But Eva Braun was there.

He had answered the first of her several telephone calls in November, allowing her to get through the switchboard in the Reichschancellery. He was prepared to quickly hang up at the first indication that she was becoming suspicious but, on the contrary, it was she who suggested that the conduct of the war was to blame for their being apart and that she understood completely. He could not agree more, he said.

She had called several times since then and, to his surprise, he began to enjoy the conversations. It was all one sided at first, with Eva telling him all of the little events of her life, both in the city and while she was at the Berghof. She did not complain of anything but only related positive, lighthearted things for him to think about. Eva and her sister, Gretl, had visited the Tea House in the Eagle's Nest which had just been finished. It was beautiful, she told him, and she couldn't wait for him to spend time there with her.

On another telephone occasion she told him that she had spent the day with Emmy Göring, the once well-known actress Sonnemann. She had made a great number of films, Eva said, and she secretly missed her career even though she enjoyed making a home for the Reichsmarshall and her daughter, Edda. Archie found himself wanting to visit with Emmy Göring himself, and was tempted to drop everything in Berlin and decamp for the Alps. But he was not yet so courageous.

He spent part of New Year's Eve at a Reichschancellery party that was blinding in its profusion of brass and braid, but his appearance was perfunctory and he left the celebrants early. By now he was aware that the presence of the Führer was not always a guarantee of frivolity for those around him. Smoking was popular with most people and Hitler was violently opposed. He was also a non-drinker and a vegetarian, complexities of character that Archie easily attached as his own, and he used them to advantage. In short, when Hitler wanted to be alone, he was not missed.

In spite of his distaste for the task, Archie began reading the Bormann reports again and, as he turned one page after another, a sense of horror crept over him, a chill that seeped into his bones coming not from the temperature of the Führerbunker, but out of the words before him of which he tried to make sense. The post-action reports from Poland contained suggestions that were incomprehensible. In his need to illuminate the confusion in his head over the virulent antisemitism that had become the bedrock of Nazi social policy and laws, Archie read prior speeches made by the man whose body he took. In one of them, given in January of 1939, the dictator said "Today I will once more be a prophet. If the international financiers inside and outside Europe should again succeed in plunging the nations into a world war the result will not be the Bolshevization of the earth and thus the victory of Jewry, but the annihilation of the Jewish race throughout Europe."

Archie shuddered as he quickly scanned the printed material for a second time.

There was a thing called the Nuremberg Laws of 1935. He had not read them all but Archie knew that they stripped Jews of everything. They could not own property, they could not hold passports, they had no civil rights at all. But it was the activity of the German armed forces in Poland that had made Archie's head swim in a sea of tumultuous confusion.

It was not Archie's habit to sleep late in the morning, as it had been the real Adolf Hitler, and Archie looked forward to those hours to be totally alone, at whatever form of peace he could find away from the press of state business. But this morning, at 0600 hours, he picked up his telephone and called his driver, Colonel Erich Kempka. He informed Kempka that he intended to travel to the Luftwaffe base at Bergues, France. He wanted to get there as quickly as possible and, Archie said, that would probably best be accomplished by airplane. Arrange it, he said to Kempka.

Within minutes, even before Archie had begun to shave and touch up the roots of his hair, keeping it quite dark, his phone began to ring insistently. He knew intuitively that it would be Martin Bormann.

It was. Archie confirmed to Bormann that he had ordered Colonel Kempka to arrange transportation to the Channel fighter base in Bergues, and had to assuage Bormann that he had not by-passed Bormann's office with travel plans but that since the journey was to be quite brief and not far, there was no need to take Bormann away from his much more important duties at the Reichschancellery. Archie listened patiently as Bormann wheedled away, reminding Archie that Bormann's office only existed to provide for the Führer so it was therefore no trouble at all, on the contrary. In the process, Bormann insisted that he accompany the Führer even though he was true that managing the affairs of state with which his department had been entrusted was at a harrowing level, he would hear of nothing that would keep him from his Führer's side.

Archie, taking the risk of turning the Deputy Party Secretary into an outright foe, gently ordered Bormann to remain in Berlin so that the Reich would remain in his capable hands. Thus mollifiéd, Bormann suggested that the flight be made in Hitler's personally configured Fock-Wulf FW 200 Condor 'Immelmann III', a comfortably appointed four engine aircraft that had only recently been outfitted with gun positions. Not that they would be needed with Luftwaffe fighters that would fly cover for Germany's leader. Archie agreed and said that he wanted to leave for Tempelhof within the hour.

19

Dietrich had flown two Channel sweeps beginning at dawn and would fly two more before the day was done. His Me-109 was shot full of holes on his last sortie and he had landed on but one gear when the other main gear would not extend. His canopy had two bullet holes in it and the cooling system had been all but shot away. He had lost all of his glycol and his engine, overheated, had seized four miles short of the runway. He had bellied his stricken machine into a ploughed field and, when the aircraft ground-looped, Dietrich was hanging upside down from his harness. Had there been a fire he would have died in the flames. Before hitting the ground, however, he had shut off the master switch to prevent sparks when wires were ripped from their termini, but Dietrich, covered with aviation petrol from ruptured wing tanks, could only thank Providence that another source did not spark.

He was resting in his small quarters, freshly showered but very tired, when his squadron adjutant knocked on his door per protocol, then opened it and stepped inside.

"Herr Major," he said in a state of undisguised excitement, "the Führer is coming!"

"Hitler?" Dietrich responded, propping himself up on one elbow. "You don't say. Standing in the *Bedienungen Platz*?" Operations Room.

"No, sir, he will be touching down any time now. His pilot called three minutes ago. It is a Fock-Wulf FW 200, the Führer's own airplane, you know," the adjutant said. "And he wants you!"

"The pilot?" Dietrich teased.

"No, sir. The Führer wants you."

"Very well, I will get dressed and meet him. Tell the base commandant that he had better round up some kind of honor guard. Whoever is available."

But the SS-traveling security force of the RSD was taking no chances on a forward operational base having available an honor guard. The 100 man-strong bodyguard had arrived minutes in advance of the Führer's aircraft and were smartly formed in front of the area where the FW-200 would park. Dietrich was still buttoning his tunic and buckling his uniform belt when the Führer's pilot shut down the final two outboard engines. The passenger door was opened from the inside and Archie was the first to deplane.

To Dietrich Archie looked pale. There were dark half-circles under his eyes. His shoulders seem to have slumped forward as he looked around at the fighter strip and at its utterly rapt personnel. Dietrich stepped forward, not as though to be presumptuous, but near enough to make himself convenient for the nation's Führer. Archie brightened measurably at the sight of his London contact. He moved forward with deliberate, dignified steps, returning Dietrich's extended-arm Nazi salute.

"Well, Major Dietrich," Archie said, pretending much more jocularity than he felt. "Good of you to take your busy time to show me your fighter base."

"I am honored, Führer, and I know that I speak for the entire base staff, as well. What would you like to see first, sir?" Dietrich said, moving to Hitler's left, per protocol that requires junior officers to walk to the left of those senior.

"Ah, the cockpit of your plane, of course," Archie said for all to hear. "Obersturmbannführer Vass," Archie said, turning to the SS officer near him, the man who today was commanding the traveling security force.

"*Jawohl,*" Vass said, snapping his booted heels together, pulling in his chin and standing ramrod straight.

"Allow your men to stand at ease. I want to visit with the major,"

Archie said, strolling along the flight line of parked fighter aircraft. "I hate that man," Archie said to Dietrich under his breath.

"The Obersturmbannführer? But why?" Dietrich said.

"I don't trust him. He has beady eyes. You laugh, but he is a bully. He slops up beer and then rides around with his bully boys to smash windows and steal money from the Jews. It is all in his dossier, but of course it is meant to applaud his dedication to the Reich," Archie spat the words.

Archie glanced casually over his shoulder to ensure that they were not being trailed too closely by members of Archie's bodyguard.

"Here," he said, this is my plane." They stopped by a squat, fierce appearing Messerschmitt. Archie was impressed, despite his total ignorance of airplanes, with its all-business look. "Let's take a look inside the cockpit."

By climbing onto a wing and putting their heads inside the cockpit, Dietrich could appear to be explaining the functions of the various gauges, handles, buttons and switches in the complex machine while they spoke unheard by others.

"You did an incredible job with the Luftwaffe High Command," Dietrich said. "We are no longer hitting airfields. We are pounding cities, especially London, but at least the RAF is recovering. Good work," he added.

"It would be ironic if I killed my wife and child in the process," Archie said, his eyes falling.

"I think your wife and child are being very well looked after, Archie," Dietrich offered, totally ignorant about how indeed Archie's family was being dealt with. He had never thought of it before. Good God, what were the odds?

"Yes," Archie said without passion, "I'm sure they are."

"Well, then, shall I try to find out about them?" Dietrich offered.

"You could do that?" Archie said, suddenly brightening.

"I don't see why not. I'm going to be on the air with London tomorrow night. It wouldn't hurt to ask. Consider it done, Archie." Dietrich wanted to pat the man affectionately on the shoulder but of course he could not move out of character.

"I'd be ever so grateful, old man. Really, I...." Archie suddenly stopped, emotionally overcome. Dietrich pretended to point to various areas of the Me-109's cockpit to keep the act alive.

"Hang on, Arch," Dietrich said.

"I'm all right," the actor said.

"You're way ahead of the game. No matter what happens now, you've pulled it off. Even if...." "Dietrich almost bit his tongue in instant regret. "That is..."

"I know what you mean. Even if I'm caught now, it doesn't matter," Archie said bravely, but immediately depressed again.

"That is not what I was going to say," Dietrich lied. In fact that was exactly what he was thinking. The Luftwaffe had stopped short of its dedicated task of wiping out the RAF and Wehrmacht troops along the Channel had been withdrawn. There would be no invasion of England. No one on the face of the earth but Archie Smythes could have done it.

"Dietrich," Archie said, gravely, "you have to tell the people in London, the Prime Minister, or whoever runs the bloody place, that evil things are being done in Eastern Europe. I would give the orders but I do not know where to begin. It was all set in motion, you see, before I..."

"Wait, Archie," Dietrich said, suddenly concerned for Archie's badly traumatized nerves. "What evil things?"

Archie paused to gather his thoughts. It was a bit of a struggle. "I'm not sure, really. What I know, or what I read, is never quite written, or said, in clear language. It's as though they speak in euphemisms."

"Who is 'they'?" Dietrich asked.

"The Party. The Nazis. And mostly the SS, I suppose," Archie said, still struggling in his own mind to clarify what were, after all, emotional issues. "They're killing people. Jews, mostly, I think, and they build these concentration camps, they call them. They are all over Europe, now."

"People die in wars," Dietrich said, cautiously.

"I'm not talking about battles. You know, bombs dropped and guns going off. Look here, Dietrich, I've never been much of a Jew lover. Truth to tell, I suppose I've been something of an anti-Semite most of my life. Not that I'm proud of it, you understand, and I've tossed off my share of slurs about Hymie's and Jew jokes, but I never went out of my way to... to...."

"Yes?"

"Well, we Ger... these Germans seem to be positively crazed on the subject. They took away everything they owned, the Jews. Stole it, actually," Archie's voice dropped to an almost inaudible level so that Dietrich had to lean quite close to hear the man.

"Yes, I know. Let's walk. Pretend you are interested in other parts of the base".

The two men climbed down from the wing of the Me-109 and began to stroll along the flight line toward the maintenance hangars, little more than camouflaged netting. Thundering sounds of multiple engines being either ground tested or from aircraft landing or taking off made it possible for Archie and Dietrich to keep their heads close together and to mask their conversation from trailing bodyguards and staff officers, constant figures among Hitler's entourage.

"One SS report I read only yesterday referred to 110,000 Jews emigrating from Austria and another 35,000 that had emigrated from Moravia. But where did they go? To 'relocation areas,' the report said. Camps, is what I believe. What happens to them there, I wonder? Did you know that the political governor of Poland is forcing thousands of Jews into a ghetto in Warsaw? It must be horrible. They are ordered not to own a business, they cannot work...."

"Archie," Dietrich interrupted, "you cannot afford to get emotional. You are under a great deal of...."

"They are forced to wear yellow stars. Arm bands, too. And it isn't only Jews, it is others. Political leaders... wherever the army goes, the SS sends special units to 'deal' with them. They have all of these terms and words that mean something else. It is like an inside joke, a secret of some kind. You have to tell the people in London. Churchill has to be informed. Don't you agree?"

"Of course. Churchill and London want to know everything that...."

"I have to do something. Give an order. I did it before. Twice. And I can do it again," Archie said.

"You'll do no such thing," Dietrich said.

"Eh? What's that?" Archie said, clearly surprised. He was no longer accustomed to receiving prohibitions in any form.

"Wait until you hear from the SOE. That's who we work for, you and I," Dietrich said, pointing his finger as though explaining part of the Luftwaffe station activities to his Führer.

Archie considered for a moment. "Of course. I am quite aware." He lifted his chin and, for the first time since he arrived, gazed at his surroundings with the arrogance Hitler would have displayed at inspecting his personal property, over which he was undisputed master.

To make Archie's visit look complete, he lunched with Dietrich and his fellow pilots in the squadron mess. He chatted with them about their flying tasks as well as asking about where they came from and about their families. He asked them what, if anything he could do for them when he returned to Berlin. Was their food all right? Did they get enough leave? How was their morale? he wanted to know. There were fleeting moments of embarrassed silence, especially when the question of leave was raised. They virtually had no leave, not in months, anyway, and it would be a very long time before they could imagine combat requirements easing to the point where they could get away for a few weeks or even a few days. But the moment of discontent passed and, when Archie signaled that it was time for him to leave, he sensed that he had truly lifted the spirits of these very young men who were giving their uttermost for the Reich.

Indeed, as Dietrich walked at Archie's side toward the Führer's FW-200, he smiled broadly as he said "Well, Arch, you've made a lot of people happy today. I would think my boys will tear through the skies tomorrow with completely renewed vigor. We might even shoot down a few extra RAF planes as a result."

Archie stopped, stricken, and stared at Dietrich. "My god! I never thought of that," he said.

Dietrich was more than a little amused. "Don't worry a bit, my Führer. I try to think of something every day that will keep their spirits up. I want as many of them as possible to come out of this war alive. Even if they are German, they are fine young men."

Archie nodded his head as he regarded Dietrich for a long moment. "You are, too, Stephen," he said.

Dietrich came to attention, took one step back, extended his arm and said, "Heil Hitler!"

The house in Belgravia had now completed its installation of a signals center sufficient to handle its Special Missions Section. The basement had been expanded by excavation and concrete walls and ceilings had been reinforced to protect against aerial bombs. Nothing less than a direct hit from a 1,000 pounder could penetrate to the nerve center of the building. Indeed, the object of the engineering feat was to shield the delicate tubes and circuits of the short wave radios that operated around the clock in the bowels of the house. Not that the operators who listened for and transmitted messages to the teams sent out by SOE were easily replaced, either, so that when the air raid sirens went off around the city, an increasingly frequent event, Mssrs. Elliot, Schuyler and Wiles could usually be found down among them.

Those three men, however, had been two floors above the ComCenter for several hours pondering its latest product. They had received a disturbing signal from "Greek," the code identifier assigned to Dietrich. Greek had paraphrased Archie's misgivings about almost all of German social and political malignancies in cryptographic form and delivered it to SOE for their evaluation and, if need be, action.

At first Archie's concerns seemed to be the result of what must be the unbelievable stress of pretending to be another person, within the very center of the enemy camp. Now that he was in charge, they agreed, Archie would quite understandably want to make changes.

"He can't do that," Sir William Schuyler said, dismissing Archie's most heartfelt concerns. "It was his... I mean Hitler's... idea in the first place. About the Jews. Bloody nut case, the man is... I mean was, but Archie can't just...." Sir William waved a long arm in a sweeping gesture before being interrupted by MacLean Elliot.

"I wonder just how bad it all is? I mean, good heavens, I would have been the first man out of Europe in 1932 were I a Jew. But there it is, isn't it? They had all the time in the world to get out."

"With respect, MacClean, I don't think that is the point. For whatever reason, or reasons, most Jews who lived in Europe in 1932 still do. Many of them left, without question, but what's to be done with them now?" Edward Wiles said. He played with a watch fob, a harmless affectation he allowed himself to appear a bit more conservative, perhaps even a little older, among his colleagues.

"I hope you aren't suggesting that the SOE, and in the specific, we three, dispose of the Biblical conundrum of Jewish persecution? I mean, isn't that a philosophic question?" MacLean Elliot said to Wiles.

"Elliot's right. It's bloody nonsense to think that we can send some bloody message to Archie the actor in Berlin and accomplish what Moses failed at! Eh? What does the man expect?" Sir William said, blowing his nose into an appallingly overused handkerchief as he treated his first cold of the season.

The discussion was interrupted by the appearance of a non-uniformed staff officer who entered the room after a single knock on the door. "Excuse me, but the Prime Minister's office called to say that Mr. Churchill has experienced an unavoidable change in his schedule. He suggests tomorrow morning at ten, if that is convenient, and he offers to come here."

"Ah, saved by the bell," MacClean Elliot said.

"We shall be honored," Sir William said to the junior officer, dismissively. As they were left alone once again Sir William said "It isn't our decision to make in any case and we should be grateful that it is not. We'll let Winston call this one."

Edward Wiles had been depressed for several weeks even though he should have been ecstatic with the recent turn of events. SOE had, after all, supplied the vital relief in what very well might have been the collapse of the RAF and, almost certainly following that, the loss of the war itself. If that seemed too dramatic to imagine, it was a thought shared by most of the Crown's best informed military minds. Indeed, it was a common perception quietly sweeping world public opinion. So Britain had managed to dodge the German poisoned arrow but found itself still clinging to a very small raft in a giant storm of military might. It would take many months, perhaps years, before Britain could rebuild anything that remotely looked like an army capable of invading Europe, by which time it shall have witnessed an ascendancy of Germany's naval power and the inevitable strangulation of trade. Trade from abroad was as fundamental to life on the British isles as air to breathe.

The simple fact was that Germany, in its present form, was far too big for Britain to deal with alone. The odds were that Archie would be found out at any time. It would be foolish to continue to believe that with Nazi Germany's leader in their pocket they could sit back and forever call the tunes to which the Huns could be expected to dance. It was already clear that Archie was suffering from the strain of his impersonation. And who could blame him? If he didn't crack soon, it would be later.

When Wiles at last fell asleep in the early morning hours, it was a fitful rest that he endured. He rose early, still troubled, looking forward to his own hard to find brand of Continental coffee. Hardly waiting for the percolator to finish its work, he poured the black liquid into a wine glass and sipped. He ran a shallow bath, taking little pleasure in removing the invisible grime of the office from his limbs and loins, and avoided looking into the eyes mirrored before him as he shaved. His driver cum security guard was waiting in the foyer of his apartment as he shrugged into his camel hair overcoat, and as he followed the man out of doors he was even more depressed than ever. The reason for his increased despondency, however, was not because the scenario he had ruminated upon the night had proven impossible to solve. On the contrary, he had arrived at an idea that could very well provide British deliverance.

And the very thought sent tremors of horror through his body.

The Prime Minister was an avid participant in a breakfast of scrambled eggs and bacon provided by the SOE headquarters cook. Immediately upon the outbreak of hostilities Sergeant Dennis Lamar had volunteered for hazardous duty in the army. Because of his extraordinary courage in the face of all odds, and because he had once been certified as a master chef in pre-war Switzerland, he was snatched up by SOE's housekeeping director, Sergeant-Major Robert Bickford, and put to work in its kitchen.

"I don't think I've ever tasted scrambled eggs quite like these," smacked the PM. "Incredible. Tell your cook that I said so."

"I would rather not, Prime Minister, if you don't mind," MacLean Elliot said, dabbing at his mouth with a linen napkin. "The man already has an insufferable ego and anything we say only expands his sense of self importance."

"Too bad. Based upon Napoleon's counsel that an army marches on its stomach, you have a superior weapon at your disposal." The bacon that Winston Churchill was just finishing was pepper cured. With MacLean Elliot and Edward Wiles looking on, Sir William and Winston had wordlessly battled for the lion's share of the delicious meat. Even the most malevolent stare by the Prime Minister aimed at intimidating his cunning adversary failed to achieve victory in the Battle of the Bacon. Winston may have had the last piece but Schuyler had devoured the most, his skinny frame supporting a bloated gut.

Still, the Prime Minister had digested not only his breakfast but the fullest possible meaning of Archie's dilemma as it had been encrypted and signaled by Dietrich. They had begun to repeat their own assessments of the Jewish condition in Europe by the time a third round of coffee was served, this time with a stimulant added.

"You didn't have time to do a psychological evaluation of the man, did you? No, of course not. I do not for a minute believe that any of us thought that the Raven ruse would work as well as it did. Archie...?"

"Smythes, Prime Minister," Wiles prompted.

"Smythes. Enormous asset, this Archie. Enormous. He is concerned, and rightfully so, about Europe's Jews. But what can we do? That is to say, we can't very well order him to feel better, can we? Nazi Germany has outraged the world with its atrocious behavior toward the Jews and other minorities. They have built a party of hate and that hate has spread, like an infectious plague, to all of the German people who support it! Shockingly dreadful. So here is our man, Archie, sitting in Berlin, entirely innocent of what was wrought by his, ah, predecessor, if you will. Eh?" Churchill looked to each man at the table. He almost invited interruption by his pause, but Sir William merely rolled his eyes, MacLean Elliot nodded in sage agreement.

And Wiles waited.

"Obviously, if we signal to Archie that he is to save the Jews at all cost, along with the other afflicted souls selected by the Nazis for persecution, we have thrown him away. We have denied not only this country of its greatest secret weapon of the war, we have done as much to the world. Well? Perish the thought, gentlemen. Perish the thought."

"And the reports are apocryphal," Sir William Schuyler sniffed. "We hear that the Jews and others have been mistreated. But which reports are true and which are hysteria? Oh, some were put into camps, for the duration, I suppose. Not very pleasant, to be sure, but that's what war is, isn't it? I say we're doing our best. Blast it, we've gone to war in their defense, have we not?"

It seemed to Wiles that he had just heard a decision made purely on military consideration. It must have been this way in the last war, at Verdun, at Belleau Woods, the Somme or Amiens. With little effort Wiles could see himself as one of the aging, gilded generals, ordering men to their deaths over poached eggs and croissants. And not a few soldiers would have died carrying out orders to go "over the top" from the trenches. There would be thousands. Hundreds of thousands, their bodies torn to pieces by the new invention, the machine gun, their eyes burned, their lungs seared by poison gas. Decisions of this sort were made not in the mud and among severed body parts where they should have been made, but in ornate dining rooms among baroque furnishings. That's where death is truly palatable. And it was so easy. Effortless, actually.

Well. What *could* be done for them? If Archie suddenly became a champion for the Jews he would certainly be found out for the impostor that he was. Churchill was right about not taking the risk. There was too much to lose should Archie be allowed to make an ill-advised decision about extending mercy to the Jews.

"Prime Minister," Wiles said at last, "our strategy of using Archie the actor as a stand-in for Adolf Hitler was essentially a temporary one. That is that he was to give a single order, and if that worked, just that once, we were way ahead of the game. He succeeded in directing the German High Command back from Operation Sealion and, as a very large bonus that none of us could have even imagined, he supervened in the Luftwaffe's war plans."

"Yes, we're way ahead of the game, Edward," MacLean Elliot agreed, somewhat paternalistically.

"I say we continue to roll the dice, if you will accept what I believe is an appropriate gambling metaphor. Let us assume that Archie will soon be caught in the act, but that before he is unmasked he has given one more order, an order so dramatic that we succeed in once again misdirecting the German armies. In other words," Wiles said in measured word, "if he is going to be caught, let's make his last shot a big one."

"That makes sense, Wiles, but where are you going with this?" MacLean said.

"A second front," Churchill interjected, leaning back in his chair, fingers interlaced on his bulging middle.

"Yes, sir," Wiles said in response. "But not just any front. Not, for example, the Balkans, or Greece or Africa...." He had their undivided attention now. "I believe Archie should send his armies against Russia."

Sir William turned to look at Wiles as though he had lost his senses.

MacLean Elliot swallowed cold coffee down his wind-pipe and coughed into his white napkin.

But the Prime Minister smiled broadly. "I like the scope of your thought, Edward," Churchill said, "but why don't we consider might be accomplished realistically."

Wiles shrugged his shoulders. "Read the man's book, *Mein Kampf.* Listen to his speeches. The only people who approach the level of hatred for the Jews in Hitler's mind is a Communist. On a list of life's lowest animals he ranks Slavs and Russians and Jews in about the same order. He has declared for years that *Lebensraum* lay to Germany's east. Poland was the first part of the plan Hitler had for the total subjugation of the Slavic race to support the Aryan people. Hitler's Germany. I suggest to you that it was an obsession with Adolf Hitler and that Archie should study that part of his role."

"And," Churchill finished, "give the order to invade the USSR."

"Precisely so, yes, sir."

For very long moments Wiles' words hung in the air like the Devil's own artwork as each man considered 'what if?'

"Russia is a non-belligerent," MacLean Elliot said to no one in particular and without much emotion.

"We'll note that for the record," Sir William said, caustically. "I'd rdly call the Soviet Union a friend."

"I didn't say that they are anything of the sort," MacLean Elliot said, defensively. "But since Wiles here brought it up, what we are discussing is the thing that war crimes are made of!"

"The idea is insane, at any rate," Sir William said, shifting uncomfortably in his chair and recrossing his stork-like legs. "Not even Hitler, and I mean the real Hitler, could convince his generals to march on Russia. They are not that stupid."

"I'm not so sure, Sir William," Wiles said. "The General Staff pledged unqualified allegiance to Hitler. Not to Germany, but to Hitler."

"Yes, but...." MacLean Elliot began to protest the incongruity of such a notion.

"I put it to you, Sir William. You were a field grade officer in the last war. If the Crown ordered you to attack nation X would you have refused?" Wiles asked.

"I think I might have if the nation had been Russia," Sir William answered, his eyes looking at a distant object in the room. Then he said "No, of course I would not have. Neither would any of us."

"Then we agree that the OKW would obey Hitler's command if he gave it?" Wiles said, the back of his neck beginning to feel prickly.

"They might," Sir William said.

MacLean Elliot only nodded his head, deep in thought.

The decision, of course, was not theirs to make.

"If you were not men sworn to the Official Secrets Act under penalty of prison or death, I would demand that you take such an oath now," Churchill said, his voice hardly above a whisper. "For what we are talking about in this room is no longer a war between England and Germany along with its conquered territories, but a world war. A world war, gentlemen. Are we prepared to fling the bloodthirsty Nazi armies against an unsuspecting nation, however we disagree with their system of government? I do not see Joseph Stalin allowing Adolf Hitler to march into Red Square and to sit his ass inside the walls of the Kremlin. No, I see a war that would be a fight to the finish, and great loss of life."

By the end of February, 1941, the Luftwaffe was continuing its "Blitz" against the city of London and surrounding areas but with a lack of focus by target planners as well as aircrews. Dumping thousands of tons of bombs into concrete rubble was neither satisfying for an aircrew risking their lives on the mission nor to air marshals whose job it was, after all, to shorten the war and to do it by making their side the winner. While the spring of 1941 lacked the intensity of the six hundred planes per day by which the war had been prosecuted four months prior, though German Luftwaffe casualties remained high, the outlook for Great Britain was only slightly less grim.

Submarine activity had become Germany's not-so-secret weapon and the tonnage of shipping sunk while Britain attempted to keep itself supplied with vital war material was reaching a critical mass. U-boats, now hunting in packs, prowled and terrorized the seas virtually at will. It seemed a very real possibility, at least to Grand Fleet Admiral Raeder and U-boat chief Admiral Dönitz, that the Unterwasser fleet could sever the island nation's lifelines completely. Their reports submitted to Archie, if one discounted the losses of the battleship Bismarck and the pocket battleship *Tirpitz*, should have been immensely uplifting. However, the admirals received little more than polite smiles and rather forced verbal pats on the back as they brought into the daily staff meetings the activities of U-boat captains.

Hitler was not a nautical man and never pretended to be. Still, while Hitler was awed by the great ships he had no idea how to evaluate their role in his war. Nevertheless the German admirals knew that when England eventually capitulated, and it would, the German navy would have contributed a major part in that victory.

Continuing an almost non-stop travel schedule , Archie "inspected" the U-boat complex at Lorient, France. He had to admit that the "pig pens," as they were affectionately called by men of the Unterwasser force, were exceptional engineering achievements and that the submarines were equally fascinating. Archie, with the obligatory retinue of staff and bodyguards in tow, Archie personally reviewed a U-boat crew and decorated several of its members. As he talked with a young captain around whose neck Archie had hung a Knight's Cross, he could not help but be impressed with their raw, quiet courage, and while they were hunters of the high seas they paid a terrible price when they became the hunted. Archie could only imagine the horrors of depth charging, of gasping for clean air when, after two days or more of being forced to the bottom of the ocean, of waiting for the immense power of the sea to crack the pressure hull like a peanut shell.

He was sorry for them. He wanted to tell them that they were no longer following a madman but that he, Archie Smythes, was going to somehow save their lives. Given time.

When he returned to the Reichschancellery, the thoughtful Berta Holz had his favorite tea waiting for him on his desk. Berta had turned out to be one of his better appointments when he assumed the Führer's position. She seemed to be the soul of discretion, someone in whom he could confide all but the most obvious lies of which Archie obsessed and he treated her with deference.

"There is a special message for you, Führer," she said as she sat at the side of his desk establishing a paperwork triage.

"Berta, everything considered, I think you might call me something other than 'Führer,' at least when we're alone in this office," Archie said to the younger woman.

"I will try. What would you like me to call you, sir?" she said, amused but embarrassed.

"Ah, some of my friends call me 'Adie,'" he said.

"Who? Miss Braun?" Berta blurted, curious enough to border on an invasion of the Führer's private life.

"Yes, she is one," Archie said, wondering how, indeed, he would feel when he would come face to face with Eva. His current plans were to visit the Berghof the coming week.

"I could never do that. Herr Hitler? Would that be appropriate?" Berta asked.

Archie wondered if he was being teased. "I suppose it would. Better than...."

Sensing that the most powerful man in Europe had more important work to do, Berta sobered. "Major Dietrich sends you his deepest respects. He asks if it is convenient for you to sign an autograph on a picture of one his pilots who was killed. He said that it would mean a great deal to the man's mother and father."

Archie brightened immediately. "Is he here? In Berlin?"

Berta nodded. "He is staying at the transient crew quarters at Tempelhof."

"Call him at once and tell him that a car will pick him up. No, wait. Instruct the Major to have someone at Tempelhof drive him here. That will save time. Then arrange for a light dinner in the bunker. Dietrich will be my guest," he said.

"You like the Major, don't you, Herr Hitler?" she said.

"Yes. He's a very good... Nazi. And I like to have a first-hand account of the war," Archie answered. He did not add that he would be literally lost without the Luftwaffe major.

The days were getting longer. Archie anticipated the coming spring days and Berlin, a city of rivers, lakes and plentiful greenery, was beginning to fill his nostrils. They were the kind of smells he remembered when his mother and father took him on a train to visit a distant cousin who lived well away from London. The cousin, even older than his parents, lived on a farm where Archie saw a cow and sheep for the first time in his life except in picture books. On those very infrequent trips to the country it seemed that the days lasted forever and he was tucked into bed while it was still light.

But in the basement of the Führerbunker day and night were the same. He and Dietrich sat down in his work room where the table, normally overlaid with maps or papers, was now covered with a sparkling linen cloth, polished silverware and crystal goblets. Archie knew Dietrich enjoyed wine so he made certain that the best French selections were available.

After the last plate had been cleared and butterscotch ice cream dessert had been left, Archie gave instructions that there were to be no further interruptions. He gave the communications room operator the same orders, that he was not to be disturbed except in an emergency. Archie turned his radio onto a Berlin station that played classical music. He was all but certain that his rooms were not spied upon or wired for sound, nevertheless they two men spoke in subdued tones.

"Well?" Archie asked, anxiously. "What did they say?"

"First, let me tell you that your family is quite safe. Your daughter..."

"Rose," Archie interrupted.

"Yes. Rose is living in the country with a farming family. I understand that she is happy and that she is attending school. Many thousands of London's children have been moved to the countryside to avoid the bombing," Dietrich said.

Archie once again felt lashed by guilt, as though the city was being crushed solely because of his orders. He said as much to Dietrich.

"You can't think that, Archie. The Luftwaffe was fully engaged against England before you arrived on the scene. Try to remember that."

"I know," he nodded, but did not feel buoyed.

"It isn't possible for the SOE to make special provisions for your wife. Laverne, you know," Dietrich said.

Archie nodded.

"Which is not to say they are not looking out for her, because they are. But she still works. The Wartime Housing Agency has miraculously found her an apartment that is considerably finer than where you lived before. It's in the Rotherhithe district. Do you know where that is? I'm not so familiar with London myself. I understand she's within walking distance of a park. And she..."

Dietrich broke off as Archie had suddenly placed a napkin over his eyes which he had closed tightly. The Luftwaffe pilot was on the verge of asking the actor if he was quite all right before realizing that the ersatz Führer's eyes had filled with tears. After a moment Archie opened them again and nodded vigorously.

"Sorry," he said.

"I'm sure it's a relief to know that your wife is all right," Dietrich said. Then, "Look, Archie, they've handed you a tough one. I don't quite understand it myself but then that isn't my job. Maybe it isn't even your job. We just follow orders, you and I, and we have confidence that those above us have done all of the strategic thinking for us."

"What is it?" Archie said. "You're talking about the Jews and the others, aren't you? The ones in the camps. I know it isn't going to be easy but I... well, I'm ready for whatever the consequences are going to be."

"So, you realize that if you attempt to come to the aid of the Jews you'll certainly be discovered. Is that right?" Dietrich said.

Archie nodded again. "Not exactly. That is, it seems to me that there are orders I could give, small ones, directly to certain people, not sweeping changes in the laws. Not right away, anyhow. Naturally, I'll have to move as quickly as I can because...." Archie stopped speaking when he realized that Dietrich was not in agreement. Archie might as well have been talking to the concrete wall. For a moment he felt resentment. He took a deep breath, feeling a surge of anger rush through him. This was the Reichschancellery, after all, and he was in charge, here. His lips parted then closed again when reason again quickly took hold.

"I can see that you don't agree. All right, then, what do we do? What do I do?"

"How many contingency operational plans have been drawn up by the OKH and submitted to you?" Dietrich asked.

"I'm not sure. I haven't ordered any such things to be done," Archie said, unsure what Dietrich was getting at.

"Of course not. They would have been ordered by your predecessor. Probably many months ago. Even years. But they are at your fingertips," Dietrich gently urged.

"Yes. I've seen some of them. That's what the OKH does, you know. It does battle planning. And they are quite good at what they do, I understand. I've been informed that the German General Staff is among the best, if not the best, war planning group in the world," Archie said with a measure of personal pride recognizable in his voice.

Dietrich nodded his agreement. "As a matter of fact that's true. So here are your orders from London, Archie. You are to order the Nazi war machine to concentrate on an entirely new enemy. Right out of the contingency files."

"I don't understand," Archie said.

"What we are saying... what they are saying, in London, is that Germany needs to have a second front. A front that will divert their armies and air forces in another direction. Away from England," Dietrich said, hoping that what he was relaying in the form of SOE orders made more sense to Archie than to him.

"You mean *expand* the war?" Archie said, incredulous. "How? Where?"

"Russia."

"What about Russia?" Archie said, the enormity of what Dietrich was suggesting not taking shape as a real proposition.

"In its simplest form," Dietrich said, lowering his voice to almost a whisper despite concrete walls that diminished the range of his voice, "find the OKH invasion plan for the Soviet Union and order your armies to march."

Archie slowly stood up from the table and began to pace the room, his hands clasped behind his back. He would occasionally glance in Dietrich's direction but did not speak until he had made several circuits around the room.

"They won't do it," he said, at last.

"I think they will," Dietrich said, with more conviction than he felt.

"Ah, advice from the great military mind of Stephen Dietrich," Archie snapped, not in the least sorry for sarcasm directed at his SOE operative. "That would about wrap it up, then."

"Sorry, Archie. Of course you're right. It doesn't matter what I think. What matters is what you think. And what London thinks, of course. It isn't that the Russians are innocents in all of this. They've attacked Finland, annexed eastern Poland, the Baltic states as well," Dietrich said.

"God," Archie said, collapsing again into a stuffed chair placed against a concrete wall. "They would shoot me," he said, almost to himself.

They probably would, Dietrich thought. He could easily see the rationale behind SOE's decision. Archie was going to be caught and shot. That was a given. But, as before, if he could issue one more order before that event happens, then it was a bonus. A huge bonus. Everything he did under the direction of SOE was an unexpected reward, far above what had come the day before or the day before that.

"Well, I won't do it. I asked you to tell them about the concentration camps and about the Jews and about other people in eastern Europe that are suffering, probably dying. Those code words they use. Well? What instructions did they send? What ideas do they have about that? Surely they have *something* to say? Well? I'm listening," Archie said.

For a very long moment Dietrich could not respond. It would have been easy for him to agree with Archie on both counts, that the order to attack Russia was absurd and that the failure to take proper account of the Jews of Europe was inexcusable. Still, had he been given Edward Wiles' place in SOE, would he have been able to suggest a more effective antidote for the approaching annihilation of life of the British Empire? They, Dietrich was still aware that he was American and America was not at war with anyone, were by themselves, with France a conquered nation, alone against the German juggernaut which was incredibly strong and getting more so every day. No, he could not come up with a better idea. And it might not matter even if he could.

"Archie, it should be obvious that the best way to help Jews or whoever it is the Nazis hate, is to end the war as fast as possible. Unless somebody comes in on our side and helps, we could lose. No, not maybe, we would lose. Soviet Russia could be that ally. And one more thing," Dietrich said.

"Yes?"

"You can trust Canaris."

21

I t appeared to Archie that German panzer forces with infantry would strike deep into Russian territory along a gigantic front ranging from east Poland in the north to the Ukraine and the Caucasus in the south. The onslaught called for no less than three million men and all of the machines and materiel required for blitzkrieg tactics.

He was trying mightily to concentrate on Barbarossa, the OKH plans for war against Russia, but his thoughts were pulled toward his morning conversation with Mussolini. Il Duce was a regular caller, especially now that his armies were bogged down in North Africa. The Fascist dictator had bitten off more than he could chew, again, but would not admit it. As usual. He was arrogant, petulant, vain, but for some reason that Archie could not put his finger on, he liked the Italian leader. He was not held in high esteem by the German General Staff, and God knew that Mussolini was no more gifted as a military strategist than Archie was. *Maybe less,* Archie thought, giving himself the benefit of the doubt. But Il Duce, as a private man, enjoyed much of life that Archie thought was droll. He complained about his mistress. Not his wife. His wife was a wonderful woman, but of course she had lost interest in sex. At least sex with him, Il Duce laughed at himself. What kind of music did der Führer like, he asked Archie one day, catching the actor off guard. When Archie recovered he said that he liked much of the Italian opera. While Mussolini waited Archie struggled to recall even one. "Verdi!" he blurted. Rigoletto also came to mind.

Yes, the Italian fascist sighed, recalling the love story of a high priced courtesan. And of course Otello, Mussolini urged. Archie had never seen or even heard the opera but agreed that it was one of Verdi's finest works - how did he ever allow himself to fall into a trap of lies? Then he admitted that he was not familiar with Requiem - Te Deum or with Puccini's Tosca, Archie feeling relieved with each confession of ignorance as Il Duce rhapsodized on each.

As Archie listened he could not help but recall that the man's armies were being beaten all over the Sahara. Marshal Rodolfo Graziani, Mussolini's commander, was a laughing stock at OKH. Even while operating with sub-standard equipment and weapons, Graziani had redefined the concept of leadership. Il Duce, exasperated with the man's lack of zeal in facing his enemy, had messaged him "It is not a question of aiming for Alexandria or even Sollum," Mussolini said. "I am only asking you to attack the British forces facing you."

Despite his boss's urging, the Italian Marshal set the tone for his commanders and their men. He remained as far from the fighting as possible and often fabricated action reports to Il Duce in Rome.

In fairness, it was an ill-advised military adventure handed from an egotistical tyrant to a romantically inclined career army officer whose ambition in life was to avoid war at all cost. The Italians had no national interests to protect nor any ideological quest in their aggression in North Africa.

Still, Graziani's army of 250,000 faced a British force of only 30,000 on the Libyan-Egyptian border. The Italians fielded 300 tanks to 150 British and 190 fighter aircraft to the British 48. Yet at one point in the British offensive the Coldstream Guards reported capturing "five *acres* of officers and 200 acres of other ranks."

While Archie's senior officers counseled him to let the Italians bleed to death on the hot sands of the Mediterranean, Archie was considering doing exactly the opposite. But not for the reasons the OKH assumed. Like the generals, Archie saw little strategic value in that part of the Middle East but it was, if you were working for SOE, a good place to misdirect German troops.

But he was in no hurry to give the order.

It was true, Archie knew. The General Staff had discussed Operation Barbarossa many times since he had arrived at the Reichschancellery. He knew that there were plans for the invasion of all of Germany's neighbors including the Soviet Union. Just as Case White was the code name for Poland, Case Yellow for France, Barbarossa was chosen for a blitzkrieg to be launched against Russia. The size and scope of the invasion plan was staggering even to the military dilettante that Archie, by necessity, had become.

His eyes swam at the scale of the Russian campaign map. It was a simple enough plan in concept, but he was able to appreciate the incredible, almost breath-taking detail of the blueprint involving timing, logistics, materiel movement, panzer repair support, medical battle stations and their supply, uninterrupted fuel transportation, Luftwaffe targets and coordination with ground units. And the list went on. There would be three army groups; the North, commanded by Field Marshal von Leeb, Center, commanded by Field Marshal Fedor von Bock, and South, commanded by Field Marshal Gerd von Rundstedt.

Barbarossa called for 183 divisions facing 170 divisions of Russian troops. These, Archie read, represented over 50percent of the Soviet Unions total strength. The Russians had a vast population from which to call upon to train more troops, Archie knew, yet he gulped at the thought of the entire German military machine aimed at the relatively small island of Britain. In that moment of realization, Archie no longer had qualms about bringing Russia into the war. The SOE was right; the Soviet Union, with his help, could deal with Nazi Germany, Britain alone could not.

Archie considered how best to start the invasion machinery. Should he bring together the entire OKH staff and simply order the generals to proceed? It occurred to Archie that C-in-C Werner von Brauchitsch and the Chief of General Staff Franz Halder, were often in agreement with Hitler's vision both in the strategic as well as the tactical sense. Archie remembered that von Brauchitsch once remarked that he shared Hitler's total disgust for Communists and that it took a very low order of human to support it. He, von Brauchitsch went on, understood Hitler's statements contained in *Mein Kampf* that Germany should look toward the east for its necessary expansion. Halder, likewise,

worked with fervor with General Paulus on the planning for
Operation Barbarossa and said it was the best that he, and others, had
ever done.

Archie had Berta invite the two generals to dinner that very night.
He called Martin Bormann and asked the arch schemer, as Archie was
beginning to realize, to join them. He considered allowing Göring to
sit in but quickly decided against it. Göring was currently out of favor
as a military strategist and what Archie needed were people with just
the right combination of Nazi ideology and solid military tactical
knowledge to support the scheme. And he wanted the micro-gathering
to be intimate. The dinner would be in his Führerbunker and served
by Reichschancellery staff.

Later, at the table, Archie was basking in the compliments extended
to him by everyone present regarding the brilliance of his statesman-
ship in completing the Axis, or Tripartite Pact, with Italy and Japan,
by bringing Hungary, Romania and Slovakia into the political equa-
tion. It not only secured their southern flank but provided for an
uninterrupted supply of oil from the Romanian fields for Germany's
voracious war economy. Of course the Balkan "Protectorate" involved
sending troops, equipment, aerial defense guns and their crews to
augment existing indigenous forces, but the gain was certainly worth
the effort.

Archie noticed that von Brauchitsch was playing with his pheasant.
He refrained from wine with his dinner, unlike Halder and Bormann,
who were generous to themselves.

"Are you feeling well, Werner?" Archie asked solicitously.

"As a matter of fact, Führer, my stomach... bothers. But it is nothing
new," he said.

"Have you seen your doctor?" Archie persisted.

"Oh, yes. Several times. But nothing is wrong, they say," the general
officer said, uncomfortable even to talk about a matter so trivial.

"Could it be your diet?" Archie probed.

"Diet?" the general echoed, genuinely surprised. "No, I don't think
so. My diet has remained quite consistent since I served with the 3rd
Guards." Brauchitsch allowed himself a slight smile. "I was in superb
condition, if I do say so myself."

"Hmm," Archie mumbled, unsupportive. "A young man's body can
endure almost anything. But as we age nature takes its revenge. I

urge you to purge your system, Werner. Get yourself away from dead animals. Reject flesh and I guarantee that you will feel fit again in no time." Archie relished the idea that the obsequious general might become a vegetarian simply because a British actor prodded him. Personally, Archie yearned to eat meat again.

"I have to admit, Führer," Bormann offered, "that I have cured myself of discomforts from time to time just as you suggest. It is only my pathetically weak will that brings me back to the butcher's menu." The Reichsleiter said, then finished a glass of French red wine in two swallows.

"I find that hard to believe," Archie said. "Your willpower makes me cower."

Appreciative laughter lilted its way about the table with a beaming Bormann shaking his head. He raised his glass, "Thank you, Führer. I am flattered."

"Martin, do you still carry your gun?" Archie said.

Bormann's smile vanished as though a light had been turned off. It was common knowledge that Bormann was never without his compact Walther 9mm pistol carried in his coat pocket.

"Why, yes, I do," he said.

"Then if I ever lie to you, Martin, you have my permission to shoot me," Archie said.

The table collapsed in nervous laughter, Bormann leading the outburst.

The conversation, somehow, turned to Italy.

"I like the man," Archie said of Mussolini. "He reminds me of the Caesars. I think he may be a direct descendant. The Roman Empire was the greatest of them all. We owe much to it."

"They have fallen on evil times," Bormann inserted, rather brainlessly, Archie thought.

"But the magic of Florence and Rome," Archie said, remembering his brief trips through those cities while he toted scenery. "And Siena. Lovely!"

There was a protracted silence that preceded the dessert. Archie realized that his guests were waiting for something of greater moment.

He cleared his throat. "Gentlemen, I believe the time has come to carry on with my most important work. But first, let me put what I am about to say into perspective. France is a defeated nation. It is supporting Germany with food and war materiel with which to carry on our mission. Poland is a vassal state, as are Norway and Denmark and, though neutral, so is Sweden and Switzerland. Britain continues to hold out but hold out, against what? Air activity. I have been very patient with our Aryan cousins across the Channel because they are no longer a threat. I expect them to collapse at any time. Within weeks, certainly months. They are of no military consequence. They have been reduced to begging the Jew Roosevelt for help. But America sits like a bloated toad on the other side of the Atlantic Ocean, its confused government will never allow its president to venture into European business. My business. In the south of Italy is our fast ally, and through them we control the Balkans and North Africa." Archie paused for dramatic affect.

"All of you know, after reading *Mein Kampf*, that Germany's destiny lies to the east. Our volk need lebensraum and that is why we have taken Poland into the Reich. My vision, as I cast my eyes eastward, is to rid the world of the odious existence of Bolshevism. They are barbaric little commissars who, like their top bureaucratic clerk, Stalin, has enslaved their own people in foolish schemes designed to enrich the few at the expense of the many. Well, I have my eyes on the grain harvests of the Ukraine. And Germany needs the ores of the Urals and the oil of the Caucasus.

"I see no reason to wait. We have planned long and well for this hour and it has arrived. Gentlemen, I am informing you that very soon I will sign Führer Directive Number...."

Archie paused, looking at Bormann.

The Reichsleiter took his cue. "Twenty-one, my Führer."

"Twenty-one. The world will once again awake to the rumble of our panzers and the fury of our Luftwaffe, and the nations will know that all that has gone before was nothing. The Third Reich will wipe out the last great cancer remaining in Europe. Well?" he said, turning to Brauchitsch, "how long will our victory take?"

The senior general managed to close his slack jaw long enough to make it open again. "Ah, what date, exactly, do you have in mind, Führer?"

"Date? Tomorrow, Brauchitsch. Tomorrow! I want you to execute Barbarossa at once!" Archie demanded, unsure that he would not get a bullet from Bormann's pistol.

"With respect, Führer," Brauchitsch said, "I assume you mean to launch Barbarossa this year, 1941. But you had said that we would not attack Russia until 1943 or even 1944."

"I am quite aware of what I said, Brauchitsch, but for the reasons I have just outlined the time to move is now," Archie said, rather enjoying the obvious discomfort on the faces of the generals.

"Yes, but we need time. It is February," Brauchitsch said, turning to Halder for support. He got it.

Halder leaned forward in his chair. "I'm afraid I have to agree with General Brauchitsch, Führer. We have not made preparations...."

"You mean you have not made preparations for the preparations," Archie interrupted.

Halder smiled, wanly. "I suppose that is one way of putting it. But Barbarossa is massive in every respect. We must move troops, equipment... "

"Don't patronize me, Franz. Barbarossa calls for one hundred eighty divisions to launch on the eastern borders. Twenty of those divisions are panzers. Three thousand tanks. Seven thousand artillery pieces, and twenty-five hundred aircraft," Archie said, quoting from Canaris's intelligence estimates as though they were gospel. "We have almost half of those forces already located in the east where they would be used. By April we can have them all on line," Archie insisted.

Brauchitsch cleared his throat, finally finding his voice. "There can be no argument that the Soviet Union has twice those forces to stand against us, Führer. In fact they have almost three times the aggregate of troops as well as three times the quantity of tanks. We are outnumbered. The figures are not even close."

Brauchitsch was visibly upset, knowing that he was speaking for the entire General Staff with whom, if he lost this argument, he would be forced to deal. Those officers often outranked him, and they included Gerd von Rundstedt and Fedor von Bock, both Field Marshals and neither man with a passive temperament. And they, Brauchitsch knew, were only the tip of the iceberg.

"Nonsense. Soviet forces are inferior in every respect," Archie argued. "Stalin has murdered his most capable officer corps, and his aircraft were obsolete shortly after the last war. Not only is leadership in the Soviet army rotten, the people over whom the Commissar swine have power will revolt if we show them the way. All we have to do is kick in the door and the entire house will collapse."

Archie knew that he had made strong points. There was no disputing that Soviet leadership was almost non-existent. It was commonly known that the vast majority of Russia's officer ranks had been purged. The paranoid-schizophrenic Stalin had outdone himself by eliminating imagined threats to his power by killing those who might have now saved his regime. Archie warmed to the ironic idea. Admiral Canaris, Chief of German Abwehr, Military Intelligence, had provided Archie with a brilliant summary of Russian shortcomings that he needed to justify the attack now.

"I am not interested in excuses for delay. I asked you how long it would take to achieve victory. Well?" Archie demanded.

"The plan calls for penetration to Moscow in less than three months," Brauchitsch said, "but the weather in Russia can turn into an enemy...."

"It is winter for the Soviet army at the same time it is winter for our army, is it not, Herr General?" Archie dared.

"Of course, but we are not fitted for a winter campaign," the general said without enthusiasm, sensing that he had already lost the argument to proceed cautiously.

"Winter will not arrive until December. You have ten months to equip the Wehrmacht with winter provisions. By that time we will have won the war. Is that not right, Martin?" Archie said, turning to Bormann.

"The Führer is right," Bormann said to the others. "He has not been wrong yet. And you, yourselves, have designed Barbarossa. Unless you do not know what you are doing, victory is assured."

"So," Archie said, signaling that the dinner was over, "I urge you to lose not one precious minute of time. Martin will bring me daily reports of your progress."

When the last German general had left, Archie congratulated himself on one of his best performances. His ability to memorize was working well, even if not all of the facts were understood. His audience had bought his act.

Or so he thought.

22

Hess was one of the Reich's easily recognized figures. His visage had appeared in hundreds, perhaps thousands, of newspaper and newsreel pictures over the many years that Hitler had struggled to power. Hess could be seen, always behind the Führer, but never far from his person. His party rank and responsibilities required that he be assigned a large and effective bodyguard drawn from the Reichschancellery RSD. Berliners gawked as the solitary man walked the approximately two kilometers from the banks of Die Spree through Kurfursten Platz and down Wilhelm Strasse to the main entrance of the government buildings. His bodyguards, following his orders, remained at discreet distances, front, back, and on either sides of the streets that he walked.

Always a serious, highly dedicated servant of the German people and his Führer, Hess was today a specially troubled man. A number of OKH high ranking officers had approached him. General Warlimont was one. And if Warlimont was considered something of a plain speaking departure from the more rigid, austere Prussian generals who comprised the weight of the General Staff, Hess knew that Warlimont spoke implicitly for younger generals such as Rommel, Guderian, and Model. Also present had been Field Marshals Gerd Rundstedt and Günther von Kluge, each of whom had argued vocifer-

MICHAEL MURRAY

ously with the Führer after receiving the order to put in motion Operation Barbarossa. Even while Kluge and Rundstedt, two of Germany's most respected military minds, attempted to convince the Führer that the invasion of Russia at this time would be a disaster of the first magnitude, Hitler seemed to have a closed mind.

"He is like a deaf man," Kluge said, angrily. "He thinks he can give orders without consulting us."

"That is exactly what he can do," Hess said.

"You know what I mean," Kluge said in his own defense.

Rundstedt, a taciturn personality, cleared his voice. "Then perhaps he doesn't know what *I* mean. If our Führer doesn't need my advice then he should allow me to remove myself from the active roster so that he can go right ahead on his idiotic military adventure."

"Watch how you talk!" Hess responded savagely. "You are speaking of the greatest military mind of the century. How dare you refer to his decisions as idiotic!"

Rundstedt was not cowed in the least. It was almost as though he enjoyed the opportunity to prick the pride of the Number Two Nazi.

"Before the Führer displaces Alexander the Great allow me to point out that the Wehrmacht has not yet been challenged. Unless you want to discuss the success of our tanks against Polish cavalry," Rundstedt replied.

"And France!," Hess said, raising his voice.

"Oh, yes, France," Rundstedt said, dryly, "I almost forgot."

"I think what Field Marshal von Rundstedt is attempting to point out," von Kluge said, "is that the Soviet Union is not France. And it is certainly not Poland."

Hess could not argue with simple facts so he did not try.

"So?" he said, "what do you want me to do? I am not a military man, as you know."

"If I may," General Warlimont spoke for the first time. "I believe the OKH needs reassurance that the Führer has a complete and total grasp of what he is ordering us to do. That is, that there is no possibility of launching Barbarossa prior to early May, perhaps even later. We will have to fight in winter weather and... "

"You do not have to tell me the obvious, General Warlimont," Hess said, fighting down a cool chill that traveled down his backbone. "I think the Führer has made allowances for that fact."

For a very long moment no one in the room spoke, then Warlimont said "Tell us, Herr Hess, is the Führer fully... ah, recovered from the attack on his train?"

"Of course he is recovered. A ridiculous question. The Führer's command of memory and all of his faculties is a tribute to his iron constitution. You have been in his presence. It has been five months," Hess said, dismissing Warlimont's suggestion. "Let me give you some advice, gentlemen. You are quite lucky that you brought your... concerns... to me, and not to some others in the Reichschancellery. I will not report your disloyalty to him, but you are in danger if you continue this kind of second guessing."

Even the courageous and authoritarian Rundstedt seemed to have been silenced by Hess's warning. But now, as Hess slowed his pace near the main entrance to the Reichschancellery, certain fears were awakened within him by the generals. Even they had pinpointed a date and time.

The attack on the train.

True, the Führer had suffered a concussion. Head injuries were difficult to diagnose with precision. The doctors had advised Hess that Führer might show mild psychological lapses. Indeed, Hitler had confided to him that such was the case and asked that Hess be patient. But there were other things that niggled at Hess. The Führer seemed unwilling to engage in substantive conversation, the kind that he once was eager to discuss. Party matters, for example. And the Jewish question. It was almost as though he had lost complete interest in settling the problem of Jews in Europe. The SS and the SD were working around the clock to develop plans, to build more physical facilities, and to put in place transportation schedules and rolling stock to transport Jews from various parts of German spheres of influence.

But it was all done without the Führer's participation, as though he had completely lost interest. Or was it that he did not want to know?

Martin Bormann, to Hess's grudging credit, had done yeoman work in authorizing the necessary documentation to keep it all moving ahead. Looking back at the hours Hess had spent in Hitler's close company he could hardly have imagined that the Führer would have lost a single ounce of passion in dealing with the remaining Jews.

They were so close. Of course he had lost no determination in his desire to deal decisively with the Russians. There was no question about that. No one who knew Adolf Hitler ever doubted that he meant to bury the Slavs and the Communists to his east. He loathed them as much as he loved his Germany.

But invade Russia now? In 1940? Even to Hess's untrained military mind the venture seemed rash. The Wehrmacht was not up to full strength, Hess knew. Far from it. Nor was the Luftwaffe's new bombers, capable of carrying larger bomb loads off the drawing boards. And tanks. Invading a country the size of the Soviet Union without the new Tiger model, at least a year away from full production, seemed highly risky. Hitler, contrary to the opinion of some, was not a risk taker. He knew exactly when his enemy would fight and when he would not. That confidence came from knowing in advance whether he could win a fight once started. He had proved that in Poland, in Norway, Denmark and in France. It was not bluff.

But Russia?

It was out of character for the Adolf Hitler that he knew.

There were two tea houses in on the Obersalzberg mountain. One was located on a wooded hill at Mooslanderkopf, within easy walking distance from Hitler's Berghof. Among the Obersalzberg's elite residences. It was a popular place to visit. They included the Herman Göring family, the Joseph Goebbels, the Bormanns, and other several, assorted, and important personages of the Third Reich.

The other "teahaus" was built under the slavish direction of Reichsleiter Martin Bormann. Bormann employed Dr. Fritz Todt, Reichsminister for armament and ammunition, and Chief Engineer Hans Haupner. These men supervised hundreds of workmen almost around the clock to complete the task in record time in order to please the Reichsleiter. The teahouse was also referred to as the Eagle's Nest because of its perch at the very top of Kehlstein mountain. The Eagle's Nest project was huge, elaborate, accomplished at the expense of numerous injuries and even death to its laborers. Like most buildings erected with Adolf Hitler in mind, the Eagles Nest was grandly designed and expensively furnished. The view of the Alps was unequaled anywhere in Europe.

Hitler hated it.

Among other reasons for avoiding trips to his seemingly idyllic place of meditation was the rarified air existing at 1900 meters above sea level. His lungs, damaged in the first war, suffered at that altitude.

The arrival of Adolf Hitler was always a closely guarded secret, especially following his near death experience in his private rail train. But the entire Obersalzberg complex, since it had become a favorite home away from Berlin for important Party members in the mid-1930's, had become one of the most secure locations in Europe. Underground tunnels, bunkers and guard resources criss-crossed the beautiful Bavarian countryside, patrolled assiduously by special troops of the SS. Indeed, a large SS barracks, the size of a small hotel, occupying a central place within the compound, was always fully staffed.

At his own invitation, Hess had accompanied Archie to Obersalzberg. Their traveling retinue numbered more than one hundred ninety including the RSD bodyguard that followed Hitler's car driven by SS-Colonel Kempka. This customized Mercedes-Benz 770 KW150 limousine featured 40 mm bullet-proof windows and manganese-treated anti-armored piercing plating throughout.

Archie and Hess had talked almost unceasingly about the forthcoming invasion of the Soviet Union. Archie had become intimately familiar with all facets of Barbarossa and found that he enjoyed the complexity of the massive undertaking. War planning, raised to an art form by Germany's General Staff, was an incredibly complicated discipline. Archie had come to admire the work the same way in which a dilettante becomes conversant with the subtleties of opera or Shakespeare while not being expert. He even experienced the emotional stimulation that the real Adolf Hitler must have tasted while he was the undisputed head of his nation's armed forces. He was able to point weapons at anyone or anything that displeased him. The heady feeling was intoxicating and Archie found himself counting the days until Barbarossa would commence. And he had ordered it!

The two men enjoyed the breath-taking scenery en route past the Bodnerfarm toward the huge Untersberg Mountain. The sight of the lofty crag caused both men to pause in their conversation. As the car passed through Berchtesgaden toward the Berghof, it was Hess who broke the silence.

"Too bad Heinz could not be here to watch our Wehrmacht in it's greatest triumph," he said.

"Heinz?" Archie said, turning away, looking out of his side window.

"Scholler," Hess said, resting his head back against the padded seat.

"Ach, ja," Archie said. "Well, life goes on, eh, Rudolf?"

After a moment of creeping uneasiness, Archie felt compelled to turn back toward Hess. The Party Deputy's eyes were regarding him steadily, without blinking.

"Surely you have not forgotten the Chipmunk? The one who would chew food with his front teeth?" Hess said.

"Certainly. I...." Archie began, a chill of apprehension moving through his entire body. "That is, I don't remember as I should. The train, you know," he said, nervously.

"Of course," Hess said, but as they continued to make their way up the mountain Hess lapsed into a prolonged silence.

Archie felt suddenly clammy. Surely he had made a mistake in recalling, or failing to recall, a name he should have remembered. He heard Hess speak again.

"What was that?" Archie asked.

"Your favorite place in Obersalzberg. The tea house on Kehlstein Mountain. I suppose you miss it terribly while you are in Berlin," Hess said.

"Naturally. Who would not?" Archie said, turning his head back toward the passenger side window, away from Hess's penetrating gaze. "I miss all of Obersalzberg when duty keeps me in the city."

The seconds began to tick by like hours inside Archie's head as he listened to the gentle hum of the limousine's engine, the swishing sound of its tires pushing aside remnants of snow slush still on the roadway after it had been cleaned. He waited for Hess to speak but he did not, yet Archie could not bear to turn his head toward the Party Secretary lest his fear show through and his grand pretense be revealed.

Weeks prior, on the pretext of looking through security measures, Archie had arranged to read the history of the Obersalzberg complex. He knew, therefore, that he was passing through farm land that had existed for almost three hundred years as well as villas and pensions. Moritz, the famous piano producer, once had a retreat there, Hotel Antenberg and Lindenhoehe also had occupied choice areas in the community before they were confiscated by the Nazi party in 1936 and 1937. More than 400 people had to leave the Obersalzberg to make room for Hitler's chosen few.

A contingent of SS guard sprang to attention, giving the Nazi salute as Archie's motorcade passed through the final security barrier before the Mercedes-Benz turned into the circular driveway in front of the Berghof at the foot of Hohe Goell Mountain.

As Archie stepped out of the car he looked up at the great house before him, now mis-termed as a berghof as, when its smaller size ten years ago it would have been accurately regarded. From the outside Archie appreciated how its architect, Delgano, had attempted to retain the mountain chalet affect on a house that was anything but a small mountain retreat in the third renovation of the house. The Berghof spread itself at the foot of a snow capped mountain at the Kehlstein summit more than a mile above sea level. Archie passed by the giant picture window which, he knew, could be rolled down for a clear and uninhibited view of the surrounding mountains and valley.

The armed SS guards had fallen back once their Führer was safely delivered to his residence, leaving the uniformed members of his inner circle, and some dressed in civilian clothes, to continue on. He knew the way through the main entrance. Bormann, who had a large house nearby, had turned away from the convoy promising to appear at the Berghof later. Aides and secretaries, not including Berta Holz who remained in Berlin, peeled off in various directions while Hess and Archie ascended the Berghof's large gothic staircase that led to the reception hall. They passed by a hall, a vestibule, a dining room and a guard room on the ground floor where the conference room, and huge picture window, as well as a large kitchen were located. The first floor above ground level contained the living and bedrooms for the Führer as well as several guest rooms. These were in addition to the hotel-sized guest house located a few hundred meters down the road.

Archie strained to appear relaxed as he removed his leather gloves and Alpaca uniform great coat with its black swastika against the elegant white and red background worn on the sleeve. Servants took his apparel while he made his way into the lavishly furnished study. Its graceful appointments awed Archie who, since his first excursion scarcely six months ago to the Semley Place house in Belgravia, was becoming accustomed to wealth and splendor in various forms. There were blond oak walls festooned with paintings, inset book cases, thick carpets, a large desk and tastefully covered sofas and chairs. He was tempted to rush down the hall to view the conference room, colored photos of which had caused him to shake his head in wonder. The life of a tyrant could be very good.

But these things, the furnishings of the Berghof would not quell the rising panic inside his head.

Without looking over his shoulder Archie could sense the cause of his panic was still nearby.

"And where is Eva?" Archie heard himself say, dreading an answer that would tell him that she as on her way to him.

"She is in her apartment," Hess said, unctuously, Archie believed. "She will only come if you call, as you know."

Archie was now certain. Hess *knew*. There was not a shred of doubt in Archie's mind that he had given away the game and that the real Hitler's intimate friend was onto him.

"Put them there," Archie directed a military aide to place fully stuffed document cases near his desk. Without a word, the aide withdrew.

"I have work to do, Rudolf," Archie said to Hess. "We'll talk again at dinner."

"I am looking forward," Hess replied before nodding his head in formal acknowledgment.

Two hours later there came a knock on Archie's office door.

"Come," he said. He turned in his chair away from the window to regard one of the household staff.

The man bowed, then said "With apologies, my Führer, Herr Hess offers his regrets and begs that you excuse him from dinner. State business has required his immediate return to Berlin."

After the servant had departed and closed the door behind him Archie reached for the telephone on his desk. He hesitated when he realized that he did not know how to dial the number he wanted from this location in Germany. He impatiently clicked the receiver several times when a female voice, that of an operator assigned to the communications headquarters at the Obersalzberg, came on the line.

"Get me Standartenführer Hebert at the Reichschancellery, at once," Archie barked into the telephone.

When Standartenführer Robert Hebert replaced the telephone into its cradle his face was ashen. The conversation, if one could call it that, left no room for doubt. The traitor had been found.

Guter Gott. Rudolf Hess.

Imagine! The Deputy Party leader! Adolf Hitler's old comrade. The standartenführer, as amazement took hold, felt a kindred spirit to the Führer in that when the Führer was wounded, all of Germany was wounded. The thought of a traitor close to the Führer sent a stab of anger through Hebert that burned, then seethed. Hebert sat in his thickly cushioned desk chair looking at a point in space, his mind beginning to lay out the scenario that would have to take place. But cleverly done.

"He is a public figure, Standartenführer," Hitler had said over the telephone. "I want it done quietly and quickly. Very quickly. Can I count on you, Comrade Hebert?"

"Without question, Führer," Hebert said, still standing at attention while he held the telephone at his ear.

"Very well. Who do you have in mind for the work?"

"I am an expert in this area, sir. Consider it done," Hebert said.

When he had envisioned the action that he was about to pursue Hebert began a list of equipment he would need to accomplish his work. The list was necessarily short and took only a few minutes to commit to memory. Then he dialed a number.

"Vass, come in," Hebert said, then waited less than a minute before his deputy arrived.

"Good evening, Standartenführer," Vass said easily, crumbs from dinner still clinging to the corners of his mouth. *The man never stopped eating,* Hebert thought. *Nordrinking.* Rich food and equally rich Bavarian beer pushed at Vass's belt from the inside out. Still, Hebert knew his man. Vass had a heart like the heels of his jackboots he wore when he had been an SD Brown Shirt in 1929. He did not flinch from killing and, if necessary, inflicting maximum pain in the process.

"Listen very carefully to what I am about to say, Vass," Hebert began, slowly lowering himself into his chair. "Party Secretary Hess is to be arrested. I have just spoken with the Führer himself. He has ordered Hess's execution."

Hebert paused, waiting for a reaction from the Obersturmbannführer. Vass did not so much as blink.

"You and I will carry out that order, Vass. Do you have questions?" the standartenführer asked.

"I am sure you have considered how we are to carry out the assignment," Vass said, taking a nearby chair.

Archie felt a certain lightness possess him. Within a very short while Rudolf Hess would be dead. Or he, Archie, would be dead. Either way the gut-wrenching masquerade would be over. Peace would attach. He realized how it was that people found God in their hours of stress. When events became too great for the mind to bear, something spiritual was needed to escape. Some used drugs, alcohol, God. Archie would use death. His or Hess's.

"Hello, Adi."

Archie knew without looking that the soft voice, almost demur, belonged to Eva Braun. It was a perfect time, an epiphany had taken charge of his life and she had come to be witness. He turned, a genuine smile of amusement pulled at the corners of his mouth.

"Oh," she said, advancing to him with arms outspread, "I'm so happy you are not mad with me."

He took her into his bosom, his arms returning her embrace.

"How could I ever be mad with you?" he said, aware of the irony.

She was warm to the touch, wearing a blue and white polka-dot dress, a gold bracelet on her right arm and a tasteful gold necklace. Her light brown hair had been neatly coiffed but was now blown into a very casual, and attractive, disarray. She was, Archie thought, much lovelier than he had imagined she would be and thought the worst of the real Adolf Hitler for giving this woman so little of his life.

"You have gained weight!" she said, laughing. "I expected you to have wasted away, with all that you have been through."

"I am fat?" he said, tickled with her frivolity.

"No, no, you look much better. Don't men like to hear that?" she teased. "We notice your weight just as you notice ours."

"We men are not supposed to care. We are warriors, you know. I shouldn't have to remind you," Archie said as he led her toward comfortable chairs. Would his stomach muscles ever relax? He slipped from a state of fatalism to suddenly caring once more that he not die.

Here was another source of discovery. Another person, because of their intimacy, could now reveal him as the imposter that he was.

"Let me order something for you to drink. Have you eaten, yet?" he asked.

"Well, I.... Yes, I have eaten, but I would like to drink a cocktail!" Eva announced her wishes for a drink as though she had never had one before. Archie found that pleasing.

"Then you shall have one." He pushed a button on his desk console and within moments a white jacketed house staffer appeared.

"Miss Braun will have... ?" he arched an eyebrow in her direction.

"Gin. With quinine water, and ice," she said, making herself comfortable on the green tinted sofa near Hitler's overstuffed wingback chair.

"And I...." Archie hesitated, his mouth watering for the same drink. "Ah, bring me tea."

If Eva was disappointed in drinking alone, she did not let on in the least. She might have even been relieved that he remained in such good spirits while she imbibed so early in the day. Archie guessed that the real Adolf Hitler would have disapproved of her taking alcohol at any time. Well, hell, he thought, if he survived the next forty-eight hours she could drink to her heart's content.

"I have been very bad, Adie," Eva said as she rose from the sofa to stroll around the immense room, fingers interlaced behind her back.

"What have you done?"

"I was in Berlin. I haunted the stores on Kurfürstendamm all week! Nearly all week. I spent money wildly. Do you want to know what I bought?"

"I know everything you bought," Archie said with a sober face but secretly delighted at her shocked expression. "Gestapo. They tell me everything you do."

Her lips compressed. "They are such oafs. I see them everywhere I go. Well, it isn't funny, is it?"

Archie had never considered that Eva Braun would be under close scrutiny. But of course she would, in a dictator's state. He suddenly felt very sorry for her, loving a man, literally, from afar.

"I'm sorry, Eva. Are they really oafs?" he asked.

Eva pouted only for a moment before her face broke once more into a broad, carefree smile. "Yes. I think someone chose them for their ugly looks. I know, I know, you explained to me what would happen if I did not have snoops around me. Bodyguards, pardon me."

"I will order that your entire bodyguard be replaced with nothing but young handsome men. Handsome Gestapo men, to be sure," Archie said.

Eva's mouth fell open. "Adi, I can't believe you said that. You are teasing, but it is a very nice thing for you to say. As if I really cared about those silly men!"

For a moment Archie was struck by the sudden urge of wanting this woman. She was young, attractive, and seemed to look beyond his rather plain features. He had never been considered attractive to the opposite sex. At best their attitudes had been indifferent. But this bubbly, carefree girl was clearly genuine in her feelings for him. He rose from his chair and met her in the middle of the room. He put his arms around her and felt her come into him fully and without restraint. He wanted very much to kiss her but somehow felt that should he do so he would give himself away for sure.

Eva pulled her head back so that she could see him totally and up close.

"There is something different," she said, holding him fixed in her eyes. Immediately he released her and turned away, but she held on to his hand.

"Naturally. Since I saw you last I was in a terrible fight. No one knows how it was," he said, gently but firmly escaping from her grip.

"Yes, I suppose...." Eva began, then her voice trailed off.

He turned back toward her. "In what way?"

"I'm not sure but... oh, never mind. I'm silly, that's all. Whatever happened on that train worked out for the best. I think you look wonderful. You *are* wonderful," Eva said, drinking from her glass of gin. "I hope they caught the filthy British who attacked you. Well? Did they?"

"Without any question. We tracked them down and killed them all. It only shows how desperate that idiot Churchill is to avoid losing the war." Archie realized the irony of his notion, that he was very close to the mark.

There was a pause in their conversation, the kind that is not unrestful, and Archie found himself eager to make Eva happy. "And your sister? Will she join us for dinner tonight?"

Archie was aware that Gretl was near Eva more often than not.

"I'm sure she would be. Adie," Eva purred.

"Yes?"

"That handsome young colonel, Hans," she began.

"Be specific. How many officers are there in the German army by the name of Hans?" he teased, but sternly so.

"You know who I mean. The Waffen-SS officer, Fegelein."

"I seem to remember the name," Archie said.

"Well, Gretl is quite taken with him. Could he join us, do you suppose?"

If it was like most dinners Archie had hosted in his role of Adolf Hitler, they were quasi-affairs of state and always well attended. One more body in a uniform could not matter.

"I'll arrange it," he said.

Eva moved to face him, putting her arms around his neck once again and kissing him on the cheek. "I already have."

Hess entered the Reichschancellery from the Voss Strasse entrance. It was closer to his office. The two black uniformed SS guards came to attention and saluted. As he strode through the Marble Hall the building was full of officials, civilians, military, visitors, all trying to do business as usual. Hess even heard occasional laughter as he made straight for his office.

He waived away his secretaries who informed him of calls to return and papers to examine. Without slowing his pace he continued through the outer office and into his private, typically Nazi elaborate, office. On the way back from southern Germany he had been pondering his unique knowledge. The man who occupied Europe's throne of power was not Adolf Hitler. He was an imposter. That nonsense about Heinz Scholler. Heinz Scholler was a math instructor at Hess's gymnasium, age ten! Chipmunk, indeed. And the Teehaus. Adolf Hitler loathed the place.

But who was this man? A spy, obviously. No, much more than a spy. An agent of the highest order. British? Almost certainly so. The imposter, whoever he was, might be a Czech or an American or even Austrian. Perhaps even a German, but whatever he was, he was in the pay of British Intelligence. Hess carelessly tossed his uniformed great-coat on the arm of a chair near his desk.

So. What to do?

Kill him? Hess could imagine putting a revolver to the pretender's head and pulling the trigger. What then? Would he calmly explain that he had not killed Adolf Hitler but that he had rid the Fatherland of a British agent? He would never get the words out of his mouth before the Gestapo would have him executed.

Expose him? Tell other powerful party leaders that their Führer was not who he seemed? Then it would be his word against the imposter. Again, he had no chance in such a scenario.

And the conduct of the war: how would it go without Adolf Hitler, even the imposter, to give the orders?

The orders?

Barbarossa.

Hess slowly sunk into the chair behind his desk. Was it possible? That the German armed forces were about to march into a massive trap set for them by a foreign power? Von Rundstedt, von Kluge and the others were right! There could be no mistake that Hitler's determination to invade Russia would sound the death knell for Germany. As the generals had argued, the order was not irrational.

It made perfect sense.

There was a single, sharp rap on his door before it opened. Hess looked up, irritated at an entrance made without his permission, to see the familiar figure of the deputy RSD commander, Obersturmbannführer Jon Vass.

"I am busy, Vass. Leave and close the door," Hess snapped, reaching for his telephone to communicate with his secretary.

"With apologies, Herr Hess, but there is an urgent message for you," Vass said as he allowed the door to close behind him.

"Well? Then what is it?"

"The message was not given to me directly but is at the communications center at Oberkomando der Wehrmacht," Vass responded, his eyes never leaving Hess's.

OKW was located at Number 72 Tirpitz Kufer near the Landwehr Kanal.

"I am quite busy, Obersturmbannführer. I will authorize you to bring the message to me here, at the Reichschancellery," Hess said, looking into a drawer of his desk.

"That was my suggestion, too, Minister Hess, but my instructions were to escort you to OKW at once," Vass said, evenly, his voice not lacking confidence.

"Yes? And who gave you such an order that it should supercede mine, a Minister of the Reich?" Hess said, now standing.

"I presume it was given by the Führer himself, Herr Hess. I have a car waiting, sir," Vass said, moving a respectful half-step to one side.

"Very well," Hess sighed. "I will have to finish my work in the car."

Moving from behind his desk, Hess retrieved his great-coat from the chair and a briefcase from nearby. Now standing near the Obersturmbannführer Hess tried awkwardly to pat his pockets as though he had forgotten something.

"Here," he said to Vass, extending his coat and briefcase quickly forwarding. Vass's instinctive reaction was to accept the items with both hands. Thus occupied, he was defenseless for only one second. But it was all Hess needed.

Hess plunged a stiletto directly into the throat of the SS officer, penetrating his windpipe. Vass dropped the coat and briefcase, grabbing desperately for the steel shank in his throat. But Hess's strong hands clamped over Vass's wrists, holding him helpless, virtually paralyzed while blood began to exit the neck wound and run into his white uniform shirt.

"Tsk, tsk," Hess cautioned, "let's leave it right there, Obersturmbannführer. You are only making the hole bigger when you struggle."

Indeed, as the SS officer willed himself to engage Hess, he felt suddenly weak, his knees buckling and, with the Reich Minister's weight atop him, collapsed backward onto the floor. Hess continued down onto the carpet, keeping the SS man between his legs and holding fast to the man's ever weakening wrists.

"You are swallowing hard, Vass. The blood is rushing into your throat very fast, isn't it? In a few seconds it will enter your lungs and then you will drown," Hess said, his eyes alight, his mouth twisted into a grim smile of satisfaction.

"Fucking pig. Did you really think you could lead me to slaughter like a stupid sheep? And who else is waiting for us in the car? Would it be your superior, Hebert? Eh? Oh, you can't talk," Hess said, as indeed Vass attempted to move his lips. But no words came, only blood. Hess could feel the Obersturmbannführer's hands weakening until they fell from his throat. Hess leaned forward, peering more closely into now lifeless eyes.

In a last act of anger, Hess shoved the stiletto even deeper into Vass's throat. If he had been alive, his cervix would have been severed and death would have been instant.

Hess slowly rose from his knees. His uniform sleeves were soaked with blood as well as his hands and trousers. No matter, where he was going he would go in civilian clothing.

Standartenführer Hebert looked at his Swiss wristwatch yet again. They were late, no question. Something had gone wrong. Reluctantly, the Standartenführer stepped out of the car. If necessary, he thought, Hess would be liquidated in his office. He began to walk back toward a Reichschancellery entryway on the west side that led through the canteen, a short way to the Marble Hall and Hess's office, his boots clicking with authority on the concrete. As he neared the guarded door he looked to his left, at the subterranean auto garage. A black Mercedes suddenly emerged traveling at a rapid speed, hardly stopping at Herman Göring Strasse, then turned south. It had been an official car, one that would have been assigned to someone of high rank. But even though Hebert's view had been snapshot quick there was no mistaking the dark hair and jutting jaw of Rudolf Hess behind the wheel.

Hebert ran to his own automobile. He started the engine and, slamming the BMW into first gear, causing the rubber wheels to howl as he gave chase.

Hess turned south on Willhelmstrasse, then made another hard right turn onto Leipzeiger Strasse accelerating to a fast rate of speed. He turned onto Potsdamer, a main thoroughfare, and stepped on the gas pedal even harder. He was traveling at a speed of more than 115 kph and attracted the attention of military police on two occasions. Neither time, upon looking closely at the car and its driver, was Hess stopped or hailed in any way. He was now on a southern route out of the city that could take him either to Magdeburg or Leipzig. As he passed over a bridge spanning one of the several large railroad marshaling yards Hess lifted his eyes to his rear view mirror. A car was following, also traveling at a speed that would overtake.

Hess was not surprised. In the car was Standartenführer Hebert, no doubt. Now, with civilian traffic very light, Hess put the accelerator to the floor of his Mercedes-Benz. The speedometer quickly passed through one hundred forty kph and beyond.

Standartenführer Hebert could only watch while the bigger, faster car, began to pull away. Reluctantly dropping back, Hebert considered his options. He could not call for roadblocks. The Führer's orders were to keep the entire matter tightly secret. Nor had he the stomach for contacting the Führer at the Berghof and confessing that he had botched the assignment. He would probably be shot. Hebert briefly considered doing that to himself. The notion of a single bullet to the brain was sometimes a luxury when in the hands of Gestapo interrogators. But he dismissed the idea at once.

Where, he wondered, would he go if he were Hess? He was moving south, but that meant very little. Hess could change directions at any moment. Besides, all of Germany lay south and west. Well, he was not finished yet.

Hess raced through the town of Zwickan, then slowed only slightly while navigating Nüremburg, but found that he had to stop for petrol in the town of Aalen. He cared not at all that the station attendant recognized him. Indeed, he received the fastest possible assistance and was on his way with minimum delay. His pursuer, whoever it was, had fallen away two hundred kilometers back. There were no unusual police activity, no military units looking for him, as far as he could tell. But to remain in Germany meant certain death. A plan had now fully formed in his mind as he pushed the Mercedes down the autobahn.

He arrived in Augsburg at 5:00 pm and drove directly to the Messerschmitt factory. He knew the way very well.

Conrad Holsembach, the factory's chief pilot, did not knock at the door of Messerschmitt's aufsicht, Doktor Emile Henneberg, but walked right in.

"Reichsminister Hess is here. He wants a 110," Holsembach blurted, as though he disbelieved his own words.

Henneberg rose from his desk, slowly removing his glasses. "Hess?" he said. "I see. Ah, where does the Reichsminister intend to go?"

"I did not think it was my place to ask," the chief pilot said.

"Yes, er, that was quite wise, Conrad. Then we had better see to it that the Minister is not delayed."

Rudolf Hess was already seated in the cockpit of the twin-engine Me-110 fighter plane when Superintendent Henneberg and chief pilot Holsembach arrived on the flight line. They could do little more than smile and wave flaccidly to the second most powerful man in the Reich as Hess, all but ignoring them, set the fuel selectors on main tanks and switched on the electric fuel pumps. He set the duel mixture controls on rich, then worked the priming pumps that sent streams of raw fuel into the engine cylinders. He cracked the plexiglass canopy on the big fighter to yell at the ground crew, two of whom were standing by to heave the inertial starter into motion on the port-side engine.

"Ready!" Hess shouted.

Inside the now secured cockpit, Hess waited until the inertial wheel sounded near its maximum, then engaged the starter. The three bladed prop began to turn slowly, then coughed. White smoke arose in a large white vapor as the Daimler-Benz DB-605 engine fired, died, then fired again before rumbling into full ignition. Hess adjusted the throttle ahead slightly until he was sure the engine was running properly. He waited impatiently for the ground crew to repeat their work on the starboard engine. While they cranked on the inertial handle, Hess pulled a leather helmet over his head and, activating the master electric switch, also turned on the radio.

While the factory personnel watched with nervous interest, Hess began taxiing toward the end of the runway. Other aircraft in the area were alerted to give the Reichsminister priority clearance.

Hess lifted the Me-110 off the ground at exactly 5:45 P.M. and set course for England. The date was May 10th, 1941.

By the time Edward Wiles had dragged himself upright, and brought himself to the map room at Semley House he had expected Sir William to look even worse than he at this ungodly hour of the morning. It was 04:15 A.M. and while Wiles was accustomed to being awakened at any time, he had been without sleep for thirty-six consecutive hours and was beginning to lose track of events. He and MacLean Elliot agreed to let Sir William sleep whenever possible because of his advanced years, but the old boy seemed far more capable than they when it came to enduring sleep deprivation. They concluded that it was because Sir William had no heart to damage and that the rarefied air he breathed, untouched by the masses, kept his blue blood fresh.

But even Wiles was surprised at the state in which he found his nominal SOE superior pacing the floor, eyes on the toes of his scuffed Oxford shoes. His general appearance was unkempt, uncombed white strands of hair flopping over each ear, shirt tail out in the back and, Wiles could see, no stockings. Sir William did not look up or quit pacing when Wiles entered the room.

"Close the door," he snapped.

Hardly civil, Wiles thought, war or no war. Must be getting to the old man. Nevertheless, Wiles closed the door. He could see that Elliot had arrived before him. Wiles never regarded Elliot as a man easily flapped but tonight the Deputy SOE was literally chewing his fingernails.

"MacLean," Wiles said by way of greeting as he glanced about for a warm tea pot.

Elliot merely grunted.

"Sit down," Sir William said.

"I am sitting, Sir William," Wiles said, his hand going to stifle a yawn.

"I have something important to tell you," Sir William said.

"I should hope so," Wiles said, reaching for cigarettes that he no longer smoked.

"What's that?" Sir William said, pricking one elongated ear higher than the other.

"I said that you had better get on with it. I think MacLean is drifting off on us," Wiles observed, dryly.

"Damn it man," Sir William mumbled toward Elliot, "will you do me the courtesy of giving me your undivided attention for one moment?"

"I say, William, a little rest might do your disposition a world of good," Elliot said to the older man.

Sir William gestured with his hands as though he had given up. At last he got on with it. "At ten P.M. last night, Saturday, a German Me-110 made landfall over Scotland and was spotted by Lord Hamilton's RAF wing. An hour later its pilot parachuted out."

"Shot down?" Wiles said, beginning to come awake.

"I did not say shot down. I said that the pilot parachuted out," Sir William said, testily. "The pilot gave his name to local authorities as Alfred Horn and claimed to be on a special mission. He demanded to see the Duke of Hamilton. Getting to the nub of it, Wing Commander Hamilton informed Number Ten Downing Street that the pilot was in fact Rudolf Hess." Sir William paused for reactions. They were not long in coming.

"*The* Rudolf Hess?" Elliot said, sitting bolt upright.

"Apparently so. It seems that Hamilton and Hess had met in Berlin during the 1936 Olympics," Sir William said.

For a very long moment the room remained silent.

"Good God," Elliot breathed.

"Hess, if that is indeed who he is, is being kept in a safe house under guard. He has demanded to see Mr. Churchill who has, obviously, been informed of Hess's arrival. The Prime Minister called me immediately," Sir William added.

"I take it that the Prime Minister has no intention of meeting with Herr Hess?" Wiles asked.

"None whatever."

"What does he want?" Elliot asked of Schuyler.

"What he wants is exactly what we have feared. Hess knows about Archie the actor. He threatens to reveal the secret unless the Crown is willing to meet his demands," Sir William said, recrossing his angular legs.

"Good God!" Elliot said, sliding lower into his chair.

"And those demands are?"

Sir William shrugged. "He wants to be the Gauleiter for all of Germany when the war is over. Nonsense, of course."

"Who else knows?" Wiles said, beginning to pace the floor.

Sir William sighed. "Ivone Kirkpatrick, for sure."

"The former ambassador in Berlin?"

"First Secretary, actually," Sir William corrected.

"I assume Churchill will have the man executed at once," Wiles said, quite seriously.

"I assume that's one option, but I rather think they'll declare the man insane. That shouldn't be so hard to prove, all in all," Sir William said.

"Then deep freeze him, of course. But there is always a danger, isn't there? I mean, short of death closing the man's mouth, he could find a way to smuggle out a message, couldn't he?"

On May 11th, it was as if a bomb had exploded within the Berghof itself. Archie, equally as shocked as the others within the Nazi hierarchy, was able to disguise his emotions by making unfettered joy into the appearance of rage. He paced the conference room, flung his arms clumsily in various directions, ranted, raved, used despicable language to describe Hess's ultimate betrayal. A Judas, Archie screamed. Insane, he said, pointing a finger to his head.

Martin Bormann remained largely silent among the increasingly crowded conference room, inwardly delighted that Hess was no longer an impediment to his ever expanding personal ambitions. Bormann would now take over Hess's duties as well as his own, a rather simple fiat that would elevate him to the defacto second most powerful man in the Third Reich.

Goebbels was highly animated, concerned with how the defection could be explained to the German people, indeed, to the entire world. Various approaches to news control were raised, argued, and tossed away. They kept coming back to an act of insanity, despite the bitter truth that neither Hitler nor any one of the Party members liked the idea of admitting that a crazy man could have derived from their group.

Sometime after midnight Bormann received two men from the district Gestapo headquarters in Amiens, France. The tall one, Roul Bagasaran, offended Bormann's sensibilities. The man had about him the smell of stale body odor and an overpowering scent of garlic when he spoke. He was of Slavic origin and Bormann made a mental note to have the man's ancestry investigated. His skull measured, too. He was, indeed, a cadaverous appearing man with noticeably pigeon toed feet and a aquiline nose that seemed to almost touch his upper lip when he talked. He explained the situation to Bormann.

"The frequency always changes, but never in a pattern. The messages are sent at any time of the day or night and at any day of the month. Even the months are irregular. The transmitter operator is almost certainly using one-time-pads, as the British refer to them. That is a system of tear away pages... "

"Yes, yes, I know what they are. Continue," Bormann said, leaning forward on one of the several comfortable sofas in his extravagant home very near the Berghof.

"We are not able to decipher the code because of that. The key changes with each transmission," the gangly Gestapo man said through crooked teeth. "But we can identify the sender by his key stroke. Each operator develops an easily identifiable touch when he sends... "

"Damn it, man, get to the point. Give me facts I can use, not things that mystify you!" Bormann said, theatrically throwing up his hands.

"Yes, Herr Reichsminister," the oleaginous Gestapo man said. "Of course there are a number of transmitters that we are tracking along the channel coast. One of my intercept sergeants has been plotting this particular operator. We noticed something strange. The transmissions started in August of 1939, and continued until the end of June of this year."

"They stopped?"

"Yes, sir. Nothing since then. But there is something else," Bagasaran said.

"Well?"

"When the wireless was keyed, we would immediately send a direction finding vehicle, sometimes two, for this signal. He was never on the air long enough for us to locate the source precisely, but we were able to narrow it to about thirty kilometers," the Gestapo man said without a trace of false ego. It was a small character indication but it gave Bormann a certain sense of confidence in Bagasaran's story.

"A large area, isn't it?" Bormann asked, completely mystified about the workings of electronics.

"Yes, Herr Minister. If you will allow me...." the Gestapo man removed a map from a leather folder. The map was of France that included the Low Countries, western Germany, the English Channel and southern England.

"I have made markings on the map here, at Amiens-Glisy, and here, St. Léger, St. Omer-Clairmarais, Lille, Crécy, Villacoublay, and here, Cherbourg." The Gestapo agent leaned back in his chair to await a reaction from Bormann.

The Reichsleiter studied the map of France, following the blue ink dots made by the agent Bagasaran but if there was a pattern, he could not see it.

"So?" Bormann said. "What?"

"Well, Herr Bormann, the first transmissions began, at least as far as we can tell, just before the Reich marched into Poland. Out of self-defense, of course. The last transmission was shortly after the start of Operation Barbarossa. And these locations," Bagasaran said, waving his hand across the dots across France made by his pen, "are all within thirty kilometers of a Luftwaffe field."

CHAPTER

23

SS-Sturmbannführer Hartung was fighting his panzers of the 1/44 Regiment of the 2nd Das Reich Division against the numerous Russian T-26 and T-28 light tanks and infantry. Though the Russians fought valiantly the T-26 was no match for his battle tanks with only 15mm of armor and a 37mm gun to oppose Hartung's 75mm gun. Hartung's abteilung was destroying Russians almost at will. The T-28 was eighteen tons heavier than the T-26 but its armor was only 30mm. Its main gun was 76.2 mm howitzer, a weapon not designed for flat trajectory shooting. The tank, too, was vulnerable to a first strike against its thin armor. Hartung's regiment had killed six this day, June 27rd, as his panzers and grenadiers covered thirty kilometers at the spearhead of Army Group Center. They had been fighting virtually non-stop for a month, and while his tank crews were exhilarated by their success against the Red Army, they were also exhausted from lack of sleep, their senses dulled by the constant concussions from their own gun muzzles and incoming enemy shells. Late at the end of a typical battle day they would pause to refuel, take on ammunition for the 75mm StuK assault gun, and gulp down combat rations along with tea or coffee, and always water. Their machines were supposed to be supported by mobile field repair units but the front was far too broad for engineering teams to work the entire line, so Hartung and his four man crew aboard his command tank labored far into the night to keep their Maybach HL V-12 engine running and their track links replaced when needed. They slept, in the few hours or minutes of darkness that was left, at their combat positions.

Hartung would then visit the tanks under his command to see what they needed for supplies and repair parts. He met with his junior officers and ranking non-commissioned officers to assess the casualties they had taken and to estimate damage meted out. He collected their written reports then went over maps and time tables for planned action the following day. He made the rounds of his infantry/grenadiers, making sure their supplies were reaching them and that wounded were treated without delay. The Waffen-SS had their own medical units apart from regular Wehrmacht units and the medical staff were the best in Germany.

The Waffen-SS fighting man, a hand-picked volunteer, carried with him not only outstanding weapons but extraordinary training, both physical and mental, so that SS troops felt, and probably were, greatly superior man-to-man than most fighting forces they would encounter on the battlefield. There was no complaining among his troops as he briefed his subordinate officers, and was in turn briefed by them. Casualties had been acceptable and although they had been moved twice to trouble spots on the line, his regiment had responded quickly and efficiently to its objectives.

Hartung frequently returned to his own tank just in time to give the order to move out toward the next objective, usually a village, sometimes a particular Russian defensive line, and sometimes an airfield. Tomorrow he expected the fighting to be lighter than usual. He had been ordered to a wide bend in the German pocket southeast of Bialystok which was occupied by elements of the 23rd and 87th Infantry Divisions under Major General Hellmich and Lieutenant General von Studnitz.

The pocket thinned between the Szczara sector and Minsk. Sturmbannfuhrer Hartung was to seize and occupy the town of Kilov which contained a railroad bridge. Air reconnaissance indicated light enemy infantry and no armored units to oppose them. Hartung's orders were to hold that position until relieved by the 19th Motorized Infantry Division the following day.

Hartung's panzers were delayed several hours while they awaited fuel, resupply of ammunition for their cannons and rounds for automatic assault weapons, so that they did not jump off until 1800 hours the night of June 28th. The en route resistance was light, as promised, the entire twenty kilometers to Kilov. Still, the regiment did not arrive until 0430 the next morning. Hartung, his tank leading, raised his arm in the air, signaling for his panzers to halt.

He raised his binoculars to his eyes and scanned the town. It was just beginning to get light, the town still within the grasps of night's shadows, as though buildings were carved-out caves among the streets with telephone poles rising like fingers out of the surrounding bogs. Hartung could just make out the single track trestle on the far side of town, southeast of his position. He saw no one in the streets of the town, only a dog walking slowly, head hung low to the ground, looking for any morsel of food to eat. No lights shown. All as it should be. Very quiet. Too quiet. *Well*, Hartung thought to himself, *what do you expect? They will not send a band out to meet you.*

He raised his radio mike to his lips. "Viktor One, all vehicles, four columns, A and D will enter first. Ludke," he said to his infantry commander, "skirmish your men five hundred meters. I don't want big targets. Understand?"

"Understood," SS-Hauptsturmfuhrer Karl Ludke answered at once. Almost immediately infantrymen dropped off of their armored personnel vehicles and spread out in lines abreast on either side of the road. Panzer gunners checked their cannons and their MG-42's.

"B and C panzers stand by in reserve. Keep your fingers on the triggers, boys," Hartung said.

The two reserve columns, acting upon orders from their platoon sergeants, repositioned themselves abreast so that every gun could bear on a target. They were twenty tanks plus armored cars, having lost two panzers that had not yet been replaced.

"Boord," Hartung said into the radio to SS-Untersturmfuhrer Johanne Boord, "you will take the west side with D column, I will go to the east. Is that clear?"

"Yes. Keep your head down, Major," the junior officer said in jaunty response.

Boord was a cookie salesman before the war. It made Hartung laugh when he thought that such a mild-mannered young man, with big brown eyes and a constant smile on his face, could be such a fierce fighter in combat. If Boord lived through the war he would doubtless become the biggest cookie man in Germany.

"Hans," Hartung said to his driver, "I want you to follow that road there, on the right. Watch out for mines. Richter," he said to his gunner, "I want speed on target when I ask for it. Kraus, get your fingers out of your ass!" Kraus, the loader, waived a hand and grinned upward up to his commander. Hartung would select targets for the big gun while continuing to command his columns of tanks.

Hartung heard the rumble of guns like distant thunder as action raged in the forest region east, toward Minsk. It was a secondary distraction to the panzer commander but nonetheless it registered in the back of his mind that the battle was large, on a wide scale. He knew that there were two army corps, the XVII and XLII, the 17th, 78th, 134th, 131st, 45th and 31st Infantry Divisions were formed to do battle in that sector.

Ahead of Hartung's panzer abteilung the town of Kilov appeared deserted. Civilians invariably cowered inside their homes until the fighting was finished. His eyes scanned windows and doorways, roof tops, looking for strategically placed defensive fire positions.

At first he saw none.

Then a window swung open. Or had it? A garage door was ajar. He had not seen that before. "Boord," he said to the lead panzer of D squad, "what do you see?"

"Nothing."

"The church," Hartung said.

"*Nichts*," Boord repeated.

"Hans," Hartung shouted to his driver over the roar of the V-12 engine, "the oil spot."

"I see it," Hans said, driving around a dark spot in the road. The Russians sometimes covered mines with freshly dug earth, disguising them with a variety of innocent looking masks.

Hartung looked again at the church. It was becoming a distraction to him. He forced himself to look elsewhere; at the automotive garage, at the hotel, at large, barn-like building into which electric overhead lines ran. Probably a trolley maintenance shed. Double doors were partially open there, too. The lower part of the building was constructed of stone, the upper half of wood with a shake roof. Most of the houses behind the business district of the town were of wood construction, many with small fences around them. A civic center building, built of brick, occupied the very middle of the town with businesses down each side of the main street.

The days had been scorching hot and, despite the early hour, sweat was already rolling down beneath his black tanker's beret, its death head emblem reflecting first rays of the sun. It was a flash of light from another place that caused Hartung to drop into the turret of his tank and button up. A high velocity round bounced off the 16mm armor top hatch door of the panzer, slamming it down painfully onto his knuckles. The momentary reflection had come from the top of the church roof, probably from the telescopic sight of a marksman placed behind the orthodox cross on the church's dome.

Suddenly, within seconds the town of Kilov became live with hot gunfire from small arms as well as mortars and cannons. While Hartung's infantry dropped behind cover and began returning fire at buildings and dug-in positions between them, Hartung began fighting his machine.

"Left ten degrees, the window, machine gun!" he calmly ordered Richter who manually traversed the gun turret as ordered. Hartung immediately recognized the distinctive silhouette of the Russian 7.62mm ShKAS MG with its circular magazine atop the breach. He knew that the Soviet weapon had an 1,800 rounds per minute rate of fire and could decimate an infantry group very quickly.

As the gunsight aligned with the target Richter pulled the trigger on the 75mm assault gun. The target window and the entire side of the stone building disappeared in a violent cloud of dust and debris.

"Left five, doorway, same building, Richter. Two rounds...."

Hartung had hardly got the words out of his mouth when Richter had fired the 75mm through the doorway and was reloading for the second shot.

"Good shooting," Hartung said, slapping the gunner on the back.

Kraus slammed the second shell into the breach of the gun and closed it up. Richter adjusted his target for the movement of the tank, then fired again. The second round took the front and the back out of the building, causing it to collapse on one side into a pile of rubble.

Hartung regretted that he had wasted a second round on the building because his assault cannon was one of the biggest in his group, the other panzers being equipped with only .37mm. Most critical, however, was that his tank carried only 44 rounds where the PzKpfwIII's carried 99 each. In addition, the smaller tanks packed a 7.92mm MG34 and 3,000 rounds of ammunition, formidable weapons against an infantry unit.

"Rocket!" Hartung shouted as the snout of the Russian 14.5 mm anti-tank rifle appeared in a second story window. Hans kicked hard left and had the tanker turning as the Russian soldier aimed and fired. The tank-killer streaked toward Hartung and his crew. The reaction of Hartung's driver and the inability of the Russian soldier to adjust his aim caused the rifle grenade to hit the panzer at an angle and failed to penetrate the 50mm armor superstructure. A less oblique shot would have blown them to pieces.

"Get him, Richter! Get that son of a bitch!"

But the gunner was already traversing toward the target. When he pulled the trigger of the mighty assault gun most of the upper part of the building disappeared including the soldier who fired the anti-tank grenade.

Hartung looked through his navigation slits to see as much as possible of the fighting as he could. His other units were fully engaged. Russian soldiers, while there was no way to tell for sure, seemed plentiful in number and were fighting smart, taking advantage of cover and delivering steady rates of fire. When a round from a panzer gun blew up a building, Russian soldiers would immediately leap to occupy the rubble, increasing their concentration of fire. There was little doubt in the Sturmbannführer's mind that he would win the fight. His six hundred Waffen-SS infantry troops were seasoned fighters and could easily defeat an enemy force several times their own number. Also, the Russians, at least in this engagement, had no heavy guns to bring to bear.

But Hartung was not complacent. In fact he was concerned. Why were so many enemy soldiers engaging an armored unit with small arms fire? Why were they not in retreat? Mortars were no good against tracked vehicles and Hartung doubted that they would see many more rocket grenades. The Russians did not have them in great supply. Still, the Russians were fighting with their usual ferocity and the German unit would earn every meter of ground it captured.

"Boord," Hartung called into his radio, "turn to your left and flank these buildings; I'll take the right. B and C columns, move into the center."

Even as he gave the order, a tactic to disperse his tanks to minimize them as targets as well as surround the town so to fight the battle from the enemy rear, Hartung had sensed disaster. It had seemed too smooth, too predictable. Now that his panzers were in a line abreast, a T-34 rumbled out from behind the church.

"God damn!" Hartung heard his driver shout from below. Hans could have saved his breath; they were all gaping at the machine at their nine o'clock, six hundred meters.

Hartung knew what it was. He had seen photographs and drawings of every Russian weapons system that rolled or carried a gun. This was the newest battle tank the Russians owned, the T-34. It was 26 tons, 45 mm of armor and a 76 mm cannon. Its tracks were wider than Hartung had seen on any tank but the purpose for those wide tracks were not immediately obvious to him. What he did realize at once, however, was that the Russian tank turret was traversing toward him.

"Fire!" Hartung screamed at Richter who, in seconds, had trained his own gun on the Russian. But that was too long.

Hartung saw the tongue of flame from the muzzle of the T-34's main gun. He was only vaguely aware that in that same nanosecond he had gone deaf from the round exploding against the turret and the hull of his StuGIII. The projectile hit in the heaviest armored part of the tank and jammed the turret. Hartung's 75 mm gun was now useless in lateral movement.

Hartung thought he gave the order to fire again but he could not hear himself and, in fact, doubted whether his crew could have heard him in any case.

Richter fired. The German round struck the T-34 between the rear roller-wheel and the drive gear, partially crippling the Russian machine. Both gunners rammed new shells into their cannons and fired. This time the German round, unassisted by a turret that would not traverse, made nothing but noise as it passed harmlessly above and beyond the T-34. The Russian projectile struck the German tank slightly lower, on the hull, and the round penetrated.

Hartung felt intense heat and searing pain. The inside of the panzer was burning. Black smoke invaded his lungs. He knew that his crew had been killed and assumed that he would die with them. Whether the hatch had been blown open from the inside or that he had thrown open the lock himself he did not know, but it was open and he struggled toward the light. He rolled over the turret, slid down the hull and fell heavily onto the ground.

He became aware of intense gunfire as every gun in his unit opened up on the common enemy, the T-34. He would later learn that it was not one Russian tank but three T-34's who had waited in ambush for the Waffen-SS panzers that sought to take Kilov that day. As Hartung painfully crawled two meters toward a shallow ditch on the side of the dirt road leading off from the town's main street, his black uniform smouldering on his scorched body, he was aware that Boord's tank had found a berm on the west side of the town providing him a low profile target, and that his 75 mm gun was firing round after round down toward the opposite end of town. The T-34 that had struck Hartung's panzer, unable to maneuver with its broken drive-wheel, became an easy target for Boord to kill. Hartung rolled his head just in time to see the Russian tank hit broadside, on its thinnest armor plate, the German round penetrating through. The internal explosion blew the entire turret off the Russian machine, its crew of four killed instantly.

Boord trained his gun toward a second Russian tank, this one emerging from the town's trolley barn, then pulling quickly back after it had fired its gun.

All twenty of Hartung's light tanks were now pouring fire into enemy infantry positions rather than waste their fire on the T-34's. Hartung's left arm hung at a crazy angle to his body, both legs lacerated as though flayed by steel claws. He was in exquisite pain but his loss of blood from his leg, he thought, was manageable. With his good right arm he attempted to make a tourniquet with the silk scarf from his neck, but after several attempts he gave up.

The sound of battle would have been deafening had he not already lost most of his hearing, as round after round of cannon fire roiled the air a few feet above his head. He could feel the concussion of each round, and he could feel his body rise and slam back onto the ground as enemy mortars hit nearby. Still, the loss of blood and concussion from the destruction of his own tank did not knock him out. He was able to stay alert, his eyes wide open.

While Boord was battling one T-34 a third machine pulled out from behind the rubble of the east side of town, swivelled its big gun in Boord's direction. From that flanking position it would have been a certain kill. At that moment Hartung could see a team of his infantrymen that had crawled through the rubble of a building and set up a shot with a Panzerfaust within twenty meters of the Russian tank. An SS-Sturmann fired the rifle grenade, penetrating the hull of the T-34. It exploded the ammunition and fuel tanks of the Russian machine creating heat that would have melted the interior.

Boord had by now failed to kill the third T-34. With his own tank damaged to the point that it had lost its ability to fight, Boord and his crew dropped through the bottom escape hatch and crawled backward to the combat positions among the infantry troops.

The other light German panzers of Hartung's abteilung kept their machines in continuous motion, but the T-34s had decimated their ranks. Hartung could count at least seven of his panzers laid to waste, black smoke pouring from them, troops either dead inside or their corpses still burning nearby. He would later learn that their own casualties were 74 dead, 110 wounded.

The T-34 was far better than military intelligence said that it was. The Germans had nothing like it.

Still, the battle had been won in the technical sense. The Russians were withdrawing, the T-34 pulling out backwards, its 75.2 mm gun no longer firing. Hartung guessed that the Russian tank was out of ammunition for the main gun else it would have finished them off. Waffen-SS troops pursued the Russian foot soldiers but they were few in number and not worth the effort of chasing them all down. By 1700 hours that day the fighting was over. They had killed three hundred fifty troops, knocked out two tanks, and occupied the town of Kilov. Hartung recalled, as a morphine needle was shoved into his arm, that if the rest of their victories were to cost so dearly, the war was all but lost.

On June 29th, newly promoted Lieutenant Colonel Stephen Dietrich, recipient of the Iron Cross 1st Class for repeated acts of bravery in the operation of his fighter aircraft against an enemy of superior numbers, was reassigned from his station in France to the Eastern front. He would command 22nd Squadron of JagGeschwader 3, Luftflotte 2. Field Marshal Kesselring commanded the Luftflotte from his train near Brest-Litovsk. He had the II Air Corps and VIII to use in the destruction of the Soviet Air Force which had gone forward in the early days of Barbarossa with few serious complications.

Dietrich brought with him 24 new Me-109Fs, and their seasoned pilots from demanding and dangerous combat fought in the skies over Britain as well as in the defense of air strikes launched along coastal regions. His fighters received white paint stripes on their tail sections to designate their theater of operation, i.e., Central Group East, while the air crews were settled into their new quarters by local *Lufgau* services. Each air district was assigned a Luftgau whose business it was to provide crew accommodations, dining halls, fuel and ammunition supply sources and, generally, to execute all paperwork required of fighting units so that the unit was immediately free for combat operations.

After seeing that his men were satisfied with their new quarters, Dietrich was walking into the officer's mess when he met Colonel Möelders, a good friend and one of Germany's fastest rising aces, on his way out.

"Dietrich, you bastard!" Möelders greeted Dietrich with a huge smile and open arms. The two airmen embraced warmly. "Congratulations on your promotion, you coward," Möelders said, throwing his head back in laughter.

"I suppose they're giving Crossed Swords for surviving syphilis these days," Dietrich said, nodding toward one of Germany's highest awards for bravery worn around the neck of this young Luftwaffe colonel.

"I think you and I should find out as soon as possible," Möelders said, taking Dietrich's arm and turning back to the officer's mess.

They found a table in a corner where they took their drinks, both men ordering bottled beer. Dietrich took a good look at Werner Möelders. He was about average height, slight build, and with his gold trimmed Luftwaffe uniform that included breeches and hand-made black boots, Möelders looked like a military poster on the streets of Berlin. Dietrich, by contrast, was still wearing his flying suit which was stained with oil, reeked of aviation fuel and hydraulic fluid. His hands were still darkened by combinations of airplane grease and other liquids and his fingernails looked like they belonged on a coal miner in Silesia rather than a German officer. Also he knew that the two shared deep circles under their eyes.

Möelders had been in continuous action since Spain where he chalked up 14 victories, Poland, then France and continuously on the Channel, also stationed in France. Möelders had more than 90 victories as they toasted each other with dark Bavarian brews.

"Did you bring your squadron with you?" Dietrich asked.

"Of course. The 51st. Still the best fighter squadron in the Luftwaffe," he said.

"No question about it," Dietrich said, dryly.

"Fuck you."

"Well?" Dietrich said, eyes wide open, "where are the girls? How long have you been here? Why am I not yet getting laid?"

"Because I refuse to contribute to sin. If a Russian puts a bullet up your ass I don't want to tell your mother that you died with a dripping pecker. Where is that friend of yours, ah...."

"Friedel," Dietrich said.

"Yes. Funny man. He was flying Heinkels, I think," Möelders said.

"That's right. Shot down in September, October...." Dietrich said.

"Dead?"

Dietrich shrugged. "How are the Ruskies? I hear their machines are junk."

"Yes, nothing very good. But they have some good pilots. Someday, if they last long enough, they will get good machines for those who fly them and we will have our hands full," Möelders said, taking a long pull on his beer.

"We will be in Moscow before the summer is out," Dietrich said.

"Yes! That's right, you have the ear of the Führer, I hear. Tell me, what is he like?" Möelders asked.

"You have met him," Dietrich said, taking a long drink of his beer. He belched.

"Yes, but I was in a line with others. I mean, is he a genius?"

"He can't be too smart if he signed your promotion orders," Dietrich said.

"Göring signed my promotion orders, you ass," Möelders said.

"Then I think I have made my point."

The two fighter pilots worked their way through two more beers when Dietrich suggested they move on to cognac.

"Just one, Yank. You and I are going to fly in the morning," Möelders said.

Dietrich's eyebrows shot up. His machines had been refueled and rearmed but there had been no operation order for them at the field.

"If you get off your fat little ass and do your job, junior birdman," Möelders said, "your orders are probably waiting for you at Operations right now.

As though on cue one of Dietrich's flight-line sergeants entered the officer's mess. Spotting his C.O., the sergeant crossed the room and saluted.

"Pardon, Colonel Dietrich," he said.

"Yes, Müller, what is it?" Dietrich asked, casting a knowing eye back to Möelders.

"General orders, sir. Air Operations officer sent me for you. We, ah... "

"Yes, I know. I will be there presently," Dietrich said.

"Well, Yank, did you do the right thing?" Möelders asked.

"You mean leave my country?"

"It is more than that, isn't it? Fighting in a war for a foreign power. Serious business," Möelders observed.

"I don't think about it much," Dietrich said.

"Liar."

Dietrich shrugged. "I guess I do think about it."

"And you feel justified?"

"To be honest I had some misgivings about shooting down the Brits, you know? It is kind of a relief to be here."

"Fighting the Russians," Möelders said.

"Yes."

A moment of silence passed between them, then Möelders leaned closer to Dietrich. "You could be at that nice little college you came from... "

"Yale," Dietrich interjected.

"Yale. And you would be playing with the tits of beautiful young girls. Those ones that cheer on the football teams," Möelders urged.

"Yale is not a co-ed school."

"Co-ed?"

"We don't have girls at Yale," Dietrich clarified.

"A waste of time, then," the Luftwaffe colonel said, drinking deeply of his beer and beckoning toward the bar for two more.

"A great school. I'll miss not going back," Dietrich said.

"And why will you not?"

"Do you think you are going to survive this war? I think it's an illusion. Something to keep us going. I haven't had a leave in almost two years. A few days off, but no leave," Dietrich said. "They'll fly us until we die."

"What do your parents think of what you are doing?" Möelders asked.

"I think they are embarrassed, their son fighting for Germany. We are not so popular in America, you know. But they never say."

"Do they write to you?" Möelders wanted to know.

"No."

"Do you feel homesick?" the German ace said.

"Sometimes. It's a great country, you know, America. You should see the west. Huge mountains, deserts, beaches that go for thousands of miles. Beautiful," Dietrich said.

"And girls," Möelders urged.

"Lots of girls, and all of them knock-outs," Dietrich said.

"Knock downs?"

"Knock outs, you jerk. That means incredibly good looking," Dietrich said, explaining to Möelders.

Möelders shrugged, not understanding.

"Tell you what, Werner, if you and I survive this son of a bitch we'll go to Hollywood together. How's that?" Dietrich said.

Möelders' eyes widened, a smile pulling it at the corners of his mouth.

"Can you be serious? Dietrich, you bastard...."

"I know a movie star. George Raft. Maybe we could stay with him," Dietrich allowed.

Möelders slammed the his hand on the table. "Now you are talking, you fat little prick! And we can take out actresses!"

"Of course. I'll have to pay them to go out with you but I think you are worth it," Dietrich said. He stood, stiffly, still feeling the soreness that came from being crammed into a tiny cockpit from a long flight across Europe. He extended his hand again toward Möelders who took it. "I am off for the greater glory of the Reich. Try to keep yourself alive until you can buy me another drink."

"Stay in the middle of your squadron so you have some protection. You fly like a cow," Möelders said.

Dietrich never saw Möelders again. The young colonel amassed a record of 115 kills before dying himself riding as a passenger in a plane that was to take him to the funeral of Ernst Udet on November 22, 1941.

On June 30 Dietrich's squadron, along with Möelders' 51st and others, took part in a large air battle over the city of Minsk. The Soviet Air Force stationed in that sector was attempting to break out but was intercepted by Luftwaffe fighter squadrons that shot down a total of 114 aircraft. Möelders shot down two Russians. Dietrich shot down two and destroyed another on the ground. His air unit then rendered close ground support to elements of the 3rd Panzer Group as well as the 2nd Panzer Group, in the process destroying more than 100 enemy armored vehicles.

The German High Command believed that by the end of June the campaign in the East had been half won. Stubborn elements of Russian forces continued to hold on, but they were leaderless and would soon be annihilated.

On June 28th Moscow named Lieutenant General Yeremenko as commander of the Western Military District, a day the OKW would remember in sober retrospection. The first meeting by the general was held in the presence of Marshal Voroshilov and other high ranking officers. Yeremenko's first order was short and blunt: "Halt on the Berezina and defend."

Listening freely to BBC radios were not restricted for German POWs. Frederick Friedel, along with his fellow prisoners, had been following the war news, especially reports of the Nazi blitzkrieg that seemed to be working so well against the Russians just as it had in the West. The days of the Soviet Union seemed to be limited, just as Britain was living on borrowed time. Friedel had almost completely healed from a compound fracture of his right leg and second degree burns on his hands and neck, thence to be detained at a prison camp near Dumfries, Scotland, that was occupied almost wholly with Luftwaffe prisoners.

They had been notified early this morning that they were to board a special train. British authorities would not reveal the train's destination but rumors among the prisoners had it that the train was bound for Glasgow where the POWs would board a ship for Canada. In point of fact, the train went in the opposite direction, to Liverpool, but the final destination would prove to be correct.

The battles of Bialystok and Minsk being over, Lieutenant Colonel Dietrich led his squadron into fights over such places as Bobruisk and Mogilev while German armies advanced toward the Dnieper and Duena Rivers. Dietrich and his 22nd Gruppe flew from early morning until night. They would pause only long enough to fuel their planes and their bodies. They were constantly fatigued, critically so, by the time they had fought for three solid weeks, taking only one Sunday afternoon off. Their losses had been surprisingly light, given the state of their exhausted bodies and airplanes, while the Russians were hemorrhaging both pilots and aircraft.

While it was true that during the early months of Barbarossa Dietrich and his colleagues were shooting out of the skies with relative ease such unmemorable machines as the Polikarpov I-16, a 288 mph radial engine fighter and the 300 mph SU-2 fighter-bomber, they would also come across the occasional flight of LaGG-3s. The Lavochkin fighter was new in 1941 and it was a considerable step for Stalin's fighter defense system. It flew at 348 mph at 17,000 feet and when Dietrich and his squadron mates ran into these machines they were invariably flown by Russia's best pilots. The Russians never lacked courage in defense of their homeland and their pilots were experienced in the more elite fighter units.

On September 28th Dietrich was leading a six-aircraft sweep along the Berezina River west of Lepel. His gruppe had been assigned the job of suppressing air attacks and lending ground support for the XXXIX Motorized Army Corps and the 20th Panzer Division. Dietrich had expended most of his ammunition on a convoy of Russian vehicles and on a train. They had used most of their fuel for what would have been a 50 minute sortie when Dietrich's wing man, Flying Sergeant Ernst Meier, spotted an airfield off his wing. There were aircraft there, in various dispositions of refueling, repair. Or parked.

"Three o'clock, Yank," Meier said into his radio/oxygen mask.

"You lead, Pope," Dietrich said, using Meier's nickname given to him by his squadron mates pertaining to his religion. "I'm low on ammo." Dietrich figured he had just enough left in his 20 mms to repel one pass, should they encounter fighters.

"Follow me," Pope said, rolling in his Me-109 from 1500 meters, dropping the nose below the target airfield, knowing that as he picked up speed on his run aerodynamic forces would cause his aircraft to lift in a kind of floating motion. He pushed the electrical trim-tab button to make the stick more responsive to his touch. As his air speed indicator passed from the green into the yellow zone, a high speed warning, Meier ignored the design limits of the aircraft and allowed the indicator needle to approach red.

Keeping perfect station off Meier's right wing and slightly behind, Dietrich let Meier, now the acting flight leader, pay attention to attack angles, target approach speeds and g-force stress as they would be subject to coming off their run. His job, and he was doing it now, was to watch their six o'clock position and elsewhere for intercepting fighters. Even though he kept his head continuously turning, his eyes peering into cobalt blue skies over Russia, Dietrich was aware that the airfield in front of them was crowded with twin-engine bombers, several of which were the Petlyakov Pe-2s, a well armed and fast light bomber just reaching the Soviet front lines.

At four hundred meters Dietrich had to pull his throttle back slightly in order to keep station with Meier whose now continuous gunfire was causing his Me-109 to lose airspeed. Dietrich, in his visual sweep outside the airplane, could see that Meier was getting hits on the bombers on the ground. He also saw flak bursting nearby as well as heavy machine-gun fire, their tracer rounds stabbing up for them from the ground. Meier was not jinking to avoid the ground fire. Dietrich had his finger on his push-to-talk button, intending to advise Meier to break left when they had finished their strafing run when he felt his machine jolt.

He knew he had been hit but the Me-109 continued to respond to his ginger test of controls. As he followed Meier out of the target run he spoke on the mission frequency.

"Forget the second pass, Pope. I'm hit. Check me over."

Few fighters could catch the Messerschmitt in a climb and Dietrich and his wing man were quickly at 2,000 meters. Meier dropped his plane under Dietrich's port side and, looking up and forward, inspected the fuselage and wings.

Meier saw the problem immediately. "Fuel tank," he said. "It's streaming."

"I see it now," Dietrich said, the needle of his petrol indicator visibly moving toward the empty side of the gauge. He had used his wing tanks first, then switched to the main tank forty minutes into the mission. They were already flying on a westerly course toward the German lines, but how far out were they, he wondered?

"Reduce your power setting," Meier advised over the radio.

"Already have," Dietrich responded. He had reduced the power to lessen the pressure inside the fuel cell and he had set the propeller pitch to cruise so that he was pulling big bites of air while the engine was underpowered. Normally this procedure would have ruined the Daimler-Benz engine by "over boosting" but under the circumstances it might pull his machine an extra kilometer, perhaps two, before it dropped out of the sky.

Dietrich looked down hoping to see the sight of vehicles moving east or artillery positions firing toward the morning sun. He saw neither. He saw only small villages, an occasional stand of trees, and endless stretches of wild grass and planted fields, not yet harvested. This was a bad sign. Only recently Stalin had given an order to the Russian people. *"The enemy is pitiless. He is determined to occupy our territory, take our grain, use our oil, the fruits of our labor.... The life and death of the Soviet Union is at stake.... We must take all of the railroad rolling stock with us.... Not one kilo of corn, not one liter of fuel must fall into the hands of the enemy.... Anything of value, metal, grain and oil, must be destroyed if it cannot be withdrawn.*

The fields below were not on fire, nor were they charred. The unharvested ground under Dietrich was still under Russian control.

His engine sputtered, then coughed. No amount of emergency fuel pump operation made the slightest difference. The engine was out of fuel and Dietrich either had to jump or go down with the airplane. His decision was made very quickly. There being no fuel to catch fire, Dietrich was confident that he could land the fighter plane and walk away from the wreck.

"Pope, get a fix," he said, even as he looked at the field of wheat below. There was little wind, judging from the very gentle sway of the stalks, heavy with grain on their ends. He had been sinking at a rate of two hundred thirty meters per minute, his best glide angle at 145 kph. With the ground only three hundred feet below and coming up fast, Dietrich extended the gears, deployed his flaps 20. He could feel the effects of speed reduction as his body pulled gently against his shoulder straps. He kept the nose down to avoid a high-speed stall.

There was nothing left to say to Meier as he sensed, rather than saw, his wing man slowed but remaining 200 meters above and behind.

"Vehicles at your eight o'clock," Meier said. "I'll take care of them."

There was no time for Dietrich to respond as he deployed full flaps and made gentle control inputs to line up his Me-109 on a field that did not have tree stumps within the rows of planted wheat. The first bounce was almost easy, but Dietrich realized that the second contact with the ground would be severe. If the field was soft the wheels could dig in and turn the airplane onto its back.

Accordingly, the second bounce ripped off one of the Me-109's "legs." The 109 ground looped, spinning in a complete circle, and sliding several hundred feet before coming to rest in a cloud of dust. Dietrich's straps had held him firmly in the cockpit, and though his head struck the side of his canopy impact was softened by his leather flying helmet and the injury was not serious.

His nostrils filled with the unmistakable and highly unpleasant odor of burning electrical insulation. There were no flames, yet he was glad to be able to release his restraints and drop down onto the wing of the flightless bird. Dietrich's flight suit was festooned with an array of zippered pockets. On his left thigh, sealed with a pressure stud flap, held a flare pistol and several flare cartridges. In the same pocket was a knife with a six-inch blade. On the thigh pocket on the right leg were maps and a compass as well as five one "hundred" franc Swiss gold pieces. Yet another pocket on the hip contained a folded silk German flag to lay on the ground should friendly forces come within view. On his hip, attached to a wide leather belt, Dietrich wore a holstered 9mm pistol. There was a liter canteen of water, his own idea while flying, secured to the aluminum frame of his pilot's seat. He noted that his wristwatch crystal was shattered. The sweep-second hand no longer moved despite his attempt to make it run again by winding and shaking. He removed it from his arm and dropped it on the ground.

He did a quick inventory of these items as he pulled off his outer suit exposing his blue Luftwaffe uniform underneath. The weather was far too warm to wear both. There were, as well, emergency rations containing food that was unappetizing to think about now but which, he knew, would taste like gourmet food much later.

It was important to get away from the scene of his crash as soon as possible, but he took several minutes to consult his maps. Using a protractor, he marked the known objects on the ground that could be matched to his navigation chart that all pilots carried on clipboards in the airplane. Part of his problem was the same as that which had dogged airmen and ground forces alike: there were very few accurate maps of the Soviet Union. Returning to home bases was infinitely easier when, after an action, they simply dialed in a given radio frequency, verified its identifier, then flown home on the beam. But now, with no RDF to assist him, Dietrich had to work very hard with his few navigation aids.

In the distance he could faintly hear the attack being made on the Russian vehicles spotted by the Pope. He could count on his wing man to knock out the machines, neutralizing the Russians ability to arrive on site quickly. With any luck their radios would likewise be knocked out so that Dietrich might avoid dealing with an organized search party.

Dietrich could hear the Pope's Me-109 climbing, breaking off the attack. He knew that his comrade would be low on ammunition and fuel and would be heading for home base. There would be little chance of Dietrich making his way as far his fighter base, well in the rear of the lines, but he estimated that the town of Stolin should by now be taken by German troops, a distance of about seventy-five kilometers from his present position near the Prypyats river. Fortunately, he was on the west side of the river, his course line putting that body of water at his back. Moving west-southwest he would cross other streams, lakes or rivers before arriving, should he be so lucky, in Stolin.

He quickly dumped his parachute pack onto the ground and cut the canopy clear of the cords. Both would be useful for survival. He placed his small hoard of survival items into the parachute, folded the bundle and tied it off with several wraps of parachute cord. It was light weight but very strong. Replacing his leather helmet with his forage cap, he marked a compass heading. He peered into the distance looking for a natural marker on which to guide, but there were no mountains in this part of Russia and no other tall projections on which to head. He would therefore refer to his hand-held compass much more frequently as he moved along.

He took a deep and prolonged drink from his canteen, fully aware of the need to hydrate himself before beginning the trek.

The Eastern Führerhauptquatier, or Wolfschanze (Wolf's Lair), was located near the Polish town of Ketrzyn, 8 kilometers east of Rastenburg. Set in the beautiful Masuri Lake region in northwest Poland, the Wolfschanze was a tribute to the speed and efficiency of the Todt Reich construction organization. The complex occupied some 600 acres of ground and was a complete city within itself to serve the needs of OKW (Oberkommando das Wehrmacht) and, more specifically its commander, Adolf Hitler. Its building began in late 1940 and was continually expanded for the entire duration of the war. Over time there were more than 80 buildings erected on semi-swamp ground, including communications centers, two airfields, one with a traffic control tower, guest facilities, staff quarters, train sidings, SS barracks, a Hitler bunker, a Göring bunker, and a Bormann bunker, offices and housing for a complete stenographic and administrative staff, post office, offices and housing for Luftwaffe and Kriegsmarine liaisons, a cinema, two teahouse/restaurants, and many others.

Two special trains left every morning for Berlin while two trains from Berlin left that location heading east to the Wolfschanze. Two flights a day to Berlin made the round trip while other flights left and arrived the Wolf's Lair daily to and from various areas of the Russian front.

There were two main gates leading into the three *Sperrkreis,* or security areas, one of which was paved with asphalt and lined with cobblestone gutters. The entire complex was covered with gigantic camouflage netting that was maintained meticulously and changed to appear as foliage during the various seasons of the year. Aerial photographs were taken frequently to insure that the entire area was completely covered. While the efficacy of the camouflage was open to debate, there was never a serious attempt at bombing the *Wolfschanze.*

Archie had become almost accustomed to the frenetic pace of the Reichschancellery in Berlin with a hundred people wanting to see him each day and thousands needing to see other Reich officials. But at the *Wolfschanze* the pressure and pace was exponentially greater. There was a war going on and it was Archie's responsibility to run it. He found himself rising later each day and, like his late alter ego, staying up into the early morning hours of the following day.

Archie was thus eating his first meal of the day, cucumber sandwiches and plum pudding, at 11:30 hours on August 4th, when he learned that the Russian army had launched a counter attack on the city of Rzhev. The assault against German forces began early in the morning and had been in progress for more than five hours by the time Archie entered his command bunker. The German combat line began to sag and was penetrated by 1300 hours. Archie studied the report that was handed to him when he arrived on the scene.

"Where did they come from?" he asked Colonel Fritsch, a staff adjutant.

The tall, dark haired officer who wore an Iron Cross First Class, showed darkness around the eyes highlighted by pale white skin, symptoms of a pressure-cooker life lived away from natural sunlight.

"It must have been last night, Führer. We believe the attack is coming from the enemy's 20th and 31st Armies with two tank and one cavalry corps. They were here," Colonel Fritsch said, stepping to a huge wall map and pointing, "early yesterday. They must have moved almost fifty kilometers after dark."

Several OKW staff officers had by now gathered about the Führer, anxiously awaiting his appraisal of the situation. The report revealed that the Germans were defending that sector with XLVI Panzer Corps and the 14th and 36th Motorized Infantry Divisions.

"Who is the general in command of that sector?" Archie demanded.

"Generalmajor von Langen, sir," Fritsch replied.

"Relieve him at once," Archie said, turning toward the map as though the matter of von Langen was out of his mind.

The effect of his order, however, was electric around the room. Colonel Fritsch was stunned into silence. He looked helplessly at other officers, several of whom outranked him. One such officer stepped forward.

"Führer," said General Felix Klause, "may I suggest you reconsider replacing Langen. He is an exceptional panzer officer and a brilliant leader. Perhaps we might... "

Ignoring Klause as though he had not spoken, indeed, that he was not even present in the room, Archie directed his attention to Fritsch, the adjutant.

"And reduce Langen in rank," he said, which was followed by a collective gasp by all of those assembled. "It is quite apparent that General Langen was not alert to the dangers of what lay in front of him. Two army groups moving into position make noise and Langen did not hear it! Get him out of there. Send him back to Germany," Archie said, turning back to the accumulation of the previous day's action reports.

Not all of the news was bad throughout the rest of the day, at least from the German armed forces point of view. The XXXIX Panzer Corps took command of the south Zubtsov area and demolished virtually all of the VIII Soviet Tank Corps.

By late afternoon the front had stabilized everywhere.

"You see?" Archie pontificated within the midst of the Command Center's beehive of activity, "when a weak officer is found hiding within the larger group of brave German soldiers, he must be eliminated quickly and ruthlessly! So. Look where we are now," he boasted, scanning the masses of pins and flags and icons attached to a giant wall map indicating German and Russian forces along the entire 2,000 kilometer front.

There was not so much as a murmur of disagreement with his pronouncement among the entire staff of army, Luftwaffe and Kriegsmarine.

Reports of fighting along the front began to flow into OKW by 2200 hours, the daily action slowing with the onset of darkness.

Commanders in the field outlined battle assessment reports and handed them up to battalion, then division, and Army headquarters where they were assessed and finally passed on to OKW. Archie insisted on reading those submitted by Army groups as well as summaries made there at OKW for his and other senior staff officers.

On August 27th Major General Grossman, who had relieved General von Langen, received orders from Generaloberst Model who had received his orders directly from Archie, that no German command post be allowed to withdraw so much as a single meter (and that cooks and clerks take up their rifles, if need be), brought in forces from all possible sectors and threw them wherever there was a crisis. It took a full four weeks to win a victory at Rzhev, but at the high cost of casualties on both sides. The town itself was reduced to a smoldering pile of rubble serving no strategic value to either army. In its aftermath Field Marshal Gunther von Kluge arrived at the Wolfschanze where he proposed a limited withdrawal of the exhausted 3rd Panzer and 9th Infantry Armies for a temporary respite.

"We would all like to rest, von Kluge," Archie said to his valued general while a crowded staff room listened in embarrassed silence. "Should I ask Stalin to withdraw two of his armies while your units rest?"

Von Kluge, known to have been fearful of Hitler's crude sense of military tactics even prior to the outbreak of the war in 1939, was aghast at Archie's sarcastic response to a reasoned proposal.

"I appreciate your humor, Führer, but these men have been in non-stop combat since 22 June. And they have been in the heaviest fighting. They are at their limits," von Kluge argued.

"Are they, indeed, General? And what is that limit, precisely?" Archie asked, facetiously.

Von Kluge was a scion of an old and venerated Prussian military family who revered genteel behavior and loathed the Nazis from their earliest beginnings. He abhorred Hitler's treatment of the Jews and in 1938 he, General Beck, and others planned to arrest the Führer and other high ranking Nazis. They needed the assistance of the British government and when their cabal was refused recognition in London, the coup never occurred. General von Kluge now stood before this odious dictator like a schoolboy receiving a lecture on the importance of hard work.

Von Kluge ground his teeth and said, "My soldiers have fought bravely and without complaint. They have taken sixty percent casualties because they are a spearhead. They are quite willing to die where they stand if that is what you are ordering them to do, but they only ask to be given a little sleep first."

Archie, taken aback by the words from such a courageous man asking relief not for himself but for his deserving men, felt momentarily sick at heart. He had, since arriving from Berlin in June, become used to causing death and pain for others, but always from a distance. This time he was killing German soldiers in cold blood. He tried to respond with vigor but instead heard himself say, in a rather subdued voice, "Do what you want, Kluge."

Since Archie had turned his back, General von Kluge did not offer a salute before withdrawing from the room.

Inside his relatively small personal office, Archie turned his attention to reading Luftwaffe action reports. As he worked his way down the stack of papers he noticed, yet again, that his right hand was trembling. This was the worst it had been since he first noticed the shaking at Obersalzberg four months ago. The action was involuntary. He had assumed that it was nothing more than a nervous tic, he had a cheek muscle that had twitched years ago, the result of overwork and lack of real exercise. But this was persistent and noticeable. Archie put his right hand over his left. The tremor was arrested, but when he removed his right hand it began to shake once more.

There was something dreadfully wrong, he thought. It wasn't his health. It was something far worse. Germany was winning the war.

General von Kluge arose before morning's light and was driven to his waiting aircraft. He told his personal pilot not to return immediately to his Army Corps headquarters but to detour to Borisov, current field headquarters for Field Marshal Fedor von Bock, Commander, Army Group Center (frequently referred to as Army Group B).

"Have caviar, Kluge," von Bock said to his unexpected visitor. Von Bock was wearing a white turtle-neck sweater and breeches but had not yet replaced carpet slippers with black boots. "I'll have something cooked for you. Eggs?"

Von Kluge nodded. "That would be good. Two scrambled and coffee," he said to a soldier from the kitchen. He helped himself to the delicious Russian caviar, from the Black Sea, no doubt. He spread the stuff generously on a piece of toast.

"Where are my panzers?" he demanded, referring to 12th and 23rd Panzer Grenadier Divisions.

"Where? Do you mean exactly where are they garrisoned?" von Bock asked, arching an eyebrow.

"You know very well what I mean, Bock. I was promised those armored reinforcements three days ago!" von Kluge said, visibly attempting to control his temper.

"The Führer has instructed me to hold those divisions in strategic reserve," von Bock said, evenly.

"Ah. So the Bohemian corporal has instructed his Army commander as to the disposition of his forces. I see," von Kluge fumed.

"Now, Gunther, be careful. The walls have ears."

"I don't care if the walls have assholes! I have just come from an audience with the Corporal-in-Chief and have received a lecture in personnel staffing. Damn it, Fedor, if this egocentric moron remains in charge of the Army we might as well surrender to the Russians. And I don't care who hears me! Somebody needs to tell him that he is making the war impossible to win."

"Sit down, Kluge. Please. Drink some grape juice. It's good for you. It will keep you regular."

"That's prune juice," Kluge responded.

"You know that every commander up and down the line, and that includes North and South, not just Center, is calling for more. More of everything. More troops, more panzers, more ammunition, more men," von Bock said. "The coffee is French. Try it."

"Forgive me if I fail to see the lack of merit behind those requests. To fight a war one must have guns and bullets," von Kluge said, allowing himself to sit for only a moment before getting to his feet again to pace.

"'Ah, therein lies the rub,' as Shakespeare might once have said. We are here, dear Gunther, at least two years early. The Russians weren't expecting us but then neither was German industry."

Von Kluge stopped pacing long enough to look squarely at his Army Commander. "What are you saying? That there are no supplies to send?"

"Exactly so. I recently had a long and very serious discussion with General Stabb...."

"Procurement," von Kluge interjected.

"Who revealed the rather incomprehensible story of a nation that declared war upon most of the world while it was not yet ready. Not only not ready, but not even geared up to a war footing! Supplies? Kluge, we have a twenty-two day supply of artillery ammunition and a ten day reserve of motor petrol if there were no further trains from the Fatherland."

"Poland all over again," von Kluge said, sitting down more slowly. It was common knowledge among ranking military officers that had not Poland and France fallen so quickly the front line soldiers would have run out of many crucial parts for almost everything, including the panzers upon whose tracks the Blitzkrieg was carried.

Von Bock nodded. "I can ask the Führer once more to release your panzer divisions but I can tell you in advance that he will refuse."

"Does he give a reason?"

"Oh, yes. He expects a counter-attack in the Orsa sector. He will use those divisions to crush the Russian thrust."

"Is that so? And when was our Führer intending to share that intelligence with us? Sometime before the attack, one would hope?" von Kluge asked, sarcastically.

Von Bock shrugged and sipped his freshly poured coffee.

Dietrich's feet felt like they were wading in warm swamp-water as his fur-lined flying boots squished with his own sweat. His blue uniform was almost white with caked dust and salt from parched earth over which he walked for what was now the afternoon of the third day. He attempted for at least the tenth time to estimate the distance he had covered since crashing 90 hours ago. He believed it to be a disappointing 24 kilometers.

On the first day he was forced to deviate countless times from his dead-reckoning compass course of 230 in order to avoid enemy patrols. One of them, a twenty-man, two vehicle infantry detachment was, he was sure, looking for him in particular. To avoid them he had half buried himself in a dung pile shared by two farms in the vicinity. The houses that were built upon the farms had been burned so that nothing remained but vestiges of mud brick foundations and stone hearths. Dietrich had eagerly tested the ashes for signs of warmth, perhaps telling him that the fires were recent and that German forces would soon arrive. But the residues were cold. They could have been created two days or two months ago.

The dunghill, however, was quite fresh. Dietrich could not bring himself to immersed himself totally under the animal waste but the sight of four Russian T-24s and their accompanying infantry moving in his direction inspired him to lie in a shallow trench and to rake as much dung as possible over his body before the enemy arrived on scene.

Dietrich's mind almost revolted as his body crawled with insects of kinds that he could only imagine. But if he had moved at all the of Soviet soldiers walking only a few meters nearby would have discovered him. He had hidden in manure when the outside temperature was in the high 80s causing his body temperature to soar. When at last he could stand it no more he rolled hard to one side, prepared to run, if indeed he could.

But the Russians were gone. The sun was almost down on the western horizon and the air temperature was plunging. During the night there would come a frost, and by morning each blade of grass would show a white coating of ice. Dietrich had finished the last of his water, filled up the day before from a slow moving stream. He shuddered to think what might have died and turned rotten farther up current, but there was no choice but to drink and hope.

In the early hours of the morning Dietrich awoke, sweating, joints and head aching. Rolled into his parachute, protected by several layers of silk, he was nevertheless alternately hot and cold. His dreams had been nightmarish in quality. His airplane was on fire. The hot flames, fed by the slip stream, were reaching for his lap. They would burn his feet, already on fire, then his body and his face. He tried to put his Me-109 into a slip in order to keep the flames away as long as possible, but the aircraft would not respond to control inputs. It continued its lazy spiral down, the fire getting hotter as he descended. The fire was now intense, the pain excruciating, and he hoped that he would very soon hit the hard Russian plain.

He awoke to the sound of the crash. It was very loud in his ears. And then he heard it again, and again. Struggling to extricate himself from the parachute cocoon, he stood unsteadily on his feet. His head still swam but cleared just enough to tell him that he had not heard the crash of his dreams but rather the sound of gunfire. Heavy guns. In what must have been the last step of his journey the night before, he had collapsed into a ditch before rolling himself up. The ditch, which bordered a wide unpaved road, contained telephone poles. Wires once strung along them were cut down and lay on the ground. Dizziness and nausea came upon him with ferocity and he barely had time to remove his uniform trousers before his bowels let loose. He then collapsed a few meters away, weakened and struggling against delirium, still carrying, half-dragging his parachute silk. He fell once again into the ditch and, with early morning sun warming his body, descended into sleep.

The ground had again begun to heave, lifting him from the earth, dropping him roughly while covering him with clods of broken dirt and fine dust. He could only guess by the position of the sun that he had slept two hours when heavy shells had fallen nearby. He also began to register another sound, or series of noises, that sounded very much like vehicles. Dietrich cautiously raised his head to road level. The almost continuous noise assaulting his ears was that of vehicles of all descriptions moving in convoy in an easterly direction. While the vehicles, some of them towing guns, caissons, and troops, came into and out of Dietrich's focus, he could at once make out the fact that on their sides were vividly painted red stars.

Dietrich sought cover again in the ditch. He lay for what he estimated to be several hours before the last of the trucks and personnel carriers had passed. When he awoke late in the afternoon every muscle and joint in his body throbbed, his head ached with great intensity. He rummaged through his small medical kit and found a vial containing pain pills. The only water he had to wash it down was the remnants of that which he believed to be contaminated. He looked at it for a moment, weighing the consequences if he swallowed more. After all, it might not be poisonous. His illness could be something else. Although desperate to alleviate his suffering, Dietrich nevertheless poured the water onto the ground and put the pill into his mouth and chewed. The chemicals in the pill tasted incredibly bitter, almost making him regurgitate, but his parched throat swallowed repeatedly to keep it down.

His thirst now intensified. He knew he would have to find water soon or die. He had finished the last of his meager emergency rations last night. Dietrich determined that he would move at night and sleep during the day. He again pulled the parachute silk around his body and closed his eyes, falling almost at once into a fitful, difficult sleep.

When he awoke it was quite dark. His general body pain had eased somewhat but he used the second of five pills. Steeling himself against the awful taste, he chewed another before preparing to set off once again. There was no reason not to walk on the road, he thought. If he saw lights, or movement of any kind, he could jump into the nearby ditch. Moving with difficulty, Dietrich put one foot in front of another, continuing the process until he had achieved something of a walking pace as opposed to a stagger. With the pain pill doing its work, Dietrich stepped in the direction of either death or deliverance.

Flying Sergeant Ernst Meier reported Dietrich's crash position to Hauptman (Captain) Kurt Wenta, second in command of the 22nd Fighter Squadron, JagGeschwader3. As quickly as it took the ground personnel to refuel and rearm the Pope's 109, every aircraft in flyable condition was off the ground, wheels up, falling into formation behind Pope's Messerschmitt as he led them back to Dietrich's approximate position.

"Gruppe," Wenta said over his command frequency, "spread out. Two hundred meters."

Immediately the graceful, high-speed aircraft moved laterally, putting distance between each set of wingtips, creating the widest possible area to be swept.

Pope was painfully aware that his navigation back to the crash site was imperfect. He and Dietrich had conducted an aerial battle before rerouting their elements to the airfield where Dietrich was hit. True, Pope had been careful to get the best possible fix on his return to base but he had been forced to evade Russian fighters en route because he was too short on fuel and ammunition to fight.

Still, the airfield he and Dietrich had attacked that morning at last came into view. It must have been mind-numbing to Russian ground personnel to see an entire squadron of German 109's roar into view, only to have the aircraft bank to the right and disappear into the distance.

The northernmost element of the 22nd Stafeln found the remains of Dietrich's 109 flying west only five minutes from the Russian air-field. Hauptman Wenta resumed lead of the squadron and, with Pope, dropped to within five hundred feet of the ground to circle the site at minimum throttle while the remainder of the squadron flew top cover.

Wenta could easily read the trail made by Dietrich's downed Messerschmitt. He could see the broken parts covering the path through tall wheat, could see that the starboard wing had dug into the ground when the landing gear collapsed. He could also see that the cockpit canopy was open and that Dietrich was no longer in or near the aircraft. He was either taken prisoner or had lit out on foot. Pope had reported that he had knocked out a small Russian mounted patrol heading toward Dietrich's position. Wenta therefore assumed that Dietrich was not captured, at least not immediately.

Also assuming that Dietrich was able to walk, Wenta believed he would strike out toward the west, toward German lines.

"Gruppe," he said into his radio, "I want a wider search. Spread out."

It was always dangerous for a fighter aircraft to fly slow in a combat zone. Wenta had two of his best elements, four Me109s, fly top cover while he and his comrades flew the deck with throttles reduced in order to loiter as long as possible on station.

The gruppe flew for fifty-five minutes over countryside upon which had been fought a desperate artillery battle only that morning. There were wrecked vehicles and dead Russian soldiers along a dirt road, farm houses that appeared to be all but deserted, but no sign of Dietrich. Wenta did not believe that Dietrich had been captured by any of the Russian units along that stretch of road, but he had no rational reason on which to base that belief. By the time 22 Gruppe had to return to base to refuel, it was too dark to continue.

On the ground, Wenta strode into his operations tent and cranked his field telephone that rang in Geschwader headquarters. He was put through to Major Johanne Snell, Deputy Commander, JagGeschwader3.

"Hauptman Wenta, Herr Major," he said into the telephone.

"Ja, Wenta. Was ist aufwärts?"

"Dietrich was shot down in the Berezina sector. We have seen the site and I want to search for him tomorrow," Wenta said.

"You have mission orders for tomorrow," Snell said.

"Yes, sir, that's why I am asking you to override those orders so that we can execute our search," Wenta responded, a slight edge to his voice.

"I know how you feel about Colonel Dietrich, Wenta, but we are fighting a big war. Fly your mission."

Wenta's knuckles went white as he tightened his grip on the telephone.

"With respect, Herr Major, I request that you allow me to speak to JagGeschwader3 Commander Lötz."

"I am going to save your damn ass and refuse your idiotic request, Wenta! You may be interested to know that we knew Dietrich was shot down within fifteen minutes of his crash and that General Koller specifically ordered that no squadron missions be diverted for his search! Do you understand me, you stupid shit?"

Wenta gulped. "Yes, sir."

"Very well, Wenta," Snell said, in a markedly softer tone of voice, "Now I want to give you a piece of advice. If you don't want to receive a 'no' answer to a request, it is best not to make the request at all. Do you agree, Wenta?"

"Yes, sir," Wenta said.

"Good. Then I will inform you that I never received a request from you at all today. In fact, you never called this headquarters. Do you understand, Hauptman?"

Wenta considered for only two heart beats. "Absolutely, Herr Major."

Dietrich's feet were dragging as he walked. Even in the cool of the night he could not put aside his raging thirst, his brain pounding with each tortured step, sending the message that it needed fluid or it would quit and let him die. He began to see images floating across the road. They were ethereal, ghost-like objects drifting from one side of the road to the other, sometimes hanging suspended, waiting for him to react to their presence. At times he did. He would blink his eyes, then stumble to one side of the road to get a better view of the object, only to have it disappear when he got near. Animals grazed only a few feet away, they, too, chalk white.

Dietrich stopped at the image of still another light. This one was neither on the road nor was it white. At least not the smokey white that rises from very dry fire wood. This light was yellow, and it was dim. He shuffled to the side of the road and peered into the darkness. The light did not move. He began to walk toward it, forgetting about the pain in his feet and legs. As he neared the source of the light he became aware that the feeling of the ground had changed from hard to something softer. Then, in the blackness, he struck something with his body and fell painfully to the ground.

It was a fence.

It was not much of a fence, only the wood rail type that kept stock animals in place. After he had pulled himself to his feet he moved forward, ever closer to the light. As he came within one hundred meters he could see the outline of a house. It was totally dark except for the very dim light inside, no doubt the glow from an oil candle. He noted that there were no vehicles in sight nor were there any animals that one would expect a farm to have. Yet it was a farm. He could now see a small out-building where animals could be sheltered and fed during winter months. A feed trough stood near the out feeding shed.

Dietrich was now near the house, noting that its roof was thatch. He stepped upon its front entrance, a wood porch. Unsure how to proceed, he raised his hand and knocked softly. After several moments the light within went out. Inside was completely silent. He knocked again, and when there was no answer he tried the door knob. The door was locked. He walked along the porch and around the side of the house. There was but a single window there, and it appeared to be made of transparent leather membrane, not glass. He continued around the house to the rear until he came upon a water trough. While he could see water in the bottom of the trough he took the extra few seconds required to work a pump handle and to hear the promising gurgle of water below being sucked into the pipe.

Then water! It was ice cold and Dietrich gulped it down in the largest swallows he could manage. He choked several times but hardly allowed himself to recover from one near-drowning before he pumped still more into his open mouth. He believed he could feel his belly swell with each massive swallow and would have laughed except that he suddenly felt sick. He turned his head away from the fount and bent over. Water, once in his gut, suddenly spewed forward from his mouth, falling onto the ground under his running mouth and nose.

Even while it was flowing out like a neap tide, Dietrich realized that his life was nonetheless temporarily saved. At least he would not die of thirst. He had hardly considered his sudden upturn of good fortune when he looked up at the rear door of the house and saw the face of a woman. The woman, gray and clearly old, pulled quickly away. Curtains fell over the window.

His brain slowly beginning to work once again, Dietrich glanced at the roof and sides of the house. There were no electrical wires connected to it, no telephone lines. He was in enemy territory and had to assume that the woman inside was Russian. Even though he was sure the woman could not call out, Dietrich had to control the situation. He mounted the four steps to the door and, feeling slightly foolish, knocked on it as he had done on the front. There was no answer nor did he expect one. He tried the latch - there was no knob - but could not open it. He put his shoulder, side and hips into the door but on the first try it remained solid. He hit the door again. While it did not spring open Dietrich could feel that it was not designed to resist a determined assault. He summoned all of his strength and smashed as hard as he could. The door sagged. After a moment, breathing hard, Dietrich hit the door once more and this time, even with less force than the last, it swung open.

The woman inside screamed.

In her hand was a knife. It was a very old knife, Dietrich noticed almost subconsciously, with a carved inlaid handle, the kind a young woman would receive as a wedding gift and looking forward to cooking meals for her new husband and later her children. The knife had probably sliced a thousand loaves of bread, countless potatoes, even apples and meat.

Framing her face were heavy lines from abusive years of hard work and fierce weather, he could see lengths of white hair puffing out from under her babushka. Her once brightly colored dress was now worn, faded. She wore heavy shoes with no stockings, almost tripping over them as she retreated from the kitchen.

"Mother," Dietrich said, gently, the palms of his hands opened, "please. I mean you no harm. I wanted only water."

The woman's eyes were wide with fear. She backed away from him, the knife gripped so that the knuckles in her hands shown white, heavy veins of old age swelling with blood pumping wildly from her heart.

The woman babbled words in a surprisingly loud voice in words that were unintelligible to him. He wondered if there was another person in the house. Dietrich drew his pistol from his belt and moved, with little caution, toward the only other inside door. The woman's shrieks increased with intensity creating even more alarm for Dietrich to deal with. He flung open the door, the 9mm ready to fire. But there was no one inside the small, stark sleeping area.

He turned back toward the old lady, holstering his pistol as he did so. She ran toward the front door, a move that did not at once cause Dietrich to react. She opened the door and ran, still shouting and the top of her voice. Dietrich followed her and might have ignored her completely but he saw the narrow, slitted glow of headlights from a vehicle traveling the road. He increased his pace, reached the woman easily, and pulled her back toward the house. She raised her knife with the intention of plunging it into Dietrich, but the pilot caught her arm and removed the knife from her hand.

Now back inside the house he waited still holding the woman. As the vehicle approached it began to slow until it turned toward the house and stopped. It was a light armored six-wheel vehicle serving as a platform for an anti-tank gun. Dietrich thought he could make out four soldiers, no doubt its gun crew, all of whom stepped out of the machine and began walking toward the house. The old woman began to squirm but Dietrich held one hand firmly over her mouth while the other held one arm and a shoulder. As the Russian soldiers neared the front porch Dietrich pulled the woman backward, her unwilling legs pedaling ineffectively off the ground.

Dietrich snatched open the rear door and, hauling the old woman with him, continued to retreat outside. He passed the water trough and headed toward the small animal shelter 80 meters away. He could hear the soldiers now inside the house, could see the lamp relit. He heard Russian voices, commands given, and two of the soldiers open the back door and enter the animal enclosure. In their hands were the crudely made but extremely effective 7.62 PPD-40 sub-machine guns. Dietrich's pistol was no match for their firepower even if he were lucky enough to get off the first shot.

His hand gripping the old woman ever more tightly around her mouth, he retreated deeper into the shadows of the livestock feeder. As the Russian soldiers advanced Dietrich slid slowly onto his knees, making his body as small as possible, praying that the darkness would hide them both. One of the men stepped out from the corner of the feeder, within five feet of Dietrich and the old woman. He only had to turn his head to the left. Dietrich wanted to raise his pistol into firing position but he was afraid. The slightest motion, even to disturb the air, would have given him away.

At that moment there was a voice from within the house. Responding to what apparently was an order, the soldiers turned in the opposite direction from where Dietrich and the old lady crouched, and returned to the house.

For almost thirty minutes Dietrich continued to hold the old lady while the Russian soldiers, by the sound of their movements, took what food had been left in the house before returning to their armored vehicle. Dietrich heard the engine start, then accelerate onto the road. Eventually he could see the rear of the cumbersome vehicle as it rolled awkwardly down the dirt road in an easterly direction. It was only then that he realized that the house was on fire. He released the old woman at once, turning to her that they might combine their effort to douse the flames.

But the old lady fell to the ground. As Dietrich reached for her he could see that her body was limp, lifeless. He bent over and, taking her small shoulders into his hands, shook her.

"Wake up! Wake up, now! They are gone," he said, even while knowing that it was no use. The old woman's eyes were wide open, staring sightlessly back into his. He felt for a pulse, listened for a heartbeat, willing it to be there but it was not.

Heartsick, Dietrich sat down on the parched earth and began to weep. He had become what he loathed not only in Germany or Russia or England, but in the sick barbarism of war itself and finding the illness inside his body made him deeply depressed. The woman was about the age of his grandmother. She probably had several children, perhaps some of them also dead. Without doubt she had labored all of her life to make something of a home for her husband and her children, and he, Dietrich, had snatched away her final hours of dignity so that he could survive to continue the killing.

He gently folded the old woman's hands across her breast. He was not a religious man but he wished that he might have known enough of the Holy Scriptures to pray over her poor form. He found a crude shovel among the few farm tools near the feeder shed and began to dig a grave. The chore was specially arduous for him because of his lack of food during the past 48 hours, so he satisfied himself with a rather shallow grave. A coffin for the old woman was not possible but he wrapped her in a bed cover and managed to fashion a crude cross. He pounded the wooden stake into the ground with his shovel, hoping that whatever army swept through this area would exhume her body and give it a proper burial.

He could not bring himself to make the sign of the cross before leaving. He drank heavily of the well water then filled his canteen. His direction was again west, and his compass heading took him a full 15 to the right of the unpaved road. This turned out to be fortunate because by walking through part of the farm that now lay in smouldering ruins he came upon a ploughed and well-picked field so that in the earliest hours of dawn he caught a glimpse of a tuber. Investigation revealed a half-buried potato. Delighted and and famished, he quickly rubbed as much dirt from it as he could with his bare hands before biting hungrily into the vegetable. His sense of taste was almost overwhelmed! While his brain told him that it was only a potato and his teeth were grinding on a generous amount of black Russian soil, he could not imagine a three course meal tasting any better.

He spent a good while on his hands and knees rooting for another potato and, voila! Success. He pocketed three of the undersized and almost withered spuds before moving on, but he felt that his chances of walking out of Russian territory had just dramatically increased.

He walked with renewed energy. He could feel an improvement in his physical condition with each step until, sometime before noon, fatigue brought him down. Before succumbing to sleep he spread his not-so-white parachute silk on the ground and looked skyward. There were no airplanes above that he could see, no sounds of engines. He reasoned that Russian aircraft might see the parachute as well as elements of the Luftwaffe, but if the Russians saw it first he hoped that an Me-109 would be right on the Ruskie's tail.

He was in a coma-like condition when Oberleutnant Rudi Holsembeck spotted the white parachute on the ground. Three hours later a Fieseler reconnaissance aircraft made a short-field landing nearby while the 22nd Fighter Gruppe flew tight air cover on top. With feeble assistance from Dietrich, the pilot of the Fieseler was able to deposit the Lieutenant Colonel into the rear seat. With its 46 foot wingspan and 240 hp engine, the very light spotter aircraft was able to lift off the ground in under five hundred feet. With thirty-three Me-109s guarding the Fieseler, Dietrich was on his way to hospital at the breathtaking speed of 98 knots.

When Dietrich was informed that upon direction of the Reichs Luftfahrt Ministerium (RLM) he was being transferred from the Luftflotte Ost Field Hospital to the Wolfschanze in East Prussia, he was not surprised. After only three days in hospital he was almost fully recovered and felt guilty for taking up a bed with clean sheets. Though weak, he felt ready to leave.

He had been drinking copious amounts of fluids, though none with alcohol, and attempted to regain his lost weight by eating well. But therein was the rub, the thing that kept him off the "fit to fly" list. His gastro-intestinal track still harbored obnoxious bugs that tossed a good deal of his food back up as soon as he ate it, despite that he and the doctors were quite optimistic about winning the battle for the colon.

Exasperated at not being allowed to fly himself to Rastenburg Dietrich settled into the right seat of an aircraft assigned to OKW for special flights and courier work. With nothing to occupy his mind for the one hour flight northwest, Dietrich was contemplating the weather. It was now the second week of October and it was quite cold. Snows had begun in many parts of the front. Soon winter would fully arrive and they were nowhere near defeating the Russian bear.

Dietrich could see isolated patches of snow as they flew northward as he looked down out of the airplane's window. Then he raised his eyes. There, on their left wing was a smartly stepped formation of twelve Me-109s. On the right side was a mirror image of his fighter escort on the left. The pilots nodded their heads and saluted their grounded leader. Dietrich returned their salutes and, turning deliberately away from the plexiglass, wiped the moisture that had formed in his eyes.

The 22nd Gruppe turned back toward the east as Dietrich's plane touched down at the Wolfschanze airfield. When Dietrich alit an SS junior officer stepped forward and saluted.

"Welcome, Colonel Dietrich. The Führer sends you his warmest greetings."

Dietrich returned the Nazi salute. The SS-Untersturmfuhrer was impeccably turned out in his field grey colors, the new uniform of most SS units. He was hardly twenty years old, Dietrich guessed, and there were no visible scars, twisted fingers, sagging skin that would betray nerve damage from combat. He might even come from a "good" German family, not necessarily in Berlin, or a recent graduate of one of the state's high quality universities. It was only a deeply focused look into the young man's dark brown eyes that gave him away. While the eyes squinted at their corners there was no light within. Muscles that regulated the movement of the lips tugged in a failed attempt to reflect merriment but the effort was lost on the young man's lack of understanding humor. The Untersturmfuhrer was the archetypical Nazi.

"That is very good of him. How is the Führer?"

"He is always excellent, Colonel," the officer said as they stepped into a waiting car. "He is looking forward to seeing you at your earliest convenience. The Führer has instructed me to see that you are made completely comfortable at your guest quarters where there are two doctors and nurses waiting your arrival. The Führer is quite aware that you are still technically hospitalized."

"He is too kind," Dietrich said.

"If I may be so bold, sir, he is the kindest man I have ever known. Not that I actually know him," the SS officer quickly corrected, "but we are all honored to stand in the shadow of such a great man."

"Yes, I suppose he is great."

"We all talk about him, of course. The world will soon come to know how many of the virulent communist hoards he is annihilating. We are killing hundreds of thousands, even millions, you know," the SS-Untersturmfuhrer said, proudly.

Dietrich was struck with the man's blood-thirsty ferocity cloaked in a soft, matter-of-fact tone. It made his head swim.

"So many?" Dietrich found himself responding, somewhat stupidly.

"Yes! Of course. Well, you should know much better than I, sir. I have not yet had my chance to meet the Ivans. I can only hope they are not all killed or put into pens before I get my chance," he said.

Dietrich regarded the young man for a very long time. His desire was to simply shoot the man with his pistol and rid the earth of a pubescent vermin but he had a better idea.

"What is your name, Untersturmfuhrer?" Dietrich asked.

"Ruh, Herr Lieutenant Colonel," he said, gathering himself to attention. "Raymond Ruh."

"Well, Raymond Ruh, I might be able to use my influence with the Führer and have you transferred to Army Group B. That is my sector. Would you like that?"

It was as though the youth saw his first Christmas tree with presents laid out beneath it. "Me? You would do that for me, Colonel? I could not be more grateful, sir."

Dietrich reached out and patted SS-Untersturmfuhrer Ruh paternally on the shoulder. "I will offer to take personal responsibility for you."

"I hardly know what to say, sir. Thank you!"

"Sometimes it helps to have someone above with a little help, eh?" Dietrich said.

There, again, was the humorless smile. Dietrich shuddered.

"Are you chilled, sir? I'll roll up this window."

They passed through the outer perimeters of the Wolfschanze and wended their way through the several *Sperrkreis*, each time they were stopped and their documents thoroughly checked by RSD personnel. Dietrich was delivered to the guest quarters inside *Sperrkreis* I, nearest the Führer's bunker. His assigned apartment within the guest facilities was comfortable but Spartan in keeping with a wartime environment. While the young SS-Untersturmfuhrer moved about the rooms checking to insure the amenities were in place, Dietrich was reminded of a bell hop in a four star hotel. Dietrich sat on the edge of the bed merely to catch his breath. He realized, however, that he was quite tired from the short trip. He thought he might lie down and close his eyes for only a few moments when he became aware that other persons had entered his rooms.

"I am Doctor Morell," a bespectacled man was saying. "Please, stay as you are, Colonel. With your permission I would like to take a little closer look at you while you are resting."

Dietrich resisted the urge to sit up and allowed the doctor to feel his pulse, listen to his heart and thump his chest.

"Dr. Morell is the Führer's personal physician," the SS-Untersturmfuhrer said, as though this fact was of enormous importance. Well, Dietrich considered, in Germany it probably was.

"Thank you, doctor," Dietrich said. Then, to the junior SS officer, "Thank the Führer for me and tell him that I am entirely at his service."

The young man clicked his heels smartly and said, "Jawohl, Colonel." He then took one step back, raised his arm in the Nazi salute before marching from the room.

"Your medical records are here, Colonel Dietrich," Morell said, assuringly. "You have some nasty little bugs in your system but they will soon be gone, I assure you. With your permission, I would like to draw a small blood sample. We can do some counting, then, and we will have a much better idea when you will be fit."

Dietrich said that he did not mind a prick in the arm. A female nurse, who had been waiting behind Dr. Morell, stepped forward to do the blood work.

"And is the Führer in good health?"

"Of course he is, Colonel. The Führer is in perfect health. He has the body and constitution of a man twenty-five years younger. Why do you ask?"

Dietrich had asked out of politeness, but with the doctor's rather barbed reaction to an innocent question suggested to Dietrich that there might be something for Morell to be defensive about.

"I have something that will make you feel better," Dr. Morell said to Dietrich. "Some vitamins and blood builders." Morell rolled up Dietrich's sleeve on his right arm and stabbed a needle painlessly into his upper arm. "Now, I think you should rest for a while."

Dr. Morell reported to the Führer that Colonel Dietrich was resting comfortably. Archie ordered that Col. Dietrich be allowed to sleep as long as he liked and that when he was fully rested he was to be brought to the Führer's private quarters in the Hitler bunker.

Dietrich awoke hours later incredibly refreshed. The nap did him good and, unless he was mistaken, so had Dr. Morell's vitamin concoction. He was literally free of pain and quite alert, much more so than he had felt in weeks. He picked up the telephone in the room and informed the operator that he was now at the Führer's disposal.

Dietrich was escorted by a Wehrmacht officer from his guest quarters to the Hitler bunker, as it was named. The reinforced concrete building teemed with activity, officers in a variety of uniforms bustled this way and that. They compared battlefield locations on the huge maps that covered the walls with paper reports in their hands, and changed pins with flags attached to indicate where specific units were located. Female workers were well represented, most of whom carried with them stenographic books and pencils. There were, he came to be informed, a small army of women simply called "writers" whose duty it was to record the historic events unfolding each day within the concrete walls of the Wolfschanze. The clatter of teletype machines, typewriters, code processors and hushed conversations paused dramatically as the Führer himself strode forward, arms outstretched, to greet Dietrich.

"Stephen! How good to see you," Archie said, his lips twisting into an off-smile.

Dietrich came to attention, clicked his heels and gave the Nazi salute. "My Führer," he said, self-consciously. "I am honored to be here, sir."

The fact that he was saluting a British actor was keenly set in Dietrich's mind as he regarded the defacto leader of Germany. Archie did not look entirely well. The left side of his face seemed set in stone and his left arm moved unsymmetrically with the right side of his body. Yet, while his eyes were dark they still shone, causing Dietrich to smile even more broadly. Archie and the real Adolf Hitler shared riveting eyes and stentorian voices.

"Come," Archie said, placing his arm inside Dietrich's. "We'll have tea in my quarters. And something to eat."

Dietrich was aware that others in the bunker looked upon their Führer approvingly as the great man bestowed his friendship upon the person of a lowly fighter pilot.

After hungrily finishing a bowl of delicious potato soup and warm bread with real butter, Dietrich leaned back in his chair and regarded Archie. Archie had left orders that he was not to be disturbed for any reason. The door was closed with the SS guards posted outside, unable to hear through the sound-proofed walls. Dietrich was surprised at how often he thought of Archie, and he was coming to increasingly admire the man in many different ways.

"So, Archie," he said, "tell me how you feel. And you can tell me some war news. I don't really know what is the big picture, you know."

"I am quite well," Archie said, leaning back in a rocking chair then, knitting his brow, leaning forward. "No. That isn't exactly so. I... I'm not sure how to say this but, I have been diagnosed...." Archie hesitated.

Obviously this was something that he immensely disliked speaking about. Dietrich waited.

"Well," he said, biting his lip. He placed his right hand on a nearby end table. "You can see for yourself."

Dietrich could see that the hand was shaking. Nerves, he thought, and said so to the actor.

"I'm afraid not. I have Parkinson's disease. It is progressive, of course, and there is no cure, no treatment. It will kill me in due course," Archie said.

Dietrich's heart sank. He knew about Parkinson's but only that it was an enormously debilitating affliction and always lethal. He hardly knew what to say or that would not sound trite and transparent. So he said nothing.

"So much for that. I will deal with it as it progresses. On a much cheerier note, the war is going very well. We are advancing on every front. And it is the largest front in the history of warfare! Isn't that incredible, Stephen? Oh, we have setbacks, to be sure, but the Russians are much more unbending than any of us thought. Including me, I don't mind admitting. Human life means nothing to them. Nothing at all. They throw their bodies in front of our panzers simply because they have nothing else to stop them with. Idiots." Archie chuckled almost to himself. "Now if Stalin would kindly oblige us with the same personal sacrifice the world would breathe a sigh of relief. Eh?"

Dietrich watched Archie very closely. He could see that the Parkinson's disease had affected his face as well as the tremor in his arm. And he thought there was just the hint of foot-drag when Archie entered the room. But how much of the disease accounted for his apparent lapse into fulfilling the Führer's role for Germany's war-making public?

"And have you been getting reports from the SS, as well?"

"What's that?" Archie asked, absently.

"I am talking about the political action groups of the SS. The ones who are murdering civilians," Dietrich asked, evenly.

Archie looked at Dietrich blankly. "What are you talking about? Murdering?"

"Yes. The Special Action squads. Einsatzgruppen, they are called," Dietrich said. "They move behind the Wehrmacht and their business is to liquidate political leaders and Jews who do not die in battle."

Archie looked entirely blank. "That is not true. Not at all. Dietrich, have you seen such things with your own eyes?"

Dietrich hesitated now. Then, "No. I have not. But one hears things."

Archie exhaled with audible force. "Ah, well, there you have it. I hate to say this, my friend, but you are a victim of foreign propaganda..."

You mean British propaganda? From the BBC?"

"Yes! Well, why not? Isn't it their business to put Germany, and me, in the worst possible light? Look here, Stephen, I admit that the Jews are not having a picnic in this war. Not at all. You will remember that it was I who brought this to your attention months ago. Isn't that so? And what were the orders from London? Ignore the problem. Yes? Well, I have ignored it. But there are no mass murders. The SS wouldn't dare, nor would any other military group in Germany, without express permission of the Führer!"

"Archie, do you ever get out of this bunker? Have you been to the front? I mean to the real front where the blood flows? How can you be sure that what I am telling you isn't a fact?"

"Be kind enough not to tell me how to run the bloody war!" Archie shot back, aware that he had used a British colloquialism. "This was your idea! You and London. The Fat Toad probably ordered it himself. Churchill. Is he accepting his measure of blood in all of this?"

Archie sat back once again into his chair and began to rock.

Dietrich considered Archie's mental state. The Führer. He, Archie, felt totally responsible for the life and death of every German in uniform. Just as Dietrich was his airmen. There was no question in Dietrich's mind that Archie was entirely sincere. He even wondered if perhaps there wasn't a great exaggeration factor contained in the accounts that he, Dietrich, had heard of such atrocities. After all, he had received it not even second hand but third hand.

"Would you stop it if you could, Archie? If it were true, that is."

"What kind of a question is that? Am I a monster? Of course I would put an end to such conduct. And if it will make you feel better I'll bring it up to Martin tomorrow. Or the next day. In fact I don't want to talk with him right now. I'm tired. I want to simply visit with you and step away from my heavy tasks for a few hours. Is that selfish of me? Probably. Tell me, Stephen, how are you coming along? Is Dr. Morell treating you all right? He's very good, you know."

"As a matter of fact I felt much better after he treated me. Some kind of vitamin shot and maybe something else mixed in." Dietrich might have added that he was beginning to slump, the muscles and joints were hurting again, though not as acutely as when he had arrived.

"Yes, yes, that's it. He gives me the same injection twice a day. Once in the morning and once at night. Marvelous stuff, whatever it is. I eat like a rabbit, you know. I'm a complete vegetarian, now. I'm even getting used to it, don't think about meat very often. But I miss... " Archie's voice dropped almost to a whisper and he smiled broadly "kidney pie. I couldn't ask for that here, you know," he sighed.

Archie then listened while Dietrich told of his crash behind the lines. He briefly described the ordeal of walking west to German lines and when he had finished Archie had him tell it all again, this time in more detail. Dietrich obliged, and found that in the retelling he included the fact that he had killed an old woman to save his own life, an act that he had omitted the first time around. When he had said it all again he found that his eyes were cast down. He realized that he was staring at the floor, unwilling to meet Archie's gaze. As he rubbed away the tears he wondered if it would be this way for his entire life, that he would cry at the recollection.

Then it occurred to him that he might not have a life, might not become an old man, might not marry, might not have children. He became depressed anew but this time he was determined not to weep.

"Terrible. Just terrible that we almost lost you. I intend to issue an order immediately adding you to my staff. You'll stay right here in Rastenburg where you'll be safe," Archie said.

For a very long moment Dietrich considered the idea. For a change it seemed very sound. He had certainly done his share of killing for the Third Reich. He could justify sitting out the remainder of the war, especially if the Führer ordered it. A very large number of men had been moved to safety by virtue that a senior officer had seen fit to do them a favor of this kind. Why should he not accept? God knows London would arrange such a stroke if they believed it possible.

"Are your mother and father well, Stephen?" Archie asked.

Dietrich shrugged.

"What if I wrote to them? Wouldn't that be something for them? To get a letter from Adolf Hitler?"

Archie could only stare.

"Archie..." Dietrich began.

"Yes?"

"I have orders for you from London."

"Orders? What kind of orders?"

"SOE wants you to divert Army Group B."

"Divert? The entire Center?" Archie asked in disbelief.

"Yes. With a southern wheel, you could justify your decision to ignore Moscow in order to capture the oil fields in the Caucuses. You would then be free to turn back toward Moscow with von Bock's sixty divisions as well as Leeb's Group B."

"You mean with Leeb's survivors," Archie said, sarcastically.

Dietrich shrugged. "War has casualties."

"We are forty kilometers from Moscow!" Archie shrieked. "Who do they think they are, those idiots in London?"

Dietrich said nothing.

"Well, I won't do it."

Dietrich was determined to remain silent as Archie fell to the floor of the bunker. Then, "Stephen..."

"Yes?"

"I want you to get me a British uniform," Archie said.

"A what?"

"Any kind will do. I want to have one as a souvenir. That is possible for you, isn't it?"

"Well, I suppose it is, but..."

"Thank you, Colonel. You may go back to your unit, now."

BOOK V

CHAPTER

26

Newly promoted Sturmbannfuhrer Hartung had been given the reformed XXXIV Panzergruppen. He was more than pleased with his command after fighting with them for fifty-eight days. Upon his release from hospital and winning the Knight's Cross with Oak Leaves, he was asked by SS-Obergruppenfuhrer Paul Hausser, then Division Commander SS 2, for whatever request he wanted. He informed General Hausser, who, with several members of his staff was standing by Hartung's hospital bed, that he had only one, very modest, request. He asked that he be sent to the Mediterranean island of Capri for extended coast watching duty.

General Hausser's staff was shocked into collective silence until the room suddenly filled with the general's roaring laughter.

What Hartung did not receive was an assignment to Capri, but instead was given twenty-one brand new F model StuG III battle tanks fresh off the assembly lines from Germany and all packing the 75mm StuK assault gun.

And for Hartung, specifically upon the orders of Reichsfuhrer SS Himmler, one of the very first PzKpfw VI Ausf. A, Tiger tanks. It was so new it was, in fact, one of the prototypes. Its 57 tons dwarfed the Russian 26-ton T-34 which, German Tiger crews came to call the "Micky Mouse." There were no tanks in the field that were the equal of the new Tigers and as Hartung inspected it for the first time he was forced to admit that if one could not avoid fighting a war, this was the chariot to ride. It had a crew of five, a gunner, a loader, a driver, a hull gunner and a commander. It carried 50mm of hardened steel armor on the superstructure and the hull, with 30mm on each side and rear. And even more important to Hartung and his comrades, the Tiger mounted an 88mm cannon for its main armament. His group would no longer shake in mortal fear of the Russians.

He trudged through two feet of snow toward a temporary shelter dug into the side of a hill. His panzers had been parked for two days awaiting fuel and ammunition resupply. His men could use the rest, Hartung admitted to himself, but the idea that his unit was outrunning their supply lines did not set his mind at ease. In point of fact the snow bothered him more than the lack of fuel. He and his men were still fighting in summer uniforms and the promised fleece-lined boots and other thermal gear was long overdue.

"Stand to attention when I enter the tent, you swine," Hartung said to Johanne Boord, also newly promoted from SS-Untersturmfuhrer to the rank of SS-Obersturmfuhrer.

"You will have to make up your mind, Herr Bunny, which way you will have it. If I am on leave, then I am not going to move my ass out of this chair. If I am not on leave, then I a have deserted my post. In either case I don't stand up," Boord said.

"If you have deserted then I will have the distinct pleasure of executing you myself. You are an insubordinate dog in any case. Do you have any vodka left in that bottle?"

"No," Boord said. "And while we are on the subject of vital supplies, we are out of graphite."

"Use the regular bore cleaner," Hartung said, referring to the solvent used to clean all weapons on the panzers.

"Too cold. We put blowtorches to all the 75 mm barrels this morning. I'm not going to tell my gunners to do it again," Boord said, taking a generous swig from the vodka bottle.

Hartung snatched the bottle from his hand and took a deep drink himself.

"Karl," he barked to his radioman nearby. When the corporal looked up Hartung tossed the bottle to him. The communication man caught the bottle and drank thirstily. He recapped the bottle and returned it to Obersturmbannfuhrer Boord.

"Also," Boord drank, then belched, "we are building fires under the oil pans to keep the engines running."

"It may surprise you to know that I built two of those fires myself this morning. Kerosene gives a nice easy heat. I'm hungry," Hartung said.

Corporal Karl Schlicker rose from his makeshift stool and radio table to retrieve a Red Cross parcel and handed it to Hartung.

"We are raiding the prisoners parcels again?" he asked as he dug into the contents of the box. There was a can of corned beef still unopened and bread that might have once been toast, or toast that might once have been bread. He ate most of each but looked in vain for the cigarettes that one expected to find.

"Where are the cigarettes, Boord?"

"They are in my pocket, Sturmbannfuhrer Bunny."

"Give them to me. You don't smoke," Hartung said.

"I have taken up the habit," Boord said.

Hartung opened the flap of his holster and pulled his Walther P-38 and pointed it at his deputy commander. "Give me the cigarettes or I will kill you."

Corporal Schlicker touched his earphones, then scribbled something onto a pad. Turning toward Hartung he said "Third Army Corps, Sturmbannfuhrer. They want a position report."

"I am busy," Hartung said, his gun leveled at Boord's chest.

"Shall I send that, sir?" Schlicker responded.

"Yes. And tell them that our position is the same fucking position we were in yesterday and the day before that. If we change our position I will tell them," Hartung said.

Schlicker turned back to his radio and began to transmit.

Boord shook his head, digging the package of cigarettes out of his tunic and tossed them to Hartung. "Touchy, touchy."

"American!" Hartung said. "No wonder you were ready to die. Here, have one."

"Never mind. I don't want one now," Boord said, turning sideways and, head resting against a case of rifle grenades, closed his eyes.

When a message was received from Third Army headquarters, minutes later, Schlicker removed his earphones and spoke to Hartung.

"We are moving up, Sturmbannfuhrer. Here are the coordinates." Schlicker handed Hartung a piece of paper with map references written clearly upon it.

"Fuck," Hartung said.

Within the hour Hartung's tanks were rolling toward the Kalinin area. Of his original gruppe of 21 tanks, after hard fighting he had only 14 serviceable machines and crews. In the winter all traffic moves in long, never-ending columns on a well worn path, unlike summer campaigns when the panzers could spread out over hard-baked fields and make their own roads. He was in such a column, moving upstream against retreating horse drawn carts, trucks carrying wounded to the rear, huge 6 ton trucks mired in mud and blocking the road, wounded personnel with rags on their feet instead of proper boots, when he was caught in an artillery barrage that had that section of the road zeroed in. For twenty minutes heavy shells rained down upon them, blowing tanks, soldiers, civilians, women and children, Red Cross nurses, leaderless hordes of fleeing stragglers high into the air, to rain back down in small pieces. Then more heavy rounds would fall in their midst blowing them all skyward again, the earth erupting beneath them. The macabre scene was like a giant tossed salad being made out of human parts by unseen gods.

Tank repair shops were nowhere to be found. Headquarters had their own vehicles that needed repair and that every panzer company along the entire front needed repair.

As Hartung led his panzers out of the artillery trap he saw tanks dormant from lack of fuel, soldiers slogging along the road, heads down, insignia on their collars showing they were from signal companies, bakery companies, heavy anti-aircraft units, motorcycle companies and communications. But there were no howitzers with them, no radio trucks and no bread to eat.

On the road they spied a huge building in high flames. One sergeant leaving the scene explained that they were retreating and they had to burn forty tons of flour so the Russians would not get it. Hartung and his men had eaten nothing for two days and before that were on half-rations.

His orders were to hook up with units of LIX Army Corps that were forming into two combat groups. Major General Jaschke was in command of the northern group, an officer that Hartung new and respected as a gutty fighter and a fast-thinking tactician. Hartung was advancing his panzers in a single column regretting that he could not run on either side of a road, a technique he favored to avoid mines and zeroed enemy artillery. The road led toward the town of Novo Sokolniki and Hartung, riding high on the turret, could see it clearly in the distance. Division Intelligence had advised that the town had been secured that morning and that the Russians had reformed into a counter-strike force twelve kilometers beyond. General Jaschke was waiting.

Hartung looked over the town carefully with his field glasses. He could see most of it quite clearly. There was no place for the Russians to hide a tank. Or an anti-tank gun. Indeed, as his unit drew closer Hartung could clearly see several light vehicles parked on the south side of the town. They had German markings.

"Boord," he said into his tank-to-tank radio, "what unit, do you think?"

"No idea," crackled the reply.

Hartung had expected to see elements of Jaschke's Corps in defensive positions, but these vehicles were not recognizable to Hartung. There were two vans, an open truck and a staff car.

Hartung swung his binoculars around a 200 arc looking for any sign of enemy armor or aircraft. There were plumes of black smoke on the horizon and the sound of heavy guns could be heard, a kind of unceasing roil of thunder or the crashing of waves on a rocky beach. There was very little wind. But that would come the next morning, roaring down the steppe, seeking crannies, tearing at clothing, snatching the breath from the nostrils of troops on the ground. Hartung felt lucky that this time his command was armor only. Being responsible for foot soldiers slogging through mud one day and ice the next was more than he cared to think about.

He could hear a flight of JU-87 dive bombers working to the northeast, zeroing in on Russian tanks or, at least, strongholds in towns, one of them almost certainly being Rzhev where Hartung's unit would be tomorrow at dawn.

He swung his glasses back to the right, across the vast panorama of flat land. More smoke, more crumps of distant explosives, and the sun low in the southern hemisphere.

When the column arrived in the village Hartung was mystified by what he saw. The German troops in the town appeared to have taken a number of prisoners. The prisoners, guarded by an SS contingent, were engaged in digging a trench behind the community church. There was an officer, an SS-Untersturmfuhrer, commanding Stabsfeldwebel and 20 men, all armed with the latest assault weapons. On their caps, Hartung noted, were the Death's Head insignia, members of the Verfuegungstruppe. These were volunteers for "Special Disposition" assignments. They were fully trained military troops but used against such things as domestic disorders, concentration camp maintenance and sometimes against German enemies of the state, whoever those "enemies" were according to Reichsfuhrer-SS Himmler.

Hartung halted his tanks within meters of the "prisoners" and the townspeople who looked on. Nearby, Hartung could see yet another trench dug into the near frozen earth, this one filled with bodies. The bodies, tossed into the ditch like piles of wood from a cleared field, appeared to be not military but civilians. Hartung, his bile beginning to rise in his throat, stepped down from his panzer and walked into the center of the German troops guarding prisoners.

"Who is in command here?" he said to a Feldwebel.

"He is over there," the sergeant said, nodding his head in one direction.

"Stand to attention when an officer speaks to you!" Hartung snapped.

The sergeant immediately did as he was ordered. "*Jawohl*, Sturmbannfuhrer. Untersturmfuhrer Skufca, sir, is this way." The sergeant began to lead the way but Hartung stopped him.

"Never mind. I see him."

Skufca saw Hartung coming and snapped his heels together, but gave the Sturmbannfuhrer a very fashionably relaxed Hitler salute, the kind that a fatigued infantry officer might offer another. It was disrespectful under these circumstances. Untersturmfuhrer Skufca wore a neatly pressed uniform and a peaked hat with silver cord that had never been soiled in battle.

"What are you doing here, Lieutenant?" Hartung demanded.

"I beg your pardon? I think I should ask you what you are doing here!" Skufca said, raising himself to his toes before rocking back on his heels.

"Look, I don't want any of your shit, Skufca. You are murdering civilians. Pack up your filthy pigs and get them out of here. Now!" Hartung said.

For a moment Skufca was appalled. "Are you insane? We are carrying out the business of the Reich. Under orders of Reichsfuhrer Himmler himself! It is you who will pack up and move on. At once!"

"You son of a bitch. Why don't you get yourself into a line abteilung and fight like a man? You are brave when you can murder old men and women. Well, try it out on the Ruskies and see how courageous you are then."

"That's enough! I will not have my courage questioned. Nor any of my men. Stand back, I tell you. I am authorized to arrest anyone who interferes with our work, and that includes any military unit. Including yours, Sturmbannfuhrer."

Skufca nodded to his men, all of whom turned their automatic assault weapons away from the Russian civilians and pointed them at Hartung. Safeties clicked off.

Hartung half-turned toward Johanne Boord who stood in the turret of his tank.

"Obersturmbannfuhrer Boord," he said.

"Yes, sir," Boord answered evenly.

"Have your machine gunners target these men. The Untersturmfuhrer first. If they are not back in their vehicles when I count to ten, open fire. Is that clear?"

Boord mumbled into his command radio set. MG-42s mounted on the panzers swivelled toward the Verfuegungstruppe officer. Bolts clacked, rounds were ratcheted into breeches.

"Ready, Major," Boord responded.

The lieutenant's eyes widened. He snatched his own pistol from his holster and pointed it at Hartung. "I can have you killed!" he shouted.

"One," Hartung called, turning fully to face Skufca, offering him a better target. "Two."

"This is mutiny!," Scufka shouted. "You will all be shot! Make no mistake. Put your arms down and... and..." The Untersturmfuhrer licked his lips and looked first to his men, then at the civilians who were beginning to watch the proceedings from a fearful distance.

"Three.... four.... " Hartung continued, calmly.

The Deaths Head commander began to step backward, jerking his pistol hand toward their vehicles, indicating to his men that they should retire.

"Six.... " Hartung continued.

"You will hear about this, Sturmbannfuhrer... "he screeched, but this time from the sanctuary of his staff car.

"Seven.... Hartung. Sturmbannfuhrer Hartung. Tell that to whatever sniveling coward you report to."

After the murderers were nothing more than a cloud of dust on the horizon, Boord spoke to his leader. "He is not kidding, Bunny. We should have killed the bastards and thrown them into the ditch. They wouldn't find the bodies until next spring."

Hartung cast his eyes upon the Russian populace. He was deeply ashamed. If he had to speak to them now he could not. There were no words to express himself. So he turned toward his tank and stepped onto the tracks and up to the turret.

Boord smiled broadly. "Can I have your dress boots when the Gestapo comes to execute you? They will, you know."

For the next days the fighting for Rzhev was fierce, the Russians having split the German defenders in two. The combat became virtually hand-to-hand, with tanks shooting at each other point blank. Two regiments, one to which Hartung's panzers were attached, were driven into three small pockets. On the beginning of the fourth day Hartung's unit fought a retreating action toward the town of Burtseva, finally arriving in the second day of December One of the German infantry divisions was down to 26 officers, 118 non-commissioned officers, and 532 men.

Yet in the midst of the brutal fighting a contingent of SS officers from the Totenkopfverbaende Division (Death's Head), led by an SS-Oberfuhrer Reinhold Kress, arrived at Major General Jaschke's headquarters. Oberfuhrer Kress was there to arrest SS-Sturmbannfuhrer Bernard Hartung and SS-Obersturmfuhrer Boord.

"Are you mad? We are fighting for our lives!" Jaschke said to Kress. "I cannot possibly weaken our forces at this time."

"It is only two men," Kress said, as though the problem was a very simple one.

Thinking quickly, General Jaschke said, "Boord was killed yesterday."

"Yes? Well, then we will take only one. You will note that we are acting on the authority of Oberstgruppenfuhrer-SS Beckman. You must order Sturmbannfuhrer Hartung here at once."

General Jaschke took a deep breath. "Wait here."

Jaschke had his driver get no closer to the firefight in which Hartung was engaged than necessary. The general then used the field telephone to raise the Waffen SS tanks and order Hartung to his vehicle. Hartung dropped out of his Tiger, stepped over bodies, danced around shell holes and collapsed buildings to reach Jaschke's position.

After explaining to Hartung the situation, Jaschke had another suggestion. "I told them Boord was killed yesterday. So tell him to put on a sergeant's uniform and lie low for a couple of days. No point in giving them more than we have to. They will shoot you, of course. There is nothing I can do. They are filth, and the filth goes all the way to the top of the manure heap."

"Yes, sir, I understand. I knew what I was doing at the time," Hartung said.

"You're a hell of a soldier, Bunny," Jaschke said.

"I would have been a better pimp, sir. I could be working the streets of Paris even now. It would have given meaning to the war." Hartung tried to smile but it was hard. For both men.

"Well," Hartung said. "We might as well go, sir. Give me a moment to talk to Boord."

"Of course."

Hartung ran to Boord's panzer, scrambling up to the turret from the rear.

"The outfit is yours. The general says they wanted you, too, but he told them that you were dead. I confirmed to the general that you've been dead for thirteen months. Anyway...." Hartung put out his hand.

Boord shook it solemnly. "Don't go. We have the power right here," Boord said, patting the turret of his tank. "We'll blow the scum to hell. We should have done it back at Novo Sokolniki. Every man would be with you."

Hartung placed his hand on Boord's arm and squeezed. "You're a good officer, Johanne."

With nothing left to say, Hartung dropped off the Tiger and made his way back to General Jaschke's waiting staff car.

Because black, overcast skies and heavy snows grounded all aircraft, not because of a lack of fuel for a change, Dietrich left off reading "Crime and Punishment" in order to get a drink and perhaps something to eat at the officer's mess. He trudged through three feet of snow and ice from his igloo-like tent to a much larger igloo-like tent that served as an auxiliary mess for officers. There was another officer's club four kilometers away in the shell of a town of Bodrinski which had the advantage of standing walls and a partial roof to reduce the effects of strong, arctic wind that blew across the vast landscape. But most of Dietrich's ground crews remained near their planes with no chance to escape the cold but to crouch in holes that they dug in the frozen ground.

Dietrich was furious with the man-killing weather, with the fact that they were in Russia in the wintertime without adequate clothing and supplies, and that they were at a literal standstill in a war that was grinding up human flesh but going nowhere. Yet he had to laugh at the irony that this is what he, and London, and Archie had in mind when they caused it all in the first place! If there was a god, he would be shaking his head, long ago having turned his back on us earthly fools. There were two other officers in the mess when he stepped through the double-flap door. They were huddled in a single location, on either side of a small wooden table, wrapped in layers of every uniform they could put on, including their fleece-lined flight suits and boots.

"Ah, Dietrich. Come in and drink vodka with us. If you don't care for vodka, there is also vodka. Your choice," one of them said. He was a Ju-87 dive-bomber pilot by the name of Neitzel. A dentist in civilian life, Neitzel was regarded to be quite insane, dedicated to sex in all of its forms, and took particular delight on dropping bombs on anything so long as they exploded.

"We were talking about the mutiny. Tell us what you think," Neitzel said, his strange, slightly mad smile tugging at the corners of his mouth.

With him was a reconnaissance pilot by the name of Müller, a one-time famous distance runner who failed to compete in the 1936 Olympics because he had intestinal flu. Müller, quite tall, had not gained an ounce of weight since he was fifteen years old.

Dietrich ordered a drink and was served vodka. "Thank you. Anything to eat?" he asked the orderly.

"Yes, Colonel. We are offering bean soup today, sir."

"Ah. One of my favorites. Good, is it?"

The orderly said nothing nor did he change a rather pained face.

"In that case, make it a large helping, please," Dietrich said. He raised his glass to his fellow airmen. "To friends," he said.

"I'm going to drink, anyway," Müller said, joining them.

"What mutiny?" Dietrich asked.

"A Waffen-SS officer, we heard. Threatened to shoot an Untersturmfuhrer," Neitzel said.

"And all of his men," Müller added.

"And why?" Dietrich asked as his bean soup was served. The "broth" was almost devoid of spices and flavoring and was barely warm. But heating anything was a challenge at every level of command including the officer's mess. Dietrich did not complain.

"That is just it. For nothing," Neitzel said.

"The untersturmfuhrer was shooting civilians," Müller observed.

"But they were Russians. Jesus, imagine stepping in front of a Totenkopfverbaende unit while it was doing its duty," Neitzel said, shaking his head.

"Duty," Dietrich scoffed. "They're thugs," he said into his soup spoon.

"Like your gangsters from America?" Neitzel teased Dietrich. "Tell me, Yank, would you step up to Mr. Scarface to save some Slavs? Or Jews? Idiotic, eh? He will be executed tomorrow. Or perhaps tonight, I don't remember."

"Tomorrow," Müller said, knocking back yet another vodka and signaling for a refill. "No flying today," he said to the other two airman, as though they cared how much he drank.

Dietrich stopped the path of the spoon to his mouth as he considered the rhetorical question. He knew the answer. It was no. He, who had killed a helpless old woman to save his life certainly would not have the resolve to stop someone else's slaughter.

"Who was it?" he asked.

"Who was who?" Neitzel wanted to know.

"The Waffen-SS officer," Dietrich asked, only mildly curious. Rumors of executions up and down the line were rife.

"A Sturmbannfuhrer. He must be crazy, his men call him the Rabbit," Neitzel said, eying Dietrich's soup.

"Bunny," Müller corrected, lighting a Turkish cigarette, its pungent smell dispersing quickly in the well ventilated enclosure.

For a moment Dietrich was jarred but confused. Bunny. He swallowed, then looked at each pilot in turn.

"Bunny. A Sturmbannfuhrer? You're sure?" he asked.

"Yes, that's it," Neitzel said. "The Bunny. Müller is right."

Dietrich rose to his feet so quickly that his chair fell over backward. The two pilots looked at him in surprise.

"What's wrong, Dietrich?" Müller said.

"I have to get to a land-line," he said, muttering.

"But why? We've just started, here. We have a long afternoon... "

But Dietrich was on his way out of the tent. If he could get one of the vehicles started he would drive the three kilometers into Bodrinski. Otherwise he would walk.

The Wolfschanze operators were keenly aware that any communication from the Führer's favorite Luftwaffe officer was to be put through to him at once. Nevertheless, Dietrich was asked to leave his name. The Führer would call him back as soon as he was free, the operator said. Dietrich instructed the operator that his call was most urgent and that the Führer should be so advised.

While he waited in a single room that contained many of the headquarters staff for JagGeschwader3, Dietrich appreciated the fact that the large room was warm, that term being relative. The Geschwader's personnel occupied one of the few four walls with a roof still standing in the town and it contained a large fireplace. A huge fire was kept burning, there being no shortage of scrap wood since the entire town had been reduced days ago to nothing but scrap. The temperature inside was therefore raised from 15 below zero Fahrenheit to 10F above. Every bone in his body ached, partially because he had yet to fully recover from his body being poisoned but mostly because of the cold. Still, when he considered his plight visa vis the infantry, he would not complain.

A field phone rang. "For you, Herr Oberstleutnant," an awed sergeant said. "It's the Wolfschanze."

"Hello? Is that you, Stephen?" a voice whom Dietrich recognized as Archie exploded onto the line. He could be heard clearly although the connection cut in and out at odd intervals.

"Yes, my Führer," Dietrich said. "I hope you are well, sir, and thank you for taking my telephone call. It is a matter of great urgency, I assure you."

"Yes, yes, but make it quick, Stephen. We are extremely busy, here," Archie said.

Dietrich was immediately interested. What could possibly have happened to distract Archie from one of their infrequent communications? And whatever "it" was, Dietrich was sure that London would be at least as much interested as he was. But first things first, he told himself.

"Führer, SS-Sturmbannfuhrer Bernard Hartung has been arrested. I believe they mean to shoot him if they haven't done it already. I request that you intervene immediately. He is a much decorated hero of the Fatherland and we must not let him die over a stupid misunderstanding," Dietrich said.

For a long moment the line was silent.

"Hello?" Dietrich said.

"I am here, Herr Oberstleutnant," Archie said. Archie had never referred to him by his official military rank before. "I know of the case. Sturmbannfuhrer Hartung threatened to shoot another SS officer in the course of doing his duty, Stephen. I approved the execution."

Dietrich tightened his grip on the telephone. He felt sick to his stomach. "Is it over? Did they kill him?"

Again there was a hesitation on the line. "I don't know. He is a friend of yours?"

"A very good friend, Führer," Dietrich said, suddenly enraged that he had to bargain over the telephone with a British actor. He fervently wished that he was at the Wolfschanze. He would snatch Archie by the lapels and shake his goddamn head off if he didn't obey Dietrich's order immediately.

"Very well, I will see what I can do. I cannot promise," Archie said.

"Thank you, Führer," Dietrich said through gritted teeth. "Ah, is there anything in particular that is keeping you busy, Führer? I am only concerned for your health, you know."

"Yes, yes, I know, my boy. Well, it certainly is no secret. I plan to make a public announcement very soon. Japan has bombed the Americans at Pearl Harbor."

Dietrich was shocked into utter silence, his head swimming with the potential import of the news.

retired at his usual time, he was purposefully patient with the partyers that night.

The next morning, however, the news was sobering.

In North Africa the British and the Australians were finishing off the Italian army. To cover Mussolini's incredible debacle in the northern Sahara Archie found it necessary to send a very large investment of armor and air units (10th Fliegerkorps) and one of his most effective generals to that theater. Rather than call it for what it was, a new "front," it was referred to as a satellite operation, or simply North Africa. And while General Erwin Rommel settled down to meting out warfare on a level that the British had not yet seen in the desert, knowing military minds in Berlin (OKW) realized that supplying Rommel on the other side of the Mediterranean was at best a short term proposition. Germany had ceded naval command in the Med to the British and while the Luftwaffe could match the British in that part of the world it, too, was strung out in an unmanageable arc.

The Luftwaffe was carrying the war to the British Isles, fighting on the Eastern Front and the Balkans, and was now dispatched to finish what the Italians had begun in North Africa. Unless Rommel could win swiftly and decisively, the exposed southern flank of Germany would collapse in the end.

The British had taken Tobruk.

Archie, in a moment of insightful military wisdom, countermanded the order for German assault troops to invade the island of Malta which the British were using to stage aircraft and naval units to interdict German supply convoys going to Rommel. The consequences, at least to the possibility of German victory in North Africa, was to seal the doom of the Desert Legion.

Nor were the combat situation reports any better on the Russian front. On the December 8th General of Panzer Troops Model, who had been mounting a determined attack with the 1st, 6th Panzer Divisions and the 23rd Infantry Division on the residential area of Moscow, had his troops drop from under him like overworked horses. To Archie in the Wolfschanze he sent "... completely exhausted and, for the first time in this campaign, combat incapable...."

And from Panzer General Reinhardt ordered the suspension of his troops against their Moscow target. The Russians were fighting fanatically and, increasingly, wisely. The 44th Siberian Cavalry Division rode with *drawn sabers* against German positions in the Mussino Heights and the 106th Infantry Division, hacking their enemy in what was the last classic cavalry charge in military history.

German infantry, grenadiers, engineers and panzer crews fought through driving snow and ice in pressing their attack at the Klaisma Reservoir. A nearby sign said "Moscow - 35 Kilometers." But they penetrated no further.

On December 3rd General Hoepner ordered his men to halt when his troops, still fighting in summer clothing, experienced overnight temperatures of -34F. Truck and tank engines were frozen solid and would not start, breeches of guns were frozen shut and could not be opened to receive shells.

When Generaloberst Guderian, arguably the world's most knowledgeable army officer on tank warfare, reported to the Wolfschanze "The icy cold, wretched shelters, the shortage of clothing, the high losses in men and equipment, the lack of heating fuel made the conduct of battle a chore...."

"A chore?" Archie shouted into a field telephone at Guderian's headquarters. "You are reporting to me that your men are overworked? And you are telling me that your sector is cold?"

"It is now minus thirty-seven degrees," Guderian snapped back into the telephone. "Vehicles cannot move and the horses we use for supply have fallen into the snow, dead. Our troops immediately cut up the animals up for food! I hope that clarifies the picture for your staff at the Wolfschanze."

That afternoon Soviet forces, completely equipped for winter fighting, attacked near Venev and blew huge holes through the 17th and 4th Panzer Divisions. Guderian continued to attack the XLIII Army Corps but eventually bogged down. He ordered his commanders to withdraw to the Don-Shat-Upa positions.

While German armies up and down the front were running into solid walls of ice, snow and wind, Russian units were reinforced with fresh provisions, replacement troops, and entire new units including a complete air division and fifteen new infantry and tank divisions in the Army Group Center sector alone.

Out of 600 panzers that Generaloberst Guderian was supposed to have, he was down to 25 tanks. It was then that the Red Army launched its winter offensive. Field Marshal von Bock reported to the

OKH on December 9[th,] "The army group is no longer in the situation to withstand the enemy attack!"

On December 19th, Archie relieved Army Commander in Chief Field Marshal von Brauchitsch and took over OKH himself. He began to issue "no-retreat, stand and fight" orders at every sector. Yet commanding generals, disdainful of OKH orders that lacked strategic insights, nevertheless passed them on to their subordinate commanders.

But the front, to Archie's frustration, continued to deteriorate. On December 28, Archie put this order in writing: "Strip Generaloberst Hoepner of his shoulder boards and send him home. Effective immediately, he has been discharged by me from the Wehrmacht!"

He also relieved the brilliant Guderian of his command.

By now Army Group Center was defending an 800 kilometer front and its six armies were fighting without heavy tanks, without fuel, virtually without food and without Luftwaffe support. Arrayed against them were 16 Soviet armies who were fully equipped and trained for winter warfare.

Good man, Archie, Dietrich thought.

He just hoped his generals didn't kill him before the Russians did.

The weather in Vancouver, British Columbia, was far from the numbing cold of Europe in the winter. The Japanese current flowed up to Alaska then followed the North American continental shelf clockwise, taking with it the warmth of the great Pacific ocean. It rained a great deal on North America's northern west coast, but showers did not bother Fred Friedel as he busied himself at Camp Edward. There was a good number of POW camps strung out along the breadth of Canada, some containing mostly Luftwaffe personnel, others were German sailors and soldiers defeated in combat from various parts of the world.

Escape was a frequent topic of conversation among camp prisoners. Most plans involved getting over or under the wire, then making south to slip over a border into the USA, then on to Mexico or South America. But now that America had entered the war an escapee had another sixteen hundred miles of enemy territory to traverse, a much more difficult journey. Friedel, however, was motivated to escape to America but no farther. He had got to know a good many Canadians in recent months and regarded them as very pleasant people. They were quite similar to Americans, he understood, in that they were relaxed and fun to be around. He had worked hard to learn English, and had created the German/Canadian Exchange Club that met in the prisoner's day room twice a week.

Their goal was to cultivate various Canadians who lived in the nearby communities in order to provide mutual assistance. The fundamental tenet of the club was to acknowledge to the people of Canada that the war was over for the prisoners, that whatever civilian skills and expertise the POWs possessed was offered to the community. This benign attitude was not shared by a majority of prisoners but Friedel could not have cared less.

Over a period of time German "trustees" were let out of their camp confinement to perform chores such as milking cows twice daily, or plowing land, thus providing relief for dairy farmers whose men were off fighting a war on the other side of the Atlantic. Prisoners also repaired lawn mowers, electric irons, vehicle parts for civilians for whom replacement items were impossible to obtain for the duration.

It was during a visit by a young American woman, Margo Henningson, that crystalized Friedel's post-war plans. Margo, visiting her Canadian cousin, Dorothy McTaggart, went along to the German POW camp with Dorothy who stopped at that place every other Tuesday. In her capacity as a nurse for the Red Cross she insured that the prisoners had medical attention. But she did more than assist doctors who treated the POWs as required. Dorothy oversaw the distribution of parcels.

The POW compound consisted of six acres of ground surrounded by two fences of coiled concertina wire and was guarded at four corners by manned towers. There were gates at the east and west ends of the encirclement. In the middle of the fences were ten buildings that resembled Canadian military barracks which, in fact, they once were. They were built of plain wood outer and inner walls and insulated with a kind of paper batting. The trick for escaping POWs did not lie in breaking out of their living quarter, the doors were never locked, but getting through the fences. Those were guarded by foot patrols and, ironically, German Shepard dogs.

Friedel was planting flowers near the front steps of his barracks when Doctor Major Raymond Oakes, RCAMC, accompanied by Dorothy

McTaggart who in turn was accompanied by Margo Henningson, entered the barracks to make his weekly rounds.

"Oh," Margo said, hesitating on the steps of the barracks. "I love Tickseed."

"Is that what they are?" Friedel responded, rather proud of his English.

"Sure. Didn't you know that?"

Margo was perhaps 5'2" and with coal black hair that framed one of the most beautiful faces Friedel had ever seen in his life. Her eyes were dark, dark brown, and her skin was fresh in appearance but still tinged with last summer's tan. Friedel had seen photographs of American Indian women and wondered if she might have been a tribal woman. Squaw?

"No. I do not know the names of anything I plant. They all die, anyway."

"That's terrible," Margo said in real horror.

"That I am ignorant?" Friedel asked.

"Yes," Margo said, lifting her nose into the air before continuing into the barracks behind her friend.

In a few minutes she was back, again trailing Canada's medical contingent.

"Would you like to see something else I planted?" Friedel said as she passed nearby.

Margo hesitated. "Is it still alive?"

He led her a few steps around to the north side of the barracks building where he gestured toward an attractive green plant that produced luscious white leaves.

"I know what this one is," he said to Margo.

"I'll bite," she said.

"Bite?"

"Yeah. I give up. Tell me what it is," she said.

"A Bellflower," Friedel said, gravely.

"Very nice," Margo said.

"I also know where it came from," he said.

"Arizona?" Margo guessed.

"No. The Caucasus," he said.

"Caucasus? Where is that? Somewhere around...." she searched her memory but in vain.

MICHAEL MURRAY

"The southern part of Russia. That is why we invaded the Soviet Union. We already control tulip production in Holland and now, if we defeat the Soviet Union, we will conquer flower sales all over the world," Friedel said, arching an eyebrow.

Margo smiled despite herself, but turned away.

"Please," Friedel said, causing her to hesitate. "I was only a humble bomb-dropper but I never dropped one on an innocent person."

This time Margo laughed out loud. Then left the camp.

CHAPTER

28

The courier plane from Generalmajor Felix Loz's headquarters of V. Fliegerkorps arrived unannounced, ostensibly to refuel at Dietrich's fighter base at Aleksin. Its pilot, Captain Konrad Schul, was personally known to Dietrich. Schul advised Dietrich that the general was aboard the aircraft and wanted him, Colonel Dietrich, to join him.

"All right, Schul," the general said over the intercom as soon as the cabin door closed behind Dietrich.

Without further directions the pilot spoke briefly with the control tower while advancing the throttles. The aircraft quickly lifted off the icy runway but only to begin flying in a large circle high above the aerodrome. The engines on war aircraft were virtually unmuffled and the fuselages were never insulated. The voices of the two men seated in the rear of the plane were therefore impossible to overhear.

"We can talk better up here, Dietrich," the general said, turning toward his subordinate.

"Yes, sir. And what is it that we should discuss?" Dietrich asked, genuinely at a loss.

"I am not supposed to be here, Dietrich. Talking with you might be a very dangerous thing. You will understand when I tell you that yesterday I had a visit from the Gestapo. They were men from SS-

Obergruppenfuhrer Heydrich's department and they were acting upon his explicit instructions. The reason for their visit was to question me about you."

"Me?" Dietrich said, his heart suddenly leaping to his throat.

"They wanted to know what kind of officer you were and if you had ever done anything that could be construed as disloyal, no matter how trivial. They were suspicious of the fact that you are also an American, of course, and they wanted any information I might have about your political attitude. Naturally I told them that you were a first-rate fighter pilot, an excellent leader and that your squadrons were among the most effective in the Luftwaffe."

"Thank you, Herr General," Dietrich said, truly grateful.

"Don't thank me. It is the truth, but that is not what they wanted to hear," General Loz said. He found a package of cigarettes in his breast pocket. He offered the pack to Dietrich who shook his head, then lit one for himself. The aircraft continued to drone in a wide circle just outside the operational approaches of the airfield at Aleksin.

"They asked me something else," Loz said, blowing smoke from his lungs.

"Yes?"

"About your radio," General Loz said, pausing to regard Dietrich before going on.

Dietrich was not mystified but attempted to maintain a look of innocence. "Radio, sir? I don't understand."

"The Gestapo wanted to know if the radio in your plane could contact London while it was either on the ground or in the air. I told them that our radios were capable of that transmission but that other aircraft would be listening to whatever calls are made. They seemed to accept that stupid statement at face value but they will no doubt check with their own communications experts back in Berlin."

General Loz continued to smoke his cigarette but remained silent, at least for the moment.

"Well, sir, I don't know what to say...."

"There is nothing for you to say to me, Dietrich. Why? Because I am not even here talking to you so what could you possibly have to say?" General Loz held Dietrich's eyes for several moments before picking up a microphone attached to his command radio set. "We go down, Schul," he said.

Dietrich remained silent until they had landed and he was reaching for the door lever.

"Be very careful, Stephen," Loz said. "Don't get too far away from your aircraft. Once they arrest you, there is nothing we can do to get you out again. Do you understand?"

Dietrich nodded, then saluted by touching the brim of his hat. The engines had been kept running and as he closed the aircraft's door, the pilot throttled up and, lining up with the runway, roared off toward the north.

Standing on the frozen runway at Aleksin, Dietrich considered following Loz's opening. He was tempted to climb into his Me-109F and make a dash for England. His head was almost singing as he mentally computed fuel and speed components, considering where he could refuel and the time it would take to reach the channel and beyond. As heady and as compelling as the prospect loomed in his psyche, he realized that were he to run now it would certainly seal Archie's doom.

It was probably the case that Archie had already guaranteed Germany's eventual destruction, but he remained critical to the Allied cause. Should the "Führer" suddenly die, the clever and fanatical Nazis might find a way to negotiate a truce of some kind and rise again later. Or, failing that, would certainly fight to the last man and thus cost the Allies millions of additional lives. No, Archie was still vital to England and now to America, as well. And if Archie was to survive, Dietrich must survive.

But if he did nothing, the end for him as well as for Archie would not be far off.

Sir William Schuyler raised his nose into the air as though he had been confronted with a smell so odious that his sensitivities would not and could not deal with it. "Good God," he said, collapsing into his favorite chair. "What does Elliot say about this?" the SOE man said in a somewhat shaky voice.

"He said that he would have nothing to do with it," Edward Wiles said, evenly.

"Does he offer another solution?" the older man asked.

"Yes, but none that I think are practical. For example, he is for sending a submarine to retrieve them both. He has several suggestions of how Archie might detach himself from his retinue long enough for him and Dietrich to sneak away completely undetected. It's rubbish, of course."

"Hmm," Schuyler agreed with a grunt.

"Let me put it to you in another form, Sir William. I am quite prepared to put my plan into action without your.... shall we say, 'knowledge'. The same is true as pertains to MacLean Elliot. I don't know of any administrative need for either of you to be involved."

"We are bloody well not involved, Edward. I choose to forget that you suggested that we do such a... a monstrous thing. I want nothing of the sort to be discussed again my presence. Do I make myself clear?"

"Quite clear, Sir William."

Wiles worked late into the morning hours on his plan to save Dietrich and, far more important, Archie Smythes, from discovery. He was under no illusion that to do so would be difficult, even unlikely. But not impossible. So he had to try. After emergency meetings with his document forgery department and his Special Air Operations people, there was still one more very important SOE worker with whom Wiles had to coordinate. His name was Robert MacClure, an American whose devious mind would send ripples of joy through the heart of Niccolo Machiavelli himself. MacClure was an American Irishman who had a love for intrigue for its own sake and whose nerves seemed absent from his body. MacClure had fought the fascists in Spain and had helped the Czechoslovakians lay an assassination trap for Hitler in 1939 that almost succeeded. He was at once a cryptographer, radio engineer and linguist, an intelligence expert who was also blessed with a memory that could only be described as extraordinary. MacClure ran several of the espionage teams operating in the Low Countries and parts of northern France. Without committing anything to paper, McClure knew the complete names of almost two hundred operatives, their entire backgrounds, their codes and radio frequencies, contacts, training credits, and a thousand details that went into their lives before and during the war. And, almost to a man, he spoke their languages.

MacClure's hair was totally black despite his forty-plus years, wore glasses that slipped precipitously toward the end of a pointed nose, and walked with great care, as though avoiding land mines. He was a chain-smoker in the throes of quitting and while he sat in a chair opposite Edward Wiles he habitually slapped his breast pocket to either insure that he had got rid of his pack or perhaps hoping that one would somehow magically appear. His eyes wandered the room but Wiles was absolutely sure that MacClure was missing nothing in their exchange.

"I want your unqualified advice on this one, Robert. If you don't think you have the...."

"Guts?" MacClure suggested.

"I wasn't going to say that."

"Yes you were," MacClure said, only half of his mouth trying to form a smile.

"I was going to use a far different phrase," Wiles said, admitting that what he was asking MacClure to do was more than difficult.

"You want me to choose the man," MacClure said and crossed his legs.

"Yes. He has to have courage, but not too much courage. To be honest with you I was thinking of Denise," Wiles said, gritting his teeth. Denise Littrel was French. Her husband was captured by the Germans with the fall of France and put to work as a slave laborer in Germany. Her hatred for the Nazis was profound and she was fully trained in all of her spy craft assignments including the parachute.

"Sure," MacClure said, managing to dismiss Wiles' suggestion while agreeing with it. "But that might just go around and bite you in the ass." MacClure continued when Wiles's eyebrows arched. "She's tougher than you think. She just might not crack. Or she might find a way to kill herself if she thought she'd talk."

"Are you quite sure of that?" Wiles asked.

"Hell, no, I'm not sure. But let's scratch her off the list, anyway," the American said.

"Right," Wiles said, falling silent, waiting for MacClure to tender a name.

After a reflective moment MacClure sat up straighter in his chair. "My vote goes to Robert Vossler."

"The Dutchman?" Wiles asked.

"Yeah. We've got two busted teams there now including Vanden Eykel."

"We are not sure... " Wiles interjected.

"I'm sure and even if I weren't certain, we have to assume he's turned," MacClure said, speaking absolute logic, Wiles knew. "Somebody in the Gestapo is doing good work in Holland. I say we drop Vossler on Vanden Eykel."

Edward Vanden Eykel was parachuted out of an airplane into occupied Holland ten months previously. He was twenty-four hours late in making his first broadcast which was enough to arouse the suspicions of SOE handlers. He then failed to transmit the "safe" prefix before he sent the entire message. Agents working in occupied countries were instructed to insert a code word or phrase somewhere within the body of the message to inform the wireless receivers in London that the agents were operating of their own free will. That is, if the code word or phrase is in place, the agent is presumed not to have been caught by the enemy. If the "safe" sign was not included, it meant that the agent was operating, literally, with a gun to his head. Vanden Eykel's "safe" sign was not included in the first message but was contained in the second. That, and other idiosyncracies from Vanden Eykel's work made MacClure certain that the agent had been turned by the Gestapo.

"Very well, Robert, you know best," Wiles said, not entirely sure but faced with no other choice. "Another thing about Vossler...." Wiles bit his lip.

"I don't know why you're laying on this mission, Eddie," MacClure said, using a sobriquet that Wiles would never allow anyone else to exercise, "and I sure as hell don't want you telling me now."

Wiles was certainly not going to reveal the Raven operation, but he was probably looking for some kind of absolution for murdering one of his own kind. Wiles knew that he would live with that for the rest of his life. He wished he could see into the future to know if it would be worth it. "I was only going to say that we have to replace his 'C' pill."

All agents that jumped into enemy territory had a cyanide deposit built into their dental work so that if captured, they could relieve themselves of unbearable torture by crushing the capsule with their teeth. Death was almost instant and relatively painless.

Vossler was roused from sleep at 0500 and told that he had a mission. While he reported to Mission Processing his MP quarters would be cleaned entirely so that when he departed into the night there would be no trace of him in London. At MP he was issued clothing made in Europe before the war, carefully examined for any traces, no matter how minute, that might indicate that he had been in England. He showered with harsh soap of the only kind that could be found in Europe, and then dressed under the supervision of a Dutch team expert. In his well-worn wallet he carried recently obtained Reich Guilders to replace pre-war Dutch money now banned in occupied Europe.

Into the linings of his clothing were sewn silk maps of Holland and France, finished but unset diamonds (for use as an international currency) and a smoking pipe which, with its stem removed, fired a 9mm bullet. Vossler was also supplied with a cigarette lighter that doubled for a miniature camera. Wiles knew that the Gestapo would find all of these items on Vossler, thus rendering them superfluous to his mission, but not to have included them might give the game away. So he possessed the full compliment carried by any other agent.

"Remember," Wiles warned Vossler in his final briefing, "you must arrive in Lille no later than the 13th. His leave will be over by then. Arriving sooner would be even better."

"I understand," Vossler said, nodding.

In point of fact it did not matter a whit if Vossler arrived at that time or not. Or if he ever arrived.

"Good," Wiles said, offering his hand, feeling every bit a despicable monster. As the Dutchman took it, he exuded confidence not only in himself but Wiles, as well. "Good luck, then," Wiles said.

As Vossler opened the door to leave the final briefing room he turned to Wiles. "Thank you for believing in me," he said, simply.

Wiles averted his eyes to hide his shame.

The Gestapo moved with alacrity.

"Oberstluetnant Dietrich?" the angular man wearing civilian clothes said in the form of a statement rather than a question. At shoulder level the man held a small metal identity tag which Dietrich knew, without looking at it closely, was a Gestapo mark. His pretentiously relaxed attitude struck Dietrich as theatrical but the man was a member of an obscene organization. He would not be one to take lightly. His dark complexion, comb-like mustache, and aquiline nose gave him a Slavik appearance, very similar to Joseph Stalin. Dietrich wondered how he managed to be tolerated within an organization which was dedicated to the eradication of his ilk. "My name is Bagasaran, Gestapo," he said.

Bagasaran was in the company of another man. Shorter, but unlike the Slav, had no expanding waistline and appeared to have had a recent shower.

Dietrich turned directly toward him. "And you are?"

"Hans Loetz," he said, pulling back thin lips over uneven teeth. Loetz was rail thin but sinewy, heavy hair low on his forehead. Loetz appeared older than his partner, yet neither appeared to have passed age forty.

"I was once in U-boats," Loetz said, as though in so saying he had apologized for his current sad state of subservience to the Nazi cause. "But now," he gestured toward his head, "my ears will not take the pressure."

Dietrich said nothing to put the Gestapo man at ease, on the level of a fighting man. He suddenly wished he had accompanied other members of his squadron on their leaves to Lille where the Luftwaffe maintained a French chateaux for the rest and relaxation of its pilots. But the moment passed as he realized the Gestapo could reach him as easily in France as here, in Russia.

"I was in your country, once," he said, still trying to make his lips work into a smile.

"My country?" Dietrich said.

"America. They call you the Yank, I believe," Loetz said.

"I was born in Germany."

"But raised in America, eh? It has such beauty. Like Germany. I worked for General Motors. That is in Detroit."

"Doing espionage, I assume," Dietrich said.

For an extended moment the smile on Loetz's face turned to ice while the Gestapo man attempted to determine if the remark was praise or something else.

"You will come with us, now," Bagasaran said, doing his best to sneer.

"I'm much to busy to go with you, Herr...." Dietrich began.

"You will do exactly as I tell you to do, you son of a bitch," Bagasaran said, spittle appearing at the corners of his mouth. Dietrich smelled garlic in the air. Bagasaran was not assiduous about brushing his teeth. The Gestapo bully began to move toward Dietrich who had a table between them in his makeshift headquarters tent.

Out of the corner of his eye Dietrich saw his communications sergeant, Kurt Parmalee, rise from his place near the radio, a machine pistol in his hands. The movement caught the Gestapo men by surprise. Bagasaran halted in his tracks.

"You are in a combat area now," Dietrich said to the agents. "You will respect military rank whether you like it or not."

"What is your name?" Bagasaran snarled at Sergeant Parmalee.

Before the sergeant could answer, Dietrich responded for him. "His name is Schmidt. Now, you two, what is your business here?"

It was the turn of Loetz to take a different tack on events. "Herr Oberstleutnant, the Gestapo is authorized to make an arrest of any citizen or military man under the laws of the Reich. You know that. We are giving you the chance of coming with us for questioning on a matter most urgent. If you force us to notify Berlin that you are uncooperative, your entire unit will suffer the consequences. Even Sergeant 'Schmidt' here."

Dietrich knew that Loetz was exactly right. He was painfully aware that the Gestapo was not restricted in any action they saw fit, including immediate executions for real or imagined crimes against the Reich. More out of deference for the men under his command than to appease the bullies before him, he nodded his agreement.

"Very well, where do you wish to talk?" Dietrich said.

"We have a plane waiting," Loetz said, undertaking still another smile that was more a grimace.

Dietrich nodded toward his sergeant. "Put that away, Schmidt," he said. "I'll go with these men. Notify General Loz that I have been...."

"He knows where the hell you are going," Bagasaran snapped. "Come. We have no time."

Swallowing his rising fury, Dietrich accompanied the two men through the entrance of the tent, then hesitated. "One moment," he said, and reentered the tent before the Gestapo men could restrain him.

"Parmalee," he said to his communications man. "Tell Hauptman Kraus to transfer you to another squadron immediately. No, make that another Fliegerkorps."

"Colonel," Parmalee began.

"Do it quickly, or your wife will never see you again. Do you understand?"

"Yes, sir," Parmalee said, saluting.

Dietrich's cell at Gestapo headquarters in Krakow was one of hundreds in a three story brick and concrete building. There were two levels above him and the lowest level, to which he was consigned, was a basement. There would have been standing water in his cell as well as in the walkway between cells directly across but for the cold. The temperature in the cells was always below freezing. To keep from dying from exposure Dietrich had a blood and mud-encrusted wool rag that was once a blanket and his uniform coat that he was wearing when he was tossed into his dank dungeon.

His floor space was seven feet by four. There was no window that opened to the outside. There was only an eighteen inch square opening on an otherwise solid steel door through which jailers could observe him or issue orders at their pleasure. Food, what little there was, was shoved through a four inch slot at the bottom. There was no communication allowed between cells, no rapping on pipes, no shouting, no talking.

There was no toilet nor sink. In Dietrich's cell there was a drain hole in the cement floor into which went his body wastes. The hole was always plugged and his vomit, his sewage and the vermin he destroyed went into this central receptacle. The stench was overpowering. He received a bucket of water on days when the guards were generous. The bucket, if filled, contained about one litre. But it was seldom full.

There were no lights inside his living tomb and what illumination existed oozed under a quarter inch space at the base of the door.

Every centimeter of his body hurt beyond his ability to quantify. His left arm had been separated from its socket at the shoulder. His ribs were either broken or cracked and he breathed only with great difficulty, each labored breath stabbed at his lungs. The bottoms of his feet were raw and broken from the beatings and he could not stand on them. He had swallowed two of his teeth and others had fallen to the floor of one of the interrogation rooms. His testicles were raw from copper wires that shot voltage through his body. On those exquisite occasions his mouth would open and he would try to scream but if there was any sound that came out he could not hear it through his broken ear drums.

And the worst was yet to come. They had promised it and Dietrich believed them.

He wanted to die and spent lucid moments considering the problem. He had no rope with which to hang himself. He had nothing sharp to open his veins. More than once he attempted to strangle himself with his own hands but he would pass out only to awaken later. Throughout the days and the nights he would hear the sharp, cracking sound of jackboots worn by the Gestapo guards as they strode the concrete corridors between the cells. He would begin to shake as the steps came nearer and nearer, then sob with relief when they halted by another soul's cell. Waves of guilt would wash over him when that door was unlocked and the pitiful moans from within could be heard. Each time a prisoner was taken from his cell for interrogation, Dietrich died by inches, by anticipation. He knew that sooner or later his antagonists would increase the level of torture and he would talk. Or die.

It was Bagasaran who delivered most of the pain. Not a man of towering intellect, it seemed to Dietrich that the man's source of amusement was in causing misery, and this was his physical outlet for incoherent rage. While Gestapo agent Loetz did little to administer torture, he was far more interested in results. It was a good division of labor. While Bagasaran pounded Dietrich with rubber hose, struck him with his fist, and attached the electric leads to his testicles and screamed insults, Loetz almost quietly prodded Dietrich with cogent questions.

"You are an agent of the British, Dietrich. We know this. We will stop the punishment when you are honest with us. Hmm? Do you wish to speak now or to speak later? It is your choice."

Almost at once the cosh would swish through the air and onto his bare back, again, again, again, and yet again.

"That was unnecessary Oberstleutnant Dietrich. You are an American and you are at war with Germany. I understand that. Who is your controller in London?"

The lashings would resume and they would continue until Dietrich would pass out. Then ice water would awaken him, then the questions, then the beatings. Again, again, again and again.

He had protested his innocense, of course, until the energy to do so was simply too much. He remained silent not from a sense of duty but from a kind of morbid curiosity about how long he might live. He began not to fear the pain because he *was* pain. He was the embodiment of pain. There was no universe that was not pain so that should the pain cease his world would cease and he would no longer *be*. The syllogism was not something that he worked out inside his head but rather it was his experience. It took no conscious thought at all. The pain merely became a solid entity, the ferocity of which almost blocked itself out. When he realized that the pain was becoming its own anaesthesia his swollen lips pulled back in what might have appeared to be a smile and he heard laughter, not realizing that the strange sound came from his throat.

Bagasaran flew into an uncontrollable rage as he intensified the blows to Dietrich's body.

His invectives ratcheted up and sweat poured from his glutenous body as he pounded on the inert Luftwaffe pilot. He was only stopped by Loetz who stayed his hand while shaking his head.

"We don't want him dead," the Gestapo man said.

"I want him dead," Bagasaran spat.

Dietrich had been a prisoner for approximately five weeks when there was a sudden and dramatic change. He was removed from his cell by medical orderlies and driven by ambulance to a hospital in Krakow. As he was being wheeled on a gurney into a private room, an officer dressed in immaculate field grey walked by his side. Three aides and a coterie of white-coated medical personnel kept nervous pace with the gurney and with the SS-Standartenfurher.

"My name is Hebert, Colonel Dietrich. I am here at the direction of Reichsleiter Bormann. Minister Bormann has found you by following a trail after he learned of your false arrest. I assure you, Colonel, that the Gestapo agents responsible for this horrific mistake have been arrested and will be shot."

The medical orderly steered Dietrich into a position next to a pristine white bed. Doctors, nurses and orderlies worked together to move Dietrich's prostrate body onto the bed. Dietrich was only partially conscious and instinctively knew that he was closer to death than to life. What once had been his Luftwaffe uniform was now unrecognizable tatters. The medical staff went to work cutting the rags from his body while Standartenführer Hebert looked on. He could feel the pleasant sensation of warm soap and water being administered to his flesh while an I.V. was placed into one of his arms and a solution started.

"Sir," a doctor said to Dietrich, "can you hear me?"

Dietrich felt his eyelids move.

"Good. My name is Doctor Reiner. You are dehydrated and we are giving you fluids now. You would be in pain from your... ah, crash. I am going to give you something for that now. You will feel better in only a few minutes," Dr. Reiner said and proceeded to insert a hypodermic needle into a cleansed area in Dietrich's elbow.

"This man is to have 24-hour care. Is that understood?"

"Of course, Standartenführer. He will be our most important patient," Dr. Reiner said.

"I don't care if everyone else in this hospital dies while you are tending to Colonel Dietrich. It is Minister Bormann's express orders that the colonel has everything that he wants. If there is anything you lack here, you are to advise me at once and we shall see to it that you have immediately," Hebert said.

"I understand, Standartenführer," Reiner said dutifully.

"Of course I moved immediately and decisively when I learned of his arrest, Führer. Himmler's idiots had covered their tracks, of course, but I put my own men to work and we located him at Gestapo headquarters in Krakow. I assure you that..."

"I want them shot! Do you understand me? Shot! No, not shot, hanged! Do it at once, Bormann! This is a sacrilege to have a hero of the Reich dishonored. I want the names of all of those implicated in this filthy plot!"

"The executions have been carried out, Führer, of that I can assure you," Bormann said, standing by his desk at the Reichschancellery. Indeed the executions had been carried out. Not as punishment, but to cover Bormann's tracks. Gestapo agents Bagasaran and Loetz had done nothing more than they had been ordered to do. But in his zeal to unmask the man he was certain was a traitor, Bormann had erred.

"The spy has been found, Führer. Again, it was my men who made the discovery. It was a pilot in Colonel Dietrich's squadron. His name is Ernst Meier. They called him the Pope. Yes, he has confessed to everything. I will have a complete report for you within the week. Good night, Führer.

The winter was merciless. Hartung had been stripped of his rank and assigned to a disciplinary battalion. His work was ceaseless, beginning before dawn and ending late at night on the burial detail. For the first month he had been assigned to mine clearance. Along with his fellow prisoners Hartung would move along roads and the shoulders of the roads on their hands and knees, probing before them for buried mines. In less than 30 days his entire penal battalion had been killed and replaced. Their numbers were augmented with military and civilians from conquered territories, mostly Slavs. The life span of a mine clearance person was measured in hours.

Hartung's friend, Foss, was previously a medical corpsman who had struck an officer. Their association of 58 days seemed a lifetime in the mine clearance business and they were reassigned to Graves Registration together. It was difficult to break through the frozen ground near Kltskaya where their business was very steady. Where possible mass graves were dug by heavy equipment. Hartung learned that it took sixteen cubic yards of human flesh to fill the grave. By direction of the Graves Registration Office Company commanders were to be wrapped in shelter halves before burying, enlisted men of the panzer divisions were to be wrapped in blankets. Hartung usually tried to comply but only after ensuring that he and Foss had a blanket in which to sleep each night.

An infantry regiment with its artillery was blown up, all of its men, all of its guns. The pieces, including human parts, rained back into the very craters caused by the shells. Hartung and Foss fell to work shoveling dirt over them before it could freeze again.

Hartung and Foss were ordered to clear the dead from a field hospital. "Get them out of here," one of the surgeons said to Hartung, sweeping his arm over an assemblage of wounded men.

"Some of them are alive, I think," Hartung said.

"I don't care. Get them out," the doctor said.

"But they are here," Hartung responded. "We can't bury them alive."

"We can't treat them here. Fine. Come back in the morning. Then they will be officially dead," the medic said, referring to the wounded men's inability to survive a night outside in the -40 weather.

A general officer appeared, ignoring Hartung. "Where are the doctors?" he said to the doctor.

"There are no doctors," the doctor said.

"Are you a doctor?" the general wanted to know.

"Yes."

"These men have come all the way from Tovarkovski. They have been here for days. Can't you do something?" the general asked.

"We are full, general. You see?" the doctor turned so that the general could see the entrance to the main operating tent. Bodies were everywhere. Some were standing, sitting, lying down, all covered in mud, and blood was everywhere.

"But you cannot simply let them die," the general said.

But die they did.

Bumper to bumper, horses pulling sleds, long trains of ammunition carriers, field kitchens, staff cars, only to slide and slip off of icy roads into ditches, or career into a shell crater. Walking was faster than riding and the lack of fuel obviated the choice. Panzers were scattered around the moon-like cratered landscape, idle because of fuel starvation, gun breeches frozen closed. The same was true with trucks and even small vehicles. They were simply abandoned while their crews walked west, whence they came. The lines were collapsing in every direction and German divisions had no other objectives but to avoid encirclement.

Hartung and Foss slogged along with the others, stacking bodies, going through their belongings to retrieve identity tags, unmailed etters to loved ones. They would occasionally find uneaten pieces of ood on the bodies and, without a moment's hesitation, consumed hem on the spot.

"Look," Hartung said to Foss. He was pointing to a body covered y only a thin layer of snow. It was a bomber crewmember and, Hartung could tell, his flying boots were still attached to his feet. As hey rolled him over they could see that his crushed body was inside uniform blackened from fire. His parachute harness was secured round him but there was no canopy at the ends of his shroud lines. t was not unusual for a pilot or gunner to jump from a burning air-lane and have his parachute burn up in a matter of seconds, long efore striking the ground.

The large sized fleece-lined flying boots appeared to be a fit for Hartung but he handed them to Foss.

Foss shook his head. "My feet are too small," he said.

"Put them on."

Foss shook his head again. "I don't want them."

n Hartung's sector, the "Briansk Front," Major General Kolpakchi's 40th Army broke through the XLVIII Panzer Corps (General Kempf) outheast of Kursk. Rifle and ski regiments reached the Kursk-Oboyan oad and penetrated into the suburbs of Oboyan.

The German forces, the 239th, 299th Infantry Division and the 16th Motorized Infantry Division, stood against crashing waves of the Soviet armies fighting, per Archie's orders, to the death. Hartung stood watching as his old unit, the 3rd Panzer Division, were brought up in the final hours of the battle to hold the potential breech in the ine. While the positions at Seim were held, Russian elements of the II Guards Cavalry Corps, as well as the 5th, 6th Guards and 32nd Cavalry Division broke through the German front within forty-eight ours. While Major General Breith, commander of 3rd Panzer Div. Received the Oak Leaves to his Knight's Cross during that battle, a Führer Order arrived along with it. "Your sector is to be held under all circumstances!"

Still, fresh Russian troops, winter equipped, continued to attack the German lines, the Russians now using superior numbers to press their ssaults. Generals Nehring and von Gilsa, despite Archie's orders to he contrary, attempted a breakout from their surrounded positions.

After the first effort failed, the second succeeded despite suffering heavy casualties.

Along the entire front, in every town and city, in response to every suggestion by field commanders, there was but one order that was sent out from the Wolfschanze: "Hold at all costs!"

Amazingly, when the first winter of the war on the eastern front had settled into a frozen stalemate, military tacticians, including Russian ones, had to admit that it was precisely the correct order to give.

BOOK VI

T he winter of 1941-42 was exceptionally harsh in a country where cold, ice and snow were routinely forbidding. To the north where Army Group A was operating along its six hundred kilometer front, Leningrad, the principle city of Russia after Moscow was under siege. That part of the German war machine operating nearest the Arctic Circle, after a non-stop gallop across the vast Soviet landscape in the summer months of 1941, was slowed, then halted altogether at the city gates. The siege of Leningrad would last for most of the war with enormous casualties on either side. Almost a million Russians would die of starvation. Furniture was taken part and boiled for the contents of the glue which held it together, and that was drunk. Wallpaper was stripped from houses, boiled and eaten. The citizens of the surrounded city ate every morsel of food including work animals and, eventually, their dogs and cats.

The German army was only a little better off. By the middle of December the snow was 80 cm deep and the Wehrmacht was still fighting in summer clothing, and it was supplied only sporadically with sufficient food. Then, by the end of that month, the Russian army seized the initiative and went on the attack.

Archie sacked Field Marshal Ritter von Leeb in January of 1942. Von Leeb was one of Germany's brilliant tacticians.

When the summer was exhaustively spent in see-saw battles moving the lines only a matter of meters, seasoned officers and men were reminded of the trench warfare of the previous war. As the winter rain approached Army Group A was now outnumbered. The XXVI Army Corps surrounded the Oranienbvaum bridgehead while the isolation of Leningrad from the south was delegated to the L Army Corps with the 58th ID, SS Police Division and the 121st and 122nd Infantry Divisions. The XXVIII Army Corps near Mga, had only the ,th and 1st Infantry Divisions available to oppose Leningrad while the 227th Infantry Division stood on Lake Ladoga.

Opposing the 28 German divisions on the 600 kilometer front were Soviet divisions, most of whom arrived fresh to the battle and very well equipped. Archie informed his generals that the German army had to fight where it stood! There would be no retreat, not a single meter of ground. Further, he said, all available formations were to be transported from the Reich and the West to the Eastern Front. Accordingly, the 218th Infantry Division arrived from Denmark, sent not en masse but divided into four combat groups and each sent to different sectors of the front.

The 9th SS Regiment came from Finland, the 5th Mountain Division from Crete, the 81st Infantry came from France and the 7th Air Division (paratroops) from Germany.

During the winter of 1942-1943 the temperature dropped beyond 2F. The construction of shelters for the soldiers made slow or no progress and fighting units used snow banks for protection against Russian shells and small arms fire. Motorized battalions fought the Russians in front of them but lost the battles of fuel, weapons grease and anti-freeze. Weapons no longer operated and engines could not turn over.

Horses fell by the hundreds from exhaustion and were immediately eaten by hungry troops. The withdrawal of wounded was always a race against freezing to death. Medical supplies were in the shortest supply or did not exist. Diseases became rampant. More German troops were lost to frostbite, fever, and complications from malnutrition than from enemy gunfire.

The Russians, keenly aware of the dire German conditions and stretched supply lines, wanted to wipe out Army Group North entirely with fresh winter-mobile armies. This they methodically undertook while Archie replaced von Leeb with General von Kuechler as the new commander of Army Group North.

In November 1942, America landed troops in North Africa and those divisions. After suffering a bloody nose at the Kasserine Pass the Americans quickly learned the business of war. As Rommel's supplies diminished with each pounding by Allied air units over the Mediterranean and British naval forces, the Allies aimed directly at what Winston Churchill called Europe's "soft underbelly" and a major landing at Sicily and then Italy came as no surprise to Archie's staff.

But a decidedly bright spot on Germany's otherwise problematic military adventures came with the positive activities of Admiral Karl Doenitz, commander of the Reich's Undersea boats that roamed the oceans in "wolf" packs.

"It was another excellent month," the slight and rather short admiral said in his typically clipped delivery.

"I can count on you, Doenitz," Archie said, attempting to smile but quite aware that his Parkinson-stricken face was set in stone. "So? Tea? Something stronger. Go ahead, if you like." Archie nodded his head toward a white coated waiter who was poised to take their lunch order. While Archie enjoyed taking his meals in the officer's general mess, he had lately secluded himself in the conference room adjacent to his small bedroom and office in the Hitler Bunker.

"Well," Doenitz pursed his mouth, "perhaps a cognac before we eat."

The admiral followed Archie's lead in ordering soup and salad acquiescing to the waiter's suggestion that chicken could be added to the green salad.

"It is official, now. Our boats sank five hundred and ten ships to date," Doenitz said in obvious pride, "and it is only November!"

The U-boat fleet would later refer to 1942 as "the happy times."

"That is wonderful, Doenitz," Archie said, truly amazed at the visualization of that many ships sliding under the waves throughout the world, especially in the cold Atlantic. "The English are on their last legs, you know," he said without enthusiasm. "We are far under our requirements for new boats, of course," Doenitz said, "but give me one hundred more boats and by this time next year the British will run totally out of food and ammunition. They cannot fight a war on blood alone."

"Yes," Archie agreed. "It is only a matter of time." Archie attempted to think of his wife, Laverne, and his daughter, Rose, without food. The idea was abstract and unreal, but more troubling were their images. He could see neither face. Young girls were amorphous by nature, he supposed, but it troubled him that the chiseled features of his wife never quite came into focus. As he kept his shaking right hand under the table out of view, he wondered if the disease had begun to effect his mind. His memory had always served him well. But England was increasingly foreign to him, squeezed from his consciousness by the pressure cooker of the Eastern front.

It was a giant maw that consumed human flesh and it required round the clock feeding. His responsibilities of providing for the murder machine far outpaced all other earthly concerns. It was certainly more important than his wife and daughter. He loved them still, in a kind of distant way, but his emotional juices were committed to the gourmet feast of the two monster armies that faced each other here, in the east.

"What's that?" he said.

"I have brought with me a list of special citations for certain U-boat captains," Doenitz said, relishing his garlic bread. "If you could find the time to look at them...."

"Of course, Karl. They are good boys. All of them, good boys."

The offensive against the city of Stalingrad in the Southern salient, the key to the entire Russian campaign, was going well for the German 6th army, over 340,000 men and equipment. General von Paulus was in command, and he was determined to route the Russian defenders from the city. And after the city would come the riches of coal and iron ore in the Don basin, and the oil fields beyond.

In September while the weather was still fair, the fighting was fierce. German and Russian troops fired at each other at point blank range, often hand-to-hand in cellars, sewers and buildings that were nothing more than rubble. Yet this time, Paulus guaranteed his command staff, they would succeed.

But by November heavy snows had fallen, the temperature had dropped to -10F, and Zhukov's defenders were still fighting tenaciously within the city. Von Paulus, ill- supplied, was considering withdrawing his forces to enable linking his army with other units from Group Center, then remount an offensive that would crack the backs of the Russian forces.

Lieutenant Colonel Stephen Dietrich was in his sixth week of an extended convalescence. The best dentists in the Reich had constructed a temporary bridge to cover the gap in his upper jaw. Wires had been removed from his jaw several days before and that morning he had enjoyed his first full meal without the discomfort of shooting pain each time he chewed. True, his breakfast had been modest by current standards of field-grade officers of the Reich, but the marvelous fresh bread dipped in wonderful red wine did as much for his heart as it did for his emaciated body. He had lost thirty pounds since his encounter with the Gestapo and he had only just found the will power to gain back as much weight as he could as quickly as he could. He relished cheeses and olives and egg-plant fried in oil, seasoned with garlic and other herbs he could only guess at.

His rich diet came to him despite the deprivations of the general Italian population. His uniform caused these delicacies to appear at his table without reference to local menus. His broken bones in his rib cage were still healing and he moved with a certain caution, not wanting to jar himself unnecessarily. He carried with him a letter addressed to any government official ordering that Colonel Dietrich be extended every courtesy of the Reich and its associated administrations. The letter was signed by Adolf Hitler. Further, all SS and Gestapo offices in Rome had been put on the alert that Luftwaffe Colonel Dietrich was a highly decorated hero of the Third Reich and a very close personal friend of the Führer.

What he wanted most, Dietrich had said to Major Friederich Burckhardt, chief of Gestapo in Rome, was privacy. He intended to take in the city's sights, soak up as much sunshine as possible, and in general to be left alone to forget about the war until it was time for him to return to the front. Burckhardt assured Dietrich that he understood completely and that the services of his office were as near as a telephone should there be anything, anything at all, that the colonel might require.

It was not a coincidence that Dietrich met with an old friend from pre-war times. The two of them lunched at an outdoor café on del Palazzo de Venezia. Dietrich ordered rice and lamb while his friend contented himself with bread and cheese. Their table wine was, Dietrich thought, exceptionally bad. Nonetheless, they drank without complaint under the watchful eyes of a glowering waiter who, no doubt, was getting his petite revenge against his unwanted Teutonic ally.

"How do you travel so easily, Se or Philippe?" a bemused Dietrich asked.

"We have important contracts with the German Reich," Edward Wiles said in mock seriousness. "Spain regrets its failure to throw in with El Maximo Hitler."

"Well," Dietrich smiled ironically, "you had your chance. Now Franco and the rest of you will have to stand by while we Germans finish off the Russians. And the Brits. Almost forgot about them."

Wiles' eyes examined the patrons at other tables without appearing to do so. Dietrich did the same on the opposite side of the outdoor table area. There was literally no possibility that their conversation could be overheard but they were wary, nonetheless.

"So. How did you arrive? Or shouldn't I ask?" Dietrich said to the SOE man whom he had now known for almost seven years.

"You shouldn't ask. But the answer is Portugal, Lisbon, then Madrid. Then here. I represent the Spanish trade legation, you see. At the moment we are supplying you supermen with strategic materials, in case you didn't know. And I have the papers to prove it," Wiles said, grinding his cigarette into an ash tray.

"I'll bet they are well worn, rather ragged at the edges from being removed and replaced in your wallet, eh?" Dietrich suggested.

"How are you, Stephen?" Wiles asked.

"Just wonderful."

"You look better than I expected," Wiles said.

"You should have been here last month," Dietrich responded, his smile no longer reflecting real humor.

"I'm sorry. We worked as quickly as we could." Wiles tore a small piece of bread and washed it down with the acidic wine. He looked up at an exceedingly bright blue sky, touched only slightly by wispy clouds that appeared not to move at all.

"I know that," Dietrich said, swallowing the rice without excessive chewing.

"And I'm sorry about Meier. I know that...."

"Shut up," Dietrich snapped.

"I'm sure that he...."

"I said shut up! You're not sure of anything. Nothing." Dietrich's rib cage revolted at his effort to put force into his words.

Wiles leaned slowly back in his chair, saying nothing.

The pain remained intense for several moments but it was not all physical for Dietrich. He willed his heart to slow its pounding lest his headaches resume. Within the silence that contained the two spies were words that had to be exchanged, but Dietrich struggled to find them.

"The Pope was... was my wing man," he said at last. Then he snorted at the inadequacy of his description of a kind and generous friend. "He should never been asked to go to war. He should have been home building houses. He was a mason. Well, he will never build another wall, will he? Germany has plucked the eyes and torn the limbs from one of their very best builders. The country will need men like Meier after the war, won't it?"

There was nothing Wiles could say.

Dietrich raised his glass. "To the Pope."

"The Pope," Wiles responded.

In the ensuing minutes during which time neither man could find a voice, the waiter appeared at their table. He removed their carafe of ill-tasting wine and replaced with another. He put fresh glasses before them and poured the new wine with flair.

"Gentlemen," he said in Italian, "men with good souls need equal nourishment. To your good health."

Dietrich and Wiles tasted the new vino.

"Ahhh," Wiles said, raising the glass to the waiter, responding in the man's own language. "Excellent wine. Thank you very much for your kindness."

After he had retreated Wiles and Dietrich exchanged wondering looks. "It must have been the pope," Wiles said in almost a whisper. "We toasted the pope."

"Sometimes I wish I was not a skeptic," Dietrich said. "At least God can get you a drink. I didn't know that." He relished the smooth, fruity, fully delightful quality of a superb vino.

"Tell me about Archie," Wiles said.

"I don't see much of him," Dietrich said, somewhat evasively.

Wiles waited.

"It would be an understatement to say that he is under stress," the Luftwaffe pilot said.

"I daresay," Wiles responded, quietly, waiting patiently for Dietrich to continue.

"He's sick, you know," Dietrich said.

"No, I didn't know," Wiles said, leaning forward. "What is it?"

"Parkinson's disease. His hand shakes. Getting worse all the time. And other symptoms, I suppose. He's beginning to drag his right leg a little. At least I noticed it. It's a fatal disease."

"Yes, I suppose that I had heard that. How is he dealing with it?"

"He doesn't appear in public anymore. No speeches. The disease effects his vocal cords. Hard to think of Hitler losing his voice," Dietrich smiled sardonically.

"I'm very sorry to hear it. Will he be able to...." Wiles began.

"Win the war for us? Oh, I think so," Dietrich said, bitterly.

"That isn't what I was going to say."

Dietrich leaned slowly back in his chair, closing his eyes, visualizing the thespian from London who once scratched for a living on the boards of any theater that would have him.

"He's into the role," Dietrich said at last. "It isn't easy, for him."

"I know."

"No, you don't."

"Sorry."

"It's killing him. Even without the Parkinson's, it's killing him. He's... losing his grip. He's beginning to think he's responsible for *his* men dying for the greater glory of the Reich. Imagine ordering tens of thousands of men into battle knowing that they'll die. In the role he's playing they are his boys. Some of them are richly deserving Nazis, but others are...."

They walked near the Colosseum between the Caelian and Esquiline hills on top of what used to be the Stagnum Neronis, a lake in Nero's Domus Aurea. The sun was low in the sky. There were no other persons within shouting distance as they strolled in the still warm winter's sun.

"I won't see you again until this is all over, Stephen," Wiles said. "Too dangerous for both of us. And there is only one more job for you."

"You mean for Archie," Dietrich said, dryly.

"Yes, I suppose that's the whole of it. When you see him.... well, try to express the profound gratitude that the Crown... " Wiles looked away, then tried again to form the right words. "We can't give the man the medals that he deserves."

"Then how about something for his widow?" Dietrich asked, blandly.

Wiles dropped his eyes. "Of course. Tell him that, too."

"So? What is it?" Dietrich wanted to be gone, to find his soft bed in his Reich requisitioned hotel. He would deal with his guilt later, after he had slept.

"Stalingrad."

"Yes?"

"The information you sent us was incredibly accurate. We passed it on to Marshal Zhukov. But our General Staff thinks the battle could go either way. Paulus could win. Especially if he gets help. Archie has to see that he does not."

Wiles waited for a reaction from Dietrich. When there was none he continued. "What the Germans do not know is that within the next week the Russians will have brought in forty divisions of crack troops. He will have Paulus in a pocket. Stephen, we don't want Paulus out of that pocket."

"Am I to say that to Archie?" Dietrich wanted to know.

"Yes. Von Paulus is a very bright commander. He will learn what he is facing and he will want to withdraw to a stronger position. Archie can insure that von Paulus stays where he is."

"You talk as though von Paulus is all by himself out there in the snow. Maybe with his aide."

Wiles said nothing.

Dietrich could feel the tears forming in his eyes. He rubbed them quickly so that the British spy could not see that he, along with Archie, was also losing it.

31

A t 0500 hours on November 19th 10,000 Russian guns of all calibers began firing their shells into positions held by Germans, Italians, and Rumanian troops on the Don Front. Three cavalry corps and two Air Armies, the 2nd and 17th, as well as the 24th and 65th Armies, supported by the 16th Air Army attacked General von Paulus simultaneous with the advance of forty rifle divisions and three tank corps.

The Rumanian positions were crushed at once. They died or were taken prisoner or scattered into a white expanse of ice and snow, their bodies to be discovered the following summer.

By the evening of the second day of battle, Von Paulus still had not realized the strength of the Russian offensive. But the officers and men manning the trenches at the front did know.

On the 20th the Russians broke through German lines and struck toward the southwest aiming to cleave in two the XLVIII Panzer Corps and the 29th Motorized Infantry Division. Lt. General Heim from Army Group B, 22nd German Panzer Division with the 1st Rumanian Panzers in support, set forward immediately to plug the hole, facing Russian General Romanenko.

While the battle raged, Bunny Hartung and Foss moved slowly behind the soldiers, almost catching them as they fell. They searched the bodies for their Wehrpass, the basic field record for all active-duty German soldiers, and would snap in two the Erkennungsmarke, the military identification tag worn around the neck. The "dog tag" was metal and could be broken into two pieces, each piece having stamped upon it the soldier's serial number, blood type and the like. Hartung and Foss would slip the tags onto a thin wire and keep them until they could deposit them with regiment. Then they would dig holes or find shell craters, shovel the heavy black soil over the faces of their comrades and move on to the next killing ground.

Once, in the industrial area of the city, a rifle squad led by a sergeant was battling for a few meters of a deserted factory. The enemy was in the opposite end of the building shooting back with automatic weapons and grenades. Hartung and Foss had stumbled into the building in an effort to get out of wind that was blowing ice and snow sideways in temperatures that were already minus 30F. Bullets ricocheted off the concrete walls, shrapnel from hand-grenades screamed around them but Hartung and Foss were too tired to move. Instead they remained motionless, watching the battle like two spectators at an indoor tennis match.

During an inexplicable lull in the wild carnage, both sides looked back at the two grave diggers. They might have been vultures sitting atop a fence waiting for carcasses to become available. The combatants, unblinking, turned back to their work and resumed shooting, then stabbing, and finally, strangling as three German soldiers joined forces to choke the life out of a Russian soldier before smashing his skull to jelly with the butt of one of their rifles. The German sergeant, blood oozing through his field green uniform, winked at Hartung then died.

On November 22nd two massed Russian forces closed the pincers and the Soviet armies made contact on the Don. Thus, von Paulus's entire 6th Army, the IV Army Corps of the 4th Panzer Army, and the 1st Rumanian Cavalry Division were completely encircled. 250,000 soldiers, 100 tanks, 1,800 guns and 10,000 vehicles of all types were caught in the Stalingrad pocket.

Dietrich had regained much of his lost weight. He had begun taking walks around Obersalzberg, each day attempting to increase his pace and the distance that he traveled. Archie often accompanied him when the press of his duties allowed. There was, of course, the inescapable body of military staff and attaches who maintained a steady stream of urgent requirements that could only be executed by the Führer himself. Within the scenic valley nestled into the southern alps was an immense military complex carefully disguised to make it seem to be nothing more than a tranquil residential retreat. Archie by now felt quite at ease at the Berghof and among his "neighbors," the Bormann's, the Göring's, Goebbels, and others. There was also a luxurious guest house in the complex for visiting dignitaries and high ranking officers, but Archie would not hear of Dietrich keeping himself so far away. Dietrich stayed at the Berghof.

"There is no need for you to fly again, Stephen," Archie said as he spooned peanut butter onto a length of celery. "You are a full colonel, now."

Dietrich looked sharply up at Archie, clearly surprised. Archie was delighted at the Yank's reaction.

"Your new tunics will be ready before dinner tonight. Well, you deserve it! And the Knight's Cross with Swords! How about that, Colonel Dietrich?" Archie said, glowing. The award was Germany's highest.

"What for, Archie? Resisting the Gestapo?" Dietrich asked, leaning back from his cup of real coffee.

Archie's face clouded. "Führer. Please. We, ah, might be overheard," Archie said, his eyes shifting about. "That damned Bormann. He thinks he is responsible for the entire Reich. Well, I suppose he runs most of it. I haven't the time for details. The Gestapo is all his and he is welcome to it."

They were sitting easily in Archie's lavishly furnished study. While large and rich, the room was pleasantly intimate. And at the moment, totally deserted save the two of them. "Worried that Himmler might have installed listening devices?" Dietrich said.

"Don't be ridiculous," Archie said, turning back toward a tray of custard truffles. "I am in charge here, not Heinrich."

"Sorry, Führer, I forgot."

Pathetically, Dietrich realized that Archie was trying to smile while he touched his arm with his palsied hand, but his stricken facial muscles could only form a grotesque, rictus mask. Dietrich suddenly felt like a bully, a spoiled brat who was thinking only of his own skin and his own comfort.

By unspoken communication, they leaned back in their chairs. Dietrich did not feel that he could bring up the subject of Archie's disease.

"And Eva? How is she?"

For a long moment Archie looked upward at the ceiling.

"She knows," he said.

Dietrich's heart skipped a beat. But only a beat. Of course she would know. How obvious. Still, Dietrich had to ask. "She can't know everything, can she?"

"No. Not who I really am. But she knows who I am not. She knows I am not Adolf Hitler," Archie said, his voice turning to a soft whisper. The Parkinson's disease had long ago attacked his vocal cords.

"What will she do?" Dietrich asked.

Archie's gaze, unfocused, drifted to the picture window. He made no attempt to answer Dietrich's question. His eyes slowly closed and his head eased back onto the soft cushion of his chair. Dietrich was unsure whether to leave the room and let him sleep or...

There was a sharp knock on the paneled door. Archie quickly sat upright and Dietrich, somehow galvanized by the firm rap, rose to his feet.

"Come!" Archie said, his voice thick and, Dietrich thought, rather weak.

The door was opened by Wehrmacht Hauptman Engel, one of Archie's several adjutants, whom Dietrich had once seen at the Wolfschanze. The military nerve centers, of which there were several, Bad Polzin, the Western HQ at Wiesental, Bad Nauheim, also in the West, Tannenberg in the Black Forest, and Wolfschlucht II in France near Margival, in addition to the Wolfschanze on the Eastern Front, the place he spent the vast majority of his time directing the war, like their staffs, were ubiquitous.

Hauptman Engel acknowledged Dietrich with a curt nod of his head but turned immediately to Archie. "A communiqué from General von Paulus, sir," he said, handing over a red folder marked Most Urgent! and Achtung Führer. Archie opened the folder and quickly scanned its contents.

"Tell Jodl I will join him directly," Archie said to the aide who took a single step backward before turning and leaving the room.

"Bad news?" Dietrich asked.

Archie was scowling. "Bad. Very bad. Von Paulus is cut off at Stalingrad." Archie passed the message over to Dietrich.

"*Request permission to withdraw to more favorable defensive positions west of Don. It is my intention to fight my way south to join Manstein's Army Group Don.*" It was signed simply Paulus.

"It was expected, Archie," Dietrich said, softly. He noticed Archie's distasteful reaction at the use of his true given name. He was totally immersed in the identity of Adolf Hitler and all of the appellations that go along with being the supreme leader of a dictatorship. Nevertheless, Dietrich held his gaze steady.

"We are fighting on a 50 kilometer front at Stalingrad... "

"*They* are fighting, Archie," Dietrich corrected. Archie immediately flared, his face becoming even more rigid, his hands gripping the arms of his chair until the white of his knuckles shown through the skin.

"Von Paulus is fighting. And his men are fighting with him. Courageous troops! In the snow and ice! An entire army, Stephen," he snapped.

Indeed. Von Paulus's 6th Army Command included the IV, VIII, XI, LI Army Corps and the XIV Panzer Corps; the 14th, 16th, 24th Panzer Divisions; the 3rd, 29th, 60th Motorized Infantry Divisions; the 44th, 71st, 76th, 79th, 94th, 100th, 113th, 295th, 297th, 305th, 371st, 376th, 384th Infantry Divisions and the 20th Rumanian ID; the 648th Army Signal Regiment; the 2nd and 51st Mortar Regiments; the 91st Air Defense Regiment; the 243rd and 245th Assault Gun Battalions; the 45th, 225th, 294th, 336th, 501st, 652nd, 672nd, 685th, 912th, 921st, 925th Army Engineer Battalions; plus 150 independent army artillery units, construction battalions, military police battalions and others.

"Leave them where they are," Dietrich said, his voice soft, just above a whisper.

Archie drew himself up, shoulders square. "That is a decision I'll make. I do not appreciate directions from...."

"From a lowly Luftwaffe Colonel?" Dietrich smiled without mirth. "It isn't my choice, either. The order comes from London."

Archie's eyes widened. He had not thought about the SOE for days, so completely involved in "his" war in the East that the hundreds of decisions he made each day were his alone.

"London," he repeated.

"Yes. Your plans for attacking Stalingrad were sent by me to London, then they went on to the Russians. And it all came from you, Archie."

Archie's eyes became intense flares of light as they penetrated into Dietrich and through his body. "You! We talked of that in confidence! We...." Archie fell back into his chair, still clutching the urgent communiqué in his hand.

"You'll have to give the order to stand and fight, Archie," Dietrich urged, firmly. "We can't have the 6th Army escape."

There was no reaction from Archie whose eyes closed again, perhaps blocking out the incursion of reality.

"Betrayed," he whispered.

"No. You're not Adolf Hitler." Dietrich watched as Archie's right hand trembled violently as it rested upon the black uniform trousers with red piping.

A telephone upon the Führer's desk broke the silence of the room. The Führer had left strict orders that he was not to be disturbed except under the most dire circumstances.

He picked it up. "Yes?" he said, irritably.

Archie listened for several moments without speaking, then squared his shoulders. "You will wait. Von Paulus is to remain where he is until further orders. Is that clear? He is not to retreat one meter. Not one step."

Archie dropped the telephone into its cradle. He turned back toward Dietrich.

"I have murdered a half million men," he whispered.

"Archie," Dietrich began but did not finish.

"I'll have a car drive you to the airfield. Don't come back, Stephen."

CHAPTER
32

Field Marshal von Manstein's heroic effort to fight his way through the Russian encirclement to rescue von Paulus and his army was foredoomed.

Choosing his own posting, Dietrich returned to the Western Front, back to France. He did not lead squadrons in the air but occupied himself in the administration of running a jagdgeschwader from the ground as Vice-Commander of JG5 in Luftflotte 3. Most of his gruppen were equipped with the newest Me 109J models, 350 mph aircraft that were pure joy to fly, but Dietrich had little desire for shooting down Americans who were flying B-17s over Europe.

The JG commander was General Manfred Diamant, a tough, aggressive fighter pilot who was one class ahead of Dietrich's training class of 1937 and was a year older than Dietrich's 27 years.

"The bastards are dangerous, no mistake," Diamant said as he hung his flying gear and helmet on a hook in the small office they shared. "Each has ten gun positions and they cover each other. We lost four today. And that was in three gruppen. We still have the staffeln that recovered at Abbeville."

"They called," Dietrich said. "They lost two."

"That is six. Who were they?" Diamant asked.

"Jung and Bartolame."

"The Frenchman? Damn, I liked the man. Good pilot, too." Diamant placed his backsides near a coal-fired stove burning in a corner of the hut.

"You may see him again. He bailed out and Reddimayer saw his chute open over Compiègne."

"Good. Where is our brandy?"

"I drank it for breakfast."

"If you lie to me once more I will demote you to airplane flogger. Ah," Diamant said, accepting the bottle Dietrich produced from his bottom drawer.

Diamant poured two drinks and pushed one of the glasses across their desk toward Dietrich.

"To the Führer," Dietrich said, hoisting his glass.

"The Führer," Diamant said, and they drank.

"He is your friend, yes?" Diamant said, pouring two more drinks. "I mean, he likes you."

"That's right. And he doesn't like you, Diamant."

"I am a hero. He loves me," the general said.

"No. He thinks you are a swaggering imposter. He says when the war is over and Germany is triumphant he is going to get rid of all the homosexuals in the Luftwaffe. You will be on your way out, of course."

Diamant rose from his chair to put a record on their electric player. It was *Lilly Marlene*.

For long minutes the two men sipped their cognacs and listened to the words of the French chanteuse.

"We blew up five B-17s," Diamant said, apropos of nothing connected to the music.

"We should be proud," Dietrich said, knocking back another drink.

"They are your countrymen," Diamant said as he studied Dietrich's face.

Dietrich said nothing.

"Well?"

"Well what?"

"How does it make you feel?"

Dietrich thought about the American bombers and their crews, ten men to each aircraft, some living after they had been hit, some dying.

He had never been in the air during an American raid. He had been in Germany for seven years and in many ways felt more German than American, but he had also seen the Nazis at their best and he detested everything about the regime. They were lower than vermin, but that did not apply to all Germans. Not even to German soldiers. He liked Diamant. Diamant had plans to become a lawyer when the war ended. Dietrich smiled at the thought.

"What's funny, Yank?"

"You are funny, Manfred."

"Why am I funny, Dietrich?" Diamant said, feeling the liberating effects of the alcohol surging through his veins.

"Because you have a big nose. I had a nightmare last night and it was full of people with big noses. I killed a woman in Russia once. I think it was because she had a big nose."

Diamant nodded, sagely. "After the war I want to see America," he said. Then, after a long moment when Dietrich only sat in silence, Diamant said "What am I saying? I will not be alive after the war."

Dietrich followed the battle of Stalingrad, but not by German propaganda accounts. He listened to the BBC, spoke with pilots that occasionally rotated in from the east, and talked with Luftflotte Intelligence personnel. The battle began in mid-September and was continuing in January as Dietrich watched from the safety of France.

Combat Group Strack, a battalion of the 15th Panzer Division, had run into heavy Russian tanks near Barbukin. Strack Group had no anti-tank guns set up and no artillery so they ran for their lives. Half of the combat group was wiped out in the rout. Among the dead were Hauptman Mutius and Lieutenant Kirchner. When night came the remaining three tanks, two of which were Tigers, were leaderless. When Bunny Hartung came upon them they were preparing to abandon one of the tigers because it was out of fuel.

He spoke to their ranking non-commissioned officer, an unterfeldwebel. "Stay with the panzer. You will live longer."

"What's that? We are out of fuel. Go away and leave us alone," he said, turning away from Hartung.

"Your gun breeches. Are they frozen?" Hartung pressed.

"Yes. Engines too," the sergeant responded, rubbing his hands and stamping his feet against the cold.

"Over there," Hartung pointed to a wrecked personnel carrier. The tire. Pick up the pieces. Just the shreds. Hurry!"

The sergeant did not move but two of the tank crews sensed that Hartung knew something that they did not. They scrambled to the destroyed carrier and snatched up armfuls of rubber tire shreds.

"Put them under your Tigers," Hartung said to the men. Then he turned back to the unterfeldwebel. "There is an eight-ton truck full of petrol. Over there," he pointed at concrete rubble that was once a brick factory. The heavy, unceasing rumble of heavy incoming Russian artillery rounds continued to explode nearby. Each time a round exploded the feldwebel flinched.

"So what? The Ivans are there, too," he said scornfully, appraising Hartung who stood before him in rags, without insignia or rank anywhere on him.

"They are two blocks away. Put that Tiger over here," Hartung indicated to a spot near a street intersection. "Put the other one there. Leave only two men in each panzer and the rest of your men can bring the petrol from the truck to the panzers. You can do it in forty minutes."

The feldwebel licked his lips but shook his head. "No. We'll die. They are coming!"

"Yes, and they will run you down on foot. If you fight your tanks you might survive. Put your Tigers where I tell you and you have a complete fire radius. You can kill the Ivans if they come between the buildings. Move your ass. Now!"

The sergeant jerked almost physically backward at the crackling sound of knowledgeable authority in Hartung's voice. He turned reluctantly toward his nearly exhausted panzers.

"Johanne! Karl! Did you hear? Move your panzer. Over there, Johanne." The sergeant glanced over his shoulder at Hartung who nodded his approval.

"You men," Hartung said to the skeleton Tiger crews, "set fire to the tire pieces. Hurry, now! I want them burning nicely when we get back."

Hartung grabbed the arm of one crewman who seemed to be utterly confused. "What is your name?"

"Hokenbach," he said, opening his eyes somewhat. A good sign, Hartung thought.

"All right, Hokenbach, I want you to take two pieces of that rubber tire, this size," Hartung held his hands to show the dimension he wanted, "then put one on each gun breech. Just lay it on top. Got it?"

"Yes."

"Then set each one afire. Make sure you leave the hatch open on the panzer. We want the breeches hot. We don't want the tank to explode. Understand?"

"Yes, sir," Hokenbach said.

"Don't 'sir' me. Move quickly, now."

Hartung grabbed a fuel can in each hand and led the men toward the abandoned truck. There were more cans aboard the truck. On each side of the vehicle were two hundred litre tanks. Hartung spun off the fuel caps and satisfied himself that the tanks were mostly full. He directed the panzer crews who had accompanied him, seven men, to fill the five-gallon cans by opening the petcocks. They had made one complete trip from truck to tank before the Russian soldiers at the end of the rubble-strewn street caught sight of them and began to lay in automatic fire.

Hartung jumped onto the turret of one of the Tigers and indicated toward the source of Russian small arms fire. "I want you to set up on that doorway. Shoot everything around it."

He leaped off that Tiger and sprinted to the other and told the two-man skeleton crew the same thing. "Cover those windows with your thirty-four," he said, referring to the 7.92mm machine gun, without argument the finest and fastest firing weapon of its kind in any theater of war. "I want you to reflex this gun. Don't shoot the 88 unless you see their tanks. Got it?" He dropped back to the ground and ran with another empty fuel can to refill.

When he arrived at the panzers he spoke again to the feldwebel. "I estimate we have almost 800 litres. Make sure each Tiger has four hundred before you fill the StuG."

The StuG had a maximum fuel capacity of 310 liters, and it had a formidable 75mm assault gun, but it did not have any machine guns and it lacked the heavy armor of the Tigers. Nor did it compare in firepower to the Tigers that brought the incomparable 88 to the party.

The Russian tanks now began firing down the street, blowing huge holes in the few walls that were standing near Hartung's position. Their rate of fire was about 25 seconds each, and Hartung estimated that only two could get into position at a single time, leaving the other Ivans blocked out by the huge piles of rubble around which they were operating.

"All right," Hartung said to the sergeant, "they are T-34s." They were big Russian tanks, 26 tons, excellent machines, but they were early models with the short barreled gun. "They are going to lose this shoot-out. When I give you the word, you..." Hartung pointed to the loader, "pull the tank forward ten meters. Don't hesitate. I'll load and shoot. After I fire I will reload and fire at the second Ivan. We'll get them both," he added, patting the loader reassuringly on the shoulder as the man slid behind the controls of the Tiger.

"You," he said to the sergeant. "You take the other Tiger. When my Tiger pulls back you roll in right where I was and fire down the street. If there is anything left alive, you get it. All right? Now go!"

While the tank crews with full fuel cans crouched behind piles of twisted iron and broken concrete, Hartung waited for the Russian tanks each to fire. After the second tank fired, their rounds five seconds apart....

"Now!" Hartung shouted at the driver who stomped on the throttle of the Tiger sending it forward, then slammed on the stops. Hartung had the 88 loaded and only made a 6 adjustment on the turret to line up on the Russian T-34. For him he was at point-blank range, less than five hundred meters. He chose a spot just above the tracks of the Ivan and below its heavy body armor. Hartung pulled the trigger.

There was an almost simultaneous explosion on the unsuspecting Russian tank, and while it was shrouded in the smoke and debris of the 88mm armor piercing shell, Hartung traversed the turret to bring his gun to bear on the second T-34. Like its companion machine, it too had been rolling in and out from a wall of rubble. It now presented a full deflection shot. With seven seconds to work with, Hartung slammed another shell into the breech of his gun, calmly fine-adjusted the sights of the flat trajectory gun, and pulled the trigger.

There was an instant explosion at the other end of the street and, as Hartung shouted "Back!" to his driver, he saw that the second tank had remained motionless in its tracks. From the first one he could see flames shooting from its hatch and could see one of its crew tumble out, his body consumed in flames. He fell to the ground and began running aimlessly.

The feldwebel, per Hartung's instruction, had run his Tiger into the firing position and fired down the street at the second T-34, catching it just below the traverse ring and blowing the turret straight into the air.

"Stay on the machine guns!" Hartung yelled to the driver while he, Hartung, hoisted himself out of the tank. He motioned for the crews to run forward. "Quickly! The fuel! We need to get the hell out of here!"

In the midst of the heaviest fighting of December 1942, troops in the northern sector of the city, where Hartung was located, were in non-stop combat. The Russians attacked Hill 147.6 repeatedly in company strength and each time the German defending abteilung would throw them back by counterattacks that involved bayonets and face-to-face gunfire.

Heavy caliber artillery rounds failed to arrive by air and even the light gun batteries were limited to 16 rounds. Heavy guns received only two rounds. Of the promised 500 tons of daily supplies to be delivered by air, only 100 tons arrived. Artillery regiments were transformed into infantry units when they ran out of ammunition.

Hartung would find himself among engineers at night, showing them where they needed to lay their mines. Temperatures were -20F and running gunfights with alert Russian outposts was the rule of the night.

On the 29th of December Hartung was awakened in his ice hole by the sergeant whose Tiger tank Hartung had fought free.

"They want you at HQ," the man said, stomping his feet slowly, left then right, like the mummified dance of the dead every line troop had adopted.

"Me? Why?" Hartung said, hardly opening his eyes. He had slept less than an hour, he guessed.

The sergeant shrugged. "Right now, they said."

Headquarters, 15th Panzer Division, was located in the basement of a totally bombed-out building whose original function was impossible to discern. What had once been streets were now piles of debris, concrete, pieces of shattered war equipment, and frozen bodies. Nevertheless, Hartung found his way and gave his name to one of the unit sentries. He was examined by a skeptical guard. Hartung looked like a dispossessed 16th century urchin rather than a member of Germany's Third Reich military machine. But at last he was allowed to descend concrete steps that led down into a basement.

He repeated his name to a lieutenant who occupied a table in the front part of a huge basement room. Appropriately, the room appeared to have once been a meat storage area with thick doors still hanging on bent hinges that led to walk-in freezers. It was far colder now than when the building had been in operation. The lieutenant told him to wait, then walked deeper into the bowels of the building. Hartung could see, in weak light from a gasoline lamp, a group of officers gathered around still another table. One of the officers carried an arm in a sling, another's leg was splinted, confining him to a chair.

There were a number of enlisted personnel who manned radios and acted as runners as well as maintaining division records.

Hartung noticed that the lieutenant had a morsel of bread left on his "desk." It seemed to Hartung that the bread had been smeared with something resembling lard and that it was rancid. Still, Hartung was extremely hungry and the sight of the bread made him salivate.

"This way," the lieutenant said, beckoning to Hartung to follow.

Near the gathered group of high ranking officers, Hartung waited silently until there was a lull in the conversation.

"This is the man, Herr General," the lieutenant said.

The Oberstgeneral turned toward Hartung, appraising him. The other officers, two colonels and three majors, remained silent as they awaited the general's pleasure.

"What is your name and rank?" the general said, his voice very firm despite the deep black eye sockets that revealed extreme fatigue.

"Private Hartung, Bernard, sir," Hartung said.

"And your unit?" the general asked.

"One hundred Thirty-fourth Disciplinary Battalion, sir."

"Is that so? And your former unit? Which was that?" the general asked, leaning back against the map table.

"It was the XXXIV Panzergruppe, sir. I was its commander."

"Of course!," a colonel said, his face beginning to glow in the dark. "You are the Bunny!"

The colonel turned toward the general. "General von Klossen, this is the Sturmbannfuhrer who turned his guns on the Einsatzgruppen in Group Center!"

"Jesus Christ," the general said, his eyeballs rolling heavenward. "We heard that you had been shot."

"That was my sentence, sir, but they changed their minds."

"Damned idiots in Berlin," the general said, throwing up his hands. "They have nothing better to do than kill off our own officers because the Russians have missed some of us!" The general shoved his hands into his uniform pockets and paced the room.

Then he turned back toward Hartung. "Sit down, for God's sake, Major. Are you hungry? Fessler!" he shouted at the lieutenant near the door. "Get the Sturmbannfuhrer something to eat. And make it hot."

The general then turned toward one of the corporals in the room. "Hauser," he said, "find Major Hartung a clean uniform. Make sure it has the proper rank insignia. And he'll need a panzer beret."

"Yes, sir, general," the corporal said and hurried toward the main entrance door.

The heavy thump of enemy artillery rounds landed with such frequency that the incoming was completely ignored.

"He will have no trouble finding the correct uniform. He will strip it off a body, you see," General von Klossen said, sardonically. "I am Oberstgeneral Erik von Klossen... sit down, Hartung, sit down... commander of this division. I will notify General von Paulus that we have rescued a qualified officer from our own army! Eh? How is that for total insanity?" the general waved his hand vaguely in the air.

"Well, then, Hartung, we heard about your action with the Tiger tanks four days ago. We have been looking for you since then. To say that we are desperately short of panzer officers is an understatement. Now you are working for me and I have a plan. Step over here."

Hartung joined General Klossen at the map table.

"See here?" the general placed a finger on the map. "Field Marshal Von Manstein is here with Army Group Don. He is attempting to fight his way to us. He has the LVII Panzer Corps and the 23rd Panzer Division to attack in the northeast. Now, Hartung, we have assembled our surviving tanks, twelve of them. They have full fuel but there are no reserves. Do you understand? And ammunition. There are approximately fifty rounds for each gun." The general paused, glancing sideways and giving Hartung a chance to interject a question.

Hartung said nothing.

"I propose to send this force out with grenadiers to open a wedge, here, five kilometers south of von Manstein. Behind this spearhead I will bring my forces, fighting Ivan here and here," Klossen pointed at either side of his proposed wedge. "If we succeed we have a road out for Paulus's 6th Army. You see what it is needed, Hartung. Tell me what you think."

Hartung studied the map. The picture before him was a clutter of marks indicating opposing forces broken down into types of major units. It was difficult to read because the marks were moved as units moved into and out of the line. This was especially true of the Russian side simply because they had a great number of units coming in while the Germans had few coming in and none going out. But Hartung could easily see that the Russians were closing a pincer around the Hungarian units that defended the southeast salient.

Hartung shrugged as he leaned closer to the map. "I agree, General. It has a chance."

Oberstgeneral von Klossen waited, sensing that Hartung was still considering the proposed engagement. He did not have long to wait.

"I have one small suggestion, sir, if you don't mind?" Hartung said, looking up at the general who was even taller than Hartung.

"Yes?" the general snapped as his staff moved slightly closer to Hartung's finger as he referred again to the map.

"I would not fight for this road. Let the Ivans have it. It is winter now, General, and it does not matter what is a paved road or a frozen lake. Our panzers will roll over either. I would also bet that the Ivans have zeroed in their heavy guns over this area, and here, and here. They would have one-seven-fives and Stalin organs, no question about it."

"We considered that they would," the general said, "but it also means that you have fewer Russians to fight going down that corridor. They don't want to be any closer to their own artillery than we do."

"That's true, General, but we would lose half our panzers before we reached the gates of the city. If we go here, we face their tanks and their infantry, but if we can punch the first hole, there is nothing in front of us. Then your forces follow-up close on our asses."

Von Klossen looked at the map for a long moment, then leaned over for an even closer look.

"You don't know what Ivan has there. They have had time to dig in their tanks," one of his staff officers observed.

Hartung did not reply.

His food arrived, steam wafting up from a bowl of what was referred to as lentil soup but which was little more than boiled grass and lichens. But there was a bit of bread and it was flavored with a gritty lard. Hartung was grateful for the nourishment and said so.

Hartung's unit was formed into the 10th Panzer Regiment. On the afternoon of January 1st, he gathered his tank commanders, some of them no more than corporals, his non-commissioned officers and his single officer, Untersturmfuhrer Ruh. Hartung's quick appraisal of Ruh was that he had either contracted an illness or that combat had given him a permanent case of the shakes. He would have liked to leave the man behind but he had not a single position to spare.

"We are going to sleep all day today and all night. Then at 0100 we warm up our panzers." The men knew that Hartung was speaking about lighting fires under the bellies of their tanks so that the engines could turn over. Once the engines were started they would run continuously until the panzer was destroyed by enemy gunfire or it ran out of gas. "Gun breeches, too. 0200 we move out. Keep your formations. Lead tanks remember that when you get down to five rounds for your main guns, you drop back to your partner's flank, then he does the shooting. Save the 88s for enemy armor. We'll use the machine guns on troops.

"You grenadiers," he said to the ground troop leaders who would be traveling with the tanks in armored personnel carriers, "if you lose a vehicle and cannot get to another, try to board one of the Tigers. Your only other choice is to dig in and wait for the main force to arrive. They will be approximately six hours behind us. Any questions?"

There were several, including the need for intelligence information on Russian troop strengths, possible fuel dumps, aircraft support. Hartung's answers were almost uniformly in the negative. No intelligence available, no fuel for the vehicles, no planes. "We have twelve kilometers of hard fighting. We have the best chance of success at night because they don't expect us and if they can't see us they can't hit us. All right, men, get some rest."

"Ruh," Hartung said, "stay a minute."

Hartung saw the Untersturmfuhrer's lips move but heard no sound. "Are you ill, Ruh?"

Untersturmfuhrer Ruh nodded his head, then shook it vigorously. "No, Sturmbannfuhrer."

"You are shaking like a leaf. Why?" Hartung demanded.

It was difficult for Ruh to speak, even though he struggled. "It is nothing, sir."

"You are frightened, eh?" Hartung asked in the form of a statement.

Untersturmfuhrer Ruh bowed his head, then began to sob. "I tried. Quite hard, sir. But this... this...."

"The dead bodies, yes? Men and women blown apart. Frozen. Children, too. And you think that you are next. Today, tonight, or tomorrow. You will be one of them. Is that right?"

The young officer could not look Hartung in the eyes but he nodded his head.

Hartung's heart sank. "I have been fighting since October of 1940, Ruh. I joined the SS before the war because I wanted to meet girls. When the shooting started I was terrified. Scared shitless! Well, three years later nothing has changed. I am still scared shitless and I am still looking for girls."

Untersturmfuhrer Ruh controlled his flow of tears and wiped his eyes. "You, sir?"

"Yes, me sir. The only thing that stops me from deserting this filthy assignment is you. If I leave you I know that you will die sooner rather than later. And if you leave your men in your tanks, they will die. We will probably both be killed, Ruh, but we can't leave our comrades. Can we?"

The early morning hours of January 3, 1943, Hartung's regiment started its engines. Grenadiers were ready. More than half of the men carried automatic assault rifles, and many carried the Russian made PPSh-41, a sub-machine gun fed by a 71 round drum magazine. It could fire 900 rounds per minute. Almost every Russian soldier along the entire front lines carried either this weapon or the PPD-40. The piece had been in continuous manufacture since 1938 and German troops, following a battle, would pick the weapons and ammunition from fallen enemy. Hartung insisted that his regiment, planning on a fast-hitting assault through the lines, be equipped with rapid firing guns. The bolt-action Mausers, issued to German soldiers, were slightly better than useless when firing on the run.

At 0200 Hartung gave the order to move forward. His panzers were sent out in four elements of three. Each element had a lead panzer, then one tank slightly to the rear and on either side. The lead panzer had the responsibility of finding and destroying enemy armor and anti-tank gun emplacements while the trailing panzers would suppress fire aimed at their element. Hartung put Untersturmfuhrer Ruh in command of the second two flights while he led from the front tank.

They hit the enemy lines within the first two hundred meters. Three Russian tanks, two light T-60s of the six ton class, and a 9.2 ton T-70, opened fire from Hartung's right oblique. He picked out the T-70 first, leaving the T-60s to his flank panzer since the 20mm main gun on the T-60s could not knock him out.

"Fire!" he commanded.

The 88 gun in his Tiger spit flame and smoke sideways from its flash deflector and the T-70 exploded, its turret hatch thrown thirty feet straight up when the armor-piercing round set off its ammunition.

"Echborg," Hartung calmly spoke into his inter-tank com microphone, "your ten o'clock, a big gun."

His left flank panzer was already tracking onto the target. Within seconds the second panzer gunner pulled the trigger and a 155mm Russian gun blew apart into small pieces of steel.

Hartung's machine gunners in the APCs were working selectively on enclaves of Russians fighting from behind collapsed walls and street debris. Return fire was robust but not withering. The element of surprise was working for the Germans. Within the first hour the 10th Panzer Regiment had covered a distance of one kilometer. Hartung had lost two Tigers, one in the second element and one in the last tank of the fourth element. Their infantry, the grenadiers, had lost eighteen dead and twenty-seven wounded. The 10th Panzer Regiment had only one medic, a Feldwebel, but they had scrounged a good supply of bandages and some morphine.

With the coming of dawn Hartung's regiment found itself exposed to entrenched Russian positions along the levee of the Aksai. Hartung's battle plan did not include a set-piece where he slugged it out in an exchange of gunfire with Russian forces, almost all of which would ultimately turn out to be superior in number and firepower. However, the way out of the depression in which his panzers had arrived was through a Russian defilade that protected a number of heavy guns and dug-in T-28 tanks. The enemy tanks mounted 76.2mm howitzers and, if left unchallenged, could decimate Hartung's Tigers as his formation attempted to fight his way up the river banks. He needed to gain the high ground to complete his breakout. Even as he considered his next move, a Russian big gun had managed to train in on his second element and, within the span of two minutes, blow the tracks off the element's lead panzer and score direct hits on two of the APCs, killing everyone inside.

Hartung got his own Tiger traversed onto the artillery piece and fired. His shell struck the revetment in which the gun had been dug, exploding before it reached the field piece. Though he had only three rounds left in his main gun, he fired again. This time the shell struck its target sending pieces of wheels, carriage, and personnel into the air. There was no time to exude satisfaction because now the other dug-in T-28s were turning toward him.

"Jacob," Hartung said to his port-side flanker tank, "I'm coming aboard. I'll take the lead."

Sergeant Jacob Schwitzen immediately crawled out of the lower hatch of his tank while Hartung did the same in his. The two men touched hands briefly as they crossed between their respective tanks. Inside the second Tiger, Hartung plugged in the leads of his command radio to speak to the rest of the formation.

"Give me smoke," he said to the gunners. "Put down all that you can." He knew exactly that his cause was an empty one. The smoke would work to obscure the tanks for a few minutes, but sooner rather than later they would all have to emerge from the top of the smoke onto the high ground where they would be easy targets for any well trained gun crew. And all of the Russian crews could shoot.

Within a few minutes the battlefield was shrouded in smoke and Hartung, after talking silently with his reluctant self, decided that it was now or never. There were only two directions to go, forward or back. If they went forward some of his regiment would likely get through to Manstein's forces. To go back meant certain death, probably slower and more painful.

"All crews! We're going forward! Do not stop for anything. Not for wounded, not for anything. Infantry," he said to his foot soldiers keeping pace behind the rumbling Tigers, "stay close to us. With luck we will break out within one thousand meters." His voice came across with an assurance that he did not possess. One thousand meters was nothing more than an estimate for slugging through the Russian lines, but he also knew that if it was more than that they would be dead, anyway. Ready! Attack!"

Panzer crews slammed their Tigers into a higher gear and turned their savage beasts toward Hartung's lead. Their fire remained disciplined and their gunnery was very good, Hartung was pleased to see. As the battle escalated his Tiger received non-stop hits against its heavy armor plating, creating an insane cacophony of ear-splitting clanging, ringing and shock. He was calmly picking out particular threats for his gunner or warning his driver of likely mines. He tried to keep track of his soldiers but visibility was limited inside the huge tank. He noted that his fuel was below half but, even more critical, his guns could only fire for another two hours at the outside, then the 88 shells would be exhausted. It would mean that they would then be chewed up, piecemeal.

By the time the sun was fully up behind them, Hartung could see beyond the revetments of Russian medium tanks. There were two columns headed toward them. Trucks? If so, were they German or Russian? He moved his eyes from the periscope of the Tiger, aggravating because it constantly shook, in order to use his own powerful binoculars by raising the hatch of his Tiger. As he flung back the lid, Hartung quickly focused his field glasses on the distant columns, now closing with substantial speed. Yes, he could now see them quite clearly.

His heart fell. They were not trucks but tanks. And they were not German but Russian. It would all be over very soon.

He dropped back into his tank and secured the steel hatch. A rapid 360 search with his periscope revealed to Hartung that his own panzers had been hit hard. He could no longer see Ruh's tank and estimated that no less than half of their forces were gone, including infantrymen. His element had four of its panzers still fighting and perhaps half of its infantry.

"Elements Three and Four," he said into his radio, "form up on me. Enemy tanks dead ahead. Hold your fire until four hundred meters."

He estimated that the 10th Panzer Regiment had less than twenty minutes of life remaining. He hoped he would die from explosion, not burn. And he hoped he would die like a man, not crying out for his mother.

Then it happened. He heard the high-pitched shriek, almost like a siren. Indeed, it was a siren and it was mounted on all Ju-87 dive bombers. The sirens were designed to inspire terror of those on the ground, to freeze them in place while the deadly accurate steel explosives rained down from above. The increasingly shrill sirens changed their Doppler pitch as their pilots pulled out of near-vertical descents, then came the terrific explosions. The most effective tank-killers in the world were doing what they did best, destroying the line of Ivan tanks that were advancing toward Hartung's 10th Panzer Regiment.

"Yes! Yes!" he said as he flung open the hatch once more to take in the fullest possible view of Russian T-34s literally exploding in their tracks. The skies had turned from dull gray overcast to broken blue, the half-moon easily seen in the middle of what was now a cobalt day. "Forward, boys," Hartung urged his crews and ground forces as they fired, reloaded, and fired on the move.

The 10th Panzer Regiment rolled passed burning, smoking hulks of the broken Russian tank brigade, three dozen of them, while the grenadiers leaped aboard the backs of the Tigers and fired at Russian forces who bravely stuck their heads out from cover. They fought all day and by 1000 hours that night Hartung's exhausted force had smashed through elements of the 51st Soviet Army to reach advanced units of von Manstein's Army Group Don near Kuban.

While the 10th Panzer Regiment tankers slept in their vehicles, Hartung reported to General of Infantry Zeitzler's deputy chief of staff, General Lothar Kreiger.

"General von Klossen is fighting behind us with his force, sir. If he maintains his schedule, he is six hours to our rear," Hartung said, swaying on his feet, hardly able to stand from thirty-three hours without sleep.

"Sit down, Major," General Kreiger said, motioning to an aide to bring the Waffen SS-Major a drink of whiskey. "General von Klossen is not behind you."

"Sir? He was very firm about his plans. Even as we were starting to...."

"General Klossen has been ordered to prepare for the next counter-attack on Stalingrad. General Paulus, now Field Marshal von Paulus, has been ordered to stand and fight."

Hartung was confused. He drank the whiskey at his elbow and did not resist when a second glass was poured for him. The effect of the alcohol in his system was almost immediate. Had it been otherwise he might not have spoken as he did.

"With respect, Herr General, there is nothing left to fight with at Stalingrad. Nothing."

"Nevertheless...."

"No food. No ammunition. No fuel, sir. To attack or to defend one must at least have ammunition for the guns. There must be a mistake," he said, his head starting to swim as he gulped the second whiskey.

"You are to be commended for your heroic action, Major. I will approve a citation for an award. Now get some sleep. Hauptman Gherig will find food for you and your men. You have four Tigers left? Good, we can use them."

"As far as we know," Archie droned on to an increasingly stupefied audience of high ranking dinner guests who had foregone the pleasure of liquor and cigarettes to listen to the Führer's rambling discourse at the Berghof, "the food of the soldiers of ancient Rome consisted principally of fruit and cereals. The Roman soldier had a horror of meat, and meat, apparently, was included in the normal rations only when the difficulty of obtaining other supplies made it inevitable."

Archie had become a committed vegetarian since falling from the belly of a bomber almost three years ago. He had begun reading books on the subject and could now see the sense of eschewing the flesh of animals.

"From numerous pictures and sculptures it seems that the Romans had magnificent teeth, and this seems to contradict the contention that only carnivores and animals have good teeth. The intervening centuries do not appear to have caused any changes. Travelers in Italy have noticed that the masses still feed on the same things, and that they still have excellent teeth."

Archie, rather sleepy himself given the lateness of the hour, seemed not to have noticed the drooping eyes of his guests. Eva had quietly left the room to smoke cigarettes in her apartment. She thought Archie never noticed but of course he always knew where she was and what she was doing. Her breath as well as her clothing reeked with the pungent smell of burnt tobacco. He would not hesitate to voice his displeasure with her dirty habit but she laughed and cajoled her way out of trouble with him. After all, what could he do?

"One has only to keep one's eyes open to notice what an extraordinary antipathy young children have to meat. It is also an interesting fact that among the Negroes the children of those tribes which are primarily vegetarian develop more harmoniously than those of the tribes in which it is customary for the mother to feed her infant up to the age of four or five. The dog, which is carnivorous, cannot compare in performance with the horse, which is vegetarian...."

Russian loud speakers poured out entreaties for the German soldiers to surrender. They would receive food and warm clothing, the loud speakers repeated all day and all night. They would be treated well and would be provided shelter. Huddled in burnt rubble or dug into ice-encrusted holes in the ground, German soldiers endured sub-zero temperatures, and if their brains were operating at all, the notion of relief from cold and hunger must have been overpowering. But, because Field Marshal von Paulus had been ordered by the Führer, and because his orders had been passed on to more junior officers, and on to the men, they stood in their fighting positions. Many froze to death in macabre poses of sighting along the barrels of their rifles, or with both hands around a grenade, the pin still frozen in place. Ammunition was in such short supply that heavy artillery units were authorized to fire only a single shell every other day.

There were no dogs, no cats, no mules, no animals of any kind to be seen among the rubble of the city because all of them had been killed and eaten. Along the defensive line of the Don frozen corpses were piled one atop the other to provide barricades from enemy fire.

With intelligence information supplied to them by SOE in London, Marshal Zhukov and General Vasilevsky were able to devise a plan called Operation Uranus. Zhukov knew where the Germans' weakest lines would be and he placed 14,000 heavy guns, 979 tanks, 1,350 aircraft and almost one million men in a pincer movement that had encircled Paulus's 6th Army thus guaranteeing the end of the German threat to the Caucasus oil fields and Russia's southern flank.

In the ensuing battle the Germans lost 156,000 dead and wounded, 35,000 missing, 95,000 taken prisoner including twenty-four German generals, including newly promoted Field Marshal von Paulus.

Immediately following the battle of Stalingrad, almost as a continuation of that same conflicted area, Archie launched Operation Citadel, the battle of Kursk, which would be remembered as the largest engagement of armor in the history of warfare. Involved were 7,000 tanks and self-propelled guns. In some places there was one tank for every 10 meters or, in the northern part of the 100 mile salient, the concentration was one for every 30 meters.

In the house at Semley Place Edward Wiles closed the door to Sir William's office behind him. He removed his new reading glasses he had recently been forced to use, a consequence, he thought, of too many nights with too little sleep while pouring over mountains of paperwork.

"Have you seen this latest signal?" he asked Sir William. "The one from Dietrich?"

"I thought the man was off the air. He hasn't been talking to Archie, has he?"

"No, but he still has access to Canaris's Abwehr reports. The two of them are quite friendly, now." Wiles referred to the paper he held in his hand while he plopped himself onto a comfortable sofa. "The build-up of tanks in Kursk. The Germans lost 586 tanks on the first day."

"Good God!" the older spy said, turning more fully toward Wiles.

"Seems that Marshall Zhukov has used our information to his best advantage. Incredible, isn't it? I mean that the OKH would allow it?"

"On the contrary, Edward. When you stop to think about it, the German General Staff was getting the best possible military advice available. I'm speaking of the orders coming from London, of course." Schuyler smiled, smugly.

"I beg your pardon, Sir William, but unless you sent those orders to Archie yourself, I can assure you that he was acting on his own."

Sir William sat up straight in his chair, reaching awkwardly for a teapot that was empty. "What's that? He what? You mean neither you nor MacLean....?"

Edward Wiles slowly shook his head. "No, we did not. Nor is there any way to contact Archie. And that poses another problem. We must consider how we are going to get him out."

"The Prime Minister has already considered that issue."

"Is that so?" Wiles' eyebrows arched in surprise. "Well, then, I can't wait to be enlightened. It's refreshing to think that if something goes wrong with the operation he has no one to blame but himself."

"My very thought."

CHAPTER

33

F ollowing the massive losses at Stalingrad and the battle of
Kursk, the war in the East was nothing more than a series of
German retreats under the onslaught of more than 400 Russian
divisions. For the year 1942 alone Germany had fed 1.9 million men
into the insatiable maw of the Russian killing machine. Tens of
thousands more would be swallowed up in the early months of 1943.
It was a tribute to the thorough training and discipline of the German
soldier, especially the officer and non-commissioned officer corps,
that the retreat from deep inside Russia was not turned into a total
route. German units fought bravely in what was inevitably a losing
cause.

Archie, suffering from unimaginable stress that would unhinge
even the strongest mind, quietly cut himself off from all but the most
necessary contact with his generals. He withdrew to Berlin where,
with the exception of air raids, the war was far less personal. Aides
knew that bad news was not welcome at the Reichschancellery so
that the Führer was able to dwell on positive accounts, such as individual heroism, rather than the daily defeats that befell the Germans
throughout North Africa, Italy and the entire European continent.

During late 1943 and early 1944 German intelligence sources and
aerial reconnaissance reported massive build-ups of ships, troops and

supplies around the coastal sections of the British isle. That an invasion of Festung Europa was coming was obvious, but the questions of where and when were completely unknown quantities. The entire coastline from France to the Low Countries was reinforced with heavy guns, troop assignments, and beach traps to repel the invader as he landed. Every German officer and most others knew that these measures, too, were nothing more than delaying tactics and that the Allied armies would sooner or later overwhelm the thinly scattered German forces. When the Allies landed in France on the 6th of June, 1944, German continental forces had been seriously depleted in order to continue the never-ending demands of the eastern front.

The situation in the west was summed up on July 15th by a teletype sent to Archie from Field Marshal Rommel, then commanding an army group in Normandy, when he said there "was no possibility for victory in the west" and that soldiers were "dying needlessly by the thousands every day." He strongly urged his Führer to "draw the conclusions from this situation" without delay.

On one of the increasingly infrequent visits to the Eastern front in July, Archie was going through the motions of directing his armies in the east, when a bomb exploded practically under his feet in one of his map rooms. It was a British built explosive device, placed there by Colonel Claus Graf von Stauffenberg. There were a number of plotters in on the assassination cabal, investigations would disclose, including Admiral Wilhelm Canaris, chief of Abwehr.

The Gestapo, running amok, assisted by elements of the SS and others, arrested and executed approximately 5,000 military officers, including Field Marshal Rommel, General Kluge and many others of high rank. Civilians, too, were roped into the bloodbath.

Archie had never come so close to death before and for the first time since he had arrived in Germany he was frightened to the very core of his soul. The shaking of his hand was now so pronounced that there was no way it could be hidden, as was the extreme hesitation in his dragging left side. He was even more fearful of discovery by the Nazis and now, added to his paranoia, was the obvious fact that powerful elements within the Reich who opposed National Socialism were in a position to assassinate him.

He dearly needed Dietrich.

In the middle of the night he picked up his private telephone near his bed in the Reichschancellery bunker. He informed his aide that he wanted Luftwaffe Colonel Stephen Dietrich located at once and brought to him in Berlin.

Hauptman Schaub reported back within thirty minutes that Colonel Dietrich had been shot down on June 8th while conducting a special reconnaissance sortie over the English coast. He was missing and presumed dead.

Archie knew better.

Two great armies, one from the west and one from the east, were now racing across Europe toward Berlin, and he was in the middle.

If he should fall into the hands of the Russians he would never live out the day. There were already rumors afloat about suicides among the Nazi hierarchy. As the leader of them all, he would be expected to put a bullet through his own brain, a prospect that he relished not at all.

It was later said that the Battle of the Bulge was the most stunning and the most confused battle fought on the Western Front in World War II. Archie had approved the idea of a massive German counterattack hatched by junior OKW staff officers and opposed by his senior generals which, if successful, would have split the Allied armies in half near the French town of Bastogne. The battle began on December 16, 1944, and before the Allies regained the offensive upper hand, lasted thirty full days. Germany's defeated troops, including 120,000 dead, virtually ceased to offer substantial resistance, with certain isolated exceptions, after January 17, 1945 as the western juggernaut rolled toward Berlin.

By March 23 the important industries along the Saar had been captured and in April the great Rhur industrial area was captured by Eisenhower's armies along with an entire German army group of 400,000, mostly underage boys and old men. Archie had done his work well. On April 16, strategic bombing of Germany was ended because so few targets remained.

Because of Allied political agreements the Soviet army was allowed to enter Berlin first.

It was said that Berlin was the perfect place for a fight, if such a site can be said to exist, because it was large, modern and well-planned, and despite the fact that it had been thoroughly bombed it had been so well built that the city's essential services remained largely intact. The telephone system still worked when the Russians began their assault, water continued to run. Large apartment buildings stood on strong foundations, there were deep cellars and wide street systems that gave cover to a defending army and provided them with killing zones to be used against Russian tanks and infantry. The heart of the city lay in a "V" sided by the Spree River and the Landwehr Canal.

Archie appointed General Karl Weidling to lead the LVI Panzer Corps in the defense of the city. Weidling's army, however, consisted of only two divisions, the recently formed Muncheberg Division and the 20th SS Panzer Division, the strength of which had been reduced dramatically following the battle at Kustrin. That corps was eventually augmented with two more divisions but with only sixty tanks. The Russians took a total of 12 days to capture the city but used more than 1 million men in the attack directed by the now famous Russian Field Marshal Zhukov. Berlin surrendered on May 2, 1945.

But before then Archie had figured a way out.

During the last week of March the SS formed a "Führer Battalion" headed by Lieutenant Colonel Pick to defend the Reichschancellery. SS-Sturmbannfuhrer Günsche was Combat Commandant. When the courageous but dedicated Günsche attached himself too closely to Archie, Archie calmly advised him that he did not need that much protection. Archie now openly declared the war lost and stated to the defenders and his staff that it was his intention to commit suicide. There were a few, a very few, who believed this was the only reasonable way to end their participation in the Third Reich, among them was Joseph Goebbels who spoke not only for himself but for his wife and children.

On April 30, deep underground with the Red Army only 500 meters away, Archie repaired to his quarters. Waiting for him was Eva Braun. Archie was shocked to see her there.

"I told you to go," he said as he entered the room.

"There is nowhere to go," she said, head tossed defiantly back despite the redness of her eyes.

"Eva, you could have gone to the south with Colonel Hauch. I ordered him to..."

"Yes, I know. He did not disobey. I told him to go without me."

"Your family is there," Archie said futilely, truly saddened, knowing that it was now too late for this young, caring girl to escape the Russians.

"My family? There is no one and nowhere for me, now," Eva said.

Archie was sure that Dr. Widmann had given her some kind of opiate. Her eyes seemed dilated and although Eva always exhibited self-possession, he thought her demeanor now to be almost transcendent. But he did not at once understand her fatalistic pronouncement, especially the "*now*" part of it. Then it occurred to him that "now" meant "*after*," after she had been Hitler's mistress. What indeed would happen to her, now? Would she be brutally raped then killed? Or would she be taken prisoner to stand trial as only the Russians could construct. At best she would go to jail. And for a long time.

"Eva," he said, taking her hands, looking at her evenly. "I have a plan."

"Then let us hear the plan, by all means," a voice came to them from the doorway.

Archie did not have to turn to see who it was.

"You have not been invited into this room, Bormann" Archie said, mustering indignity into his voice.

"I have invited myself into this room. Stand over there," he said to Eva, motioning to her with the pistol that he held in his hand. "So. It appears that no one is going to get out of this bunker alive, yes? Except for... the Englishman, here." Bormann hesitated, then looked quizzically at Archie. "What is your name? I certainly can't call you Führer anymore, can I?"

"When did you find out?" Archie asked, not in fear, but only curiosity.

"Months ago, Herr Führer," Bormann said sarcastically. "Hess got word through in 1943."

"And you did nothing?" Archie said, incredulous.

"I would hardly describe my work in the Third Reich as nothing. Have you any idea the fortune I have sent out of this country to various parts of the world? By the time I learned that you were not Adolf Hitler we had lost the war, of course, but it certainly was not too late too... "

"Standartenfurher Hebert, shoot this man," Archie said.

Bormann half-turned to see through the doorway behind him. There, in battle dress and accompanied by other members of his SS-Kommando, was the Commander, RSD. Standartenfurher Hebert turned his automatic weapon toward Bormann.

"Hebert, this man is not the Führer... "

Hebert pulled the trigger, emptying a half magazine into the corpulent Reich Secretary. Bormann fell to the floor, blood flowing freely from his mortal wounds.

"Filthy traitor," Archie spat. "Once again, Hebert, you are a hero of the Reich. There is one more thing for you to do, comrade."

"You have only to order, Führer," the dedicated Nazi said through steely eyes.

"Take Miss Braun to a safe place. Do not let the Russians put their hands on her. Now, I want to be alone. See to it, please."

Hebert gave his last Hitler salute before carrying out his task.

His shaking hand made the task more difficult than it otherwise would, but Archie soaped up his face and began shaving off his moustache. Suffering nothing more painful in the process than a slight cut on his upper lip, he then turned his attention to his hair. It was a simple thing to rinse his hair with a peroxide solution, then wait a few minutes before repeating the process. He knew that as it dried his hair would be blond. He might even look younger as a result he thought as he combed it back. Lastly, he went to one of his closets and removed a small trunk upon which was a lock under seal, never touched by the cleaning staff who tended his bunker quarters.

Unable to find the key in his pocket or in any of the drawers, he simply removed his 9mm pistol from a uniform holster and blasted the lock away. He reached inside the trunk and withdrew a khaki uniform. It was the complete outfit of a British army sergeant. Moving with some difficulty because of the stiffness of his right leg, he nevertheless managed to pull on the trousers, boots, and blouse, complete with three chevrons on one sleeve. He smiled to himself knowing full well that he would never have qualified for such an exalted rank in the real British army. It was now, according to his watch, 0300 hours.

He poured himself a full measure of brandy, a treat he had put off for far too long, and downed it in a single gulp. He turned out the lights behind him and exited the Reichschancellery through a secret door.

The End

L averne!"

Laverne Smythes heard her name called over the noise of the Hoxton shipyards. She had moved up from the sometimes tedious job of riveting to welding, a considerable raise in skill level and, with it, a substantial increase in pay. After attending night classes as well as on the job training, she had become a certified marine welder, capable of using the widest possible array of welding materials from Inconel to stainless steels to aluminum. She flipped up her protective mask to respond to the voice at her side of her shift foreman, Ronald Dilfer.

"Bloke here to see you, old girl," Dilfer said.

Laverne was not expecting a visitor and, even if she were, non-war effort business was strictly frowned upon during shift hours. So Laverne cocked an eyebrow.

"Says his name is Smythes," Dilfer said to the unasked question. The foreman jerked his thumb in the direction of the lunch room.

As she entered the large locker-lunch room, stifling hot in mid-July despite banks of open windows, her eyes conveyed an image that her brain simply refused to believe. She moved closer to the middle-aged man who rose as she entered the room.

"Hello, Laverne," the man said, somewhat self-consciously.

"Archie? My god, is that you?" Laverne said, almost staggering back against a wall.

"Like the bad penny, eh?" he said, attempting a smile but knowing that his facial muscles would move only slightly. He held his left hand over his right to still the shaking.

Laverne could not make her legs carry her to him but instead she sat on the edge of a table bench, hand over her mouth, taking in his image.

"I thought you were dead," she said. "And a uniform?"

"Oh, well, it isn't much for five years, is it?" He had been outfitted with a fresh uniform by the army despite his "loss" of official papers and organization. The battle of Berlin had been an incredibly confusing affair, as wars typically are, and it took him five weeks to get himself aboard a ship crossing the channel back to blimey. "I went to the old place," he said. "Wasn't there anymore, of course. Bombed, as you know. How have you been? You look... well, I think you look a knocker."

"I do? Oh, yes, well, I'm getting lots of exercise and eating better these days, Archie. Looks as though you..." She hesitated. Archie did not look well at all. She did not immediately recognize the symptoms of Parkinson's disease but she knew a sick man when she saw one. "Was it very rough, Arch? Were you wounded? Where did you go when you left.... God, it was 1940! Oh, Archie, I thought you had deserted us."

Laverne broke into tears, her head dropping to her chest, hands over her eyes as though she could stem the flood of water from them. Archie moved slowly to her. He put his arms around her shoulders tentatively at first, then firming his embrace.

"Jesus, what I've put you through. I'm such a rotter," he said, not referring to the last five years, but to the whole of his adult life. He had patronized himself first and his family last. That she no longer needed him was quite clear because he had never been there for her when she did.

She touched his arms, gently pulling away from him. "I feel such a wicked woman. I... I have a man in my life," she said, her eyes falling again.

Of course she would. How could he have thought otherwise? He had never seen her look better. There was color in her face, her hair was lush and tended, and her figure was quite firm and curvaceous for a woman in her mid-40s.

"Only what you deserve, Laverne. I had my shot, didn't I?" he said, gently and truly. "I'm happy for you."

His blessing made her sob once again. He thought she might be crying now partly from relief.

"Are you happy with the chap? You needn't tell me his name, you know."

"His name is Harry Keefe. He's a fine man. He works here, in the yard. Archie, I'm not going to leave Harry. You might as well know that... "

"Of course you won't leave him. You've waited longer than what was right. I'll not interfere. Give us a bit of time and I'll do it all quite legal."

He saw a flicker of light in her eyes and a wisp of smile on her mouth.

"What about you, Archie? Where did you go? What did you do? Was it North Africa? I never thought about you as the military type. And your age! How could they have taken a fifty year old man... ?"

"I volunteered."

"To do what?"

"It's a very long story. Where is Rose?"

"She is in the country, living with a family in Burton Heath. They sent the children to the country, a lot of them, during the blitz. She is still there." Laverne hesitated again, as though she was embarrassed, but then continued. "She is in no hurry to come back, Archie. She has few good memories of London. And the family there wants her to stay."

It was almost daylight by the time Rose Marie Hawkins had finished her story.

"It's nonsense, of course," she said to August Street. "He told the whole story many times over during the years after the war. My mother loved my father in her way but I never did. He was the one responsible for us living such a desperate life, you see, and I never forgave him for that, even in absentia." Rose offered a wan smile.

"And what did you think?" I said. "About Archie? Did he regain his health?"

"He seemed the same old Archie. He lived a life of fantasy on the stage. His problem, I think, was that he could never distinguish between acting and reality. My mother told me before she died that she might have gone back to my father until he told her the story I just told you. He was ill, she felt sorry for him, she felt guilty, as well. But even if she loved him he had not changed and she could not go back to the life that would surely have been more of the same badness."

Rose yawned. She made no attempt to stifle the involuntary reaction to fatigue and, sympathetically, I yawned myself. We both smiled.

"Sorry for keeping you up this long. But when did he pass away? And where was he when he died? In a veteran's hospital?"

Rose looked surprised. "I never thought to ask. No, he had no right to veteran's care. How could he? I have no idea what he did during the war, Mr. Street, because I think he believed his own story. But we can safely assume he did not serve in the military."

I tried to reach Jean Scheerer twice more before I left London to return to the H.P. Carlisle Foundation in Virginia. It was no use. Wherever he was he was keeping to himself.

I found myself one of the secluded office spaces in a sub-basement at the Foundation and went to work on the small mountain of notes that I had recorded from Rose's narration as well as questions that I had scribbled on a pad in my unique scratching motions. After putting it all on a disc and printing it out, there were more questions in my mind than answers. To find those answers I availed myself of the extensive library and archival research systems available to the Foundation which included access to the U.S. Department of Defense WWII archives. Some of those records, most, in fact, were committed to paper, much was on film, and a precious small amount was on computer disc. It seems that there is little value in transcribing paper to electronics about a war that has been over for more than a half century.

I ached to get back to the west coast and my very rusty golf game, especially since I was convinced I had wasted several months out of my life on a project that was a fool's errand. As far as I could tell I had discharged my assignment by cooperating with the British government and their Official Secrets declassification project. But I was not sure how I should handle the Raven file. Should I just toss it all in the nearest trash can or submit it to the joint committee who has final approval after we technical types have made our recommendations?

I asked Bradley Wallis if I could have some of his time, perhaps during lunch, to ask his advice about the Raven file.

"Are you finished with it?" he asked

"I think so. I hope so," I said.

"I'll be right down," he said, and within minutes he appeared in my well-lit rat hole.

"Let me see what you've got," he said, reaching into a breast pocket for his reading glasses.

I waited quietly while he scanned my notes. He did not bother himself by referring to my notations or the very large pile of supporting documents stacked on the vinyl covered table on which I worked. I sat, for the better part of an hour, drinking tepid coffee that would have tasted poorly even when fresh brewed. When I take over as God of the Universe I'll have the making of weak coffee placed first on the list sins against Myself and people who re-heat the stuff will be put to death. I think that's fair.

"Well? What are you going to do with it?" Wallis asked.

"I was hoping you'd tell me what I should do with it. I'm just a paid employee," I reminded the venerable masterspy.

"How good is your documentation?" he asked.

"I have to tell you that I can't find a single set of facts that does not support the argument. That's not to say that none exist. It's just that I am becoming more convinced than I want to be that Adolf Hitler was not on Germany's side. You and I both know that MI-6 has been sitting on the man they claim was the greatest spy in the history of the world. This may be that man," I said.

Bradley slowly removed the glasses still perched on the end of his nose. He folded them and replaced them into the tweed jacket pocket. "Interesting," he said. Then he rose from the table and left the room.

A decision did not have to be made immediately, I reasoned, and I placed my work into one of the foundation's archival safes. There would be three custodians of keys, one would be kept in the master file vault, one would be made available to our Secretariat, and I would have the third. I thought the whole protection scheme in this case was a waste of time. I would not have tried to divulge the information I had collected to any foreign power out of concern that my reputation as a reliable researcher would go down the drain.

I had the foundation arrange for ground transportation to take me to Washington National Airport and, within the hour, was en route to the Southwest Airlines VIP lounge. I was looking forward to a martini on the rocks, and possibly another before my plane left. And planned to have as much wine as I could get away with while traveling first-class back to the Coast.

"The least I can do is pay for your drink," Scheerer said as he slid onto the stool next to me at the bar.

He was older than I remembered him, his once bushy black hair now reduced to a thin crown around his shining pate. But his eyebrows were still dark black and as bushy as his head had once been. Somewhere in his Germanic ancestry there must have been a fence-jumping Irishman because Jean Scheerer had the impish grin of the Little People about him. His eyes, even when he was angry, seemed to laugh. Jean was a tall man who once was a talented athlete, or so I was told, who might have played the game of European soccer professionally had not the intrigues of his nation fascinated him more.

"A ghost from my past," I said. "Where did you hide while I did all of the work?"

"I'm working on a dig in Turkey, as a matter of fact. I'm not paid but when it's all finished, long after I'm dead, they promised me that I would be mentioned in its journal. I've loved ancient history since I was a freshman at university. Irish whiskey," he said to the bartender.

"So what did Bradley tell you to do with the story?" he said after his drink arrived.

"What story?" I responded, not bothering to look him in the eye. I could see his widening grin in his reflection from the mirror over the bar.

"You are upset, August? Why?"

"Since you brought it up, I am pissed, yes. You can call it a dig you were hiding in but you *were* hiding. When I needed help you weren't there. Half of the whole thing is your responsibility."

"You're right, in a way," he said. "Cheers," and he clinked his glass against mine.

"How much of it do you know?" I asked.

"Most of it," he admitted.

"So? Why did you waste my time? Why didn't you just spend a few minutes over a cup of coffee, give me the broad strokes and let me get on with some worthwhile work?" I crooked my finger at the bartender and ordered another.

"Because I didn't have the faintest idea where to find Smythes. Didn't even know his name, as far as that went. But you're such a good researcher that I was confident you'd run it all down. And I was right, wasn't I?" Scheerer said.

I would have been even more heated had Scheerer known Archie's name. Or where to start looking. "You really didn't?" I asked.

"No. And if it wasn't for you, old boy, the story would have never come out," he said.

"And why, pray, is that?"

"Because the last man to know all the facts died fifteen years ago. Edward Wiles. You might recall that he was one of the 'inside' three at SOE. He became director right after the war when MacClean Eliot was put out to pasture and Sir William Schuyler retired as well. SOE became absorbed by MI-6 and Wiles stayed quietly within the organization. He was my... mentor... back in 1952 when I arrived there from Cambridge."

"Ah." I now remembered the name that Scheerer had said more than once, a senior officer he had known long ago.

"Then you would have some answers that I don't have, Scheerer," I said, curiosity taking over from frustration which causes anger.

"I should. Let's sit over there."

We moved to a corner table where we could see the room but could remain unheard. Secrecy was more of a habit than this case needed, at least as I saw it. It was, after all, very old stuff even if true. We ordered fresh drinks and an extra basket of assorted nuts.

"What happened to Archie after the war?" I wanted to know.

Scheerer shrugged. "He tried many times to present himself to officials at Whitehall, Number Ten Downing and other places. No one would give him an audience, of course."

"Why 'of course'?"

"Think about it, August. What could they possibly recognize the man for? His mission was certainly not going to be acknowledged by His Majesty's government, now was it?"

I thought about it for a moment. How frustrating for Archie it must have been to go from one of the most powerful men on the planet to a person who couldn't get his dental work done by his own government.

"How did he die? Was it his Parkinson's?"

"He hanged himself," Scheerer said, sipping his third whiskey.

I sat upright in my chair. "Is that a sick joke?"

"If it is, the joke is on me. No, he used clothesline to tie himself to a chandelier hook and stepped off a chair. The hook pulled out of the ceiling but he simply marched downstairs to his neighbor's garage and tossed the thing over a rafter and finished the job."

I was, somehow, immeasurably saddened. I had become more attached than I had realized to a man I had never met. That Archie Smythes was, real or imagined, a tragic figure there could be no doubt, yet he was a man of more courage than I possessed. But, given that he was a brave soul, why did he then take his own life?

"We don't know, exactly, why anyone wants to kill himself," Scheerer said, "but we do know that Archie began watching newsreels of German atrocities. He would go to movies daily and leave when the newsreels were finished. He read every word of the Nürnburg war criminals trials, and even went there in 1949 to see them. He became depressed. I think that when he realized he might have prevented what happened to the Jews. He couldn't deal with it," Scheerer said.

"But didn't Churchill say that...."

"Oh, yes, I'm sure he did. And I'm sure Archie had no idea how filthy the whole thing was, the business in the Eastern camps and all. How do you think you'd feel?"

"Why didn't Churchill, or someone in SOE, take care of the man? They could have done it, unofficially, at least."

Scheerer shook his head. "You still don't get it, do you, August? Look old boy, the British government couldn't possibly allow any of this to get out. It's our darkest, bloodiest, deepest secret. Can you imagine world reaction, even now, if it became known that Churchill and three of his cronies threw away tens of millions of lives, Russians, Jews, and others, so that they could save our little island empire? Remember the July 20, 1944 plot?"

"The Wolfschanze assassination attempt? Sure. What about it?" I said.

"That was orchestrated and logistically supported by SOE on Churchill's order. By then we really didn't need him," Scheerer said, finishing his drink. "Well, good luck, August. I can just catch my flight."

"Wait," I said, rising with him, scuttling along to the door as he began to walk briskly. "What about MacQueen? Why did the RAF shoot down the bomber the commandos were returning in?"

EPILOGUE II

S S-Obergruppenfuhrer Willhelm Beckman was tried for crimes
against humanity in 1949 and convicted. He served seven years
of confinement before emigrating from Germany to the United
States of America in 1962. In an American city he resumed his old
career of illegal ownership and distribution of slot machines.

Luftwaffe Hauptman Friedel was repatriated to Germany in 1946
but returned to the Pacific Northwest where he opened a tavern in
the west hills of Portland, Oregon. The name of the tavern was The
Faucet. He located Margo Henningson in 1961 and proposed marriage.
By that time, however, Margo had married an internationally famous
skier. They remained good friends until Friedel's death in 1985 from
acute alcoholism.

SS-Sturmbannfuhrer Bernard "Bunny" Hartung was captured by
elements of Patten's Third Army in April, 1945. He was placed in
special prisoner segregation designed to hold feared and, it was felt,
still dangerous SS personnel. Hartung was detained for more than
two years without formal charges until March of 1948 when he was
ordered to stand trial. He faced the Nuremberg war crimes tribunal
for, among other indictments, "crimes against humanity."

Hartung was acquitted three days after his trial had begun in a 5-
1 vote by the court, the USSR objecting, on the grounds that the
charges against him were vague and that evidence was lacking to
justify holding him further. Following his release from prison ex-
Sturmbannfuhrer Hartung, now Herr Hartung, disappeared into the
chaos of war-ravaged Europe.

After taking several weeks off to rest and mull over my findings
connected to the Raven file, I returned to serious research in ferreting
out every possible lead that could verify the Archie Smythes/Jean
Scheerer, account. The trail wound through almost all of Europe and
Russia and, incredibly, back to Santa Monica, California.

I knocked at the door of an upscale apartment on Ocean Avenue. A rather short, red headed man in his 50s answered the door.

"Mr. Dietrich?" I asked. "Stephen Dietrich?"

"Yes. August Street, I presume," he said, responding to my preliminary telephone call. "Come in."

Stephen Dietrich Jr. served me a glass of excellent red wine as I carefully crafted my questions. He was a man of impeccable manners and, judging by all that I had learned about the man before calling for this meeting, quite brilliant. He held an MBA from Harvard and, in addition to his consulting business, taught graduate classes at UCLA. "Strictly for my benefit," he said, self-effacingly. "I assign work to my classes that I need to study myself."

"My father," he said in response to my questions, "served in the RCAF. He went to Canada when the war broke out and flew in the Battle of Britain. Later, when America came into the war, he transferred to the 442nd Fighter Wing in the 5th Air Force in New Guinea. Never got near Europe. That's a great story," Dietrich said, "But it wasn't my father."

I was disappointed and depressed after I left Santa Monica for the two and a half hour drive up the coast to Lompoc. I was so sure.... *Well*, I thought, *that's good. Fine!* It was the last straw and as far as I was concerned, it was all over.

The next morning I played in our club's morning toss-up. I thought of nothing but golf for the next several days, wondering if I would ever again shed my double-digit handicap for something more glamorous. Then, one afternoon, I stopped at our mailbox and looked through the day's take. Among everything else was a plain envelope with no return address. It had been mailed from Los Angeles.

Inside was an old photo. It was a picture of an Me-109F. On the side of the aircraft were icons of British roundels, signifying that the pilot had shot down RAF aircraft. The pilot was just climbing out of his machine when the picture was snapped and he had already pulled his leather flying helmet from his head exposing bright, red hair. Under the canopy line was stenciled "Yank."